"Terror Reigns Again"

By

RONAN STROBING

Shield Crest

ISBN: 978-0-9558557-7-1

MMIX

1st Edition

Published by
ShieldCrest

UK: Aylesbury, Buckinghamshire, HP22 5RR
USA: Morrisville, NC 27560
www.shieldcrest.co.uk

To my Grandparents Herbert & Joan
With love and remembrance always

AUTHOR'S NOTE

Terror Reigns Again is an adventure story that charts and follows events from the latter half of 2012 that are brought about by many terrorist attacks, and eventually culminates in 2013 with the final battle between the terrorist faction and the soldiers from the organisation that is brought in to fight them, in defence of the globe.

There is also a personal vendetta between two of the characters, which is sort of resolved, but not in the way anyone expects.

From the cold climate of Russia to the hot deserts of Saudi Arabia nothing or anyone is safe. Terror Reigns Again is a fast paced, high action, book

ACKNOWLEDGEMENTS

I should like to thank everyone who has helped me shape this book in the form it has taken, and who has assisted me in contributing ideas. I should also like to thank my friends, and members of my family, for being supportive of my writing of this book.

All characters are fictional as well, and any resemblance to people (both living and dead) is purely coincidental and not intentional.

PROLOGUE

Beginnings & endings!

It has taken 6 years to prepare, but now everything is ready and the great day dawns. The opening day, 27th July 2012 dawns warm and sunny, if slightly overcast, and everyone who is to be there awakes after a night of parties, most are slightly worse for wear having consumed too much alcohol.

As the day wears on they get ready to fulfil their duties, as they leave their residences to travel to the ceremony people line the streets, waving flags and cheering. They are met upon their arrival by the man who has organised everything, he will also give the other three a guided tour of this, great, finished project; by mid-afternoon the four men: the British Prime Minister, the Culture Secretary, the Deputy Prime Minister, and The chairman of the Olympic committee, together with the whole of the royal family, except Princess Sarah's daughter, Charlotte Pendragon, are seated on a platform overlooking the new Olympic facilities, spectators are kept away but can see everything that is going on; the media are also there with cameras and tape recorders, interviewing the dignitaries that are gathered. At around 4pm the Prime Minister steps forward and begins his brief speech, "We are all here today to salute the workmen who have worked tirelessly, over the last 6 years, to build the Olympic village and bring the Great back into Great Britain"

"Here, here!" the others all shout.

Princess Sarah turns to her estranged first husband, Mark Pendragon, her second husband Timothy Smith is also present but is seated behind his wife, – he is there to support his first wife and to represent both their daughter and her elder brother, and whispers, "It's a shame Charlotte, or Samuel, can't be here to witness this, but we must let them lead their own lives and make their own choices."

"I totally agree," she answers in her, flute like, high voice." Suddenly, there is a great cheer in the crowd and many rounds of applause. Even the security people who are keeping the crowds back relax a little; the people, in the crowd, are that happy and show no sign of any violent behaviour whatsoever.

However, in one of the windows, in one of the buildings, a lone gunman waits silently, a rifle at his side and a small control box at his side. His mission is simple, kill everyone there and destroy the Olympic village; total destruction.

More speeches follow, once the speeches are over the present monarch, supported on one side by the Prime Minister, and the future monarch on the other, steps forward slowly and brandishes a pair of scissors, handed to them by the chairman, to cut through the opening tape. Before cutting through the tape they turn to the crowd and the monarch says, in their strongest tone of voice, as their voice has become decidedly weaker through age, "And now I declare these new facilities…"

As the monarch is speaking the RAF's world famous aerobatic team, the Red Arrows, appear and begin performing a display. As the planes are performing their famous crossover manoeuvre a squad of 4 other planes, Russian MiG-29 FULCRUMs, suddenly appear on the horizon. No-one in the crowd sees anything amiss, as the people on the ground think that these aircraft have arrived, and are to be included as part of the show.

However, quite suddenly and without any warning the lead MiG launches its 2 AA-8 missiles, which streak toward the display planes and strike Red 1, which becomes a huge fireball. Screams come from the people below.

The other pilots in the Red Arrows panic and try to turn their planes to head away from the scene, but the other 3 MiG pilots are faster and launch their 6 AA-8 missiles at the display team; 3 more of the team fall as the squadron of 4 MiGs then release their AA-10 missiles, 4 more of the team's planes explode and become fireballs. The remaining Red Arrow accelerates away, but one of the MiGs breaks off and goes after it, travelling at a speed of mach 1 it soon catches the sole plane and fires its 30 millimetre cannon at the plane, destroying it slowly. One of the shots catches the fuel tank and the plane explodes. Their mission complete, the MiG-29's turn and fly away, at an altitude of 40,000 feet and a speed of mach 1.

As this atrocity is happening in the air a shot rings out and strikes the monarch of Great Britain in the head and they fall. The sniper fires 2 more shots, the first hits the Prime Minister in the back and he falls, the second shot strikes future monarch and he like the Prime Minister and the sovereign ruler of the country before him, falls, all three of them are dead!

There are screams from the crowd, and some from the female dignitaries. Everyone, in the crowd, whirls around, searching the grounds to see where the shots have been fired from. Security men herd the dignitaries to the waiting cars that will speed them away from this awful atrocity, committed on British soil; the crowds of people panic and try to flee, many getting crushed in the ensuing melee, as they try to reach the exits.

Up in his location the gunman sees his prey are leaving, he knows they will escape if he doesn't act quickly, he gathers up the small control box and activates the switch on it. A thunderous explosion is heard; triggering several more blasts and the whole of the surrounding area explodes and becomes a huge inferno, even the gunman is killed as the building he is in collapses to the ground, but as he dies he knows he has completed his part of the plan.

The remainder of the crowd, the ones that haven't been killed by the falling masonry, and one or two remaining security officers, together with newly arrived armed police officers, watch as suddenly a helicopter flies overhead; one of the security officers identifies the aircraft as a Russian Mi-24, HIND attack and transport helicopter, and six men slide down ropes that are hanging from the helicopter, each man is similarly dressed in a blue combat suit, black boots and black gloves, each is wearing a helmet with a half-mask covering the lower nose and mouth, they are all carrying Russian built AK-47 assault rifles, and they open fire spraying the weapons 7.62 bullets and killing the startled security men, the police officers and the remainder of the crowd of people. Once they have finished firing there is human blood everywhere.

The men, satisfied with their mission outcome, climb back aboard the helicopter and await stage two. The mission leader gives the pilots the order to leave. To avoid the flames, the pilot and his co-pilot operate the helicopter's controls and the aircraft climbs higher. Soon the machine aided by its thrusters, speeds onward on its journey towards London. The helicopter used, in the attack, was a Mi-24 HIND helicopter, class D.

Now the first part of the mission is over the pilots land the helicopter, collect the occupants who have helped kill the civilians, and then the aircraft rises back into the sunny, nearly cloudless now, sky. The whole episode, from start to end, had taken roughly three quarters of an hour.

The Mi-24 was first built in 1976 and was the first helicopter to enter service with the Russian Air Force as an assault transport and gunship; it was developed on the basis of the Mi-8's propulsion system. Additional missions include direct air support, antitank, armed escort, and air to air combat. The helicopter was used extensively in the Afghanistan War, becoming the *signature* weapon of the conflict. The Mi-24 is a close counterpart to the American AH-64 Apache, but unlike this and other Western assault helicopters it is also capable of transporting up to eight troops. The Russians have deployed significant numbers of HINDs in Europe and have exported the HIND to many countries including Bulgaria, Cuba, Georgia, Germany, Iraq, Nicaragua, Poland, Slovakia, Syria, and Vietnam.

The five-blade main rotor is mounted on top of the fuselage midsection, while short, stubby, weapon-carrying wings are mounted at the fuselage midsection. Two turbo-shaft engines are mounted above the body midsection with two round air intakes located just above the cockpit and exhaust ports on the sides of the engines. The older HIND A fuselage consists of a large, oval-shaped body with a glassed-in cockpit, tapering at the rear to the tail boom. The HIND D fuselage features nose modification with tandem bubble canopies, and a chin-mounted turret. The swept-back tapered tail fin features a rotor on the right on some models, with tapered flats on a boom just forward of the fin.

External stores are mounted on under-wing external stores points. Each wing has three hard-points for a total of six stations. A representative mix when targeting armour formations would be eight AT-6 ATGMs (Air to Ground Missiles), 750x 30-mm rounds, and two 57-mm rocket pods. The aircraft can store any additional ammunition basic load in the cargo compartment in lieu of carrying troops. Their armoured cockpits and titanium rotor heads are able to withstand 20-mm cannon hits. Every aircraft has an over pressurization system for operation in an NBC environment.

The HIND's wings provide 22% to 28% of its lift in forward flight. In a steep banking turn at slower airspeeds, the low wing can lose lift while it is maintained on the upper wing, resulting in an excessive roll. This is countered by increasing forward airspeed to increase lift on the lower wing. Because of this characteristic, and the aircraft's size and weight, it is not easily manoeuvrable. Therefore these helicopters usually attack in pairs or multiple pairs, and from various directions.

The HIND D is primarily to give direct operational support, and features twin mounted 4 barrel 12.7mm Gatling type machine-guns, as well as 57mm rockets, AT-2C/SWATTER ATGMs.

Sensors on this helicopter include FLIR, RWR, and a laser designator. It is primarily a daytime aircraft only. Two pilots use tandem cockpits.

During the previous couple of weeks mysterious workmen have been working on specific sites in London. Once their work is done they load their tools in the back of their nondescript, Transit, work vans, and then drive away. Each of the work crews is to rendezvous at an old farmhouse in the country to await further orders.

They arrive at the farm at night and drive up the dirt track which leads off the main road; the vans, there are several, park in the barns and the men leave the vehicles and enter the house. There is dust and dirt coating everywhere; as no-one has inhabited this place for years, even the windows are covered in thick grime, this is the perfect place. The men discard their work clothes to reveal similar combat suits that were worn by the men who attacked the Olympics, except one who is dressed in a pair of jeans and checked shirt – the sort of clothes a farmer would wear – to avoid the suspicion of any passer by. Then this man leaves the farmhouse and crosses to an outhouse/shed, he goes inside and gathers his colleagues and his AK-47 assault rifles and places them in a golf bag, again to avoid suspicion, and returns to the house carrying these weapons.

Whilst he is away his colleagues have been surveying their surroundings again: the farmhouse is much the same as most farmhouses, wooden beams are built overhead, these should burn easily – when the time comes. An oak dining table is situated in the middle of the room, set upon this is a standard radio set, however, this has been adapted as a communications radio; there are some, other, nice pieces of wooden furniture set about the main room, many are built from wood and will burn easily: To the far side of the room is an old, wooden, staircase leading to the upper floor. The soldiers don't venture upstairs unless they have to.

Upstairs there are 3 bedrooms, which serve as observation posts from time to time; and a bathroom. All the floors upstairs, as well as any furniture, are wooden; the floors had been reinforced by the soldiers, with strong timbers.

Another wooden staircase, set on the far side of the largest bedroom, leads up to the attic. Again the floor is made of timber, and the attic also makes a good observation spot giving a panoramic view of the surrounding area; to the north and west are thick woods, to the east lay open fields, whilst to the south is a line of trees which the dirt road runs between. The barns, where the vehicles are kept, are situated just east of the house, but due to the barns not being very high buildings the open fields are clearly visible.

Situated behind the main room, back downstairs, is a large, L-shaped, kitchen. Much of the cooking equipment is reasonably old but still usable.

The 10 combat soldiers sit in the main room and relax. The house is also equipped with an old, black and white, television.

The helicopter gradually moves through the air and starts hovering near to Big Ben. The men on board gather round, as best they can, and watch out the forward cockpit window, ready for the fireworks; people on the ground look up, as they hear the noise of the twin rotored machine, wondering why it is just hovering there, all are unaware their lives are about to be cut dramatically short.

The main pilot of the aircraft flips open a compartment of concealed switches and smiles to himself, a hard cruel smile, as he flips the first switch; there is another explosion as, in the distance, the Financial District of London is reduced to rubble; great chunks of masonry fall from the buildings, luckily many offices are empty, into the surrounding streets and roads, crushing vehicles, killing passers-by and generally causing mayhem and panic.

The pilot then flips all the remaining exposed switches and several more explosions are heard. The explosions destroy and devastate: Clarence House, Marble Arch, the Houses of Parliament, together with the House of Lords, and Downing Street, in fact most key buildings are reduced to rubble, the transport and communications networks are in total disarray.

Bombs placed at either end of Tower Bridge are detonated and the bridge over the Thames, connecting the north bank to the south bank, totally collapses swamping and crushing boats, and killing many.

The final switch is only to be flipped to *active* if the rescue attempt fails. Knowing this the helicopter pilot relays the information to the rest of the other combat troop's radio in the farmhouse, that the destruction of London is nearly complete, this is done via the encrypted communications link, He then lines the HINDs missiles up on the great clock building, known affectionately as Big Ben, and lines the crosshairs on the helicopter's targeting mechanism up, on the clock face, and releases two missiles from the craft's 80-mm S-8 rocket pods. The twin streaks of flame from the missiles, that have just been released, are seen heading towards the face of the clock, just as the clock strikes five o'clock the missiles hit. Big Ben's top section and it explodes, throwing chunks of masonry outwards which fall and crash down to the surrounding street, killing commuters and burying cars. To escape the explosion and the flying chunks of masonry, the pilot pulls on the control stick to bring the Mi-24 class helicopter to an altitude of 12,000 feet, and flies away at 250 miles per hour.

Finally, the pilot flips a few more switches, causing more buildings to explode and block off the roads, there is panic throughout the nation's capital. London is, effectively, now cut off, and facing a massive tidal wave. The tidal wave surges westward, now released from the Thames Barrier. With the sudden tidal surge of water the Thames barrier cannot cope and so water surges onward into London. The wave flows *upstream* toward the west bank, and eventually crashes against the bank; rising up into another great wave, for a split second, and then smashes down, causing mayhem, killing people and swamping any vehicle in its way; it is of such a force that some vehicles are carried further away. There is complete carnage in England's capital, and surrounding areas.

Satisfied with their work the pilots take the helicopter 200 miles northward to land on an air strip, at the old, unused, RAF base at Hemswell, Lincolnshire, to await further orders. He lowers the landing wheels (the gear) to bring the helicopter to its full height of six and a half metres. The helicopter is steered into one of the old hangars, all painted on the outside, in the distinctive army green; the colour has faded somewhat over the years and is more a faded yellow. As the HIND is being linked up for refuelling the pilots take themselves off to one of the officer quarter buildings for a rest, and clean up if the facilities are still there and working. One takes a radio with him, this is linked into the machine's radio systems, so if any orders do come through they can be relayed through to the radio, and all systems are encrypted.

Charlotte Sarah Georgia Pendaragon, now aged 31, is, at this moment, out breaking in her new stallion, Hercules. She is a natural on horseback, all of the stable staff agree, both of her parents are accomplished equestrian sportspeople, so Charlotte is following in their footsteps. She has won many medals, both silver and gold, in this illustrious career.

Having been out riding for much of the day, naturally she does not know of the events that have happened at the opening of the Olympics, she brings the new stallion around and back to the stables, where she dismounts and comments to the stable hand, "He is a very different ride from my other horse, Starsmalt, but I feel, in time, he'll come around."

"Right you are Miss Pendragon," the stable hand responds, "he just needs a little extra coaxing."

"Hmm," she murmurs absently, and walks towards the house, on the estate, where she lives with her mother, Princess Sarah and her step-father, Timothy Smith. Her father left her mother for another woman to which he has a further daughter, plus yet another two daughters, who are her half-sisters, to his former mistress.

When her mother and step-father return home later on they are to have a small party, to which a select few are invited, including her boyfriend Gareth Andrews, who plays Cricket for Gloucester.

As she approaches the house the butler, Jenkins, appears; Charlotte halts for a second as he says, "Miss Pendragon, I'm very sorry." He looks upset for some reason.

"What is it, Jenkins?" she asks, puzzled.

"I have got the Palace on the phone; there's been some sort of accident."

"Is mother okay?" Charlotte asks him hurriedly, worried now. "What's happened?"

"I don't know, they wouldn't tell me, a mere butler. They need to speak to you," replies the butler hastily.

Charlotte is almost running towards him now. She bolts past him and rushes to the sitting room, where the phone is located, rushing across the room she snatches up the receiver, "What's happened?" she almost screams into the receiver. The butler, Jenkins, appears at the doorway, and watches quietly.

"Is that Miss Charlotte Pendragon?" a male voice, at the other end of the phone line asks.

"Yes it bloody is," she snaps hotly, her emotions are in tatters now and she is highly strung. "Now what has happened?"

9

"May I suggest you watch the newsflash on TV, and then you will understand better. Needless to say you are asked to return to the Palace at your earliest convenience." Then the phone is put down at the other end.

"Damn bureaucracy!" Charlotte snaps as she slams the handset back in the cradle. "He didn't tell me anything, just told me to watch the bloody television!"

"Then perhaps you should," Jenkins says gently to her, striding further into the room.

"Switch it on then," she replies, now less angry than before. "Let's see what this is all about." Jenkins crosses the room and presses the 'on' switch on the TV. Instantly it flickers into life and a newsflash comes on screen.

It has been confirmed begins the newscaster *that a huge explosion has devastated the new Olympic village, and killed everyone in its vicinity. This dramatic footage was recorded just before the explosion.* The screen then shows the destruction of the Red Arrows, the reigning monarch being shot, and then the explosion. Just before the camera, which has filmed this footage, is destroyed a dark coloured helicopter flies into the picture.

Charlotte and Jenkins, both, watch this then the newscaster returns to the screen and continues *It is believed no-one survived. Whoever is responsible for this atrocity, and the other attacks on London that have taken place today is not known, though it is believed it may be the work of the new terrorist group, Proagnon, who are believed to be a splinter group related to Al-Qaeda.* Then the newsflash ends and an alternate programme schedule resumes.

The eleventh in line to the throne, now the automatic heir, turns to the butler, tears in her blue eyes, "What do I do now, Jenkins, old friend? My mother's family are all dead, together with my father. Even my own brother is in Canada with that Anna woman, he probably doesn't know what's happened, and cannot help."

"Might I suggest ma'am," the butler replies, "that you return to the Palace for further information portraying to this matter, and to see what they can advise now."

"Of course, you are right, but look at me. I must get changed into something more suitable for this occasion." She is still dressed in her riding outfit: including her helmet, jacket and jodhpurs. Quickly she darts from the room and upstairs to change.

As soon as she has changed she returns downstairs. As she reaches the foot of the stairs, Jenkins back is turned towards her. "I have taken the liberty of arranging a car to take you on your journey to the Palace ma'am," he turns to face her. "Oh ma'am," he says when he sees her in a full-length, gold, dress, "you look lovely, every bit the young Princess, your mother would have been proud." Her mousey blonde hair is neatened out and has been placed in a 'bun'.

"Thank you Jenkins," she says to him politely. "Now I must begin on the long journey to the Palace. My fur, if you please, Jenkins."

The butler passes her, her fur, though in reality it is a covering that goes around her shoulders, fastening in the middle with a metal clasp. She is escorted to the waiting car, a chauffeur driven limousine, with bullet-proof doors and bullet-proof, tinted, windows. In fact the car is a safer place to be than most houses. The chauffeur, as with most chauffeurs, is nicknamed James, though his real name is Tony.

Charlotte knows the man has a, regulation, service pistol in a holster situated inside his jacket in case of any assassination, or kidnap, attempt. The security officers, in the following Range Rover are all similarly armed, though they also carry UZI sub-machine guns. Knowing she is perfectly safe she settles into the leather seat and tries to relax.

The leaders of the two remaining opposing political parties have also seen what has happened and are at this moment, meeting in secret. "I believe," announces one to the other, "that, due to earlier events, we should combine the remaining MPs, along with those of our own parties, and form a coalition government. What are your thoughts on this?"

"I think you are right," replies the other. "However, I have one question, which one of us shall lead and be Prime Minister?"

"That is a good question. In answer, I think we should hold an election, between us two, like a general election, and whoever wins takes control of this new party for four years, whilst the other is Deputy Prime Minister, then after the four year term is up the roles are reversed and so on. And any MP who disagrees we should join everyone together may leave if they wish."

"A good idea, I agree," the other announces, sitting back in the high-backed, leather, chair, and sipping at his tumbler of whisky. He settles the tumbler on a side table, looks up at his counterpart, and then says, "I suppose you know Downing Street and Parliament were destroyed."

"I did," announces the standing man. "While these are being rebuilt, we could stay in our own homes, admittedly they are not as large as number 10 Downing Street was, and we could use the Millennium Dome for Parliamentary meetings, just temporarily."

"I totally agree," said the seated man, swallowing the last of his whisky. "Now I am afraid I must leave, but I will spread the word, of what we have agreed upon, within my own party. Goodnight." He gets up and prepares to leave the room.

"Goodnight," responds the other man. Once the door has been closed he thinks *Our policies differ greatly but I'm sure we can reach a compromise.* A few moments pass and then the door opens, revealing the man's wife.

"I hope you had a good evening," she says to him, and then crosses the room and kisses her husband.

The car carrying Charlotte Pendragon (MBE) finally reaches Buckingham Palace, and drives down the long gravel drive towards the main building. The car pulls up outside the front of the, majestic, looking palace – the official London residence of the Royal family since 1761, although the place was originally known as Buckingham House but has had many alterations, in its time. The door opens and a footman comes to help her out; she is ushered, quickly, inside and led into the throne room, why has she been brought here, Charlotte wonders, where several servants and footmen are awaiting her arrival. As soon as she enters they all turn to look at her. One of them, she recognises his voice from the phone call – evidently he is the head footman, turns to her and says, "As this is an emergency, that this terrorist action provoked, we have decided to hold your coronation here, instead of at Westminster Abbey where most coronations occur. Please step forward and take your rightful place on the throne Queen Charlotte Pendragon."

"But I am not worthy to be the queen yet," she protests.

"Who else is there?" the footman asks her.

"My brother, Samuel," replies Charlotte.

"Your brother is in Canada, and anyway he is married to Anna Noble and she didn't renounce her Catholicism, forcing Samuel to forfeit his right to the English throne. So you see, Charlotte, you are automatically next in line."

Charlotte knows about her brother, but this is still a shock to her to hear this.

Reluctantly she seats herself on the throne of the sovereign ruler of Great Britain and all of its empires. The crown is placed on her head and the sceptre in her left hand. "All hail the new queen." The footman and male servants swear their allegiance and bow before her, while the female servants all curtsey before their new queen.

The head footman steps before her and announces, "Today marks a new beginning, the reign of the house of Santo is over, now begins the reign of the house of Pendragon."

The new queen rises from her throne, "My first instructions to you are, would someone please contact the estate where I live, sorry lived, and ask that everything of mine be brought here, including my horses."

"Of course your majesty," says one of the servants and rushes off to obey.

"Next I wish someone to contact my elder brother and to inform him of the day's events. Tell him if he wishes to keep the house he may. Thirdly, I require someone to contact my boyfriend, Gareth Andrews, and, again, inform him I am here; if he wishes to join me, as my consort, he would be more than welcome."

"Of course your majesty," and servants and footmen rush to perform these duties.

"Finally," announces the new queen. "I shall meet with the, remaining, two political leaders in due course to discuss where we go from here."

The next day the new queen meets the two political leaders, in Buckingham Palace's White Drawing room – this is the grandest of all the State rooms in the Palace, and also serves as a Royal reception room where members of the Royal family gather before State and official occasions - and asks, "How do you think we should proceed now?"

"Well ma'am," answers the first, most senior, figure, showing the same respect for the new young queen as he would have shown any ruler of his country. "We propose, having had negotiations, that, if your majesty does not object, to put ourselves up for democratic election, and whoever is elected will be Prime Minister for four years and then the deputy will become Prime Minister and so on."

"I do not object to that, but tell me, as the Houses of Parliament have been reduced to rubble, where do you intend to hold Parliament?"

"Again if your majesty doesn't object," the other political leader replies, "we intend to use the, now empty, Millennium Dome."

"I do not object either, you have my full permission. Now, who are these terrorists and, more importantly, what do they want?" the new sovereign then enquires.

"That ma'am," the politician answers, showing the same respect as before, "we are unsure of, but we believe they, the terrorists I mean, are members connected with the new terrorist group called *Proagnon*, and judging by the aircraft we saw on TV they are Russian. However," he opens a folder, "as we know, from our Russian friends both the MIG-29 FULCRUM and the HIND class helicopter are also used by many other countries, and he reels them all off: Belarus, Bulgaria, CIS, (Commonwealth of Independent States), Cuba, the Czech Republic, Germany Hungary, Iran, Iraq, North Korea, Poland, Slovakia, Syria, and, the Ukraine. But I thought these countries had agreed to the new peace treaty that has been outlined, the one, one of us two," he nods at his counterpart, "is to sign in a few days time, along with the other world leaders."

The other politician then adds; "I shall consult with our minister for foreign affairs and ask him to enquire as to whether our Russian friends and the other countries that use these aircraft are sticking to the terms of the peace treaty."

"Thank you both of you," the sovereign responds. Both men bow respectfully before her, turn on their heels and stride through the double doors and leave the new queen, alone with her private thoughts.

The *Proagnon* combat troops, down at the farmhouse, have been issued with orders to leave the building where they are, leaving no trace they have been there, and move up north to rendezvous with the HIND D helicopter. Some of the men remove their helmets, revealing young or youngish faces; once they are all ready the *farmer* takes the golf bag containing the others and his AK-47 weapons, also a couple of the other combat troops accompany him.

Once they enter the outbuildings, where the vehicles are stored the *farmer* opens the rear doors of one of the Transit vans, all are totally nondescript, and places the bag inside; his fellows, meanwhile, produce large signs, from the rear of the buildings, all say *Morgan's Transport* and have a telephone number underneath, both are bogus. Once everything is ready all three of them return to the main building, and then 9 of the troopers troop out the building and on to the outbuildings, they board the three vans and await the arrival of their comrade.

Back inside the farmhouse the final terrorist, who is also an arsonist, groups straw, grass and paper around all the furniture; once he has done this he turns on the gas, leaves the building through the front door; outside he takes a matchbox from his pocket, produces a match and lights it, and puts it through the letterbox.

The farmhouse then explodes, and a fire starts. Satisfied the final man runs to join his comrades in the Transit vans, one of the vehicles slows down enough, so he runs and climbs aboard, then all three *Morgan's Transport* vans drive down the long dirt track to connect with the main road, and so each van begins its 250 journey. Around 9 hours later, and after much grumbling and swearing, mainly at other motorists, they arrive at their destination. The troopers leave the vans and climb aboard the newly refuelled HIND D. Although the helicopter is only really meant to carry 8 troopers, all 10 manage to squeeze in.

However, before he boards the helicopter the arsonist torches all three of the Transit vans belonging to *Morgan's Transport*. The helicopter then rises to an altitude of 4000 metres (13120 feet) to begin its journey back to *Proagnon* headquarters.

The next day the new Queen has to face the media and give a *live* television announcement, to the nation, detailing the events, and what her government intends to do to track and punish these terrorists. As everything is prepared she looks at her speech again, and feels again this is too great a burden for such a young monarch. This speech will also be going out via radio linkup so, hopefully, most if not the entire nation will hear it, or see it.

Once the cameras are in place she waited for the countdown from the person behind the camera, As soon as she was given the word, plus the *red* light started flashing, just above the main lens on the camera. Charlotte then began, "Ladies and Gentlemen, wherever you are, I am your new Queen, due to yesterday's tragic events. The terrorists, connected with the new group *Proagnon*, yesterday destroyed the Olympic village that many people had helped to construct over the previous six years. In doing so they killed many friends, relations, and, possibly, members of immediate family. Many of my own family were killed along with the others who were there. These terrorists have crushed our spirit for now, but we shall do as we always have done, become stronger and a more united country."

"Why did they do this? It is too early to tell yet. How do we strike back? I have consulted with the remaining two political leaders, and they have, unfortunately, informed me that our own military forces are depleted, and the vehicles woefully out of date – as are the rest of the worlds. Therefore, we must call in help from further a-field. That is all for now, I am sorry I cannot allay your fears any further – I wish I could, but to keep you informed either myself or one of our political leaders will keep you up to date on this situation. Thank you for listening to me, I wish you all, my loyal subjects. a peaceful day."

"And cut," the cameraman announced, and the little, *red*, light went out above the main, camera, lens. "Thank you your majesty," he said and stowed his equipment away; "that was a brief but thoughtful speech. You'll probably make many more speeches during your reign as queen; some good, some not so good." Once everything had been put away, he, and the rest of the media people that had been present, left the new monarch, upon reaching the main reception area each of them was searched by the security men, as they'd been when he'd come in. Satisfied everyone was clean they were allowed to leave.

Back in the Drawing Room, where many speeches have been given from, over the years, Charlotte removed the, jewel encrusted, cloak that has been worn, over the years, by several different monarchs of the United Kingdom; underneath she was wearing a, plain, green suit with skirt and stockings. She then turned and looked up at her consort, and boyfriend, "Oh Gareth, when will it all end?"

"It will end in time," he assured her, coming over and giving her a big hug, "but for now life must go on as usual."

Whilst all this is happening in Britain small groups of terrorists, of the same organisation, are being called into action from their sleeper status and performing atrocities across the world.

Hotels are attacked, together with numerous apartment blocks. Houses are destroyed by explosives killing any occupants who happen to be inside, many people are killed, and many vehicles are bombed killing their occupants. Palaces in varying countries, along with famous monuments, are reduced to rubble by missile strikes. There is chaos everywhere. Only a few places are left untouched, many places in Russia survive, along with the people there.

Apart from Russia there is destruction all over.

In the United States of America that same evening, a band of terrorists armed with several mortar rockets, together with a launcher, are preparing to attack the White House.

Security Service agents are patrolling the grounds around the White House, even though the President has been called away to Camp David for a secret meeting, and also to relax with her lesbian girlfriend. One of the agents is patrolling on the outer perimeter of the grounds, the outer grounds are dense with bushes and trees; he, suddenly, spies the *Proagnon* group with their missiles and launcher, and realises that they must be plotting an attack on the residence of the President.

The agent, Edward Browning, pulls a radio from his inside jacket pocket, together with his, faithful, service revolver and points it at the man he can see, "Do not move," he instructs, "or I fire."

"Why should I move my friend?" the terrorist asks in an Iranian accent. "It is you who have lost." Just then the security agent feels a sharp pain in his back and he crumples to the floor, quite dead. Standing behind him is another *Proagnon* trooper, holding an AK-47 assault rifle with a specialised silencer built on – its barrel smoking from the shot it has fired – to prevent the gun from *jumping* to the left and upwards, "Good work Sergey," says the Iranian leader.

"I only did what I had to Comrade Abdul," replies the man, who is evidently Russian, from his accent.

"Now let us get back to our work," announces the leader of the group, picking up the agent's fallen Beretta pistol, and then along with Sergey they rejoin the other two members of the team, Domingo and Fritz; the two men are Brazilian and German, respectively.

Once the two men are back in the group Abdul outlines his plan, "Sergey, you and Fritz move around the outer perimeter area, providing covering fire from your assault rifles, if necessary, while Domingo and I move the SMAW rocket launcher and missiles in close enough, hopefully with as little opposition as possible, to fire at the White House. If anyone tries to interfere kill them."

With nods the two terrorists move, stealthily, away; Fritz moves off to the left while Sergey moves off to the right, both are very quiet. Both Domingo and Abdul collect both the launcher and missiles, from where they are concealed, and move forward to a small wooded area; both move cautiously, in the hope of a successful attack. Abdul, being the commander of the team, has a radio inside his jacket; to contact an attack helicopter also of Russian design, the same sort as was used in Britain, but is a slightly different model as it is the HIND E variation of the attack and transport helicopter, which is located at an unused and, now, deserted Air Force base, and is therefore available to provide air support, and also aid the terrorists on the ground, should anything go wrong with their mission.

The helicopter is, at that moment, being refuelled to its maximum capacity of 4,067 litres; 1,840 litres in it internal fuel tank; 1,227 litres in the internal auxiliary tank, which is located in the cabin; and 500 litres in each of the external fuel tanks, located under the main five bladed rotor.

The helicopter being used, this time is a Mi-24 HIND E, this is a slightly updated version of the helicopter used in the attack on London and the Olympics; this helicopter is the most proliferated version.

The only, real, difference is the HIND E possesses a twin barrel 23mm turret gun, and, AT-6C/SPIRAL ATGMs (anti-tank guided missiles).

Once the refuelling has been completed the two pilots aboard wait to see if Abdul sends a signal requiring their assistance, if no signal is received within the next hour the pilots will know they will only be required to transport the four, or however many terrorists are left, back to *Proagnon* HQ.

Abdul knows the White House is steeped in history, he has learnt about his target via information from the internet. He knows the construction of this great and famous building, the residence of the head of these infidels, was started in 1792 and finished in 1800. Many of the USA's greatest men, together with their women, have lived at the White House, which is addressed as 1600 Pennsylvania Avenue, and the current occupant is a woman, *a woman! Will these Americans never learn?*

19

Putting these thoughts aside Abdul tries to concentrate on the task in hand. Then he remembers that the President, and anyone close to him/her, is always guarded by the faithful Secret Service bodyguards, most are even willing to die in the line of duty, to protect her, or any President, this one a mere infidel woman, how stupid! The Secret Service also patrol the vast grounds that the building occupies, even when their President is not there; she is not there at the moment, it would have been better if she'd been there but a mission was a mission.

Secret Service agents are on duty and are watching, with hawk-like eyes, for any movement within the lawns that surround the President's main residence.

Suddenly, one, a young agent, named Mark Daniels, spots a movement within his peripheral vision. Instinctively, he draws his revolver and fires at the movement.

"Don't go wasting them bullets, lad," says the senior agent and also Mark's partner for this evening, Tony Lewis; then curiously he asks, "What was it you were shooting at anyway?"

Mark re-holsters his revolver and puts it inside the shoulder holster, which is situated inside his jacket and under his armpit; he always wears this round him, and then looks up at his older partner, "I'm positive I saw something move out there."

Tony looks behind and all around them, "Ain't there now, lad, come on let's keep moving, it's getting cold." Mark has to agree with that, the temperature has dropped somewhat. "Anyway," Tony continues as they continue their evening patrol, "I hear you and your wife have just been blessed with a new baby."

"Yes we have," confirms his younger partner. "A daughter no less! In fact I'm going to the hospital to see them both as soon as my shift ends." Mark, Tony knows, lives only a few blocks away. His spouse and daughter are in the main Washington hospital and are being extremely well cared for, due to the significance of Mark's job.

Both men halt as they hear a quick burst of machine gun fire, and look at each other, a look of disbelief on each man's face. "I told you I saw something," says Mark matter-of-factly.

"That you did," replies the senior agent. "We'll turn you into a good Secret Service agent yet."

"Yeah," says Mark jokingly, and brings his Beretta pistol out from inside his jacket again. "Let's take a look, I think it came from over there," he carries on. Tony draws his pistol and together they move, slowly, toward the source of the noise.

Fritz, whose gun it was, looks down and curses himself. He has, accidentally, taken the trigger guard off and has the machine-gun loaded. He has, evidently, caught the trigger, accidentally, and the weapon has gone off. It has only been a short burst, and if it had been heard there would have been Secret Service agents all round him – pistols drawn. However, what Fritz doesn't know is that at this moment two agents are coming to investigate.

Even though the President is at Camp David, the Vice-President, Sam Davis, has been given the use of the White House whilst his superior is away. He is, at this moment, holding a cocktail party in one of the large dining rooms, with the chairmen of large companies together with many Wall Street bankers and brokers, all of them are blissfully unaware of the danger lurking outside. The time is about eight in the evening, the terrorists have picked that time as many people will be inside.

Tony and Mark are now within 500 metres of Abdul and Domingo's position; however, the two terrorists are in an area of the lawns that is heavily shaded by trees. Abdul, slowly, raises himself up on one knee, and shoulders the shoulder-launched multipurpose assault weapon (SMAW) rocket launcher.

The Shoulder-launched Multipurpose Assault Weapon has an 83.5 mm tube and fires 83 mm rockets. It is a man-portable weapon system consisting of the MK153 Mod 0 launcher, the MK 3 Mod 0 encased HEDP rocket, the MK 6 Mod 0 encased HEAA rocket, and the MK217 Mod 0 spotting rifle cartridge. The launcher consists of a fiberglass launch tube, a 9 mm spotting rifle, an electro-mechanical firing mechanism, open battle sights, and a mount for the MK42 Mod 0 Day Sight and AN/PVS-4.night sights. The SMAW MK153 Mod 0 launcher, based on Israel Military Industries B-300 weapon, consists of the launch tube, the spotting rifle, the firing mechanism, and mounting brackets. The launch tube is made of fibrelass-epoxy composite material with a gelcoat on the bore. The spotting rifle, a British design (derived from the LAW 80), is mounted on the right side of the launch tube. The firing mechanism mechanically fires the spotting rifle and uses a magneto to fire the rocket. The mounting brackets connect the components and provide the means for boresighting the weapon. The encased rockets are loaded at the rear of the launcher.

The spotting cartridges are stored in a magazine in the cap of the encased rocket. The launcher has a 9-mm spotting round is ballistically matched to the rocket and serves to increase the gunner's first-round hit probability. Each round consists of a 22 Hornet blank cartridge, crimped into a 7.62-mm NATO casing with a special 9-mm tracer bullet as the projectile. The system can be used in conjunction with the AN/PEQ-4 aiming light in place of the spotting rifle.

Training is accomplished with the MK7 Mod 0 encased common practice rocket and the MK213 Mod 0 noise cartridge. At 187 decibels, the weapon is one of the loudest on the battlefield, second only to a mine-clearing line charge.

The launcher fires three different types of rocket; there is The High Explosive, Dual Purpose (HEDP) rocket which is effective against bunkers, masonry and concrete walls, and light armour. Initiated by a crush switch in its nose, the HEDP rocket is able to distinguish between hard and soft targets, resulting in greater penetration into soft targets for increased damage potential. The HEDP round is capable of penetrating 8 inches (20 cm) of concrete, 12 inches (30 cm) of brick, or up to 7 feet (210 cm) of wood-reinforced sandbags. Second is The High Explosive Anti-Armour (HEAA) rocket is effective against current tanks without additional armour, and utilizes a standoff rod on the detonator, allowing the explosive force to be focused on a small point, allowing for maximum damage against armoured targets. The HEAA round is capable of penetrating 24 inches (56 cm) of armour steel.

Finally there is The Novel Explosive (SMAW-NE) rocket is effective against caves and bunkers. The SMAW-NE uses a thermobaric warhead (PBXIH-135 explosive) which produces an overpressure wave capable of collapsing a building. The Naval Surface Warfare Center teaming with the Marine Corps Systems Command, NSWC Dahlgren, and Talley Defense Systems responded to an urgent US Marine Corps used for a shoulder-launched enhanced-blast warhead in 2003. It was used in the battle for Fallujah, Iraq, in 2004. for this operation they are using the HEPD rocket, and if necessary, the SMAW-NE rocket as a follow up.

His companion then unscrews the rocket cap, and screws the round into the rear of the launcher. Domingo then extricates the spotting rifle rounds, as he has been trained to do as the assistant gunner; and Abdul charges the charging lever on the launcher. His assistant then inserts the spotting round cartridge into the spotting-rifle, and his direct commander cocks the rifle; taking aim Abdul fires the spotting rifle until the tracer rounds are on target, with Domingo as spotter. Once the launcher is lined up Abdul's companion clears the back-blast area, ensuring no one is in the back-blast area; however, it won't matter if the grass burns. Once Abdul has been told that the area behind is clear of people he calls to his companion, in a hushed voice, "Rocket," thus indicating a rocket is about to be fired; his assistant repeats that the area is clear, and Abdul depresses the launch lever and pulls the trigger. As Abdul prepares to pull the trigger, he thinks it ironic that they should be attacking the American President's residence with an American made weapon.

The weapon fires and the blast deafens them, for a few seconds. As they watch the projectile streaks towards the intended target.

Mark and Tony hear the blast and, both, collapse to the ground, clutching their ears. Suddenly, Fritz appears, and guns them both down with a burst from his AK-47 assault rifle. Secret Service agents alerted by the noise start to appear then, and manage to terminate Fritz's life.

Abdul and Domingo see their German comrade cut down in front of them; after the initial shock the Brazilian whispers to his leader, "Why don't you call the helicopter now?"

"No," Abdul whispers harshly to his comrade. "All is not lost, and, anyway, I have a plan."

More Secret Service agents, having been alerted by those outside on their radios, rush into the, vast, dining-room and try to get everyone out and to a place of safety, fearing an attack may be imminent. At that moment the HEPD comes crashing through the outer window; everyone tries to get out its way, fast, but as it carries on and strikes the far wall, exploding. masonry crashes down, crushing the Senators and the Vice-President, together with his wife and many of the Secret Service agents.

Abdul peers up from his hiding place noting the building is damaged but not destroyed. Luckily, the terrorists also have an NE projectile to follow up if the HEPD didn't destroy the building. The leader turns to his assistant and asks him to load it; Domingo loads the rocket with the thermobaric warhead. The procedure for firing is followed, correctly, again, the projectile streaks towards its target and hits one of the outer walls. The overpressure wave is produced and the rest of the building collapses inward.

Abdul is delighted at the success and hugs Domingo, what Domingo doesn't realise is that in his leader's hand is a short, stubby, knife. As they part the assistant looks at his leader, with vacant and glassy eyes, and then looks down at his chest; a red stain is appearing over his jacket front. Sightlessly now he crumples in a heap on the floor; the last conscious thing he does before he dies is look up at his leader and mouths the words, "You bastard!"

The Iranian leader looks down at his, now dead, Brazilian comrade and smiles coldly and cruelly. He then opens the back of his radio and activates a switch that will alert the driver of a car, that the mission has been successful, and he now requires collecting from his position. As he operates the switch a,small, red light starts flashing. Satisfied Abdul replaces the cover on the radio and cliambers over the perimeter railings, that surround the lawns of the White House, crosses the road, and hides in shadows behind a house.

As he is waiting he watches as emergency vehicles arrive at the scene to see if anyone is still left alive, or anyone requies medical assistance. Suddenlly, a new vehicle arrives with a flashing blue light; seeing this Abdul emerges from the shadows and, casually but calmly, opens the rear right door and equally as calmly climbs in.

The other police, and emergency, vehicles make a space for this new one, assuming as it is a, white, Mercedes Benz with sherriff's signs on it, it must be a sherriff's car. Once there is a wide enough gap the Mercedes Benz shoots off into the night; once the driver feels they are far enough away, and the darkness has enveloped it the light is removed and the car draws to a halt, both men step out into the, cool, night air and the signs, on the doors, are removed and placed in the *trunk* of the automobile. Once this is done the Mercedes looks like any other vehicle on the road, plain and ordinary.

Back at the scene of the devastation FBI agents, assisted by the remaining Secret Service agents, are searching ffor any clues as to who committed this atrocity. From out of the blue Sergey appears, with his AK-47 assault rifle.

As soon as the men see him all of them raise their guns and point them at him, "Drop your weapon or we fire," calls one of the agents. Sergey, knowing he cannot dispose of them all before one of them extinguishes his life, calmly he places his weapon on the ground and raises his hands; "Get up or die, dog," the same agent commands. Slowly the terrorist raises himself up. FBI agents handcuff him and take him away in a waiting patrol car.

Meanwhile, the Mercedes carrying Abdul arrives at the deserted Air Force base, a few hangars still stand, the automobile draws up alongside the waiting helicopter, and Abdul is transferred aboard. This done the chief pilot activates the control that will activate the main rotor. Once all five blades have started turning, to his satisfaction, he engages the three blades on the tail rotor; once everyting is shown to be turning satisfactorily both pilots pull their control sticks (yokes) back and the HIND E helicopter lifts off, to begin its journey back to *Proagnon's* secret, underground, base.

The driver returns to the Mercedes, gets in the front, left hand, seat and proceeds to drive away. The driver then drives the vehicle to the nearest large river, knowing his orders are to dispose of the vehicle afterwards, knowing this is a suicide mission, for him anyway, he lines the Mercedes up and slams his foot down, hard on the accelerator; the car speeds forward at 160 miles per hour and is launched off the Western bank. Hoping the car has been launched fast enough, and, silently, praying he will reach the other side, the driver begins to breathe more easily. However, the automobile just hangs there for a second, which seems like an eternity for the man behind the wheel, and then it falls into the river below, breaking up on impact, the driver is killed instantly. No-one is around to witness the event.

An, almost instantaneous, message relaying these events reaches the President at Camp David. Upon reading this message the President, understandably, is distraught, "My Vice-President is dead, along with most of the Senate, plus several of the Secret Service Detail assigned to protect them, and the White House has been reduced to rubble, and I have that conference in England next week. How can I go now?" With that she collapses into her partner's arms.

Her partner, Sarah Zabu, gently kisses her President, and holds her in her arms, "Don't worry, darling, everything will be fine."

A colonel, aged about 50, of portly build and with a bushy white moustache, suddenly, appears at their side, "Ma'am, Air Force One is waiting to whisk you both back to Andrews Air Force Base." He salutes his commander-in-chief, smartly, and leaves them both.

"We will need time to pack," Sarah says, realisation quickly crossing her face.

"Already done," replies the colonel, "now would you prefer to travel to Andrews's in Air Force One, or in a motorcade?"

"Which would you advise colonel?" asks President Mary Sullivan, unsure which would be the safer. If anyone knew it would be Colonel Barry Green, in charge of the running of Camp David.

"I, personally," says the colonel, "would choose the motorcade, as it gives you both the option to travel in one of five vehicles, so if someone were to attack you they'd need to guess which vehicle you were in." Then the colonel stopped and thought about it some more," However, the aircraft is quicker, and if you will allow it I will give the order to send up some Apache AH-64 helicopters to escort you in Air Force One."

"I think, on hearing that," remarks Miss Sullivan, "it would maybe be better if we," she looks at Sarah who nods, "were to get back to Washington as quickly as possible, as the American people will want a strong leader at times such as these."

"Right you are ma'am," Colonel Green replies straightaway. "I shall see to it at once."

About an hour later both women climbed aboard the customised Airbus A380 aircraft, the Air Force had given it the designation of a VC-25A. This aircraft is referred to as Air Force One only while the president is on board; it's sister aircraft –another Airbus – is used by the Vice-President. Both aircraft are maintained by the U.S. Air Force for these purposes.

Once aboard Air Force One Mary and Sarah are shown to their seats, and directed on how to reach their cabin by a Secret Service Agent, Tom Little, his nickname among the Detail is 'shorty', even though he is 6 feet 5 inches. As they are walking towards the plane Mary asks him, "How goes everything Tom? Do we have an update on the, present, situation?"

His voice is grave as he replies, "I have consulted with our intelligence people upstairs Madam President, neither we nor any of our partner agencies have had any further news. Whoever committed this atrocity is long gone; however, we have had news that one of the terrorists has been arrested, he is Russian apparently, and he now languishes in FBI custody."

"Thank you Tom," Mary says in reply, reaching their cabin and leading Sarah inside.

The President, surrounded by so many Secret Service agents feels safe as the two women enter their cabin; both make themselves comfortable for the journey back to Washington, stopping off at Andrews Air Force Base and then continuing their journey onward to the capital in the helicopter Marine One.

Mary glances out the window and sees a couple of F-16, Falcon, jet fighters escorting the latest incarnation of Air Force One. The President knows if she is needed an agent (preferably female) will come and rouse her; she knows this is the part of being the President's partner Sarah dislikes, but as Miss Sullivan is the President of the United States Sarah will have to get used to it.

The next day dawns warm, but not sunny. Miss Sullivan, after breakfast, asks that the watch officer be sent to her quarters, the watch officer arrives, agent Alan Delta, and asks what his commander-in-chief requires of him. "Alan," Mary begins, "is it possible to get a camera crew prepared for our landing in Washington?"

"I will see what can be done, but why?"

"Yes, why?" echoes Sarah, now curious at her President's, and lover's, behaviour.

"I wish to make a speech to every citizen of our nation," the President replies, simply. "May I remind you both that it is my duty, as President of this nation, to give reassurance to our citizen's that this action will not go unpunished, plus the nation's government may be reduced in number but this country will be strong again, this is only a minor setback."

Upon landing in Washington, aboard Marine One, the President exits the helicopter onto what remains of the White House's South Lawn and is, immediately, surrounded by her Secret Service Detail, a number of shouts from the reporters that have already gathered, "Do you have any comments you'd like to make Madam President?" Flash bulbs start 'popping' as cameras begin clicking. As she pauses to collect her thoughts, after seeing the devastation around her, a CNN camera looms into view and starts making its way through the crowd.

"Just a moment, got to take a leak," and Sarah grabbed Mary's hand and they disappear inside the main building. In the toilets Mary adjusts her make-up and turns to her partner, who is washing her hands. "How do I look?"

"You look fine Mary," Sarah responds, "but tell me Mary, why do you do it all when you could have a nice, uncomplicated, life with me?"

"As you know I was a politician before I met you, and then I got the job as President, and as President I agreed to take on all the responsibilities that go with the job."

Just then the door opened and a female agent, Marcia Hunter – she had long brown hair, green eyes, and wore round, black framed, glasses – other than that she was just another Secret Service agent, told them," They're waiting for you."

"Let's get this show on the road then!" said Mary, and strode, purposefully, back outside, not waiting for Miss Zabu.

Miss Zabu followed in her partner's wake, momentarily pausing at the door she, deliberately, lowered her voice and said to the Secret Service agent, "Later." Marcia nodded, in understanding, and then followed the two women into the main conference room, where the press and reporters had been ushered.

Mary seated herself behind the main desk. When all was ready she came round to the front of the desk and began, and like the new English Queen's speech this would be going out on radio as well, "Ladies and Gentleman, my beloved citizens, yesterday a terrorist attack was committed on our shores resulting in the destruction of my home, the White House, killing my Vice-President, Sam Davis, his wife, a number of Senators, and several Secret Service agents."

"The terrorists, who we believe, are members of *Proagnon*, did not leave without casualties of their own. We believe that they were a small group of four, two were killed; one by Secret Service agents, the other either committed suicide or was killed by one of his fellows."

"I did mention there were four, the third is now in FBI custody, he is a Russian citizen. The fourth, sadly, escaped. My fellow Americans, we believe this sort of act should not go unpunished, but our armed forces are very depleted in numbers; therefore, we must seek outside help."

"Unfortunately, this could not have come at a worse time as the conference for World peace occurs in a few days. Therefore, what do I do? If I stay the rest of the world leaders may feel we Americans are responsible, if attacks are happening in other countries. However, if I go, I may be seen as callous and unfeeling by some citizens."

"That is my dilemma and I have come to a decision; it may not be the best or right decision, but it is the one I have made," there was such a silence in the room you could, actually, hear the sound of a pin drop. "I feel," Mary began again, "that it is my duty, and would best serve the United States of America, if I attend the conference, I shall, of course be taking my partner, Sarah Zabu, together with the Secretary for Defense, Edwin Brown. Whilst I am gone I will leave my Chief of Staff, Arnold Smee, in charge as temporary president."

A few days later a secret meeting is to be held at Drimsey House, which was situated in the English countryside. Every world leader, together with the new Prime Minister and his Secretary of Defence arrived to decide how best to deal with this new menace, and to sign the peace treaty.

A car from the nation in question was, usually, imported from that country to meet the representative and his/her bodyguards from the aeroplane they were arriving in. Most had private planes; the car would transport them to the desired location. Any back-up cars are also, usually, imported for such an occasion; however, if the country happens to only have bicycles/mopeds as the favoured mode of transport then, usually, a ministerial car is laid on for that dignitary.

However, as this was the American President's first trip to the UK five Chevy Suburbans had been imported for this event; the vehicles were kept in storage for her arrival. A few days before the meeting, Air Force One arrived carrying President Mary Sullivan, her partner Sarah Zabu, Secretary of Defense Edwin Brown and many Secret Service agents. As the plane touched down the Chevy's were brought out, onto the tarmac, to meet all aboard.

Two Secret Service agents walked down the steps in front of their commander-in-chief, two more followed behind, then down the stairs came the President's partner – again flanked by two further agents; each agent was wearing his or her trademark sunglasses; finally, a further fourteen agents emerged from the aircraft and proceeded to descend the steps. As the President finally reached the tarmac and gazed round at the view, as best as she could, a band started up and proceeded to play the American anthem, the star spangled banner. Every Secret Service agent had drawn their automatic weapon, just in case there may have been an assassin in the crowd.

Once ready both her partner, together with Mary, was escorted by Secret Service agents into the third car in the convoy of Chevy's, the President always boards a different car for each journey, thus making it harder for a would be assassin to predict which car their target is aboard. Agents board the remaining four cars, four in each, and a couple board their Commander-in-Chief's car, to provide extra protection. Every car has tinted windows, again for extra protection. Once everyone is ready the convoy of five Chevy Suburbans pulled away and drove out of the gates of Manchester (International) Airport. Due to the attack in London and the surrounding area, all internal flights have had to be diverted to various other airports.

The President and Miss Zabu have been booked into the Majestic hotel for two nights, the first night before the meeting, and the other night before they fly back to America., a further five rooms have been booked for their protection agents. Upon their arrival the receptionist welcomes them as Miss Smythe-Porter and friend. It was felt by their bodyguards, who made the booking that they should use aliases.

Once they have both retired to bed the agents began to move off to their rooms and relax, tomorrow will be the hardest day. Most make use of the mini-bar in their rooms, the drinks in Britain aren't as good as what they're used to, and then they retire themselves.

The next day is warm and sunny, just the hint of a cloud in the sky. President Sullivan, alias Miss Smythe-Porter, and her partner, Sarah, rise, dress, and are then served breakfast in their room. "Isn't it a beautiful day," she remarks, to no-one in particular.

"It is that Ma'am," responds a new, young, agent. The Special agent, who is sort of in charge of the other agents - who is standing just inside the door - gives him a look as black as thunder.

"What?" asks the agent; named Harry Jones, as he catches sight of the look his immediate superior is giving him.

"Never answer your commander-in-chief back unless she asks you a direct question."

"Sorry," he says meekly, and his shoulders slump.

"That's okay Jones," the latest CinC says, "you're new here, and you were only replying to my rhetorical question. Therefore, we'll let it go." Miss Smythe-Porter looked across at her Special agent, "Let it go, Price."

"But Ma'am," Debbie Price started, as if intending to object.

"Let it go, and that's an order." This President, Price notes, is much easier to get on with than some of her predecessors, though she can have a sharp tongue at times. Debbie has served several presidents.

Both President and partner finish breakfast, and then get ready for the long and tiring day ahead. After a few minutes waiting Edwin Brown joins them – looking as smart as ever in his brown three-piece suit. A further agent, Mike Kuscweski, appears and announces, "Ladies, Sir, our transport has arrived. There are no people that I can see, either in the foyer or the lobby, but we may leave the back way, if you prefer." The back way he is referring to is the fire escape, but all feel it would be easier to leave through the main way.

"Let's move people," Special agent Price says, and the leave the hotel with no interference. This time the President and Sarah board the second car in the convoy; and together with the police motorbike outriders the convoy of five cars move off on the journey to Drimsey House. As it is felt it may be a bit risky to take the southbound lane of the motorway named the M6, the procession meanders its way through the country lanes until they reach their destination, roughly two hours later. Also, this gives the new President a chance to view the countryside of England, with its green fields.

The house to be used for this meeting is a large structure, similar to a large museum; armed soldiers, along with a few armed policemen, surround the area. Many of the delegates have already arrived, the President sees.

As the convoy of Chevy Suburbans finally comes to a halt, some of the Service agents escort their President and her partner, plus SecDef, up the steps and into the house, the rest stay outside to assist the army and armed police personnel in guarding the house. President Sullivan looks round in awe, the house has many rooms, a second floor (upstairs), and a basement (cellar); the party proceed to the large drawing room, where the meeting is to be held, and both are led to their seats; both partners are seated at their designated place, indicated by a model flag of their country. SecDef, Edwin Brown, is seated just behind.

Once everyone is seated the English Prime Minister rises and looks around the table, he sees Kings, Presidents and Prime Ministers, together with other official representatives. The only country not represented is Russia; the Russian president is very conspicuous by his absence.

He addresses the world leaders gathered around the large oval shaped, oak, table, "Ladies and Gentlemen, firstly I would like to welcome you all here. The events that occurred a few days ago, in this country, and each of yours, are unlike any threat our nations have ever faced. These talks were, initially, to find world peace, but events of the past week or so, in all our countries, have changed that. I believe that unless this new threat is dealt with and quickly the whole world may be in danger. We believe, but have is no tangible evidence yet, that the threat may be of Russian origin; and as you can plainly see, the President of that country is not here." No one has really noticed this, but as soon as the Prime Minister mentions this, all heads turn to look.

The Prime Minister, of Britain, then turns and looks, sharply, at the Israeli Prime Minister, "Has *Proagnon*, as they are

called, got anything to do with your country's Mossad?"
Mossad is the Israeli intelligence agency; known for,
occasionally taking part in terrorist activities.

"Not that I know of. If this terrorist organisation is linked
with the Mossad agents, in any way, I have no knowledge of it.
However, that does not rule out the fact that there may be
rogue agents at work within the organisation. So I can, really,
neither confirm nor deny it. However, as I said if it is
connected with Mossad I have no knowledge of it."

"Okay, so we don't think it is connected with any Mossad
agents; that still leaves the problem of how to deal with this
threat."

He looks around at the world leaders or their country's
representative, who all nod their approval. "But how?" one,
suddenly, asks in alarm.

"Madam President," the Prime Minister starts, "our army,
in the UK, is woefully depleted and therefore we cannot raise
an adequate fighting force, can anyone else?" Everyone at the
table shook their heads. "Then there is only one option
available to us, and that is, we must call in HART."

HART (Human Army for the Retaliation against
Terrorism) is a semi-secret organisation, made up of personnel
from various countries, that has been performing covert
operations for the past five years. Not much was really known
about the group, except that they recruited many people with
specialist skills and put these skills to good use. They have
operated in Afghanistan, Iraq, Iran, Cyprus and Israel, usually
covertly. However, now they are needed to combat this new
menace.

The assembled leaders agree that this is the best option
open to them and they should use it, though some have never
heard of HART, however after some explanation everyone
agrees.

The Prime Minister brings out a *red* telephone, from under
his desk, and picks the phone handset up and dials an
international number. The phone rings at the other end, then a
voice says, the world leaders all hear this as the phone has been
switched onto speakerphone, "HART HQ here, who is that?"

"The Prime Minister of Great Britain, along with the rest of the world leaders," the Prime Minister says, identifying the assembled group. Everyone nods.

"And what is the problem?"

Before anyone can reply a thunderous explosion is heard, rumbling under the house, then the room explodes in flame, and slowly the whole house is blown apart, killing everyone assembled in that room, ironically only the phone survives, "What is the problem?" the secretary's voice repeats again and again, it is obvious she has heard the explosion.

All the armed personnel outside are killed in the explosion, plus every vehicle surrounding the house is utterly destroyed.

CHAPTER 1

Meetings & plans!

Prisoner AZ6012 walked along the high gantry, overlooking the main exercise yard at HMP Belmarsh, high-security, Prison; the prison consisted of 4, cross shaped wings, or residential units, the two main buildings enclosing the exercise yard of the prison. Each of the six buildings in the compound contained three floors of cells; each building had a, sloping, tiled roof. The prison could hold a capacity to hold nine hundred and fifteen prisoners, comfortably, but up to nine hundred and twenty at full capacity.

Each wing is joined onto one of the two main buildings. The prisoner in question, whose real name is Adam Barker, made his way through 'C' wing on his journey to the visiting room where today he was expecting a special visitor. He had been put in this prison, wrongly he believed, for plotting and inciting terrorist acts; but he had also blown an apartment apart – thus killing the sole occupant. Even though much of this is true he has always, flatly, denied it, the plotting of terrorist acts anyway. He looks at his watch and checks the time 14:00, he needn't rush to the visiting room as visiting hours start at 14:15 and end at 16:00 in the prison; as he is walking along he is joined by several more prisoners – they are all heading in the same direction, yet all the prisoners keep apart from Adam.

A visitor's car park is situated beyond the perimeter wall.

This prison serves the South East of London and the South West of Essex. The prison also contains an education facility, some workshops and two gymnasiums; the gymnasium staff work in partnership with Charlton Athletic Football Club and deliver F.A. accredited coaching courses qualifying prisoners to become football coaches once they have served their sentence, and are released. Much help is offered the prisoners to help them develop skills that will enable them to integrate easily back into society.

Adam Barker continues along the metal walkways, now passing many other prisoners and warders on his way. They all ignore him as he is just another inmate residing at Her Majesty's Pleasure; of course they all know of the happenings at the opening of the Olympic village.

He arrived in the visiting room to await the arrival of his visitor. 14:15, finally, arrived and a, new-looking, young prison officer opens the metallic door to allow the visitors in; many are: wives, girlfriends, or just friends; they all recoil at Adam's bandaged face. She enters the room, following the others, and spots him. Thankfully, she doesn't recoil in horror, just walks over to the table - where he is seated - and awaits the invitation to sit down opposite him.

Her hair is jet-black and shoulder length, she wears square, framed, glasses but behind them her eyes are a light green, and they shine, like a cats eyes. With a young face, Adam knows this woman is, slightly, younger than him at 32 years of age. Combined with the slim, petite, figure she is a very attractive woman; in fact Adam knows she could have any man that she wants and usually does. Her name is Tanya Roberts.

Adam looks at her and says, "This is a most unexpected pleasure. Please sit down Tanya."

Once Tanya is seated opposite him she begins by asking, urgently, "What happened to you?"

"Ah, this," he indicates the bandage, that covers the most of the left side of his face – his mouth is still visible though. Plus another strip of bandage material runs around his head, to hold the other one in place as they are pinned together just above the left eye – safety pins, of course. "I came across another prisoner who'd heard what I'd done, and he decided to teach me a lesson. He came to my cell one evening and beat me up badly, and then he filled my water jug with hot water, put a couple of sachets of sugar – which he'd taken from the kitchen - and poured the mixture onto my face. My left side took most of it."

"Didn't the screws do anything?" Tanya replied peering into his, once, proud face. Even though she'd only, really, known him when he'd been in prison she knew he was a proud man, with a past. Well everyone had a past, of some sort – whether it be good or bad.

"No, because I didn't – actually – report it. When one of the screws found my on my cell floor I was rushed to the infirmary, but when they asked me about it later I simply said it'd been my fault."

Tanya now looked angrily at her friend, "But he could have killed you."

"Yes I know, but that's where he was clever – he knew I took sugar, he didn't – so when the screws found sugar residue in the bottom of the jug they assumed I was telling the truth about my accident."

"Anyway, changing the subject," Tanya smiled, her white teeth gleaming. "Did you see what happened at the opening of the Olympics?"

"Yes I did, everyone here did," replies Adam, in a flat tone. "Wasn't it awful?"

"It certainly was," agrees Tanya, and they both shared a giggle.

They were both aware of the prison officer, observing proceedings and ready to step in between any of the several couples who were seated in the room in case a scuffle, or fight, broke out for whatever reason; also there was a guard at the door, again ready to help. However, Tanya and Adam are, totally, unconcerned about this as they know these men are just doing their duty.

Adam then asked her, "And how are the family?" Though he hasn't any 'real' family anymore Tanya knows who he is referring to.

"They are all fine, and are awaiting your homecoming."

"Oh, I received news, from the governor, yesterday that I'm being transferred to Park Hurst Prison on the Isle of Wight tomorrow. I was taken to see the governor, by one of the screws, and she gave me the good news. Does that inconvenience you, or the operation, in any way?"

"No it doesn't," Tanya answered, honestly. "I'll just have to use the family helicopter to reach you." Miss Roberts was a first class helicopter pilot, just like most helicopter pilots. "Just one question what time are you being transferred?"

"I think it's about ten in the morning from here, by prison transport, we reach the port at Portsmouth, at about twelve –

38

maybe later, then across to the island, by prison boat, with an escort of police launches. Anything else you wish to know?"

"No," his visitor replied, and then she assured him, "but don't worry we'll be there somewhere."

The two of them then exchange a little small talk, for a while, just to allay any suspicions the guards may have, or may have had, to pass what remained of their time together. As the clock reached four, plus time was called, Tanya got up, from her chair, and said to him, "It was good to see you Adam, pity we can't have longer together. I'll pass on your regards to the family, and we'll see you again real soon."

"It was good to see you Tanya," the prisoner remarked, before allowing himself to be led from the visiting room, with the other inmates. He smiled to himself and started to walk back to his cell - after the usual strip search, just in case any of the visitors passed something over to help one of the inmates in a bid to escape.

The next day dawns and prisoner AZ6012 knows this is the day of, hopefully, his release. He is up early, does his early morning exercise routine, under supervision, and then returns inside the main prison building for his morning meal. Once everything is ready, he is taken, along with his belongings, down to a small holding area, another cell, to wait for the transport that will take him to Portsmouth to start the long journey that lies ahead of him.

At ten-thirty, or thereabouts, the prison van, an old group four one, arrives and the guard who is to accompany Adam shoves the prisoner, roughly, inside and into the compartment Adam will be travelling in - commonly known as the sweat box for obvious reasons; the compartment is a mere four feet wide and three feet in depth. After fifteen minutes of travel Adam begins to feel nauseous, and he is sweating profusely. He is, however, able to look out one of the small, tinted, windows; Adam can see out but no-one can look in. He notes they are travelling along minor back roads; probably this is to avoid any nosey onlookers, as much as possible.

The prison van arrives at the port town where Adam is released from his compartment and led onto the boat that will take him across the channel to the Isle of Wight. Once he is out of the sweat box he regains his composure and takes in the salty sea air, as he looks around he takes notice a clock above the main wheelhouse, it shows twelve-thirty.

"You'll be safe with us laddie," says a voice with a Scottish accent. Adam turns and sees the captain of the vessel striding up to him. "I be Captain Abraham, your pilot for this pleasure cruise, while my friend," Adam notices a burly man approaching him, younger than the captain, "is Mr Smythe, my first mate. The other two," again Adam notes the presence of two prison officers, dressed in their uniforms. "Are Mr Shaw and Mr Shanks, your escorts." Adam, politely, shakes hands with the three men, and then hears a snapping sound. He looks down and sees one of the three men has handcuffed him to the rail of the vessel.

"Bastard screws," he shouts at them, now realising all their politeness was just to lull him into a false sense of security. Just then he hears the prison van start up in readiness to leave. "What about my things?" he shouts after it.

"All safely stowed below," answers the captain, "now just shut up and let us do the worrying laddie." Adam soon quietens down once the boat's diesel engines start up, and they slowly move away from the mooring where the boat is situated.

When the boat is out at sea the launches that are to escort the vessel appear; suddenly, a small helicopter appears far on the South horizon, approaching rapidly. "Smithy, binoculars," calls Abraham. Once the binoculars are found he raises them to his eyes. "That isn't one of ours," he exclaims to his first mate. "What the hell's it doing out here."

"Probably a pleasure flight or a pilot in training," replied the first mate in answer. Adam smiles, realising who it is.

"But surely not out here; and why is it headed straight toward us?"

Just then another set of rotor blades are heard approaching the vessel, this one sounds like a big one. Abraham swings round and sees a huge twin rotored helicopter gunship. "Christ," he swears, "that's all we bloody need, break out the guns first mate." He hands over a key and Smithy races below deck.

The smaller helicopter has by now drawn level with the boat. "Get down Adam," orders a female voice, amplified by a megaphone. Her next order is to the captain, "We do not wish to fight you or your men, surrender your prisoner to us and we shall leave without bloodshed."

"Never," retorts Abraham, having to shout to make himself heard over the sound of the, hovering, helicopter gunship behind him. Adam gets down on the deck as best he can, out of the corner of his eye he sees Smithy reappear with two handguns and two rifles.

"You leave me with no choice captain. Don't forget I offered you a way out." The helicopter she was in flew higher to avoid the main fighting.

The HIND class D helicopter, that had been steadily hovering behind the vessel, at a level of 1.500 metres, opened fire with its twin 30-mm guns hitting Smithy in the chest, killing him instantly. Then the helicopter peppers the deck with shots, as the gunfire came nearer to the captain, who was carrying one of the rifles, he retreated back into the wheelhouse and opened the communications channel, and switched to the police emergency frequency. Quickly he said into his radio handset, "Mayday, repeat Mayday, prison transport vessel Delta Oscar Lima zero-six-two is under attack from unknown hostiles. Any available cruisers or launches please supply assistance immediately. Repeat we are under attack." As he finished speaking a burst from the helicopter's twin guns tore into the wheelhouse, obliterating it.

However, by some miracle, Abraham managed to stagger forward from the wreckage and fires his own gun at the helicopter. His shots hit the base of the cockpits of the machine, but as they are reinforced, the bullets are totally ineffective He then staggered and collapsed on the deck, dead!

Of Shaw and Shanks there is no sign, whether they'd decided to jump ship or had already been killed and fallen overboard, Adam didn't know. Just then he saw police boats arrive all around the vessel he was on. So the captain's message had been heard, a pity.

Adam then became aware of a helicopter hovering above the vessel. "Rope ladder coming down," Tanya's voice called, "climb aboard."

Adam realised, with a start, that the piece of piping he'd been handcuffed to was now loose, with a good tug he was free. *A stray shot from the HIND must have hit it and loosened it.*

He made his way, as best he could against the wind that had risen, across the deck, or what was left of it, to the rope ladder, he reached up for it and missed, he tried again and caught it. Slowly, and carefully, he began to climb. He nearly fell off at one point when a voice bellowed through a megaphone, "Halt or we fire." Adam, regaining his balance, saw the voice had come from an officer, on one of the vessels that had drawn alongside. Quickly he increased his rate of climb.

Finally, he reached the open helicopter doorway, and flopped inside. "Thanks Tanya," he gasped, once he was properly in the vacant seat she flew the smaller machine away. Once they were far enough away Tanya turned the helicopter round so they could witness what was about to happen.

The HIND helicopter hovered just above sea level; once it had the attention of the four police cruisers the pilot lined the targets up and fired four missiles from the 80mm rocket pods, one located under each wing. As each of the S-8 missiles struck its selected target the cruisers exploded in four different fireballs, though they seemed as if they were one. Satisfied with their handiwork the pilots pull their aircraft back up at a rate of 15 metres a second, and flew away.

"That's some impressive hardware," Adam exclaimed to his pilot. "You've been busy while I've been inside."

"We have," Tanya's voice replied through his set of earphones. "Now let's get you somewhere where you can change out of those ridiculous clothes, and I think you'll want a shower too." She patted him on his knee, "It's good to have you back."

Tanya landed the helicopter at an old, now, disused airstrip just outside of what remained of southern London; once the chopper had touched down, Adam got up and climbed out the vehicle, and then crossed to a run-down block of flats. Even though all the tenants had now left the building, he had been assured that, the amenities were still working: gas, water and electric.

Once the chopper's rotors had stopped rotating and the aircraft had been fully shut down Miss Roberts exited the vehicle and followed her companion into the building. She looked around, and after ascending the stairs, as the elevators no longer functioned and after checking each flat she found him in flat number 18. All the flats were the same; all had a basic kitchen/lounge, two bedrooms, a bathroom with shower facilities, and a utilities room.

Tanya Roberts walked in and walked into the bathroom where she found Adam, preparing to remove his prison overalls and get a good shower; the shower was running and water was splashing into the bath. As she entered Adam looked up, knowing he needed his privacy at the moment and seeing his glance she turned and left, first of all reassuring him that they would discuss future plans when he felt completely ready.

He acknowledged what Tanya'd said and continued to undress for his shower. Tanya exited the bathroom, closing the door behind her. She knew he would come to her when he wanted to but for now she would allow him to adjust to the outside world again, along with his freedom.

Thousands of miles away, at HART HQ – outside Geneva, Switzerland, the receptionist just stared at the phone as, what seemed to be, a very loud sound was heard at the other end. Knowing this was the sound of an explosion she patiently waited until the noise had died down, and then she tried over and over again to raise the party at the other end of the line by repeating her question, "What is the problem?"

Recognising that this was an explosion, and a rather large one at that the main HART receptionist and secretary, Gwyneth Jones, traced the call back, with the help of satellite downloads to Drimsey House, situated in the heart of the

English countryside in Berkshire. Presuming no one at the other end was left alive to answer her question she replaced the telephone receiver, and moved across her desk then pressed the button that would alert the rest of the HART personnel that they were needed.

Throughout the several blocks, in the compound, that housed the separate teams in the organisation, there were a total of five teams in all, an alarm bell sounded; however, each team member also wore a wrist communicator that emitted a 'red' flashing light, together with a buzzing noise, like a mobile telephone, in case they were out performing some aspect of the rigorous training program HART had them do every day to keep in top form. Upon hearing the alarm's sound, or seeing the 'red' light, every man, or woman – there were one or two, had to return to the main command centre's conference room to be briefed on what sort of emergency was happening, and where.

As soon as everybody had assembled around the table in the conference room an internal door opened and in walked two men and a woman. The two men were HART's overall commander, Peter Roberts, and the organisation's psychological profiler, second in command, and chief medical officer, Dr Hans Schaiffer, both were in their mid to late fifties. Of course, the woman, Gwyneth Jones, was there to report how things had come about; and whereabouts in the world.

Roberts had joined the organisation when it had first been set up in 2006. He was an ex army colonel and had been appointed after two recommendations to try and help build this new organisation up, to high standards. Having served as a sergeant in the police force, and then in the army, it had been felt he would be perfect for this job. He had been married but his wife had been killed when their apartment had been blown up.

The perpetrator, of this crime, had been caught and imprisoned, as far as Peter knew.

Dr Schaiffer had been approached and joined in 2007 as a junior medical officer, but over time he had been promoted to senior medical officer, and then his skills as a trained psychologist had been recognized and now he was now

HART's criminal and terrorist psychologist, plus chief negotiator, and right hand man to HART's commanding officer, Peter Roberts. He still assisted with medical emergencies, but as he had trained the medical team to a high standard he was needed less and less on the medical team.

The woman was Gwyneth Jones, who was the organisation's main receptionist, and as she had taken the initial phone call it was felt she should be present at the briefing. Of course, the organisation had many other receptionists/secretaries, but Gwyneth was the chief receptionist.

"Gentleman, ladies," began Commander Roberts, "please be seated." Each of the 100 members of HART personnel that were present, this excluded the five team leaders of the organisation, who were taking a break from duty, seated themselves around the, large, mahogany table. "Please tell us about the phone call Mrs Jones," said Roberts.

"Well Mr Roberts, everyone," Gwyneth replied in her Welsh accent, "I received a phone call at around 15.00 hours from the British Prime Minister, who told me he was with the other world leaders, who were meeting, I believe, to discuss last week's terrorist attack which resulted in the destruction of the new Olympic village, in which the British royal family was killed; also, together with attacks in many other countries, and also to discuss the latest peace treaty. Anyway, several seconds later a very loud noise was heard, I had to hold the phone away from my ear until the noise had died away, and then when I tried to raise the world leaders again I couldn't raise anyone, so I, naturally, assumed a bomb had exploded wiping everyone out," Gwyneth took a drink of water. As she'd been speaking there had been nods from some of the members of the teams. "The meeting," she carried on, "was at a place called Drimsey House, which as we know, is in Buckinghamshire, in England. This was confirmed by one of our overhead, orbiting, satellites," more nods. "Also, as you will recall, on the same day as the destruction of the Olympic village many landmarks in London were destroyed by explosions, as was stated on the news that day; we believe this is the work of *Proagnon*, a splinter group of Al-Qaeda. We believe the perpetrators to be of

45

Russian origin, as they used MIG-29 FULCRUM fighters, together with a HIND class D helicopter; both are Russian aircraft. That, people is as much as we know for now."

The room was silent for a moment as everyone took the information in. Finally, Peter Roberts spoke, "Gwyneth, please recall the five team leaders: Ronan Strobing, Celia Most, Mark Schnieder, Lucy Lang, and, Leon Bigship; however, as the FBI managed to capture one of the suspects who helped destroy the White House, you may leave Miss Lang in her home country for now to assist in interviewing the suspect, if needed. In case you're wondering how I know Mrs Jones, the FBI Director has a phone line direct to my office, just in case. Everyone else, please return to your separate blocks to collect your equipment together in case we need to send you overseas, and await your team leader's arrival. Then you'll receive further orders."

"Yes sir!" each of the soldiers replied, saluted, and exited the conference room.

Ronan Strobing was at his home, in Eastern England, sat working on his latest book; his wrist communicator lay on his desk. "Dinner's ready," his wife of the past 10 years, Mandy Strobing, called; they also had two lovely children, Simon and Zoe.

"Coming," he called, shutting his computer down. He reattached the communicator to his arm, and then walked into the kitchen, where his family were waiting. Ronan had just got sat down when his communicator started to flash and buzz. "Sorry darling, children, but duty calls."

"Ronan," Mandy said, "are we ever going to be able to sit down to dinner as a family?"

"Obviously not," was the absent reply as he got up and left the room. He, hurried upstairs, once inside the main bedroom he closed the door and then activated the *talk* feature of the communicator; "Yes Gwyneth."

"Good evening Ronan," she replied, in her Welsh accent, "as you are aware terrorist attacks have been taking place all over the world – except in Russia, for some reason. It was felt, therefore, by the British Prime Minister – together with the other world leaders, that HART be brought in to find, and punish, these terrorists. You are asked to return to headquarters, as soon as possible, for a full briefing."

"We would also request that you also bring in Mrs Most, as you live quite near her. We expect you both within the next six hours. Thank you."

Ronan, hurriedly, packed what he felt he needed, as every mission was, mainly, in foreign parts. Once he'd packed he returned downstairs to bid farewell to his family. They were gathered at the bottom of the staircase waiting for him, he kissed them each in turn; the two children on their heads, and then he turned to Mandy, "I'm sorry, babe, I don't know how long I'll be away, but take care of yourself." Then he turned to the two children again, "And take care of yourselves, and your Mum too."

"We will Dad," they both chorused like the good children they were; that would change, in time, Mr and Mrs Strobing knew.

"Here are your car keys and coat, honey," his wife said to him, and then as an afterthought, as he was stood in the doorway, called, "Try not to be away too long this time; and look after yourself."

Ronan held the car keys above his left shoulder and rattled them in acknowledgement, and then went to the garage and got his, flame red, Hyundai 4x4 out, packed his suitcase in the boot, and drove the three streets to Mrs Most's house, which she shared with her husband, Peter – who was a long distance lorry drive, and her son, Mike. Her two other children, both girls, had left home.

Celia and Peter were standing, on the kerb, outside their, terraced, house. Ronan pulled up and helped Celia load her suitcase in the boot. Peter came up to them and said to Ronan, in a friendly way; "Now just you look after her; she'll soon be all I've got."

"I will, and you know I will."

"Oh darling," Celia said and kissed him, "I'll be okay." With that he smiled and returned inside.

Celia and Ronan had known each other for many years, in fact, when they first met he had developed a crush on her and they'd had a, brief, affair; later Ronan had proposed, just once, and she'd turned him down; and even though she was now married to someone else they were still good friends.

He helped her into the passenger seat, returned to the driver's side and got in. Then they set off, "Wonder where we'll get sent this time."

"Yes, I wonder," remarked Celia absently, in her squeaky, childlike, voice.

"Must be big if they're bringing us both in, I wonder if they'll be bringing the other team leaders in," Ronan remarked, as he turned onto the M1 (northbound), after following a few local roads, toward Doncaster/Sheffield *Robin Hood* International Airport, situated outside Doncaster. As they pulled up one of the two garages to one side, it was opened by one of the airport staff - all the staff had been trained to recognise the HART vehicles. The other garage was for Leon's vehicle, a black Ford Zetec, not quite as fast as Ronan's vehicle, but still fast.

The two occupants climbed out of the vehicle, collected their suitcases from the boot, and then walked inside the airport building; they showed their HART passes to the check-in operator at the luggage desk, just as Leon's Zetec, with Mark and himself pulled in. Again, as Ronan and Celia had done, moments earlier, they got their luggage out, walked inside, and flashed their passes at the check-in operator.

Robin Hood Doncaster/Sheffield airport was fairly new, having only opened on 28th April 2005; it had been built on the site of the old R.A.F. Finningley airforce base.

R.A.F. Finningley had a long, military, past to it. At the start in 1920, just after World War I, the Government of that time had asked the local authorities to assist in the formation of a chain of airfields so the country would not lag behind other nations in the provision of civil air services. The Doncaster authorities, of that time, had taken heed and, with expert advice from a man named Alan Cobham, on 26 May 1934, opened a grandly called 'aviation centre'. Development of the airfield continued and on 1 July 1936 an international service was opened to Amsterdam. On 1 November 1938, after long discussions with the Air Ministry, the 616 (South Yorkshire) fighter Squadron of the Auxillary Air Force was formed; shortly after the outbreak of the Second World War in 1939 the squadron went to its battle station and played an honourable part in the Battle of Britain

After the departure of 616 squadron its place was taken by the formation of the 271 (Transport) Squadron, which was, composed mainly of requisitioned civilian aircraft and, some, obsolescent twin engined bombers. 616 squadron should be noted as the first Allied jet fighter squadron, who were equipped with the Gloster Meteor, famed for using their wingtips for throwing German V-1 "buzzbombs" off course.

In 1944, after being re-equipped with Dakota aircraft, the squadron moved south to take part in what was known as 'Operation Overlord' and later in the airborne invasion at Arnhem where a Flight Lieutenant named David Lord was awarded a posthumous Victoria Cross. After the war the airfield reverted to civilian flying and it finally closed in 1994, and that was when the base was redeveloped into an airport.

The operator had been instructed to fast track all HART personnel, often to the annoyance of the other passengers, and directed them to departure lounge C. The four of them, three men and one woman, were led through to the departure lounge, which was a small, private, lounge reserved by HART, and any celebrities – located on the first floor, which could be reached by the escalator, lift or steps - along with their luggage, and sat down to wait for their aircraft which was being refuelled.

After about half an hour's wait, they were directed to a security checkpoint; after, again, flashing their passes at the security guards, they were directed to the main, airside lounge. After another quarter of an hour they proceeded outside to board their aircraft, a Gulfstream G-150; this plane had been invented and launched in America 6 years before – a modern type business jet – it was based on the old G-100, however, now six years later Gulfstream was working in partnership with Boeing, they were working on the next generation of business jets, had supplied England with a fleet of old G-150s, of course they could have supplied newer versions but Boeing seemed to be happy with the -150s. Of course HART had some newer, Gulfstream, models in Switzerland, but these were mainly used in emergencies.

The G-150 had an overall length of 17.30 metres, a height of 5.82 metres, and a wingspan of 16.94 metres. The four members of HART took their places, also aboard were two stewardesses and the pilot. The pilot went into his domain, the cockpit, and politely, relayed instructions for them all to fasten their safety belts for the 1091 kilometre flight to Geneva, Switzerland, where HART headquarters was located. As they buckled in the pilot started the 2 Honeywell, TFE 731-40AR 200G, engines, each one located either side of the tail unit.

Each engine was capable of putting out 4,420 (pound-force) or 19,66 kilo-newtons of thrust, the aircraft taxied onto the main runway, to await a vacant air slot. As soon as a slot became available and the pilot, Captain Earnshaw, was given the information the aircraft lined up on runway 2, and then the captain engaged the thrusters, a slight roar was heard as the engines powered up, again, and a slight vibration felt inside the main cabin area. Once the engines were up to full power the aircraft lurched forward, and then thundered down the 2,893 metre long runway.

Earnshaw pulled back on the control column and the aircraft rose into the air; once the plane had levelled off the captain's voice told the passengers, over the intercom that they were flying at an altitude of 33,000 feet, and at a cruising speed of 850 kilometres per hour, therefore they should land in Geneva in a time of just under an hour and a quarter. If they wished to move about the aircraft they may; the two stewardesses got up, and one went to the front of the plane, whilst the other headed to the rear. Then, of course, the one at the front began the, usual, talk of what to do in an emergency; where different items were located; and so on.

Whilst they were flying the four HART members were served with tea or coffee, whichever each preferred – although there were some alcoholic drinks, together with a meal and a copy of one of the latest, daily, newspapers. Eventually they all felt the aircraft drop speed, a little, and assumed they would be landing shortly.

In the cockpit Captain Earnshaw radioed the control tower at Geneva's *Cointrin* International Airport, "Delta Lima Six-Five-Two requesting permission to land."

"Delta Lima Six-Five-Two, this is *Cointrin* tower, permission is granted. Please be advised the wind here is strength seven, from an easterly direction. Happy landing. Tower out."

"Thank you *Cointrin*, Delta Lima Six-Five-Two out." Earnshaw then, opened the intercom channel, "Would all passengers, and crew, please return to their seats and fasten their safety belts. We are now approaching *Cointrin* International Airport." Everyone resumed their seats, along with the stewardesses, and fastened their belts, and then they felt the aircraft start to descend.

The landing gear was lowered for a smooth, if not slightly bumpy, landing; the plane was back to its full height of 5.82 metres. Captain Earnshaw, in the cockpit, pulled back on the main control column and brought the aircraft's nose upward, and then brought the G-150 onto the single runway; this one much longer at 3,900 metres long. The wheels *bounced* on the concrete for a start, and then Ben Earnshaw brought the nose down and they were, safely, on the ground, once again.

The captain of the G-150 then engaged the full stopping system, and the twin engines started to *scream* with the reverse thrust that was being applied to slow the machine down. Once the aircraft had slowed sufficiently, Earnshaw radioed the tower to confirm they were down in one piece, and then he taxied the business jet to the main terminal.

A set of steps, on wheels, was brought to the plane and the four passengers, together with the two stewardesses disembarked. The HART members were greeted by members of the Swiss police force, some armed, while the stewardesses walked into the terminal. The HART team leaders were then escorted to a waiting BMW 4X4 and were driven away, onto headquarters.

In Russia the President, Vladimir Krushkev, was finishing up for the day, when he noticed, out of the corner of his eye, a yellow piece of paper sticking out from under the pile of papers on his desk. Intrigued, he took the yellow paper out and looked at it; it was a note informing him of a conference at Drimsey House, in England, several days ago now. Why hadn't he been reminded?

Armed with the paper, but concealing it in his hand, he left his office and walked up to his secretary, "Yes sir?" she asked him politely as she saw him approach her desk.

He produced the paper, "Don't you think I should have been informed of this?" he thundered, showing her the paper.

The secretary recoiled in fright, "I am sorry sir, I thought I put it in your diary." The President, along with other senior ministers kept a day to day diary, informing him or her of their day's appointments or meetings; at the start of the working week these senior officials would hand their diary's to their secretary's and the secretary would write in all official appointments and meetings, and then hand the diary back to their minister.

"I am glad you didn't, if what I hear on the news is correct, I probably would have been killed along with the others. You will be rewarded for this service, in due course." The secretary knew his wife had died many years ago, but surely he wasn't suggesting that sort of reward.

Vladimir left the Kremlin and began his walk home, even though he had been allocated a Mercedes, as all high-ranking ministers were, for travel purposes, to and from his home, he barely used it, preferring to walk the distance, as he only lived a couple of blocks away. He paused, briefly, to look into a shop window; the shop sold electrical goods and he realised he must get a new television set soon, as the picture on his kept fading; inside was a brand-new, so the shop said, *Toshiba* colour television, 32 inches wide – no less.

Suddenly, a shot rang out, startling the President, as it, narrowly, missed his right ear and hit the shop window; the glass smashed instantly, and Vladimir, as if an instant reaction, covered his face with his hands; next a shot rang out and whizzed past his elbow, grazing it, and he fell. People passing by didn't recognise him as he'd fallen face down, but one helpful citizen turned him over, just out of curiosity, and got the shock of his life. He contacted the emergency services immediately, on his mobile phone, and soon thereafter an ambulance arrived, along with a police car and fire engine, "Has anyone moved him?" asked a paramedic quickly.

The helpful citizen, Boris Golovko, stepped forward, "I'm afraid I did, I merely turned him face up."

The paramedic replied, "As he doesn't seem to be, that, badly injured, I don't think that should've harmed him; but please don't do that in the future." As he was speaking the second paramedic was loading Krushkev's prone body onto a stretcher.

Boris nodded meekly at the paramedic and moved off. The policeman, having finished securing the shop front, along with the firemen, and taken a few notes, got back into his car, and drove back to headquarters, the firemen did the same. Once the stretcher, with Krushkev's body on it had been secured in the waiting ambulance, and the paramedics had climbed back in their vehicle the ambulance moved off, lights flashing and siren blaring.

The ambulance stopped at Moscow General Hospital and the paramedics moved the stretcher onto a metal gurney and wheeled it inside.

Back in England, once the helicopter had finished refuelling, and Adam had showered and rested, he and Tanya left the, disused, block of flats and climbed back aboard the chopper. Tanya then operated the controls that would start the rotors turning, once they were up to full speed she pulled back on the yoke and the helicopter rose into the evening sky.

The distance was 2738 miles to where they would be heading, maybe a little more, therefore with the chopper's, maximum, flight speed of 500 miles per hour, which he assumed they'd be flying at, the flight should last approximately 6 hours; maybe more, maybe less. Still he had all the time in the world, now he was a free man.

The helicopter flew, on its journey, eastward over the North Sea, and then turned South-East and flew over a number of countries until it, finally, entered the airspace of the country where their final destination lay. The helicopter flew low, less than 3000 feet, to avoid radar detection by the, main, tower located at the capital's airport. They flew southwards now, into a desert area, where the main headquarters of *Proagnon* lay. A sand coloured panel slid open and the chopper descended into it; as soon as the panel closed lights in the walls were illuminated to help the helicopter's occupants find their way about.

Adam climbed out the vehicle and walked off down a side tunnel, Tanya, who had also emerged from their transport, made no attempt to follow him – as she knew Adam knew where he was going – and instead walked down the main tunnel, but turned down a side tunnel of her own.

In the main conference room, the main 25 *Proagnon* troops, though there were many more scattered across the globe, awaited the arrival of their leader and the second in command; a few minutes later the double doors, which were located at the far end of the room, were thrown open and two figures walked in and sat down, at the head of the table. The leader was dressed in a, blue, combat suit, not dissimilar to the combat troopers with a complete, silver, face mask, while the second in command was dressed in a complete, black, suit. It had no insignia on the front, neither of them did.

At HART HQ the four team leaders, everyone knew Lucy was helping the FBI question their prisoner, were transported in the elevator to their leader's, Peter Roberts, office; upon entering they were greeted, warmly, by their commander. "Please be seated," he said to them, the four of them seated themselves, in the chairs, around the desk; "you know why you are here. In case not I will explain." He re-explained the situation, and then added, "We believe this threat may either have originated in Russia, or be aided by disillusioned Russian KGB members. Therefore, we will have to place an agent within the Russian ministry for foreign affairs, to gather intelligence. This mission could, and probably will, be dangerous."

"As you may know or not know Lucy Lang is not here; that is because one of the terrorists who attacked the White House, a Russian no less, is now in FBI custody. She has been asked to liaise with them and help with the interrogation. Back to the matter of who we put in the Russian foreign ministry, we would prefer a female, do any of you have any suggestions?"

Leon stepped forward, "What about Alice Stronglove? As we all know she's one of our latest intelligence gathering operatives, and has always wanted to prove herself in the field."

"A good idea, but as she is relatively new will she be reliable enough?"

"I believe so sir."

Peter glanced up at the other three team leaders, who all nodded in agreement with their comrade, and good friend. "As the majority are agreed we shall give Alice a chance to prove herself."

At that moment the office doors burst open, and in rushed Gwyneth Jones, "Sorry to disturb you, but we've just had a report that the Russian President, Vladimir Krushkev, has been assassinated!"

"What?" thundered Commander Roberts, rising from behind the desk.

"We only have preliminary reports, at the moment, but, apparently KrushKev was walking home after his day's work, and he paused to look into an electronics shop; the assassin, so we hear, fired and the bullet, apparently, whizzed past his ear,, and shattered the shop window. Then the assassin fired again, and Krushkev fell, eventually a citizen passing by, a Boris Golovko, recognised him and phoned the emergency services. Of course, these are only preliminary reports."

"Thank you Gwyneth," Roberts said, she turned and left the office. All the time she'd been speaking, the four team leaders had been looking at each other. "That proves it, I'm certain" began Roberts, "of Russian involvement."

"But sir," Celia objected, looking at the others, "all it proves is they, *Proagnon*, have assassinated, or tried to assassinate, the Russian president. It doesn't prove any sort of Russian involvement." Ronan, Leon and Mark all voiced their agreement.

"Okay, I'll agree with you on that; but they are certain ministers, or their aides, who may be involved. However, the sooner we get someone inside their foreign ministry to confirm this the sooner we get to the bottom of this. How soon can Alice be ready?"

"As soon as you want her to be, she's off site at the moment, but can be contacted right away," answered Leon with a smile. "I'm sure she could use her charm on some of their ministers, and maybe some of her physical attributes, to get them to loosen their tongues."

"Thank you Leon," said their commander, "if we are all agreed," everyone nodded, "you may contact her at your earliest convenience."

"Thank you sir."

Alice Stronglove was of a smallish size, and only 23; due to the absence of a man in her life she had joined HART as an intelligence gathering operative. Due to her small size her physical attributes were extremely pronounced, and she could often loosen a man's tongue this way. As she was still fairly new she had only been on two assignments: one in Japan, she'd found the Japanese very accommodating, in both senses of the phrase; her second assignment had been in Germany, and again she'd found this race very accommodating.

She had been given a wrist communicator, along with the rest of the HART members, and at that moment she was in the shower, when she heard the communicator go off. Quickly, she turned the water off, got out the shower, threw a towel round herself and then pressed the *talk* button. "Evening Alice," announced Leon's strong voice, full of authority. "Sorry to disturb you but you are required to use your skills, to gather HART some information from inside the Russian foreign ministry. You are asked to be able to leave as soon as possible. Commander Roberts will contact the ministry ahead to provide the necessary cover."

"Okay Leon," she giggled, and, with a mischievous grin, accidentally let go of her towel and it fell to the floor, Leon's face was a picture, of surprise, mixed with shock, just before she turned the communicator off. She could now imagine Leon wondering if the towel drop had been an accident or not.

She, then, picked her towel up from the floor, and dried herself off, once she was dry Alice put her, now, wet towel over the radiator, in the bathroom, to dry. She went through to the bedroom and started to put her clothes on, however, she never wore underwear unless she really had to, for whatever reason. Once she was dressed she got a medium-sized suitcase from behind her, wooden, chest of drawers. *Now what will I need for this assignment?*, she wondered, then she thought, *I'd better take my fur coat because the weather's cold in Russia, so I've been told; I'll take my blue dress with the low cut back, for functions, I'd better throw in another dress, just in case. I'll put in several pairs of trousers and some skirts. Oh, I think I'll also, put in a few pairs of hot-pants and other sexy clothes, well you never know.*

Once Alice'd finished packing she moved the towel from the radiator and hung it over the back of a chair to drip dry, once she'd done that she picked up her suitcase and left the room, and walked down the staircase, gripping the handrail in her right hand whilst holding the case in her left. At the bottom of the stairs Alice put the case down, whilst she got her coat, a black leather jacket, and her car keys. One she'd got her jacket on Alice checked she'd got everything: HART pass, passport, her pistol – a 9mm Parabellum, together with cartridges – again just in case. With her, mental, checklist complete Alice, again, hoisted her case and left her little house in the Geneva suburbs. She climbed into her BMW, coupe, car, and drove to the airport; as it was evening the roads were mostly deserted, so she arrived at *Cointrin* International Airport in around 20 minutes.

She got her case out the car boot and entered the airport. She walked up to the check-in desk and showed her pass to the operator behind the desk, all the while Alice was conscious of many sets of eyes on her – she assumed the eyes would belong to men: either single or married.

Assumedly, the married men's wives would have a few things to say to their husband's, later, for ogling another woman's backside, and a younger one at that.

Once Alice had been fast-tracked through the main airport and its security, she seated herself in the airport's airside lounge. Eventually, another Gulfstream business jet pulled up alongside the lounge, this was the same one that had been used earlier, but Alice didn't know that, it had been refuelled and was, now, ready to go again.

She was led out the gate to the airside, where she boarded the plane, aided by the mobile staircase. The pilot, Captain Sean Rickman, greeted her as she boarded, along with the stewardesses. He had already filed a flight plan, with the tower, from Geneva to Moscow.

Alice sat back in the seat designated for her. Once the pilot had done his pre-flight checks on the aircraft, the plane started taxiing to the top of the 3,900 metre (concrete) runway. As soon as a *slot* became free in the air traffic, the aircraft thundered down the runway at 1,200km/h; once the aircraft had reached 30,000ft the pilot levelled the plane off and set the auto-pilot at the cruising speed of 850km/h.

Rickman activated the communications equipment, and his voice was relayed into the cabin area of the jet. "We are now cruising at 850km/h and so should reach Moscow *Sheremetyevo* Airport in roughly 2 hours, maybe a little more, where I am told it is sunny at the moment, but they are experiencing a cold spell. Winds are light and variable, but may increase the nearer we get to Moscow."

Alice thought she would have to put on a longer, and warmer, coat; luckily as well as her fur coat (synthetic) she'd packed her long, brown, duffel coat; so she unzipped her case, which was situated on the seat next to her, got the coat out and lay it over the seat arms, and then she got up, unzipped her leather jacket; this showed her body off to its best advantage, particularly as she was wearing a white t-shirt.

There were the occasional murmurs from the stewardesses aboard, and they even whispered amongst themselves. It wasn't as though Alice were a flirtatious person, but she liked people to know what she'd got; once she'd slipped the duffel coat on she sat back down again.

In *Proagnon* HQ the commander, known as Dr Q, who sat at the head of the table, turned to the second in command, known as Squeeze, and said, "How are the attacks progressing?"

"Well, as you know, leader," Squeeze replied, in a voice full of respect for the *Proagnon* leader, "we have destroyed the, English, Olympic village, killing the Royal family of that country in the process, thus forcing them to choose a new monarch. The attack on America went well, as well, destroying their president's residence, the White House; however, one of our agents, a Russian named Sergey, was captured."

Two questions: What is the mettle of the new English monarch? And will Sergey talk?"

"Firstly," the black clad figure answered. "The new, English, monarch is young and unstable, no more than a child in some respects. Secondly, Sergey may talk, but as he is Russian, there is little to link him with us."

"Is there anything else to report that is of interest to our cause?" the, blue, uniformed figure of Dr Q asked.

"As you also know," answered the black clad figure of Squeeze, "our attack on the world peace conference was a success, all of the world leaders were killed in the initial explosion. Anyone who managed to survive, somehow, will be dealt with, in due course. Finally, we have a report, preliminary at the moment that our agent in Russia assassinated the President; of course, he didn't linger around after the president fell, in case someone saw him and connected him with the shooting, That is everything, for the moment, Dr Q." The other troopers, together with Squeeze, waited for their commander to speak again.

"This new monarch of England, you say they are young and unstable," Dr Q said to Squeeze, "do you feel the time may be approaching to activate our agent over there?"

"I believe we should think about it, but not at the moment" Squeeze answered. "What should our next move be?"

"I have learnt, through certain sources, that the French intend to launch a new line of pleasure cruisers, they are testing the prototype in a couple of weeks from now. I think we should get some of our agents aboard, covertly of course, and blow up the ship. I'm sure there will be many passengers aboard." Everyone gathered around the table smiled at that thought.

"Also I've heard that the Americans are building a new super-tanker, and sending it to the oil fields of Saudi Arabia, in order to collect 65,000 tonnes of crude oil for their refineries. My idea is to get three of our agents, place them, again covertly, one at American Airlines, as an engineer, one in the Subway System, again an engineer, and one aboard the super-tanker, again an engineer; each will place a bomb on their assigned transport, all three will be armed with a fail safe device. Only one of these three bombs will go off, but whichever it is will cause absolute devastation, causing many to be killed."

"How will we know which it is to be?" asked one of the troopers, nervously.

"I will have the trigger mechanism, so only I shall know," said the leader in response. "Now you are all dismissed." All the combat troops nodded and left.

"Now Squeeze," Dr Q said, "I may have a little job for you."

"What is it?"

"I am assuming HART has been called in to deal with us and our attacks."

"I am assuming they have Dr Q, well if they haven't already they soon will be. Anyway what is this job you would like me to perform?"

"I require you," answered Squeeze's superior, "to find one of their agents and make them talk, discover their plans and find out information, any way you can, and report to me."

"Any way I can, that'll be a challenge," and Squeeze laughed.

"That is your mission, you may go as soon as you are ready," Squeeze rose from the seat, saluted Dr Q and left. Behind the mask the commander of *Proagnon* smiled.

The Gulfstream jet, with Alice on board, touched down on Russian soil at around 10:30, (local Russian time) in the evening. Once the mobile staircase had arrived Alice gathered her case up, thanked the stewardesses, together with Sean Rickman, and walked down the staircase and went into *Sheremetyevo*'s Terminal 2.

She hadn't walked very far inside when a man's voice said, "Ah, Miss Stronglove, we've been expecting you, this way please," and Alice was led through Terminal 2 and over to a waiting Mercedes Benz, white in colour. She immediately became a little suspicious.

"Before I get in what is the codeword?" Alice demanded, only the man who'd come to meet her would know it.

"Gwyneth," he answered. Knowing this was correct, she allowed the man to open the rear door for her and she got in; he closed the door after her and got in the front passenger seat.

The driver, of the vehicle, then drove from the airfield, and then the man who'd initially greeted her turned to face her, "I was instructed to greet you at Mr Robert's request. My name is Provalov, should you encounter any problems please let me know; this is my contact number," and he handed her a card. "Your mission, as you know, is to infiltrate the foreign ministry, and gather intelligence, however you can; your cover name on this mission is Maria Bondarenko. The minister you will be working for is Oleg Ayanseikov."

"You will, for the duration of your stay, be staying at the Belgrad Hotel; this will be paid for by HART, also it is very near the foreign ministry building. However, you are asked to find out the information HART requires as quickly as possible. The foreign ministry is located in this separate building and not in the Kremlin; you start tomorrow at 9:15am. That concludes your briefing." He turned to face the front.

They reached the hotel about an hour after they'd left the airport, Alice was starting to get a bit weary by then, travel did that to her; Provalov escorted her to the reception desk. "Miss Bondarenko," he said to the female receptionist who was working behind the desk.

"Yes," smiled the receptionist, she was only young Alice noted, "room 314," and she handed the key to the room over.

"Thank you," said Alice, smiling back, then Provalov led her over to some elevators, in the far corner. The elevator ascended and took them to the third floor, and halfway along the corridor they found room 314.

Provalov then left to return downstairs; Alice entered the room and closed the door, the locking mechanism was automatic; she sat down on the bed and had a long think about how she was going to get the information HART had requested she get; finally a plan formed in her mind. With this plan thought through she undressed and climbed into bed.

Back at *Proagnon* headquarters similar thoughts were running through Squeeze's mind. She knew the HART compound was in Geneva.

Over in the United States of America the FBI had had no luck, so far, in interrogating the Russian *Proagnon* trooper, Sergey. All they could get out of him was he was of Russian origin, and his name was Sergey; to any further questions he would shake his head, raise his hand in a *stop* gesture, and say, "I am sorry, I do not understand." Many methods had been tried, from the softly, softly approach to the threat of torture.

Lucy Lang, the fifth team leader of HART, had been called in to assist the FBI officers, with special permission of Peter Roberts. Due to her special training she could speak many languages, including Russian. She watched, through the one way viewing screen, as Sergey was interrogated by one of the American law enforcement officers. In the end, after several attempts to try and obtain the information he required, the law enforcement officer threw his hands up in despair and left the room; there was always a guard on duty so the prisoner couldn't escape. "You see what we have to put up with," he said to Lucy, in a matter-of-fact voice.

"I do indeed," she replied with a slight smile. "Tell me, what tactics did you end up using?"

"I called his mother a whore, and his brother a bastard child."

"And what did he say?"

"If that was my opinion of them, then that was fine by him."

"Hmm," murmured Lucy, thinking. "Give me five minutes with him and you'll have more than enough information to satisfy you."

"Okay you can have a go, but as you saw it's like trying to get blood out of a stone."

"Let me worry about that," Lucy replied, confidence in her voice. "Now run along, I'm sure you've got parking fines to give out."

Arrogant bitch, thought the officer, who was in reality an inspector. *Oh well*, he thought and walked away. Lucy entered the interrogation room, Sergey looked up at her. Did they really think sending a woman in, and not an FBI woman at that, would do any good, "Hello," she said, in English, sitting across the table from him, "my name's Lucy, what's yours?"

What foolery is this, the Russian thought, and decided to play along with this game, "Sergey," he answered.

Lucy sat forward and looked straight at him, their eyes meeting over the table, "What is your full name?" she asked in perfect Russian. Sergey was taken aback.

"Sergey Satov," was the astonished reply. She saw his astonishment and decided to take full advantage of it. Lucy unzipped her top, a little. His eyes saw the tiny amount of flesh and stared in wonder. Lucy saw his eyes move to her chest, *Men were so predictable.*

"Were you involved in the attack on the White House?" was the next question, again in perfect Russian. Sergey wondered where they'd found this beauty. He knew it'd be no good lying to her.

"Yes I was," he answered, truthfully, again another little unzip, she was teasing him, he was very sure of that.

The next question was again in his native tongue, "How many of you were involved?"

Four of us were in our group." Again another little unzip of her top.

"How many of you survived?"

"Only two of us survived, myself and my immediate commander." As much as Sergey wanted to protect his accomplices, he found himself wanting to tell this, young, woman everything, in the hope of gaining her trust. Another little unzip of her tunic, he was getting hot under the collar, and in his loins.

"Where is your commander now?" Lucy asked him.

"I don't know. I think he escaped and left me as a scapegoat," Sergey admitted to his interrogator. A tiny unzip; if the interrogation went on much longer she'd have to find some more clothing to tease him with.

"Your headquarters, I assume you belong to *Proagnon*, do you know where it is?" Lucy asked, hopefully.

"No," he answered, bluntly.

She zipped her top back up, "Thank you for your cooperation," she said, in English, Lucy, then, got up and marched out the room, she could feel Sergey's eyes follow her as she left. *Bloody women*, the Russian thought, *always leading you on, but when it comes to the crunch they just won't go the full distance.*

At HART headquarters, in Geneva, the next morning was just beginning. At 4am a klaxon, or in some cases the fire alarm, sounded and all the HART personnel got up, stretched and dressed. Everyone was allowed 15 minutes to dress and then be out on the parade ground. The other four team leaders: Ronan, Celia, Leon and Mark were already on the parade ground, and getting prepared to begin the morning's gruelling, physical exercise routine. Before the routine began the personnel had to perform thirty push-ups, thirty sit-ups, and then just jog on the spot for 30 seconds to get them warmed up. Then came the five mile run, with their backpacks filled with 20 bricks, to represent their kit.

Most of them handled this with ease, although there were the odd one or two who trailed behind, and had to be encouraged; even Celia managed it with ease, usually managing a time of 30 minutes; not far behind most of the men, at around 20 minutes.

Next the soldiers would tackle the assault course, where they had to use ropes to swing themselves over objects, climb frames then advance across a wooden beam, slide down fireman's poles, wade through water, traverse zip-wires, and scramble under nets.

Next came a good, hearty, breakfast of scrambled eggs, bacon and sausages, followed by toast, marmalade or jam, together with tea and coffee, or squash if the individual preferred. About an hour later came a swimming session. All personnel, unless deemed ill or unfit, had to swim 50 lengths in HART's, specially built, 50 metre pool. Everything was completed, usually, by eight in the morning, and then for the next hour they were allowed to act freely.

At 10am everyone had to be on the parade ground, for inspection of themselves and their kit by their overall commander. Once this had been completed every member of the personnel followed their leader inside the main headquarters building. They took the elevator up to the fourth floor, and walked into the conference room; finding a seat at the large, wooden, table they sat down for the morning's briefing.

Gwyneth Jones entered the room with a report in her hands, "Sir, if I may." Peter Roberts took a seat himself, and then said, "Carry on Mrs Jones."

Suddenly, the door burst open and in, rushed, the figure of Dr Hans Schaiffer, "Sorry I'm late, have you begun yet?"

"No, Doctor, please find yourself a seat," said Peter, a slight annoyance in his voice. Dr Schaiffer found a vacant seat and sat down, "Now we're all here you may begin Mrs Jones," Peter said.

"Okay," Gwyneth announced, "as some of you know we received a, preliminary, report that President Krushkev had been assassinated. It now appears this was incorrect, and the bullet merely grazed the Russian President's arm. So he is doing well and will return to his job in approximately 10 days."

"Secondly, the interrogation of the Russian terrorist, captured by the FBI, and conducted by our own Lucy Lang, went well. His name is Sergey Satov, his mission was to destroy the White House and anyone inside it, he was one of a group of four, apparently, one, besides himself, he thinks, survived and returned to headquarters; however, he does not know where this headquarters is."

"Thank you Mrs Jones," said Peter, rising from his seat. "Does anyone have any questions?"

"Yes, I have," piped up Dr Schaiffer. "why was I not informed about the Russian president?"

"It was felt," began Roberts, "that as it happened, suddenly, and we only had a preliminary report, it was best not to tell you until we had something more substantial."

"I see, now, I think" replied the Doctor.

"As for everyone else," said Peter, looking round the room, "as we have no more information on the whereabouts of *Proagnon*, or where they intend to strike next, you are all dismissed; however, please stay on site, or if you are going off site: shopping etc. please wear your wrist communicators, in case of an emergency and you need to be recalled. Dismissed!"

The 200 troopers, together with the four team leaders, left the conference room and hurried to the elevator. Many would stay on site to practice their shooting skills, at HART's, specially built, shooting gallery. However, a few would go off site and do some shopping in the shops of Geneva, buy their loved ones presents.

CHAPTER 2

Murder & the russian connection!

At 6.40am, in the Russian capital of Moscow, Alice Stronglove, soon to be Maria Bondarenko, was awakened by her alarm clock. Groggily, she got herself up, slipped on a robe – that hotels always provide – and walked from the main bedroom into the bathroom, as the soles of her feet touched the ice cold marble floor Alice winced and wished she'd brought a pair of slippers, or some slip on shoes. Luckily, the bathroom was carpeted so Alice's feet soon became warmer.

She went and turned the shower on, slipped off the robe and stepped inside; the water was icy cold at first but slowly warmed up to a temperature Alice liked, not scalding, yet not cold, she washed herself all over and in every nook and cranny that was accessible to her; once Alice'd finished she turned the water off and stepped out, suddenly feeling cold again. She dried herself, thoroughly with a hotel towel; and then she slipped the robe back on and walked through to the main bedroom area.

Alice looked in the wardrobe and tried to decide what she would wear, a top but nothing too revealing or see thru, that counted out most of her tops then. Finally, settling on a leopard skin top, with no sleeves; she took this garment out, from the wardrobe and placed it on the bed.

Next came the trousers, most of them showed her backside to full advantage, but which to choose; finally she settled on a black pair, and lay them on the bed; Alice, also, took out her pair of trusty jeans and lay them on the bed as well; then she slipped the robe off, put on her leopard skin top and jeans, she'd change into the black trousers after breakfast.

With her clothes on, now it was time to pick the shoes, Alice had many pairs of boots as well. She selected a pair of, black, fur lined ankle boots, with zips up the sides, for later; for now she simply threw on a pair of, brown, flat shoes. Miss Stronglove exited her room, locked it, and then went downstairs in the hotel elevator, to the dining room, and breakfast.

As soon as she entered the dining room, many men's eyes looked up at her; many who were without companions, beckoned her to sit with them. Alice shook her head, in refusal, preferring to concentrate on the mission in hand, for this reason she sat at a table toward the back, and ate her breakfast, in peace and on her own.

Afterwards she took the journey back to her room, and put on her pair of black trousers, and her fur lined boots, plus she donned her, elegant, fur coat. Once she was ready Alice, now Maria, left her room, locked it, and returned downstairs in the elevator, to begin her first day at the Russian foreign ministry. After handing over her key to the receptionist, this time a man, she left.

As she made her way to her place of work she got many strange looks, both from men and women, maybe they hadn't seen a foreigner so well dressed, or not, as the case may be. Alice, now Maria, entered the ministry building, at the street level entrance, showed her pass, and gave the reason why she was there, to the guard on duty; he approved both documents, and sent her down a corridor to a set of four elevators.

Maria was met by a bell boy type person, who escorted her up to level 5, which would be her place of work. Again she showed her pass and reason for being there, to another security guard; again he approved both documents, and she was directed to a couch to wait. Maria hung her coat, on the coat rack provided and sat down to wait.

Presently, a youngish, about 40 year old, man came in and hung his coat up; he looked very official, Maria thought, dressed in his, brown suit, with, white shirt and, black, tie; he, also, carried an attaché case with him, therefore Maria assumed he was the minister, or at least one of them. Noticing Maria, he asked her, "Are you Maria Bondarenko? Here for the job as temporary secretary?"

"Right on both counts sir," she responded, with a smile.

He looked across at another secretary, a blonde one, "How is my diary for today Petra?"

"Let me see, Comrade Minister, you have no meetings booked until this afternoon, and that one is only with the Minister for Agriculture."

"Very good Petra," he turned back to Maria. "Now Maria," he said, "it seems I can show you round myself; this morning. Please follow me." She hesitantly got up and walked after him, much to the annoyance of Petra, Alice couldn't understand why Petra looked put out. The minister led her to a, vacant, desk, quite near his office, his name was Oleg Ayanseikov, This will be your desk," Oleg announced. "As you can see it is quite near my office," he added, with an impish smile. "If you require any assistance, please do not hesitate to knock and ask. If I am out, however, please ask Petra for assistance, as she has worked here the longest."

"I will do that. Thank you Comrade Minister," she said. It was then she noticed a couple of young men working – at the back – on computers.

"Maria, you will be required to bring any forms that come in, over the fax machine, into my office for me to sign. Once I have signed them you will be required to: photocopy them, so we have a copy in the records, and then send the original, with signature, back to the original department, from where it came. Again if I am not available Petra will perform this task."

"Again, thank you Comrade Minister."

"Now, I wish to talk to you, in my office, more privately, to get to know each other a little better," and he strode into his office. "Chop, chop!"

"At once Minister," and Maria followed him inside, she was nervous again – especially when she caught a look off the other secretary. Oleg was already seated behind his, oak, desk, he had a globe of the world on the desk, along with several official, looking, papers; around the room were several, metal, filing cases. Maria walked in, slowly; taking everything in; she knew the information she needed would be locked away in one of those cabinets, but which one she didn't know. However, she wondered, was there an easier way to get the information?

The minister shoved several forms from the corner of his desk onto the floor, and said to her, in a purring voice, "Please close the door, and perch on the edge of the desk my dear; don't worry, I won't hurt you."

Yeah, like hell you wouldn't if it was found out that your ministry was in league with Proagnon! Maria thought, but climbed aboard anyway. "I am a single man now," Oleg said to her, "after my wife died 5 years ago, after a sudden illness." *Whoa buddy!,* Maria thought, *what you telling me this for?*

"Therefore," Oleg continued, not in the least bit embarrassed, "I still have a man's needs," his hand now stroking Maria's, right, leg. As she moved her leg, to prevent it getting cramp, his hand found her buttock.

Wait a minute mate, if you think we're gonna get up to anything in your office, you got another God damned thing coming.

"Maria," Oleg resumed, all business-like now, "would you please be my guest at a dinner function, to be held at the Rossija Hotel tonight? It is only a short drive from the Belgrad Hotel, where I believe you are staying."

"Why yes minister, I should be delighted," Maria responded eagerly, *this may be easier than I thought. And anyway, how does he know where I'm staying?*

"We shall meet in the lobby of the Belgrad at eight," he said, and then in a sterner manner, "and pick those papers up off the floor, you stupid girl!"

"At once sir," Maria replied, bending down to pick the papers up. When she stood up again Oleg's bright, green, eyes were twinkling, mischievously.

Deep down, at *Proagnon*'s headquarters, a hatch slid back, in the sand, and an aircraft appeared. The pilot of this craft had filed a flight plan, which would take it to Geneva. Thus, it would land at *Cointrin* International Airport. Once the machine had landed and had been secured, the pilot/agent aboard would leave the terminal in a special custom made, BMW coupe. As with all automobiles in Switzerland, it had CH in its registration to identify it.

The *Proagnon* agent would then find a member of the HART personnel, if they could, and *squeeze* the information that *Proagnon* required. Armed with the information the agent would then, either, contact their masters over the encrypted

VHF signal, or simply return to the airport and return to headquarters.

The agent left the airport and drove, directly, to the *Rues Basses* shopping mall, which was always a good place to find people, especially as this one was open late.

Ignoring the, brutish looking, security men, the agent continued further inside; spying a, young, man in a shop named *G-leaves* – a female underwear store - probably buying some new underwear for a loved one, the agent looked down at his wrist. *Yes!* There was a HART communicator strapped to him, it looked very similar to a watch except it had no dial or hands.

Sidling up to him the enemy agent asked, "Do you need any help choosing what garments to buy?"

The man looked shocked; someone was offering to help him. The woman he saw was, he guessed, in her late twenties; she had, shoulder length, lovely blonde hair, and had light green eyes. The eyes were concealed behind, black, square framed glasses; finally she was dressed in a black, PVC, suit which clung to her in all the right places. "Yes please," he stammered, embarrassed at being caught.

"Now, this lady friend of yours, I am right in thinking they're for a lady."

"Of course they are," he blustered. "I'm not bloody kinky or gay!"

"I never said you were, darling," she cooed, in her best female cooing voice. "Now, your friend, what sort of size is she?"

"To be honest," Mark Schneider, as that's who it was, said to this mystery woman. "She is, I would say, exactly your size."

"Well," the woman, whose name for the mission was Sarah said, "I'll tell you what, I'm shopping for some underwear of my own. If you like, I'll buy mine, and then if you'd care to meet me tonight, at the hotel where I'm staying, which is the Hotel Tiffany, the address is 20 Rue de L'Arquebuse CH-1204 Geneva. I am in room 38 of this, luxury, hotel; meet me in the restaurant, at 7pm for dinner, and then afterwards we can adjourn to my room, use the Mini Bar, and then I will give you a, private showing of the garments I have bought; see what you think, and also to see if they might be suitable for your friend."

Mark thought about this, would his fiancée, Lucy Lang, ever forgive him? Still, it was for her, in a way, he'd be doing this. "Okay," he, reluctantly, agreed.

"I'll see you at seven, in the Tiffany's restaurant," Sarah said, winking at him; then she gave him a quick kiss, and walked deeper into the shop, to select her garments.

Whoa!, Mark thought, when she kissed him, *she's one hell of a girl.* What he didn't see, as he had his back to her, was her, cruel, smile as he left the store.

At 7pm that evening Mark Schnieder left the HART compound, and drove the distance to the Hotel Tiffany, located on the Rue Des Marbriers, in the west of Geneva.

The Hotel Tiffany was built at the 19th century, and was situated in a small, quiet street close to the Grand Theatre, the Museum of Contemporary Art, galleries and other designer shops, it is also right next to the banking district. The railway station and the lake and the banks of the Rhone river are just 5 minutes' walk away; all are on the edge of the old town of Geneva, with its picturesque narrow streets, therefore the hotel is ideal for exploring Geneva.

Although the hotel was situated away from the, more, major roads it was still seen as being in the heart of Geneva.

The hotel contained 46 rooms, including two suites with a Jacuzzi and one junior suite, elegant decor, stylish furniture and a Belle Epoque atmosphere down to the smallest detail made this *luxury* hotel a haven of peace and the place to stay. Guests could also try the on-site restaurant, which offered an innovative menu with a focus on fresh produce. In fine weather the restaurant could open onto the hotel terrace. Each of the 46 rooms was air conditioned, had satellite television, a private bathroom, telephone, mini bar, hair dryer, room safe, coffee maker, a smoke detector (standard), and internet access/wi-fi.

Mark walked in, and asked the receptionist where the restaurant was; the receptionist, upon seeing his HART pass, gave Mark the, necessary, directions. He followed these and soon found where he wanted to be, upon entering he scanned the faces at the tables, eventually finding her sitting at a middle of the room table; as soon as she saw him she, politely, beckoned him over. Mark went over and seated himself opposite her.

The young woman, then, introduced herself as Sarah Taylor and asked him his name. Mark made the stupid blunder of introducing himself by his real name.

Every agent that went through the HART training programme was told you never, ever, use your real name when meeting someone, in the field, unless you were positive they were also a member of the HART personnel. Other agents, from the past, had got killed for doing that.

They had a dinner of Salmon, Shrimps, and, Baked Potatoes, topped off with White wine. The mood was then set for the rest of the evening. When they were both ready Miss Taylor picked up her handbag, slung it over her shoulder, and then they both left with their arm around each other's waist; as they were waiting for the elevator Sarah turned to Mark, "I noticed earlier your hesitation/reluctance to meet me."

"Ah that," he replied. "It's just that I have a fiancée, over in America, and I was wondering if she'd object to what we're doing, probably she would, but as she's approximately 4000 miles away, plus I'm doing this for her, in a way, I'm sure she'd understand."

"Yes I'm sure she would," Sarah assured him, even though she knew his fiancée would really object she needed him for a purpose and she'd get the information she wanted any way she could; if that meant having to reassure him many times she would. What Mark didn't know, and would have left the hotel if he had, was that Lucy was, at this moment, only 5 miles away at the airport.

It had been felt, by Peter Roberts, that since she'd interviewed the FBI's Russian prisoner, she could be brought over to Geneva, to HART headquarters in order to help in the fight against *Proagnon*. If there were any new developments, or if Sergey Satov told them anymore, though that was a bit doubtful, the FBI would contact HART and inform Peter Roberts.

However, at that moment Sarah Taylor was letting Mark Schnieder into her hotel room. "You make yourself more comfortable, seat yourself on the double bed, and help yourself to drinks from the Mini Bar," and then gathering up a *G-leaves* bag she moved off toward the bathroom. "I will try on each garment, I purchased today, for your approval, darling. I will, also, try each top with each set of bottoms, to see which you would prefer to see your fiancée in." Mark wanted to see more, but knew Lucy may end up hating him for it.

Before Sarah walked into the bathroom, to try on the first set of garments she made both of them a drink from the Mini bar; however, what Mark didn't see was her slip a small, white, capsule in his drink. The capsule dissolved instantly. She then stirred the drink to make sure there was no powder left, and then handed Mark the drink.

I don't want you asleep yet, I want you to enjoy the show!

"Thanks darling," he replied, taking the drink she offered him, he took a sip, and then set it down, "I'll just go try the garments on now," she said, moving fully into the bathroom.

"Okay darling," a slightly intoxicated Mark Schnieder replied, in a bit of a slurred voice. *Hmm,* he thought, *the drink tastes slightly off. Must be because it's continental, and why do I keep referring to Sarah as darling when I know she isn't?*

A few moments passed, during that time he kept sipping at his drink, swirling it in his glass, even stirring it with his finger; anything to see if he could get it to taste better.

Suddenly, the bathroom door opened, and framed in the doorway was Sarah Taylor, kitted out in the set of, white, underwear. She took a few steps towards him, did a little twirl to show it fitted snugly where it should, and then, when she was facing him again, she bent over to show it fitted her chest. "Nice," he breathed.

"You think so?" she asked him. "There are others." With that, she walked back into the bathroom, and, a few moments later emerged in a set of, purple, underwear. This was followed by a black set, and finally a dark red set; all the sets had matching bras with front openings.

"I like it," he enthused, trying to reach out to grab her; however, she was just far enough out of his reach, and Mark's arms felt like lead now anyway, for some reason. Why had he tried to grab her, he wondered, he should be concentrating on Lucy.

"Patience darling," she assured him with a smile, "I have one more set to show you." With that Sarah disappeared into the bathroom again, and a few moments later re-emerged dressed in a pair of sheer black, shorts, together with a white, fishnet material T-shirt. "Which set of underwear are you modelling now?" he asked, certain he already knew the answer but was curious.

"Well darling, if you care to unwrap the outer packaging you'll find out," she said, teasingly to him. Mark got shakily to his feet and wandered over to her. "Easy big boy," she said, when he nearly collapsed in her arms. He held her and they started kissing, Mark trying to pull her towards the bed – even though he knew it was wrong, and Sarah, knowing in reality who he was, allowed herself to be led.

They fell onto the bed, Sarah, the only one in full command of her faculties, kicked the bed sheets back. This man was an animal, tearing at her T-shirt; so she went slack allowing him to finish the job. Once her chest was, fully, exposed, she unbuttoned and removed his shirt; next came her shorts, revealing her full body. Next came his, dark green, shorts, and finally his underwear. All the garments were, simply, thrown on the floor in a heap.

Mark was now like a savage animal. He made love to her over and over again, each time more savage than the last. Finally, when he was calm again, she turned and said to him, "I noticed in the store today that you were wearing a watch, and still are," she brought his arm out from under the covers, to prove it. "Yet, it is unlike any watch I've seen before, having no dial, hands or numbers on it, and it is a slightly faded *red* colour. What is the purpose of it?" Sarah, a.k.a. Squeeze, already knew the purpose but wanted to see how far she could push him, the substance she'd drugged him with had helped already.

"That," he answered, gesturing towards it with his chin, as he couldn't seem to move the arm of his own free will, "is a communicator that keeps me in touch with my headquarters. It flashes *red* and buzzes, if we are needed to return to HQ. I work for HART you see, which stands for Human Army for the Retaliation against Terrorism." That was mistake number two, in Mark Shnieder's case; never reveal how you communicate with headquarters to anyone, even if they are considered a friend, or in the case of this woman, his bedfellow. Plus, as it was red, it was reasonably noticeable.

"I see," remarked Sarah. Then she asked him, "But really, do you have to sleep with it on?"

"I suppose not," he admitted to her, slipping it off his wrist and putting it on the side cabinet. Mistake number three; never remove your wrist communicator, even if you think you feel safe, and feel you aren't going to be recalled.

"That's better," she muttered, allowing him to slip inside her again.

At the end of the working day, in Moscow, Maria Bondarenko walked back to the Belgrad hotel thinking about the minister, what information she could get out of him later, and how best to use this information, and him if it came to that, he'd certainly seemed keen earlier, to her best advantage.

She, silently, went up to her room, and looked at the dresses she'd brought with her. She had the choice of the, light blue, dress, which, when she bent forward, showed her cleavage; also the dress was cut in a V at the back, exposing most of her back and the, tiny, top area of her backside, especially when she straightened up. Now the other dress was a bright green, and also full length; this would, again, also expose her cleavage, though not as much as the blue dress, if she leant forward. Did she go with the risky dress, and hope the ministers, surely there'd be more than one there, weren't too horny; or did she stick with the sensible dress, and let the evening play out as it did? Or she could always go in any number of different outfits; which would it be? Alice had not always chosen wisely, in clothes or men. This was something she would have to rectify; starting tonight.

In the end, after much deliberation, she chose the bright green full length dress; it was conservative but also a nice bright colour. She changed into the dress, after showering first;

well one didn't like to give the wrong impression, pulled on a pair of, beige, calf height boots, with fur on, and finally put on her fur coat; it wasn't that cold for her duffel, and she wanted to add a bit of elegance. She took a red handbag with her, as well; inside this she put her HART personal organiser, in case she needed to take notes.

Once she was ready she left her room, locking the door behind her; secured her room key in her purse, tonight was one night she wanted it with her, and then she took the elevator from the third floor down to the ground floor. She wandered into the lobby and sat down to wait.

At around quarter to eight Oleg Ayanseikov arrived, shadowed by two bodyguards. "Ah, Maria, you are ready, please let us escort you to our waiting car. Don't worry about my bodyguards; they are trained to protect me whenever I'm not in the office."

Miss Bondarenko got up from her seat, and started to follow the lead bodyguard out, the minister came next, and then finally the second bodyguard. The procession arrived at a, white, Mercedes Benz. The bodyguards opened the rear doors, for their passengers, who climbed in. Then one bodyguard got in the front, drivers, seat; obviously he doubled as the driver as well, whilst the other, neither they nor their minister referred to each other by name, climbed in the back with his minister, and his guest. Once everyone was in, the doors were locked and the car sped off. It was only then that Maria realised she had neglected to bring her 9mm Parabellum, still it was too late now

The Mercedes sped through the Moscow evening traffic and arrived at the entrance to the Rossija hotel at about five to eight. The bodyguards handed their passengers over to the hotel staff; all had been vetted before arranging the dinner, as presenting no threat; and waited in the car, as they had been instructed.

"Now, my dear," Oleg said to Maria, "you are about to meet some of the most influential men, and women, in Russia. *Great!*, Maria thought, *so I might meet some women who are lesbians too!*

They were escorted up to the fifth floor, where the dinner was being held, by a senior bell boy. As they exited the elevator Maria took her fur coat off and hung it up with the others, as soon as Oleg saw the dress she was wearing he was speechless. "You look very beautiful in that dress Maria."

"Why thank you Comrade Minister," she replied, blushing slightly.

At just gone eight, nothing ran on time – even in Moscow, Alice noted, they were shown into a large, function, room; with a very long and large, dining, table – with places to seat at least fifty people – if needed. As they walked in Oleg came after Maria, using the gentleman's phrase of 'Ladies first', once he was close enough the foreign minister reached forward and squeezed her buttock through the material of her trousers. Alice made no reaction, just walked further in the room, found a vacant seat and sat down

Not quite the reaction Oleg expected, as he did consider himself a bit of a ladies man – Petra had given herself to him many a time – sometimes in the office – but this Miss Maria Bondarenko was, somehow, different; either she was a spy, which he didn't believe, or she was not a girl who spread her legs that easily.

He took a seat opposite her, and then the doors at the far end of the room were thrown open and in marched several people, the lead one dressed in the Russian uniform of an officer in the army; Alice looked up, he had a square shaped face, with a thick black moustache, but his eyes – which were blue – were very icy. Once the other men, and women, were seated he sat down, himself, and banged on the table; immediately waiters appeared and served them all drinks. The foreign minister's new secretary took a sip; it was pure vodka, not the usual vodka mixed with some other Russian liquor. Disgusted she had to pour it in one of the numerous plants, in the room.

The Russian military officer noticed this, "Don't you like the drink, girl," he roared fiercely, putting her on edge straight away. "That was a waste of some good vodka."

Luckily for her the foreign minister leapt to her defence, "Comrade Minister for the Defence, my new secretary, Maria

Bondarenko, has only been here a few days, so she has not fully adjusted to our ways yet."

"Has she spread her legs for you yet?" called a voice from the other end of the table. Maria noted the voice belonged to a woman, so most of the ministers knew of the foreign minister's womanising ways; yet she hadn't until now.

"Comrade Minister for the SVR, of course she hasn't."

"But I bet she will," the same minister said; everyone laughed except the intended target girl who just went very red with embarrassment.

"We're sorry my dear," the minister of defence assured her. The main course arrived, Beef with a selection of Potatoes and vegetables, along with plenty of gravy. Everyone tucked in, even Alice, who didn't usually like Beef.

As she leant forward to help herself to more, her cleavage was revealed as her dress became slack, and many of the ministers; male and female got a good look. The minister for the SVR murmured to her, in a hushed voice, "Anytime!"

The young woman was shocked by this response, and, quickly stood up; unfortunately, she stood up a bit too quickly, and some gravy splashed on her dress. "Oh dear," said the minister for defence, and being a gentleman, handed her his napkin. She tried to rub the gravy off, but that only made the stain worse.

"That'll have to come off," the SVR minister told her. "Would you like to come with me and we'll sort that mess out?"

"No thank you," answered the new secretary. "I'll leave it as it is!"

"But it looks most unsightly my dear," the minister said again. Maria could tell that this woman was a lesbian and wanted to take advantage of her, but she wouldn't give in and let her.

"I'll take my chances," was the response, and with that she sat down and ate the rest of her meal. Afterwards, once the plates and glasses had been cleared away the Russian defence minister, Mikhail Suvorov, stood and turned to look at his counterpart from the foreign ministry, "How goes the sales to Dr. Quantum?"

"It goes well defence minister Suvorov, he and his company have placed, yet, another order with me. I hope we can meet his requirements."

Suvorov roared, "I'm sure we can. What does he require this time?"

Oleg stood and said to his military counterpart, "His company has shown interest in and has requested the Admiral *Kuznetsor* aircraft carrier, any *Kirov* class battle cruiser we can supply, any *Kara* class cruiser, any *Slava* class cruiser, any *Sovremenny* class destroyer, any *Udalov* class destroyer, plus any *Neutrashimy* class frigate. They also require many submarines: Borei class, Akula class, Typhoon class, Delta class, Oscar class, Kilo class and Graney class."

"Those we can supply," announced Suvorov. "Does he require anything else?"

"Oh yes," answered Oleg. "Several different tanks; T-72s, T-80s and T-90s. Several armoured personnel carriers, BTR-60s, -70s, -80s and MT-LBs. That is all for the moment."

"We shall supply him with all he needs," said Mikhail Suvorov, "though what his company wants them for, I don't know."

"Maybe the company collects these types, and others, of military craft for exhibitions," Oleg speculated.

Yeah, or maybe they're planning on starting a war, thought the new secretary, writing the names into her, electronic, personal organizer for later reference.

"Maria," said the SVR minister, whose name Maria now knew was Svetlana Petrova, "why are you so quiet, and what is that thing?" she asked indicating the personal organizer.

"Firstly Comrade Minister, I am being quiet, as I feel, being a humble secretary, it is not my place to speak out at these, such, meetings. As for this, this is my personal organizer, an electronic device I use to write notes, should my minister need to recall, in memory, these items in the future."

"A handy little device," remarked Svetlana. "Tell me, where did you get it?"

Alice thought of a plausible explanation quickly, "It was sent to me by my brother, Pavel, who now works in the Japanese electronics industry."

80

"I feel now, if no-one has anything further to add, may be time to bring this meeting to a close, "said the foreign minister. Everyone agreed, and the ministers rose from the table and left the conference hall. As Miss Bondarenko was getting her fur coat Svetlana came up to her and muttered, "We'll meet again, I'm sure of it."

In Geneva, next morning,at the Hotel Tiffany, Sarah, Squeeze, Taylor disentangled herself from Mark Schnieder's grip, and walked to the bathroom to shower and dress; Mark had enjoyed himself the previous night, or had it been the other way round? She took the communicator with her, but shielded it with her body, and slipped it in her handbag; then she showered and dressed, in her black combat suit; then got a pair of, white, cotton gloves, from her bag, and slipped them on.

Once she was ready she strode, purposefully, back into the main bedroom area; agent Mark Schnieder was just coming round, "Good morning Sarah," he said, once his vision had cleared. Squeeze didn't really want to do what she had to, though she knew it was necessary, considering he had pleased her over the previous night.

"Sarah," Mark said, "have you seen my communicator? It's not where I left it."

"Morning darling," she replied, cheerily, hopping on the bed beside him, and then standing up in front of him. "I've got your communicator," she replied, in answer to his question.

"You!" he said, incredulously, "why would you want it? And why are you wearing those gloves?"

Her reply made him shudder, "To stop you from contacting them, because I, yes I, am *Proagnon's* second-in-command; my real name is Squeeze. As for your other question you'll find out soon enough."

"You bitch!" he spat. "Luring me here on the pretence of wanting to help me, taking advantage of me, what are you going to do to me now?"

"This," she answered, cruelly, pulling a seemingly harmless ball-point pen from her pocket, lowering herself down to his height, and then placing the pen against his chest and pressing the top 'to *click* the pen's nib, and injected him with a drug that rendered Mark totally inactive; he could still see, but couldn't move a muscle.

The pen, in question, had been invented by an organisation in America, an agent from *Proagnon* had stolen the plans and then the pen device had been remodelled by *Proagnon* scientists, made easier to use, and equipped with a deadly, paralysing, substance, which if injected in large doses could prove fatal. The substance usually acted fast on its target, and they were totally paralyzed within 30 seconds; although sight and sound went unaffected.

Mark gasped in shock, and once she was certain he couldn't move, the substance took effect in 30 seconds, Squeeze looked him straight in the eye and said, in a cold voice, "I don't want you to stop me, but I want you to enjoy this."

He was wondering what she was going to do to him; he didn't have long to find out, she made a loop with her legs, lifted his legs and slid them through hers so her legs were looped around his. She then shuffled up to the top of his legs, looked him again in the eye and, simply, told him, "I'm so sorry I have to do this to you my darling;" and she leaned forward and kissed him.

Suddenly, she produced a knife from her tunic, leaned down and cut his member off; blood started pooling on the sheet, his face was a look of horror – he wanted to scream but couldn't.

She, then, put the knife away, and then pulled her legs tighter around him; now he knew why she was called Squeeze; his bones were crushed by the tightness as she contracted her muscles, his internal organs folded in upon themselves and then simply stopped working.

Once Squeeze was certain Mark was dead she relaxed her grip, put Mark's member in his mouth, got off the bed and covered the body with the sheets. Next she walked back into the bathroom, cleaned herself as best she could; then she gathered her bags, and then took the *G-leaves* bag, with the underwear in, and hung it on the end of the bed. Once this was done she wandered back into the bathroom, took her gloves off and dropped them into the toilet, wrapping some paper round her hand she flushed the toilet; when the gloves had been flushed away, Squeeze dropped the paper into the bowl.

Once that was done she left, using a tissue to open the door, hanging the *Do Not Disturb* sign on the door and left thinking, *such a gullible fool.* She handed her key to the receptionist, and then simply, left the hotel.

CHAPTER 3

Discovered! & danger in Russia!

Later that morning, at the Hotel Tiffany, the maid started her rounds, cleaning rooms, making beds up, replacing towels etc. She noticed that room 38 had its *Do Not Disturb* sign hanging on the door, yet clearly the occupant was in the room as the door had been left slightly ajar. Plucking up courage she tapped on the door and called, "Hello, may I come in?" The worst that could happen, she figured, was that she'd be told to leave the occupant alone, probably in more colourful language, and couldn't she read the sign on the door?

However, there was no reply, so the maid, a new one and quite young – only 20, opened the door a little more, but keeping her hand on the handle – lest someone suddenly appear from the bathroom – knocked and called her question again. Still getting no answer she opened the door a little further. That was when she saw a man's set of clothes on the floor, and the body on the bed, covered by the sheets; not realising he was dead she ventured into the room and said, absently, "I'll just put these away for you." As she lifted the shirt off the floor a pungent aroma hit her nose, a smell she associated with butcher's shops. Slowly, she looked up at the bed; the sheets were now a deep *red* in colour, the colour of blood. Thinking that, maybe, someone was bleeding she edged closer; she had learnt *first aid* a few years back and wondered if she might, perhaps, be able to help. As soon as she pulled the covers back and saw him she screamed; it wasn't the actual body she was screaming at, it was what was protruding from his mouth, and where he was bleeding from, though most of the blood had dried, or was drying, now.

She bolted from the room, slamming the door behind her; she didn't want any of the other residents to look into that room and at that poor man, she assumed it was a man judging by what she'd seen. The maid, leaving her cart where it was, virtually ran down the back stairs, and on into reception. The receptionist, and also the hotel manager, looked up as she flew across to the main desk. "Yes Petra?" asked the more senior man.

She started babbling, "Get the police! A man in room 38 has been killed, murdered, and his nob cut off!"

"His what?" asked the manager, disbelievingly.

"His nob! His dick! His cock!"

The senior man looked at the maid as if she were mad, "Impossible, there is no man in room 38."

"There is now. And believe me he is a very dead man."

He turned back and looked at the younger man, "Antonio, you stay here; I shall take a pager and investigate. If there is cause for alarm I shall page you and instruct you on what to do. Now, I believe I will need the key." The younger man nodded and handed the key over. "Lead on Petra."

Petra led him back to room 38, where he unlocked the door; before he opened it he turned to Petra, and looked at her severely, "If this is a false alarm, you will, instantly, be dismissed." He opened the door and walked in, expecting to have to apologise to the occupant on this maid's stupidity. However, what he saw was totally different; on the bed was a, totally, naked body, with something protruding from its mouth. He moved, slowly, toward the bed; as the manager looked closer he saw it was the man's member sticking out his mouth; so the maid wasn't lying. Instantly, he got the pager from inside his jacket, and dialled reception. He told Antonio, as brief as he could, to get the police and the paramedics, as what Petra had told them was true.

At HART HQ everyone, especially Lucy, was worried by Mark's continued absence. He had left at seven the evening before, telling a few friends he had a special night lined up, yet nothing had been heard from him since; as the four, remaining, team leaders, together with the Doctor, and their leader, were thinking of where their missing agent was there came a knock on the office door. "Come in," called Peter Roberts. The office door opened and Gwyneth Jones walked in with a fax. "What is it?" asked Mr Roberts.

"Sir, we have just received a fax from the Swiss police notifying us that a body has been found in a hotel room."

Roberts knew she wouldn't disturb him needlessly, "And," he prompted.

"The body is that of a man," Gwyneth continued, "I don't know if it's important, but do you think we should send someone, just in case, I mean it may not be important."

"I'll go," Lucy announced, taking the fax from Mrs Jones. Before Roberts; or anyone else could object, she left the office, closing the door behind her.

They met at the Moscow restaurant *Tinkoff* and sat in a corner booth, as most of the other tables and booths were occupied; one had a vodka, whilst the other had a vodka & orange. "Nice place," muttered the more junior. "Tell me why are we here?"

"Because, my dear, there are a few things you need to know about your employer."

The *Tinkoff*, as both knew, were a forward thinking brand who had successfully introduced its restaurant-cum-breweries all across Russia. This was no small wonder when a person considered that there were eight different beers to choose from, with watiers, kindly, supplying the ignorant with a free taster of each.

The brews on offer ranged from the Dulux inspired *Mellow Autumn* dark beer, to the lighter and crisper *Weissbier* lager, the latter was much favoured by the ladies. Plus the *Tinkoff* had as one of its other house specialities the, famous, one metre sausage.

The restaurant was located in the outer west part of Moscow, which was ideal for their little meeting; it was nowhere near the embassies either worked at.

"What else do I need to know about my employer?"

"He has fathered three children, and those weren't with his wife. I'm not saying his wife, Anastasiya and he weren't happy, but he wanted children which Anastasiya couldn't provide for him, as she was barren. Oleg knew this when they married and told her he could live with it, but it wasn't long before he was playing around."

"Who with?"

"Initially, prostitutes, but when they could no longer satisfy him he moved on." The other looked shocked at what she was hearing, but urged the other woman to continue. "He decided, then, to use his power as a minister to ensnare prospective women."

"Did he ensnare anyone?" asked the younger.

"Oh yes," came the response from the other. "His first secretary, Yekaterina; he tried it on with her."

"Sorry, just let me stop you," said the younger, "who's Yetakerina; I don't know her."

"Patience," replied the senior. "As I was saying he tried it on with Yetakerina, many times, but she always resisted or refused. In the end he pushed her too far, and for several days she didn't turn into work. Then a month later her body turned up in the woods in Siberia, in her car. According to the autopsy, which was performed on her, it was established she had asphyxiated herself."

"That's awful!" said the younger of the two women. "Was there anyone else?"

"Yes, he hired a new secretary, Petra Rumanov, this was all while Anastasiya was alive, and they would often work late together; so far, if I remember it correctly, she has given him three children, Nikolay-aged 10, Yelena-aged 8 and Aleksey-aged 6. All were conceived and born before Anastasiya died. Now, rumours are he wants another child with her," the senior of the two women explained. Then she asked, "Haven't you noticed how haggard and tired Petra looks?"

"I had noticed but I just thought it was from overwork." All the while the younger woman was trying to take everything in that she was being told. "And now what?" she asked her senior.

"All I want, my dear," said the other woman, "is for you not to follow in poor Petra's footsteps."

"And how do you know all this? You could be lying."

"The reason I know is, as the SVR minister, SVR being ex-KGB, we had a KGB agent situated, undercover, in the foreign ministry once, and he reported back, on a weekly basis, that there was something strange happening within. This agent; wasn't sure what so he probed a little deeper, and still to no avail."

"However, he'd noticed our friend Petra, hanging about the minister's office, more than a secretary should, and one day once Petra had entered the office he waited patiently; after a few moments *guttural* noises started to be heard emitting from our friend Oleg's office. Making sure there was no-one about to see him, our agent from KGB nipped over and had a peep through the office keyhole, he saw Petra and Oleg in the act of making love."

"As soon as was possible he left the foreign ministry building, and brought the information to the head of the KGB. Now KGB has disbanded and become SVR we still have certain files, usually for reference purposes. There you have it Miss Bondarenko."

"Hmm, interesting and very thought provoking. Thank you, I shall bear all you have told me in mind, and I shall be careful."

"That is all I ask, now onto more trivial matters, so as not to arouse suspicion, did you get that stain out your *green* dress?" Svetlana asked. This time, Alice noted, this question was asked totally innocently.

"No, I didn't," replied Maria. "Although I have brought with me another, more revealing, dress. I'm sure you'd like it!"

"I probably would, we must arrange something in the next few days." Both women left the café, then, and proceeded back to their places of work; neither noticed the figure in the raincoat and sunglasses watching them.

The aircraft hovered above *Proagnon* headquarters, once a pre-programmed code had been keyed in and activated, the hatch in the desert slid back, and the aircraft began its descent into the underground bunker. Once it had landed and been powered down, the pilot exited the craft and returned to their inner chamber; fuel lines were attached so the machine would be fuelled up if it were needed again.

Once she had changed into a fresh combat suit, black of course, she walked, along the corridors, to her commander's office and knocked on the door. "Come in," called his voice.

She entered and sat on the seat offered to her, he, himself, was seated behind his desk – there was a globe of the world on

his desk, and a map of the world situated on the wall behind –
there were, also, many, filing cabinets along each wall. He was
writing out more orders for extra military hardware. Once he'd
finished the request he was writing he looked over at her. "I
trust everything went well?"

"As well as can be expected," was the reply, spoken, Dr Q
noticed, with relish, and yet also with a touch of sadness and
regret. "Tell me what happened?" he purred.

Squeeze couldn't see through the, silver, face plate so was
unsure if he'd read her feelings or not. "I found him in an
underwear store called *G-leaves*, which is in the *Rues Bases*
shopping mall."

He stopped her by raising a gloved hand, "Names are
unimportant except his name. Now please carry on."

"I asked him if he wanted any help choosing the
underwear for his loved one; he looked shocked when I
offered to help, as if he'd been caught with his hands in the
cookie jar. Anyway, he agreed, saying I looked of a very similar
body shape to his fiancée, Lucy; I then mentioned I was buying
myself some underwear, and if he wanted he could meet me
where I was staying, later that evening, and I would put on a
private showing for him." She knew that Dr Q would ask her if
she had.

Not to disappoint her he then asked, "And did you?"

"Yes, Mark Schnieder – that was his name, met me where
I was staying, we had dinner together, and then went to my
room. I poured him a drink and popped a drug in it, not to
make him too sleepy; I then performed the show I'd promised,
and he, genuinely, enjoyed it. Finally, we ended up in bed
together, he was like an animal."

"When morning came I knew I had to kill him, but I
didn't want to as he'd been a fantastic lover."

"So did you kill him, or let your feelings get in the way?"

"Oh no, I killed him. First I injected him with the nerve
drug, so he could appreciate being killed, but not be able to do
a thing about it; next I produced my knife and cut his penis off,
he looked horrified, and then finally he learnt how I got the
name Squeeze. Once he was dead, just for the sheer hell of it, I
popped his penis in his mouth."

"You're a cruel killer," remarked the man behind the face plate. "But at least you've got a sense of humour," and they both laughed "Anyway, I've contacted our Russian friends and requested extra assets."

It was not so funny for Lucy, who had just arrived at the Hotel Tiffany along with the chief detective. Both were shown, immediately, to room 38, where a couple of the Swiss police force were guarding the entrance to the room. As soon as the detective, together with Miss Lang, appeared one of them announced, "Nothing has been touched, sir, ma'am, everything is just as it was."

"Thank you Jacques," said the detective; Lucy then piped up, "who found the body?"

"I believe the maid found him ma'am," replied Jacques, smartly. He could tell this woman was an official, of sorts, and, for whatever reason, needed to be there.

"Okay Jacques," said Lucy, "your superior and myself will inspect the crime scene. I think you and your colleague should get this maid and the manager together, see if they can shed any more light on this incident. Don't you agree Pierre?"

"What?" the detective turned. "Oh yes, anyone who may be able to help us in our inquiries. Here Miss Lang, best put these on," and he handed her a pair of *latex* rubber gloves. These were to protect their hands from leaving any unnecessary fingerprints.

They then entered the room, whilst the two police officers went to find the people they'd been instructed to find. Lucy closed the room door behind her, to prevent prying eyes, when she turned back she took one look at the body, and then hurriedly said to Pierre, "I think I'm going to be sick," and she rushed into the bathroom. Pierre, himself, felt uneasy about this, so he approached the body, slowly; suddenly Lucy flushed the toilet, and he spun round, alerted by the noise, and drew his service revolver. *Damn!*, he thought, and then realised, *It's only Miss Lang in the bathroom, why am I so jumpy?*

The bathroom door opened, after a few moments, and Lucy emerged, "That's better," she assured him, with a smile. "Now where were we?"

The detective looked at the corpse, "Well, I think, we can safely assume he's dead, but why would anyone want to kill him? And how did he end up here?"

"Who knows," she answered, then saw the bag hanging on the end of the bed. "It looks like he's done some shopping, let's have a look." Lucy, carefully, took the bag from where it hung, and held it in front of her, "Ah Mark, you bought me some presents," and she emptied the bag on the floor. As soon as she saw his shirt, shorts, his underwear; and then she saw a white fishnet ladies T-shirt, and a pair of, ladies, sheer black shorts. "You bastard!" she almost shouted, making the detective turn round. "You filthy, bastard; going with another woman."

"What are you going on about?" asked Pierre. "What is wrong with you?"

"I know why he's here," she spat.

"Pray tell," he replied, a blank look on his face as he looked at her. He brought in a couple of chairs from the balcony, and sat in one while she sat in the other; once they were both seated he looked over at her, expectantly.

"It's obvious isn't it," Lucy drawled. "Even a flat-footed copper like you should get it." He shook his head, "Okay, the reason he's ended up here, should I be right and I think I am, in fact I'm certain," she smiled at Pierre; it wasn't a patronising smile, but he didn't like it. "Mark, evidently by the look of the contents of the carrier bag, bought me some new underwear, in the hope of surprising me," the detective was listening, and thinking to himself at the same time.

"Anyway, he bumped into a woman in the shop or somewhere else, and she invited him here; evidently he came and brought the items he'd purchased for me. She tried some, I'm not saying all – that's for your forensics team to establish," he smiled back, this HART operative may only be guessing – even if the story fitted – there was no, real, substitute for, good old honest, plain police work – even if it did take too long in some people's eyes.

"Carry on," he said, interested now.

She poured a glass of water, and took a sip before continuing. "Okay, for some reason – we may never know how, this woman got Mark out his own clothes and into bed with her. We can only speculate at what happened next, and how it all finished."

Just then there came a knock at the door; Pierre got up and answered it; Lucy heard Jacques voice, "We've rounded up the maid, the manager, and the receptionist who was on duty at the time. Plus the morgue team are here to remove the body sir; oh yes, the forensic team's on standby."

Mark's lover, well ex lover given the circumstances, bridled at the thought of him being treated like a piece of meat and stormed out. "I'm off to do some interviews," she called back to their astonished looks.

"Not on your own," the detective said, angrily, and pushed past his man and marched down the corridor after her. *Oh well,* thought the police officer named Jacques, *Look's like it's up to me.*

Lucy stormed into the manager's office, without knocking, the detective trying to keep up behind her. She plonked herself into a vacant chair and demanded, "Who found him?" The other police officer, Claude, wondered what on earth was going on; how and why had this woman had taken – okay, she was from HART - charge in this murder investigation?

Luckily, at that moment, his superior came in, puffing and wheezing, and sat down. His officer whispered something in his ear which got the response, "She did what?"

"Come on," Lucy almost shouted, banging the table with her fist for good measure. "Who found him?" She was really fired up the detective saw when he looked across at her.

"I did," squeaked the maid, frightened by the temper on this other woman.

"Lucy, Miss Lang," said the detective. "I know you're from HART, and yes, he may have been your lover, but this is not the way to conduct a murder interview." He spoke calmly and pleasantly; he was in for a shock if he thought the reply would be as calm.

"And what is?" snarled the HART operative, peering at him with cold eyes, and then flicking back to the three people who could help.

"Like this," he answered, smiling at the others. "Good morning, my name is Pierre Armstrong. I am the lead detective in this case, and would like to know who first found the body; and in what circumstances?"

"I did," answered the maid, now visibly more relaxed, in fact all three of the hotel employees sat down. Lucy just sat quietly, watching proceedings, now realising that it had been the shock of finding Mark's body, she was certain it was him, mutilated like that that had made her act like this. "I was cleaning the rooms, when I came to room 38, the door was slightly ajar, yet the *Do Not Disturb* sign was hung on the door."

"And you did what exactly?" Pierre asked her; she was rather a pretty young maid, though he daren't admit it. He noticed Antonio, at least that's what his name badge said, move to her side, protectively.

She replied, almost tearfully, "I knocked on the door and asked if I could go in. If a voice had said no I would have apologised, closed the door, and then resumed my duties elsewhere."

"Did you get a reply?" the detective asked; Lucy looked at him, incredulous, it was pretty obvious this young maid hadn't.

"No," she answered. "So I pushed the door a little further open and called again. Still no response; yes, I admit, they still might have been sleeping, but with the door being ajar I wasn't sure."

"So I pushed the door fully open, after getting no response, and looked in. It was then when I noticed a figure in the bed, and then a dark red patch on the sheets that covered the person. I moved forward, thinking maybe the person had cut himself, I was pretty sure it was a man, and hadn't realised; suddenly, I noticed two things when I uncovered the figure, the man was laid on his back, and there was something protruding from his mouth, therefore, I walked further forward to view what was wrong, if anything. As soon as I realised he was dead, and what was in his mouth I screamed, and then fled the room, slamming the door behind me. I ran down to reception and, hurriedly, explained what I'd found. The manager, eventually, returned with me while Antonio," she placed her hand in his, "dear Antonio, stayed on reception;

once the manager had confirmed everything I'd said was true he called reception. Then Antonio called you."

"Thank you Miss?"

"Petra," she told him.

"Thank you Miss Petra. An interesting account don't you agree Miss Lang?"

"Oh yes," confirmed Lucy. "It isn't everyday you find a, dead, body in a hotel room," she added with a hint of sarcasm in her voice. "I suppose I may return to headquarters now, I'm sure you'll be in touch with us if there are any, significant, developments," and, without so much as a thank you, she got up and walked out. *She must still be coming to terms with things,* thought the detective.

He turned back to the three employees, "I must ask for any CCTV (Close Circuit Television) camera footage for that evening, I assume it was yesterday, to be placed at my disposal, until such time as this investigation reaches its conclusion."

The manager nodded.

At *Proagnon* headquarters everyone; that was the main 25 combat troops, Squeeze and Dr Q, were gathered round the conference table, which was situated in the main meeting room of the base. Dr Q opened proceedings, "We have struck a blow at the HART organisation – I shall let Squeeze," he turned to his second in command, "tell you about that, in a moment – but first I will say that, through negotiations, I have managed to secure us some land and naval assets. If our friend in Russia values his life he shall deliver these assets to our 'company' dock." That got a chuckle, "Anyway, I will be securing more assets, in due course, but these will do, for the moment; we already have the, woefully, outdated HINDs, both D and E class, plus the heavily outdated MiG-29 FULCRUM attack jet. Now I shall hand you over to Squeeze" He then sat down.

"Thank you Dr Q; for that update on where we are. I, as you know, went on a mission to Geneva, and found my man, a HART operative, buying underwear for his fiancée; I offered to help, and he readily accepted. Later, I ensnared him at the Hotel Tiffany, we spent the night together – I won't bore you with the details," although, she noticed, some of the younger troopers had grins on their faces, "the next morning I injected him with the nerve fluid, so he could appreciate his death; I then cut his member off," she noticed the grins fall, "then he found out why I'm known as Squeeze. Finally, just for fun, I popped his member in his mouth – then got my things, put the *Do Not Disturb* sign on the door, closed it and left."

In Russia Maria was seated at her desk, filing reports, checking documentation, and typing reports for her minister's approval on her word processor, when Oleg popped his head out the office, "Maria, have you got a minute?"

She looked up from her work an answered, "At once Minister."

Petra Rumanov, who had until now tried to ignore her new rival, in the office – despite Oleg showing her round on her first day, for the minister's affections, looked across as Maria got up, and said solemnly, "Be careful Miss Bondarenko."

"I will, and thank you Petra."

Maria strode towards Oleg's office door, Petra's eyes following her, every step of the way, until she stood outside and rapped on the wooden surface. Petra knew what their minister intended, but would this girl have the courage to reject his advances; unlike she had tried to do but had succumbed, in the end; however, what she didn't know was Maria had been warned, in advance, of her minister's ways. She'd given him three children, up to now, all because that cow, Anastasyia, couldn't bear children; she knew he may want a fourth with her, but now this young bitch, Maria Bondarenko, had come along he may have changed his mind.

"Come in," came Oleg's cheery response.

Maria walked in, "You asked to see me Comrade Minister."

"Ah yes, so I did," and he accidentally, though it looked more likely on purpose, knocked a few papers on the floor. "Whoops, clumsy me, please pick those up for me."

Maria was a bit undecided as to whether to pick the papers up for a number of reasons, but basically they all led to the same conclusion. He had knocked the papers just far enough

95

away so she would have to bend over to pick them up, and, today, she had decided to wear her white trousers, together with a black and white blouse, which she knew would ride up when she bent over, exposing the small of her back. She was therefore a little worried that if she wasn't quick enough he would grasp the back of her trousers and yank them down, exposing her naked flesh underneath; then he'd have her. "Wouldn't you rather Miss Rumanov came in and did this?" she asked, half hoping he'd say *yes* but she knew it was a vain hope.

"No!" Oleg snapped, angrily, at her. "Now bend over and pick those papers up girl! Oh, by the way, I want them all in order of date."

Realising the only course of action left open to her was to start to bend over, then, quickly, pretend to slip and fall over; it could work, what had she to lose? So Maria started to bend forward, she could feel the minister's eyes following her every move; then she stumbled, pretended to trip, and fell; however, she made sure she fell the way her training had taught her, thus not damaging anything.

"You stupid bitch, get up!" Oleg ordered angrily. There was real venom in his voice.

"I can't, sir, I think I've twisted my ankle."

"What good are you?" her minister asked. "Falling over every time I want you for something?" Oleg, then, reluctantly, got up from behind his desk and came round, and helped her back from his office to her desk, she was limping all the while; Petra watched them with amusement from her own seat.

Once the foreign minister had returned into his office Maria looked across at the mother of his three children and winked, and then she gathered up some papers and took them across to Petra's desk; Petra was amazed, Maria wasn't limping at all. As soon as Miss Bondarenko had returned to her own desk, and begun typing again, the minister's office door opened, and Oleg popped his head out again. "Petra, my dear, as you have worked so hard for me, in the past few days, I have decided to reward you. Please come to my office immediately."

"Yes Minister," Miss Rumanov replied, and stood up; Maria noted she had a brown skirt, and top, on, was wearing tan coloured stockings, ending in the black flat shoes that most secretaries wore. She walked over to the office, knocked on the door and entered.

Maria had an inkling why she'd gone in, but could prove nothing – would it be of any use anyway? She, suddenly, heard a scream, and the door flew open and Petra ran out, not a stitch on except her shoes; the door slammed shut behind her. Evidently, Maria realised, their foreign minister had had his jollies, and had flung Petra out. "You must help me," gabbled a nervous Petra, almost incoherently at some points. "I need to go home."

Maria, luckily, had brought a sweater, and both her coats, with her that day, as it had been rumoured a cold spell was going to hit Russia later that day, she took it and the duffel coat from their hangars and gave them over Miss Rumanov. Petra put them on, and then asked, slightly suspiciously, "Why are you helping me?"

"It's not in my nature not to help people, especially people who have been taken advantage of."

Once Miss Rumanov had put Miss Bondarenko's garments on, the sweater was slightly too long in the arms, while the coat was slightly too short as Petra was taller than her junior, they travelled down in the elevator, then left the building after passing security; the security men wondered why these two were leaving early, still theirs was not to question why.

Petra led them both over to her car, a Fiat, once they had both climbed in Petra reversed out the parking space, then gunned the engine and sped out the car park, nearly mowing a security officer down; fortunately, the barrier at the main 'entrance/exit' was up so the Fiat sped out and onto the main carriageway. Miss Rumanov sped through the traffic, as much as possible, hooting at any driver who got in their way, or was going slowly.

After about twenty minutes of hard driving they pulled into a street, on the outskirts of Moscow; finding number 27 Petra pulled into the drive and said, in as cheery voice as she could muster, "Welcome to my home." Both ladies exited the automobile once it had, fully, come to a standstill, Petra unlocked the door and they went inside; Maria was surprised the children weren't home, still they did have a couple more hours at school.

Maria looked around; Oleg had certainly looked after them. The house was fairly large, with a moderate sized kitchen, a large dining/living room from what she could see; it came as no, real, surprise to discover that the house had three bedrooms, and one, specially, built on top of the garage – she had noticed the room on arrival, plus there was evidence – out the back – a fifth room was in planning. There was also a bathroom upstairs, which was where Petra was headed now, "Thank you for all your help, Maria, I'm sorry you had to get involved. I will never be able to repay the kindness you have shown me; now please go before they discover where you are, and try to harm you."

Maria felt Petra was trying to get rid of her, for some reason; reluctantly, she held back, but Miss Rumanov then pleaded with her to go, so Maria felt she had no, real, choice but to leave. However, one thing still puzzled her; if Oleg could afford this house to house his mistress, that was how Maria thought of Petra, and her children, shouldn't he be living here as well? After all, his wife was dead. Then Maria realised, after what Svetlana had told her, she was only guessing, maybe he had an apartment further in Moscow, and the reason, if she was right, he didn't live anywhere near his mistress and children, was because he was laying a different girl each night.

She carried on walking into a, crowded, shopping area. A man emerged from an alley, which ran between two shops – he had a raincoat on, even though it wasn't raining, and sunglasses, it wasn't sunny either; he had a wrist communicator on, she saw, so assumed he was an agent from HART, and was there to give her information. Alice followed him into the alley, and behind the shops. He faced her and asked, in a pleasant voice, "Are you," he consulted some papers, "Miss Maria Bondarenko?"

"Yes, why yes I am," she answered truthfully.

"I have something for you," he said, putting his hand in his pocket and making a show of feeling for something. As soon as the man felt he had her off guard, enough, he produced a screwdriver from his pocket and attacked her. Alice, completely shocked and defenceless, had no answer to this man's, frenzied, attack. He punched her, beat her, and raked her face with the weapon; she fell onto the, hard, concrete ground and her hands shot to her face as he continued with the attack. Eventually, after approximately 10 minutes since he'd begun the attack, the man kicked her several times, she cried out in pain, and then he left her for dead. Before he left he said, menacingly, "Don't go poking your nose into our affairs, or next time you'll get more than a warning!"

When Alice opened her eyes and sat up she saw plenty of blood, mostly hers, she guessed; it was painful even to sit up, the man in the raincoat had gone. Alice got, shakily, to her feet, trying to ignore the excruciating pain she was in, and staggered back onto the street. Passing shoppers either crossed the road to avoid her, or, just walked on the road; Alice didn't think she looked that bad, so why were people avoiding her? Finally, she came to some public washrooms and walked inside; when the other women saw her they screamed and hurried out the exit.

She walked to the hand basin area and looked in the mirror, the reflection that stared back at her looked really grotesque, half her face was covered in blood, her pretty eyes were now swollen and puffy, her lips were cracked and bleeding, and there were bloodstains on her forehead and cuts on her cheek, she looked horrible. In fact her reflection was so grotesque that she, actually, vomited in the sink.

Once she felt a little better Alice set to work with paper towels, soap and water; when she looked slightly more like a human person, and not just a piece of walking meat she left the public washrooms and continued back to where she was staying. Still, some people avoided her but not as many as before.

As she entered the hotel where she was staying, she noticed all conversations suddenly cease, undeterred she collected her room key and went up to her room; upon reaching room 314 she went inside. The first thing she noticed was that, while she'd been out, her room had been ransacked; luckily, her 9mm Parabellum was locked securely in a safe in the wall. Whoever had done this was only an amateur, and not a very good one at that.

Alice, as she was now, knew then what she must do, it hadn't been necessary before now. She clicked on the communicator and called HART HQ; Gwyneth answered, "Yes my lovely," how Alice hated the Welsh. It wasn't the people she hated; it was just the fucking language.

"Alice Stronglove, in Moscow; things over here are not going according to plan, therefore, I am requesting backup." *You stupid Welsh bitch!*, she didn't add.

"I'll see Mr Roberts about that, if we can spare anyone they will be with you in a couple of hours, in the meantime just sit tight."

Not much else I can do, and with that thought Alice thumbed the *kill* switch. She then realised she still felt 'dirty' so decided to have a nice, hot, long shower.

At HART HQ, in Geneva, Mrs Jones informed Mr Roberts of the message she'd received from Miss Stronglove; her superior sat thoughtfully for a moment, and then said to her, "Bring in our remaining four team leaders!"

"At once sir," the chief secretary responded, and prepared to leave the room.

As an afterthought he asked, "Have the Swiss police been back to us yet?"

"No sir. Not as yet."

"Perhaps we should send someone over."

"That's up to you," Gwyneth said. With that she turned on her heel and left his office. Approximately ten minutes later all the, remaining, team leaders were stood in his office.

Peter stood, "Thank you for coming so promptly; firstly, we received a communication earlier from Alice Stronglove, in Moscow, requesting assistance on her mission. Therefore, as she is your agent, Leon, I propose to send you over to join her, unless anyone else would like to volunteer," the other three shook their heads, "okay, that's the first point settled. Secondly, as we have not heard anything from the Swiss police I propose to send someone to hurry them up, are there any volunteers?"

Celia stepped forward, "I'll go sir,"

"Thank you Celia. Now, as you know, I am to meet with the new English queen in two days, to see about additional funding; and then I shall be going on a journey round the world to see the state of things. I shall be taking Doctor Schaiffer and Mrs Jones with me. Therefore, I propose to leave Ronan Strobing in overall charge," Lucy began to object but Roberts cut her off, "Lucy, you will be in charge of the training side. Are we all clear?"

"Yes sir," they all said and left the office. They crossed to the elevator and began their journey to the ground floor; on the way down Celia joked with Ronan about having friends in high places. Lucy stood apart from the others wondering why she hadn't been chosen to visit the police; maybe it was because she'd lost her temper before.

Once they were outside Leon left the group and headed off to go and pack. The other three walked back to the shooting range, and continued with their target practice.

Leon drove to *Cointrin* International Airport, in his official HART car. As usual he was fast-tracked through the reception and security; he sat and waited in the airside lounge until his plane, another *Gulfstream* G-150 was ready for him. He boarded the aircraft and, immediately, noticed the stewardesses, all of them were oriental; probably it was just which stewardesses were available for the flight at that time. Leon was a, reasonably, tall man, 5'9", and towered over them, mostly each of them was a good foot smaller, evidently they had not been chosen for their height.

There was a knock on Alice's hotel room door; however, as she was in the shower she couldn't answer it, the knock came again, but again Alice still couldn't be bothered to get out of the shower and answer the door, if it was important the person would come back. Evidently, then, the person left as there came no more knocks. Once Alice had finished her shower and dried herself off, there were still traces of blood on the towel but nothing serious. Exiting the bathroom she picked up the two envelopes that had been slipped under her door, and went through to dress. Once she was dressed Alice sat on the bed and opened one of the envelopes; it had two things in it: an invitation from Svetlana, the SVR minister, to join her that evening at The Tsar nightclub. Included was a leaflet detailing the history of the place.

The Tsar was owned by the nightclub chain *Revolutionaries* who were both a group of historians, as well as owning nightclubs, bars and restaurants. This club was called The Tsar to remind the younger generation that Russia had once had a royal family.

The place had originally been another club, for gentleman only, and had had two levels to it. However, during World War II this club, R&R (Rest and Relax), had been bombed and the whole place destroyed; people had tried to resurrect the club, over the intervening years but with little or no success. Then in 2000 *Revolutionaries*, a highly successful chain, had bought it and completely refurbished it.

They had built a, main, street level entrance guarded by 'Bouncers' as the club refused access to any male who looked under 21, and any female under 18; other than that the club was open to all, even gays and lesbians, although some people objected to that. Once inside, you were also only allowed in with a pass, you walked down a flight of steps then entered the main club through a door to the left.

The main hall/room had tables situated around the edges, these were in booths with a comfortable bench. The main dance area was split in half by a, giant, mirrored partition, one side for Russians, whilst the other half was European based, and could hold up to 500 dancers while there was seating for up to 200 people in the booths; in the centre of the mirrored wall was a raised dais, from which the DJ/VJ would play their music, also overhead were many TV like screens – these would play the videos to the music being played. High above were, steel, cages, which housed the club's own, professional, dancers, mainly women but also some men.

The toilets were located toward the rear of the building, two in either half, a man's and a woman's. The bar was located just beyond the dance floor, and served many different types of drinks.

The club hadn't changed since its opening in 2000, each Friday and Saturday resident DJs would play for four hour sets.

Once or twice a month big name European and American DJs provided sessions at the club. On such occasions the stage interior, the setting and even the menu had to be completely changed; the restaurant now offered popular dishes cooked to the best traditions of European cuisine.

The club was renowned for its after hours parties that were held after its main show program, these parties, it was said, reached their height at 5-6 in the morning, and the last visitors to leave the club left at around 4pm.

Svetlana informed Alice she had a card for the club, they could get in easily. Near the club was a free, guarded, parking lot. Svetlana also informed her friend she had been many times before, and enjoyed herself immensely.

Next Alice looked at the working hours; Friday and Saturday were both 2300 (11pm) – 1600 (4pm); however, Monday and Wednesday were only 2300 – 0600, and she wanted them to go, if Maria was available, in a few evening's time, on Saturday.

She opened the second envelope and withdrew the sheet of paper inside, what she read made Alice feel, slightly, more uncomfortable. It just said that they, whoever they were, knew where she was, and to keep her nose out of their affairs, otherwise they would make her stay very uncomfortable, in fact they may even terminate her existence; and that thought really chilled her to the bone.

Who could have written it? Of course, it must be the man who'd beaten her up earlier or maybe one of the people he worked for.

The Gulfstream jet landed at *Sheremetyevo* Airport around 2 hours after taking of from *Cointrin*. Like Alice before Leon was met in Terminal 2 by Provalov; the two men walked outside to the official, white, Mercedes, once everything was loaded the Mercedes left the airport area. Of course, Leon had brought everything he needed – including his Beretta 84 pistol, which was based on the Beretta 81 *Cheetah*.

The '84' pistol, which was, usually, standard HART issue; though some members preferred different pistols, had a double stacked magazine with a 13 round capacity. It had a four inch barrel, and an ambidextrous frame mounted de-cock/safety. The frame was made from alloy and the pistol was available in black or satin nickel finishes, with plastic or wooden hand grips. The standard for the weapon was a black finish with wooden grips.

The pistol had the standard overall length of 172mm, with a barrel length of 97mm; and as it weighed only 660gm; it was very lightweight, sometimes so lightweight some of the HART operatives often forgot they carried it, and it would rarely get used. It took the .380 ACP (Automatic Colt Pistol), or the 9mm short cartridge.

Leon didn't need briefing on what he had to do, after all, he was only here to provide backup to his agent, Alice Stronglove.

He was taken to the Belgrad Hotel, where she was staying; Provalov informed the receptionist why the man was there. The receptionist phoned Alice's room, to inform her she had a visitor. While she was waiting for Alice to answer she took Leon's details.

In her room Miss Stronglove was awakened by a ringing sound – she hadn't even realised she'd fallen asleep – realising it was the phone that had woken her she sat up and answered it. "Hello?"

"Miss Bondarenko," said a female voice, Leon smiled – trust Peter, "I have a visitor in reception for you; he says he wants to sell you a boat – if you're interested, shall I send him up?"

In an instant Alice knew who it was, "Yes, please do."

"Right you are ma'am." She replaced the phone, and gave Leon directions to Alice's room; Leon followed the directions, to the letter, and knocked on the door of room 314.

"Who is it?" called a female voice from inside.

"Leon."

"Code phrase?" Every team leader had one. Leon's was 'large boat', Celia's was 'plentiful woman', Ronan's was 'flashing lights' and Lucy's was 'American woman'.

"Large boat!" The door slowly opened until Alice stood framed in the doorway, when Leon saw her face he looked at her horrified. "Good God girl! What have they done to you?"

She hugged him and pulled him inside, "It's a long story," and they went into the main room, and sat down on the chairs in there.

"Tell me everything," he told her in a concerned voice. Alice had bought some 'Coca-Cola' in bottles, and they poured the drink into plastic cups.

"Well," Alice began, "I went to my new job, as a secretary, at the foreign ministry where the minister, Oleg Ayanseikov, immediately asked me to a dinner function, to which I readily agreed."

"You say you were secretary to this Ayanseikov, did he have any others?" Leon asked his agent, now curious.

"Oh yes, a Petra Rumanov, I'll come to her later." She took a sip of Coke, "Anyway, we went to this dinner function, where I met the ministers for defence and SVR; along with several others, but thy're not important."

"The SVR doesn't have a minister," Leon informed her, "just a chairman, who acts like a minister."

"That's what she must have been, the chairman," Alice said to him, watching his face closely.

"Or chairwoman, or chairperson, depending on your view of things," He told her.

Alice then resumed her tale, "At the dinner Oleg, foreign minister, said to Mikhail, defence minister, that Dr Quantum had asked if they could supply his company with a couple of aircraft carriers; three cruisers; several submarines; some tanks; and some APCs (Armoured Personnel Carriers)."

"You made notes I assume?"

She looked at him indignantly, "Of course I did, however; there was a sticky moment when the SVR chairwoman saw my Electronic Organiser. I simply explained it was a present from a relative in Japan."

"Good girl, thinking like a true HART operative. I trust you have the organizer to hand so I can download the information." Alice fetched the organizer from the wall safe; she entered her password, Leon wasn't, in the least bit, surprised to find it was 'Peter Roberts'. Once the information was on screen Leon attached a glowing stick-like device to the machine and transferred the information; when the transfer was complete, and the stick had stopped glowing he removed it and said to her, in an orderly but not angry voice, "Wipe it!"

Alice did and carried on with her story, "Next day the SVR chairwoman, Svetlana, and myself met at the *Tinkoff* restaurant. There she told me some interesting things about our friend Oleg."

"Such as?" he enquired now even more curious.

"It seems Oleg was once married to a woman named Anastaysia, who died five years ago, anyway, it turns out she wasn't able to bless Oleg with any children. This he knew from day one and told her it didn't bother him," she paused, and took a sip of her drink.

"But it did," Leon guessed, smiling

"Yes it did, he hired two secretaries, Yetakerina Koniev and Petra Rumanov; he tried it on with Yetakerina, and she refused his advances, so evidently he got more forceful, in the end she ended up taking her own life, or so it is thought, in the Siberian woods."

"Not a nice end."

"Once this had been confirmed he turned his attention to Petra, however, she didn't refuse him – even though she knew he was married," Leon smiled, he had guessed that bit, "this we know because after Yetakerina went missing he hired a temporary secretary, apparently he was an ex-KGB officer; and he reported to Svetlana that he'd seen them in his office. So, according to the SVR chairwoman he has three children with Petra, also rumours are he wants a fourth; all three children were conceived and born while Anastaaysia was still alive."

"Moving on, earlier today, I think he intended to try and have me in his office, but I was crafty and pretended to hurt my ankle. Anyway, Oleg helped me back to my desk, and summoned Petra inside. Next I heard screams and shouts, and Petra came running out, totally naked, and begged me to help her."

"I lent her my sweater and duffel coat, to cover herself up, and then we left – no-one stopped us. We travelled, in her Fiat, to her home; it was luxury – the house had four bedrooms, a bathroom etc. and a fifth was being built. There was a garage and everything, yet Oleg didn't live with her. She went for a shower, and persuaded me to leave – I didn't want to but she assured me she was fine."

"As I was walking past some shops a man told me he had some information for me, I didn't distrust him as he had a HART communicator on. Anyway, I went into an alley with him that ran behind the shops, and he attacked me; when he'd finished I waited a minute or two, and then, groggily, got up; I wandered into the street and started back here – people in the street started to avoid me and I wondered why. I then found a public washroom and went in, nothing could prepare me for what I saw when I looked in one of the mirrors, half my face was bleeding, I had bruises on me, my eyes were either swollen or black; basically I looked awful."

"What did your assailant look like?" Leon asked; some urgency in his voice.

"I don't know," she answered. "All I can tell you is he, I think it was a he – and a young he at that, had a raincoat and sunglasses on."

"Oh well, it was worth a try."

"I washed, and cleaned, myself as best I could then resumed my journey back here. Once I got back, I showered to make myself feel better; when I came from the bathroom I found two envelopes had been pushed under my door. Here they are," and she handed them over.

Her immediate superior read the letter from Svetlana, and then the note. Looking up he said to her, "I think you should go to this nightclub and I'll come too, just for added protection. As for this note, a friend of mine has a house in the suburbs of St Petersburg; I'm sure he will let us use it for a few days."

"Plus I will hire a *Lada* and you can go to Petra's to retrieve the clothes you lent her." Leon got everything organised, while Alice packed; once everything was ready they drove away. Alice directed him to Petra's; as they pulled up she was surprised to see the sunny yellow *Fiat* gone, plus the house looked deserted, Alice got out and walked up to the door, she knocked several times but received no answer. Slightly miffed she then called through the letterbox, still no reply, finally and in desperation Alice tried the door, it was locked of course.

Leon then climbed out the *Lada* and hurried round the back; seeing nothing he returned to the front, where Alice was. "Perhaps we should go," he muttered to her.

As they reached the car, a neighbour suddenly came, rushing, out. "Are you looking for Petra Rumanov?" she asked them.

"We are," answered Alice. "I'm a work colleague and this man," she gestured to Leon, "is Yuri Padaev, my brother."

"Ah, just wait here," and the woman went back inside her own house, she reappeared carrying some clothes. "Miss Rumanov, before she departed, gave me these to give back to you – if ever you passed and I saw you."

"Departed you said?" asked Alice, with worry. "When and where?"

"Yesterday, about an hour after you both came here, as for where I think she said Arkhangel'sk."

"Thank you," said Alice then asked, "Where are the children?"

"Apparently, the woman said, "she'd phoned her parents, in Penza, and they would collect the children from school, and take them to stay with them, until their mother returned."

"Thank you," said Alice again, taking her clothes and climbing into their vehicle, "you've been most helpful." Once Leon had driven a few blocks Alice turned to him, fear in her eyes, "We must find her Leon. She's my friend and, after what she's been through, she needs a friend."

Leon agreed, but told her, "Tomorrow. We'll go and unpack first, and then get a good night's rest." She nodded.

They arrived at the house a little before 10, as the *Lada* wasn't exactly speedy, plus some roads were filled with potholes. At last they arrived and unpacked, and then, practically, fell into the two, single, beds.

Next morning they awoke, dressed, ate breakfast etc. then went back out to their transport. Leon started the vehicle and they followed the roads to Arkhangel'sk. They drove around and around the streets, asking passers-by, and then every time they spotted a yellow *Fiat* Alice would inspect it for tell tale signs. Every time she shook her head; finally, at about 7pm Leon said, as she got back in for the umpteenth time, "This is like finding a fucking needle in a haystack, let's go home." Alice murmured her reluctant acceptance.

They drove away, but Leon took them on a different route home. Reaching a deserted stretch of road Alice told her male superior she had seen something, and she wanted to investigate. He took them in an easterly direction until they could see the object, it was a small car; slowly Leon took them nearer until they saw it was a sunny yellow *Fiat*, he pulled alongside and Alice confirmed, at once, that it was Petra's vehicle, both agents got out their own vehicle and walked around the *Fiat*, that's when they saw it; it was a woman's, naked, body, or rather it had been, lying on the ground.

The legs had been ripped off at the knees, arms were ripped off at the elbows; the torso was a deep red colour, with bite marks in it. The woman's internal organs had been torn away and scattered on the ground; but most horrible to look at was the face, it was terribly mutilated; the skin had been torn away revealing the skull, the ears had both been bitten off; the teeth marks confirmed this; the neck had been bitten – exposing the arteries and veins. The woman was surrounded by a deep red stain; evidently she'd bled a great deal.

Immediately, Alice was sick on the ground; she looked up at Leon, "Who or what could have done this to her?" Both knew it was, definitely, or had been, the woman they had been seeking. As if on cue they both heard a wolf, or several wolves, howling in the distance.

"That's what did this," Leon told her, "I'm sorry, truly I am, but let's get out of here before we become their next meal," neither had brought their weapons. They got in their vehicle and tore off, just as the howling came again.

On the Saturday evening Leon took Alice, Leon was armed but Alice wasn't, as she had nowhere to hide her weapon, but her superior had brought it with them, just in case; they met the SVR chairwoman, in the lobby, at the Belgrad Hotel, at 2230. Svetlana greeted Alice, who was wearing her V cut dress, with a kiss, "It's wonderful to see you again, my dear, who's your friend?"

"Svetlana, let me introduce my brother, Yuri Padaev, my brother, he would like to join us."

The SVR chairwoman looked at him, "Yes he may, my transport is outside." They walked outside, expecting a Mercedes or some such vehicle, but all they saw was an old, covered over, truck.

"That."

"Yes that, as you so elegantly put it. It goes and there's room for three, so come on shall we go?" Alice looked at Leon who just shrugged. They all climbed aboard and Svetlana drove off.

They parked in the club parking lot and they went inside, Svetlana explained to the doormen/Bouncers that the three of them were together. Seating themselves in a booth on the European side, Svetlana and Leon went to get them all drinks, while Alice went to the ladies powder room.

Upon entering she looked around for a free stall; strangely, there were two sets of legs in most of them. When she reached, what she thought was, a free stall, she pushed open the door and found a young woman, about the same age as her, stood on the pan, urinating. As soon as Alice saw her she muttered her apologies, but the woman didn't seem bothered at being caught. As soon as she'd finished she jumped down and looked at Alice. "Wanna play?" she drawled, it was evident she was drunk. The woman was a little younger than Alice, and she was dressed in a, black, T-shirt with a skull & crossbones on the front, and, black, jogging bottoms which looked a size too small for her; plus she had, close cropped, black hair which looked dyed.

"No." The woman grabbed Alice's dress and tried to unbutton it. Alice resisted as much as she could, but the other woman had taken her too much by surprise. Unfortunately, she ripped the front of the dress open, exposing Alice's chest.

"Nice chest," the Russian woman remarked, bending and admiring her better.

"You filthy bitch!" Alice retorted, with feeling, pushing her assailant back. She exited the stall, and ran out the toilets, afraid to look back. She found the booth containing Svetlana and Leon; they looked at her chest, well it was hard to miss,

Svetlana smiled, sweetly, while Leon just grimaced. Alice looked down to see what they were staring at, "Sorry," she said, covering herself up.

It was at that moment they heard gunshots outside, together with people screaming. The door to the club burst open and three men, dressed in blue combat suits and carrying AK-47 assault rifles entered; each of them looked around and then opened fire, indiscriminately. "Down!" ordered the superior HART agent; the three of them dived down and lay perfectly still. Dancers fell, all dead with blood streaming out of them.

Once most were dead one of the gunmen advanced down the steps, and on into the toilets, both men's and women's, more screams followed, about 5 minutes later the gunman who had gone in came out; rejoining his colleagues the three men went into the other half of the club and, the three people left assumed, they did the same there; the partition smashed revealing that many clubbers, nearly all, were dead. The assassins looked around and, satisfied, left.

Once they'd been gone a good ten minutes Leon raised his head. "Oh hell!" the two women heard and raised themselves as well, all around were dead dancers, staff, the DJs/VJs and anyone else who had been in the way.

"Follow me," said Svetlana, "there is a back way out. She looked at Alice, "Don't worry, your brother, if he is your brother, has told me who you really are and what you were doing; although I don't actually approve I think I should get you out of here, and you need to get away from Russia, far away. Therefore I'm prepared to help you."

They followed the SVR chairwoman, through the multitude of bodies, and into the toilets; a woman came out a stall and Alice, instantly, recognised her as the woman who'd tried to take advantage of her earlier, though her clothes were ripped and she was covered in bloodstains. "Help me," she cried out; Svetlana pulled them past, and out into the night air.

"Wasn't that a bit cruel?" asked Leon. "To leave a fellow human being like that."

"Svetlana responded sharply, "I could've killed her if you'd preferred!" Leon opened his mouth as if to say something, but then suddenly shut up and walked to the truck. Once they were all aboard the SVR chairwoman pulled out the parking lot, and headed towards *Sheremetyevo* Airport, as fast as the vehicle would go. None of them saw the man in sunglasses and raincoat, smoking a Marlboro cigarette and watching them. He pulled a radio from his pocket and spoke into it. As they were driving along at about 70 miles per hour, as the roads were clear Svetlana said, without turning, "Oleg and Mikhhail have had dealings already with this Dr Q so they are partly to blame; the President knows nothing of these ministers betrayal to their country."

Finally, they reached the airport; Leon and Alice thanked the SVR woman and walked inside the terminal. With them gone Svetlana started to drive home, it had, certainly, been a different evening; she had not, actually, approved of Alice's intelligence gathering techniques but they had worked. If by taking them to the airport she had helped lessen this terror; that was a good thing wasn't it?

Settling back she started to drive through Moscow; a waste removal lorry was ahead of her own vehicle, this wasn't an unusual occurrence, these types of lorry were everywhere. The lorry slowed, right down, to just 20 miles per hour, Svetlana thought this strange, and then she saw him. Laid in the back was a man and beside him was some sort of tube; as the man started to rise and hoisted the tube to his shoulder Svetlana realised, with horror, it was an RPG (Rocket Propelled Grenade) launcher tube, she tried to swerve out the way but couldn't, the steering had locked.

The tube fired, creating a flash, and the projectile/grenade hit the truck, exploding and creating a fireball.

CHAPTER 4

More meetings & plans!

At *Proagnon* headquarters a reply email was received, via the secure email system, from *Proagnon's* Russian agent, and not the actual foreign minister, informing Dr Q that the Russian military had decided to supply him, Dr Quantum, and his company with the hardware they had requested. The Russians would deliver it – not all at once, though, as some of the hardware requested was undergoing major repairs or were away on exercise - to the specified point, the dock in Iraq, Dr Q smiled behind his face plate, the Russians were in for a nasty surprise soon enough, but for now they were necessary.

He summoned a meeting in the meeting hall; once everyone was there he informed them all that the Russians had decided to honour the request he'd sent them. He then asked, "Will anyone who is prepared to assist with the destruction of this line of new pleasure cruisers please volunteer, I am looking for three people; of course, you may become martyrs for our cause. Are there any volunteers?"

Three men stood, "Thank you my friends, now we need people to receive our new hardware," he looked at them all, "are there any further volunteers?"

Squeeze stood and spoke to her leader, "I would like to lead a group on this mission, sir, with your permission."

Dr Q looked up at his subordinate, in surprise, "You?" Then he thought about it, and stroked the bottom of his helmet, where his chin would have been, "Yes, of course you may lead the mission, my dear, just don't get too carried away."

"I'll try not too sir, may I pick my own troops for this mission?"

He waved his hand, as if dismissing her question as trivial, "Yes of course you may," he confirmed.

"Thank you sir," and they all rose and left the room.

In Geneva the Gulfstream jet, carrying Leon Bigship and Alice Stronglove touched down at *Cointrin*. They left the aircraft and walked down the steps; Alice was still wearing her torn dress - which had hurriedly been sewn together by one of the stewardesses – but it would still give the photographers, and any cameramen, something to look at and comment on. In fact, one of them shouted, "Did you two have a good time?" Alice couldn't tell if he was being seedy or not, she nearly said something back to him, she was still uptight Leon saw, but he persuaded her not to.

Her superior led her out, through immigration and customs, and on to his official car; there they climbed inside, there had been no time to pack anything back in Russia. Leon then started the vehicle and they began the journey back to HART HQ.

Overnight Ronan Strobing, acting base commander, had been sleeping in his private residence, and had been awakened by the ringing of the phone, "Yes," he growled, annoyed at having his peace disturbed.

"Sir," said a junior receptionist, a man, who had been called in to replace Mrs Jones, albeit temporarily, "We have just received thermal pictures, via the satellite uplink, of a nightclub massacre and an explosion, both in Moscow." The satellite HART was using was nothing if not thorough.

"Thank you Smith," Ronan yawned, I'll be right there," and he replaced the receiver. *Oh hell!* He thought with a start, *Leon's over there with his agent, Alice.* He got up, quickly washed and dressed in his uniform, and then trudged over to the main headquarters building. It was still dark, but the walkways had lights either side – much like an airport runway – to guide the personnel in the dark.

He looked over at the outlines of the other two residences, both of which were occupied by one of the two, female, team leaders; the fourth residence, Leon's was empty and dark.

The whole compound had once served as an, outlying, Air Force/RAF base; however, since HART had purchased it in 2006 and modified it, to their standards, it had been used, in the intervening 61 years since the end of the Second World War, as a place where air shows were held 4 times a year. There were also several hangars at the base, as well as two control towers, personnel accommodation and many other buildings which had been converted, and, of course, a runway.

Ronan entered the, main, office building; the security team were most surprised to see him, "Starting work early are we sir?" one of them joked, as it was, only, about 03.30. Ronan just growled at the man. "Sorry sir," he apologised quickly. The acting commander, for that's what he was, got in the elevator, which began its ascent to the fourth floor, where the commander's office was. Getting out of the elevator he wandered down the featureless corridor to the Commander's office, *I wish Mandy were here*, he thought to himself, *or am I being selfish to wish that?*

He opened the door and found Joshua Smith, one of the temporary receptionists/secretaries, and with him, to Ronan's surprise, was Leon Bigship. The temporary commander seated himself behind the desk and said to the others, "Okay, what you both got?"

"Well sir," Joshua told him. "All I have is preliminary reports, plus thermal imaging pictures of a massacre in a nightclub, in downtown Moscow, and an explosion, on the highway just entering Moscow. Looks like a vehicle, and whoever was driving, seemed to be making their way back from *Sheremetyevo* Airport." Ronan saw Leon wince at that piece of news.

"Do we have any visuals?" Ronan snapped, not meaning to but most people knew he had a mild temper, which flared up, occasionally.

"Not of the nightclub, but we have of the explosion." Smith retreated from the office and returned 2 minutes later, with a folder with photos in. He placed the folder on the desk and left.

Once he was gone Leon, who had remained silent throughout, told his commander, "The massacre at the nightclub did happen, I was there with my agent, Alice Stronglove, and the SVR chairwoman, named Svetlana."

"And?"

"Three gunmen, carrying AK-47 assault rifles, probably *Proagnon*, burst in and mowed everyone down, dancers and staff alike. The three of us dived to the floor and lay very still. Once the gunmen had left, and the coast was clear the two ladies, together with myself, escaped through the rear exit." He paused, "As soon as we were outside we were urged to board Svetlana's truck; she drove us, sometimes at speeds in excess of 70 m.p.h. to the airport."

"However, as we were pulling out the parking lot I'm convinced I saw a, pale, red glow, much the same as a cigarette that was lit, as if someone were watching us. It was probably nothing so that's why I never mentioned it to the ladies."

"Thank you Leon," said the acting commander, and then opened the folder and took out the, hastily, developed images.

The satellite, that had taken the images, was in geostationary orbit and was linked to another of the blocks a little further back. The blockhouse had a satellite dish atop its brick structure linking the overhead satellite, via the dish, to the computer terminals inside. The operators worked 8 hour shifts, in five man teams, so therefore the computers were always manned; there were six teams of operators, three teams on shift whilst the other three were relief teams – should someone be taken ill. Each man was also a trained combat troop in case there was no one ill then they may be called into action.

Once the computers had received the transmission download, the senior operator would view it on his own terminal, and if was deemed *urgent* he, or she, would contact first: the receptionist on duty, and then the duty officer at the photographic laboratory, situated on the second floor of the main building, if the transmission was image data material, he would advise them he was sending the material; he would then send the data, via encrypted email, over and make a request that they develop it into photos, quickly.

This was usually done with all haste. However, once developed it was sent, via email unless it was deemed *sensitive* material, to the secretary's computer, if the secretary felt the transmission data download could wait until morning, even though it had been developed anyway, he, or she, might leave it and choose not to wake their commander at whatever time it was, day or night.

"Yes, the explosion certainly does look at the outskirts of Moscow," announced Mr Strobing, rubbing his bristly chin, he would shave when he could. "And yes, the vehicle does look like it's coming from the direction of the airport. Plus, there looks to be a second vehicle, racing away from the scene and the explosion."

"May I have a look, sir," Leon said, even though his friend were only acting commander Leon referred to him as sir, as he would do if Commander Roberts was seated in the chair.

"Please do," replied Ronan, "See if you can shed any light on this matter." He passed the pictures over; his friend stared at them, then his face became very animated, and he looked horrified.

"Now then" he picked up a ruler, from the desk. "*Sheretemyevo* airport is only 10 kilometres (6.25 miles) from Moscow, so Svetlana left us at midnight, therefore she shouldn't have been long getting back to Moscow, about 2 minutes, considering the speed she was going unless something held her up, and Moscow is notorious for its numerous refuse trucks; so if we take it that she got held up, these pictures are marked 00.05 which is about right – give or take."

"Therefore, if I am right, this dramatic explosion is the SVR chairwoman's old red truck; and going by the heat this other vehicle is giving out to our thermal tracer, I must say this is, very, probably a refuse truck."

"Oh shit," muttered Ronan. "But why?"

"Possibly because she helped us, and they, somehow, found out she did. So they decided to terminate her existence."

"Hmm, yes, I suppose it does fit. Go get some sleep, Leon, you've deserved it," said Ronan, as Leon yawned, again.

"Thank you sir," and the older man rose and left the office. The base's acting commander looked across at the wall clock, 04.00, 0 bloody 400. Exiting the room he bumped into Joshua. "Ah, Joshua, I'm just going to have a rest, in the office. I want no disturbances unless it's an absolute *emergency*. Is that understood?"

"Yes sir, I'll hang the *Do Not Disturb* sign on the door." Ronan re-entered the office and re-seated himself. Smith closed the door, hung the sign on the door, and retired to the secretary's office.

In Geneva Celia was waiting at the police station for the forensic, and autopsy, findings for the body found at the Hotel Tiffany, these results had been delayed because the British police had refused to cooperate, at first. Now the results were in, after two long, and gruelling, weeks of waiting.

She waited, anxiously, to hear the findings; the pathologist who had performed the autopsy, ushered her into his office, and he seated himself behind the desk – whilst she seated herself in the other chair. "Now, my dear," he began. "It would seem, having made a full examination – and cross checking dental records with this Mark Schnieder – I can give you the following results. The body is that of the person of Mark Schnieder; it appears he had, from toxicology findings, a high concentration of a nerve, or blood, agent called Cyanogen chloride, this does cause paralysis, and, in some cases, death. Do you know how he may have got hold of this Mrs Most?"

"No I don't, but please carry on I'm finding this, absolutely, fascinating."

"Also we found, in the bloodstream, traces of a sedative called *alprazolam* or, the common name is, Xanax. This is a minor tranquilizer; however, it seems that later the dosage was increased. Plus, there was an amount of alcohol in his system which may have also resulted in his slow reactions – that is assuming his reactions were slow."

"What about the forensics from the *G-leaves* bag?"

"Hmm," he said, turning to another report. "We didn't find any fingerprints on the handle of the bag or the garments it contained, so evidently whoever did this was a professional. The only thing we did find, though, was this," and he passed a blonde hair across, in a plastic, see thru, envelope. "Does that mean anything to you?"

"No, all I can think of is it must have belonged to the woman he was with that night." Then she asked, "Have you still got the CCTV footage from that night?"

"Yes! At least I think we have. I shall just check with the chief detective," the pathologist told her. He phoned through and checked with his comrade. "Yes we have," he announced, turning back to face her.

"With the authorisation of HART," she flashed her pass at him, "I am hereby confiscating those tapes, and this hair, plus the autopsy reports, for further investigation. This woman, should she be on any of the tapes, is a known terrorist; and it is our duty, at HART, to track down the organisation she works for," Celia announced. She left the office, with the reports, leaving a stunned pathologist behind her. As she reached the front desk she bumped into a police detective, evidently a chief detective, by the look of his uniform. They stood at the main desk, behind which another officer was writing up a report.

He looked up and decided to deal with this, pretty, woman first, "Yes ma'am?" he asked in his nicest voice.

Celia gave him her most charming smile, and announced, "I am here on behalf of HART to collect the CCTV footage from the Hotel Tiffany." She flashed her pass at him.

"I'm sorry, ma'am, I can't allow that. You will need the permission of the chief detective on the case, Pierre Sanchez, before we can allow the release of those tapes."

"Look bozo," Celia said. "We believe the woman on the footage is a known terrorist called Squeeze."

The man who was standing next to her spoke up, "This young lady has my permission, Jacques. I know you're only doing your job but if this woman, on the tapes, is a terrorist I would rather you handed over the footage, and let the experts handle it." Jacques looked, reluctantly, at his superior, but handed the CCTV tapes over; there were only three.

"Thank you," said Celia. Then she turned to the man beside her and smiled, a pleasant smile. "And thank you, Pierre," she said.

"You're welcome," the man replied, and then Celia gathered up the tapes and returned to her car.

It was nearly time, at the *Proagnon* bunker to choose the three men who would board the American plane, the underground train, and the new super tanker – which would carry the 65,000 tonnes of crude oil from Saudi Arabia, though the super tanker's full capacity was 70,000 tonnes. Dr Q called a full meeting in the conference room; Abdul Singh, who had returned a couple of weeks ago, came to the meeting as well.

"Now," began the leader, sitting in his seat, at the head of the table. "It is time to choose which of the three agents will board which mode of transport."

"Sir," said one of the younger troopers, Mitchell Walker, "would it not be advisable to send an extra two additional agents, on each mission, to aid in the sabotage?" Dr Q conferred with Squeeze to see what she thought.

Once they'd finished he straightened up, "Yes," he muttered, stroking his, silver, faceplate where a beard would have been, "I think you may be right Walker, but tell me, what is your thinking behind this move?"

"I think sir," replied the young trooper, who was a fairly recent recruit, "with all due respect, that one saboteur may be easily noticed, and dealt with, whereas with three aboard, the explosive device could be on any of the men; one may be caught, two is a possibility, but I, just, don't feel all three would be caught. However, it is up to your judgement sir." He spoke with the utmost respect, Dr Q noted.

"I like your thinking and having conferred with my second in command, we both feel your judgement is correct in this matter. You have a great career ahead of you, trooper Walker, at *Proagnon*." Abdul Singh had been listening, intently, to this, and was seething inside again. How dare this young man offer advice to his leader; and his leader take the advice on board, when it was the job of more experienced officers, such as himself, to make these judgements and offer advice in light of their judgement.

Ronan Strobing awoke at six to begin another, long, day as HART's acting commander. The night staff had gone now, they too – like the computer operators – worked a three shift rota; the receptionist now was a youngish man, named Ben Gillespie.

He got up from his chair, stretched and yawned, then left the office, and the building, to begin the, morning, training session; he found Lucy outside, starting the warm up exercises. "Morning sir," she called as she saw him approach.

The other troops stopped and saluted, "As you were people," he said with some authority, and started the warm up exercises himself. Once everyone had warmed up, including Lucy, everyone selected a backpack, and hoisted them onto their backs; then they began the 5km jog around the grounds. Once Lucy and Ronan, Ronan was used to this having two children – though he didn't run with them on his back, reached hangar straight – so nicknamed because it was a straight patch of ground, plus it could double as a temporary runway, if needed – Lucy broke away, *It must be those powerful legs*, he realised. At the end of hangar straight everyone stopped for a minute's rest, of course, the team leaders always made it before the rest of the troops.

Once they'd come to a halt Lucy turned to her superior and said, "Ronan, as Mark's gone," he noted the certainty in her voice, "I shall be wanting a new lover. What about you?"

"No!" he answered, somewhat angrily, "I'm happily married with two wonderful children, and you know that."

"Don't you ever get that emotional itch, and crave for an extramarital affair?"

"No I don't, I'm quite happy as I am thank you."

"Okay," she sighed. "Meet you back at barracks," she laughed and ran off. Ronan felt disgusted, how could she ask him that? Oh well, and he ran off in the same direction.

Once he got back there was no sign of her, where was she now? He did his warm down, took his 20lb backpack off, and took it inside. That's when he saw her, laying topless on one of the beds! How dare she? "Lucy, if you think you're going to ensnare me like that, I'm sorry but you're mistaken."

"No I'm not. I'm just getting some air to my chest. Who knows, one day I might run round like this, or worse, I might run round with nothing on." He thought, *I wouldn't put it past you* but he said nothing. Ronan slung his backpack down, left the building and slammed the door behind him, annoyed at her, but part of him was slightly curious as well.

At the main *Proagnon* bunker the men who were to travel aboard the mode of transport they'd be travelling on, collected their explosive devices and left; in their minds six knew they'd be returning and three wouldn't, having made the ultimate sacrifice. They booked themselves on flights from Tehran's Mehrabad Airport to Dulles Airport, in Washington, via Doha. However, the three groups were booked onto different flights, so no-one would suspect them; they were just three groups of tourists returning home.

Leon, had been allowed to have a lay in, due as it was felt he needed to get his head together; he had complained that he didn't need any extra time, but it had been an order. Alice had decided that, as the mission was over – and with the approval of the base commander - she wanted to go home.

The *Proagnon* troopers, extra troops had been drafted in from around the world, so now the *Proagnon* member numbers equalled well over 3000, many with various different skills in warfare. They had all been members left over from other terrorist groups; so *Proagnon*, recognising their valuable skills had recruited them – if a terrorist refused to join they would simply be turned in, therefore it was blackmail – join or be turned in to the local law enforcement agency.

They arrived in a convoy of several cars and vans at the company docking harbour, Exhibits for all was the company name. The first of the new hardware to arrive was the newly renamed Admiral *Lazarev*, which was a *Kirov* class battle cruiser; it had originally been named Admiral *Frunze* but had been renamed in 1992 Admiral *Lazarev*, the *Lazarev* had been decommissioned five years after its name change. Once it had docked the troopers produced their M951-A or –B machine pistols and waited, slowly the hatch started to open, once it was fully open the troopers raised their weapons and fired. A scream emitted from the hatch and the dead man fell into the water.

Immediately the hatch began to close again, trying to protect the battle cruiser's full crew of 710 men from the attack, from these people; however, after the shooting had ended one of the *Proagnon* troopers fitted small, metal clips to the hatch, these were magnetic explosive charges controlled by remote control – only he possessed the remote control box, in his pouch belt lest something go wrong.

Once he had attached the charges he retired to the dock side, where the others stood; at a nod from Squeeze he pressed a combination of buttons on the control – again, only he knew the correct combination, as there were 9 buttons on the control's keypad – and the hatch exploded and flew into the water. The troopers ran across the gangplank, into the ship, and started firing indiscriminately – Squeeze stayed behind, on the dockside, and smiled her, hard, cruel smile.

After about ten or fifteen minutes a face appeared at the hatch, a *Proagnon* member, "Everyone aboard – the crew, I mean - is dead." Squeeze drew her pistol and, slowly and hesitantly, walked across the gangplank and aboard the vessel.

The Admiral *Lazarev*, as the ship was called, had 3 helicopters, probably not in working order – still she'd soon fix that – aboard. She also saw the vessel had many impressive array of armaments, consisting of missiles and guns, including, 20 P-700 Granit (SS-N-19 *Shipwreck*) ASMs (Air to Surface Missiles), 12x8 (96) S-300 MPU (SS-N-6 *Grumble*) missiles (Surface to Air), 96 S-400 SA-NX-20 long range SAMs, 192 9K311 Tor (SA-N-9 Gauntlet) point defence SAMs, 44 OSA-MA (SA-N-4 Gecko) PD SAMs; those were the missiles, she only knew because she'd read a great deal of sea warfare books when she was younger. Also she recognised the two RBU-1000 305 mm ASW rocket launchers, and the 2 RBU-12000 (Udav-1) 254mm ASW rocket launchers. The *Lazarev* had 1 twin AK-130 130mm/L70 dual-purpose gun, 8x AK-630 hex Gatling 30mm/L60 PD guns.

Squeeze walked inside to find the entire crew, dead! Also there were a couple of *Proagnon* troops laid with them – both had knives in their chests. "Throw the dead overboard," she said to one of the soldiers.

He thought it was a bit unfeeling of her but he couldn't contradict her, lest he end up with a bullet in the chest. "Yes ma'am," he said instead. "Right you 'orrible lot," he announced to the rest of them. "Our superior requests us to chuck them there bodies overboard, so let's do what the lady says." Squeeze smiled, this man even spoke like a sailor.

She turned to another member, "What are the armaments below?"

"We have 10 533mm ASW/ASuW torpedo tubes, and the Type 53 torpedo or the SS-N-15 missile."

"Good," she purred, "And what are the general statistics of this ship?"

The man consulted a clipboard, "The displacement of this vessel is 24,300 tons (standard) or 28,000 tons at full load, the length of the ship is 252m or 830ft, the beam of the vessel is 28.5m or 94ft and the draft is 9.1m or 30ft. The propulsion system is powered by a 2-shaft CONAS, and 2 KN-3 nuclear propulsion with 2 GT3A-688 steam turbines; all producing 14,0000 b.h.p. This enables our top speed to be 32 knots, or 59 km/h; the range of this vessel is 1000 nautical miles, or 2000km at a speed of 30 knots, 56km/h, that's at our combined propulsion. Yet the ship's range is essentially unlimited on nuclear power at 20 knots, 37km/h. The reactor compartment is surrounded by 76 mm thick armoured plating with light splinter protection."

"And what other devices do we have?" she asked him casually. "And does any part of the ship need a refit or update?"

"To answer your first question, radar and sonar wise we have the Voskhod MR-800 (Top Pair) 3D search radars, as you may have noticed, on the fore mast, the Fregat MR-710 (Top Steer) 3D search radars, this time on the main mast, and 2 Palm Frond navigation radars, again on the fore mast. For sonar the vessel is equipped with the Horse Jaw full sonar and the Horse Tail VDS, or Variable Depth Sonar."

"Finally," he went on, Squeeze was enjoying this – it was like one of her books had come to life. "For the Fire Control we have, 2 x Top Dome SA-N-6 fire control, 4 x Bass Tilt for AK-360 CIWS System fire control, 2 x Eye Bowl for SA-N-4 fire control, 2 x Hot Flash or Hot Spot SA-N-11 Grisom, Kite Search for AK-100 or AK-130, and 2 x Cross Sword for SA-N-9."

"Onto your second question ma'am," said the trooper respectfully. "The only, real, thing this ship requires is a good lick of paint. You can see, here and there, the paint is peeling," indeed Squeeze did. "Now ma'am, if you would care to accompany me I will give you the guided tour."

They moved off, deep into the bowels of the vessel, whilst the other troops started to bring this once great vessel, back to full combat ready life again. Every computer terminal flickered into life, all except one; the operator noted this and reported it to his superior, this systems failure would be reported to the boss. Squeeze, along with the trooper, wandered down the corridors of the ship and inspected the crew cabins, reactor room – where the nuclear reactor was, engine room and the weapons room – she inspected each missile, some of them looked as though they'd never been used. She also viewed the turbines and propellers at the rear – each propeller, there were two, had 8 blades on it, and would rotate in a clockwise direction.

Squeeze thanked the man, turned on her heel, and headed back upwards to the main control room, where it was reported to her, by the operator that one of the computer terminals, he indicated which one, had packed up. Squeeze duly noted this, then ordered a, secure, communications channel be opened and headquarters be contacted. Once Dr Q's face, or rather his faceplate, appeared on screen, his subordinate said, "Dr Q, one of the computer terminals aboard has failed, therefore I am requesting a computer technical expert be sent over to restore, or replace, the system. Also, I would request that 100 cans of paint, of gunmetal grey, be sent over, to restore this vessel to its former glory. How soon can these things be done?"

Such an impatient woman, thought her leader. "One day," he replied, consulting some papers in front of him. It would do her no harm to wait; after all he was her commander. At the other end of the connection Squeeze seethed with rage, how dare he treat her like this and make her wait.

Finally, accepting defeat she left the control room and crossed the gangplank, back to the dock side. She walked along the concrete floor, and entered the little, commander's office. Inside was just the same as a normal ship commander's office, with a desk – on it was a telephone/communicator, globe of the world, notebooks and shipping charts, most were no good for this mission but they were there – on the walls were the usual filing cabinets and so on, plus on the rear wall of the office was a map of the world. The vessel would travel in a south-westerly direction, swinging round the bottom of Africa, then in a north-westerly direction upwards, through the Atlantic Ocean until the ship reached the gap between the top westerly tip of Africa and the most southerly point of Portugal. Then the ship would enter the Straits of Gibraltar and onwards into the Mediterranean Sea, where the cruiser was, and the fun would begin.

CHAPTER 5

Discovery & the pleasure cruise, from hell!

The three *Proagnon* teams boarded their separate flights on Boeing 787 aircraft, and flew to Doha; in Qatar, where they were booked into the five star Marriott hotel, for a layover of nine hours, before completing the second stage of their journey to Washington. This second journey would be completed on the same Airbus as the Russian had used to enter the country, but no-one knew, among the nine agents – all men as *Proagnon* had only two female officers, Squeeze and Sandy Tulliver, who was a new recruit.

The men went into the departure lounge, at the airport, in their three different teams – an hour between each departure on the Airbus A320 liners for the 721 mile journey to Dulles Airport, in Washington; and the Airbus would be travelling at 594mph, therefore their journeys should take 1 hour 20 minutes. Considering the first part of their journey had taken roughly a similar time they were happy; they had arrived as a group of nine friends, but were leaving as three separate teams.

The first team of three boarded their aircraft, along with the other passengers, an A320-200; a narrow bodied jet-liner. Once everyone was strapped in aboard the plane the jet moved off on its taxiing towards the runway; once the airport terminal was out of sight the stark reality of the mission hit them, they may be committing suicide, and it scared the hell out of them. The jet aircraft halted at the top of the runway, awaiting clearance; the plane seemed to wait an eternity and the men hoped that, maybe, somehow they'd been saved, when the twin IAEV500 motors started throttling back and the A320 began to lurch forward, building up speed and built up thrust, and the jet liner took off from the west runway, using most of the 4280 metres. As the plane rose up, into the sky, the men realised there was no going back now.Whatever last minute doubts they'd had had been left on the ground.

Peter Roberts, had journeyed to Great Britain and met with Queen Charlotte Pendragon, and her consort, Gareth Andrews. The Palace staff were most courteous for this visit, giving a guided tour to the party of three, and allowing his party and himself full access to the State Dining Room, Music Room, each of the Drawing Rooms, each of the Galleries, Ball Room, Centre or Balcony Room, Chinese Luncheon Room, Principal Corridor, Service Areas, The Grand Staircase, and the extensive gardens.

Many of the Palace's principal rooms were contained on the *piano nobile*, or principal floor, behind the west facing garden facade, at the rear of the palace. At the centre of this ornate suite of state rooms was the Music Room, its large bow the dominant feature of the façade; flanking the Music Room are the Blue and White Drawing Rooms. At the centre of this suite, serving as a corridor to these state rooms, was the Picture Gallery – upon whose walls hung numerous works by Rembrandt, van Dyck, Rubens and Verneer; other rooms leading off from the Picture Gallery included the Throne Room, the HART members were refused access to this room, and the Green Drawing Room.

They were told that the Green Drawing Room also served as a huge anteroom to the Throne Room, this room in itself was very magnificent, and was part of the ceremonial route to the throne from the Guard Room at the top of the Grand staircase; the Guard Room, they were told, contained white marble statues of Queen Victoria and Prince Albert, in Roman costume, set in a tribune that was lined with tapestries. These formal rooms were only used for ceremonial occasions and official entertaining, but were open to the public in the summer.

Directly underneath these State Apartments was a suite of slightly less grand rooms known as the semi-state apartments. Opening from the Marble Hall, these rooms were used for less formal entertaining, such as luncheon parties and private audiences. Some of the rooms were named and decorated for particular visitors, such as the *1844 Room*, which was decorated in that year for the State visit of Emperor Nicholas I of Russia, and, on the other side of the Bow Room, the *1855 Room*. At the centre of this suite was the Bow Room, through which thousands of guests pass annually to the Queen's Garden Parties in the Gardens beyond. The Queen uses privately a smaller suite of rooms in the North wing of the building.

Between 1847 and 1850, when Blore was building the new east wing, the Brighton Pavilion was once again plundered of its fittings. As a result, many of the rooms in this wing have a distinctly oriental atmosphere. The red and blue Chinese Luncheon Room was made up from parts of the Brighton banqueting and music rooms, but had a chimney piece, also from Brighton, in design it was more Indian than Chinese. The Yellow Drawing Room had 18th-century wall paper, which was supplied in 1817 for the Brighton Saloon, and the chimney piece in this room was a European vision of what the Chinese equivalent would look like, complete with nodding mandarins in niches and fearsome winged dragons.

At the centre of this wing was the famous balcony, with the Centre Room behind its glass doors. This was a Chinese-style saloon enhanced by Queen Mary, who, working with the designer Sir Charles Allom, created a more *binding* Chinese theme in the late 1920s, although the lacquer doors were brought from Brighton in 1873. Running the length of the *piano nobile* of the east wing is the great gallery, modestly known as the Principal Corridor, which runs the full length of the eastern side of the quadrangle. It had mirrored doors, and mirrored cross walls reflecting porcelain pagodas and many other oriental furniture from Brighton. The Chinese Luncheon Room and Yellow Drawing Room were situated at each end of this gallery, with the Centre Room obviously placed in the centre.

They were also given a guided tour of the bedrooms, occasionally being allowed to view the inside of some of the main bedrooms; though the Palace staff, as well as the three HART members were situated in separate quarters from the main part of Buckingham Palace. However, they were never allowed to see into the Throne Room, where Charlotte's crowning had taken place.

The new, young, queen, along with her consort, had held meetings with these two men, and one woman, in the Drawing

Room, as many meetings had been held there in the past; joining them was the Prime Minister, he had been Prime Minister since the, sad, demise of his immediate superior. Finally, in the room, there was Charlotte's chief bodyguard.

Peter Roberts had asked the group, "How is London coping now?"

The young queen answered that. "Half of the main city has gone, either destroyed by the terrorists, *Proagnon*, or washed away in the flood. Hospitals are full to overflowing and some patients have had to be left, to die – if they are not seen quickly - in corridors," Charlotte began to weep and Gareth, together with her chief bodyguard, quietly led her from the room.

The Prime Minister took the tale up, "Law enforcement is at an all time low, there are looters all over. Luckily, though, this building survived intact." Then he added. "Many Londoners see this new reign as the beginning of a bad omen, and have fled the city, and I am inclined to agree in some cases. Did you know this country only has 80 MPs left? No, I don't suppose you do," he thundered. "Now a question for you Mr Roberts; what the fucking hell are HART doing about *Proagnon?*"

Roberts was surprised at this outburst. Still, he supposed, it was understandable, under the circumstances. "Gwyneth?"

"We monitored, via our satellite, these events, but as we felt, as you may have done yourselves, it was a random attack, until we noticed the attack on the White House in the United States and then we started to wonder. However, when I took the ill-fated phone call from Drimsey House we were pretty certain; and we are continually monitoring for any armoured vehicle and troop build-up. Once we find that HART shall strike at these bastards."

Mr Roberts and Dr Shaiffer looked up at her, neither had ever heard her use that sort of language. "So you're monitoring the situation," began the Prime Minister. "In other words you're doing nothing!" Gwyneth Jones looked like she was about to explode with rage, but was restrained by her commanding officer.

It was then that the doors opened and Queen Charlotte returned, along with the men who had led her out. "Sorry about that, it's just that, as you will know, both my parents were killed in the attack on the Olympics. And it is still, sometimes, painful to think and talk about that dreadful occasion."

"We quite understand your majesty," the commander of HART replied, as she was helped to her seat by Mr Andrews. "I came here to ask you for any help your armed forces, what's left, can supply."

"Mr Roberts," the queen told him, a look of determination crossed her face. "Your forces may have access to any equipment you need. My Prime Minister will give the order to the Secretary of Defence, and he will pass on the order to every surviving commanding officer in the British armed forces."

"Also, we at HART require additional funding, and wonder if this country would be prepared to assist us?"

"No, we bloody wouldn't!" snapped the PM forcefully.

"Prime Minister, do not exceed your authority!" Charlotte snapped at him. "Yes, Mr Roberts, we will do all we can to help, anything your force requires please contact us."

"Thank you your highness," Peter said. As if on cue a servant appeared with a tray of tea, coffee, biscuits and cake.

"Most hospitable of you," Dr Schaiffer said, pouring the other HART members and himself a drink, and selecting some cake for himself. Everyone joined in, except the PM, who just pushed past the bodyguard and stormed out the room. Must be something we said," and they all laughed, even the bodyguard who, normally, didn't have much of a sense of humour.

Once they'd all finished eating and drinking the six of them left the room and parted company; later on Dr Schaiffer mentioned to his fellow companions, "I would like to visit the hospitals, see what troubles they are experiencing and see if I can be of any assistance."

"Hmm, yes, that's a good idea. We'll take the car and tour the city," Roberts replied. That afternoon, after obtaining the queen's permission, the three HART operatives piled into their aged, rented, Ford Escort, supplied by Hertz – Roberts didn't want to be seen in an official car, or have an official escort. This way, he knew, they'd blend in and be seen as just three more citizens in this, once, great city.

They drove out of the gates of Buckingham Palace, and travelled into the main city, or rather what was left; buildings lay in ruins, Big Ben's clock face was now just rubble, Wesminster Abbey lay in ruins, as did the Houses of Parliament and Lords, Downing Street had been shut off; everywhere was just ruins, all three of them were shocked. Seeing this just made their resolution to find and punish these evil terrorists. At each hospital they stopped and Dr Hans Schaiffer would go into the building; every time he came out, after about 10 minutes, shaking his head. After several such occurrences his commanding officer asked, "What's wrong old friend?" Both commander and secretary looked at him with concern.

"As soon as I mentioned I was from HART I was told to leave, not always in the mildest terms, I think many people feel the way the Prime Minister does."

"That's as maybe, but they need to understand that before we can destroy the *Proagnon* forces we need intelligence as to where they may be hiding. Battles, even wars, are often won or lost on how good the intelligence is," Gwyneth assured Hans.

"Well, personally," began Roberts, "I feel it is time we were getting back as it's getting dark and nippy." They all agreed and drove back to the palace.

That evening, at the palace – as it was their last evening, a banquet had been laid on for them in the State Dining Room. When the three of them entered they all gasped in astonishment; a complete buffet had been laid on for them. Even the doctor was taken aback – even though he'd known a lot of food at one sitting – since the 1980s Germany had always prospered and once the Berlin Wall had been taken down the Germans had prospered, maybe not as much as other countries but they'd prospered – in food markets as well, however, the sight of all this totally amazed him.

There were many different foods, many from around the world. The queen came up and gave him a strange look; it was then he realised he was staring, "Is there anything wrong Dr Schaiffer?"

"No, sorry your highness; it's just that even in my native Germany I have never seen this much food at one meal."

"Enjoy yourself Mr Schaiffer," and she nudged him in the side. "And please call me ma'am, your highness and your majesty sound too formal." Then they all went round the room, filled their plates with food, and sat down to eat.

"This is delicious your maj, sorry ma'am," Gwyneth Jones told her.

"Thank you," Charlotte replied, "I shall pass your comments onto the cook. As you know we get all our ingredients fresh, and then the head cook assisted by her group of cooks, prepare everything you see before you; that is, except for the cold meats."

As always, the bodyguard was present, just in case, He was certain that if any medical emergency arose, as he was also trained to be a medic, he could rely on this Dr Schaiffer fellow to assist him – he seemed a competent enough chap, and pleasant with it. Okay, he was German but hadn't the war ended some 67 years ago; now it was all jolly hockey sticks between the two countries.

The banquet/buffet passed without a hitch, and afterwards the queen met Mr Roberts, in private; well, as private as could be if you ignored the armed man at the doors. "Mr Roberts," she began, "When you find the leader of *Proagnon*, or whoever organised the attack on the Olympics, killing many of my family, and if you can, please bring them back here before they are punished; as I want to see the face of my parent's killer. Please try."

"I will do my best ma'am," the HART commander assured her, looking into the face of this new queen. She was only young but, Roberts judged, she had a good head on her shoulders, and to coin a phrase 'the heart and stomach of a lion'. He knew her loss was nothing any child should go through, but, given time, she would get over it, and be a good monarch, perhaps as great as many past monarchs had been; but, well, time would tell, it always did.

Saluting her, as if he was on parade, he turned on his heel and marched out, the bodyguard holding the door open for him.

At HART headquarters Leon was going over, more thoroughly and in more detail, the events that had happened, in Russia, with acting commander Ronan Strobing. Lucy Lang was present as well, perched on the desk, listening in, when Celia Most walked into the office, Ben Gillespe holding the door open for her; she was carrying the CCTV from the night before Mark Schnieder had been killed, and she produced the blonde hair. "These are everything – footage wise, of evidence, relating to the evening before our fellow agent, friend and fiancé to Lucy, Mark Schnieder, was killed. Yes, I'm afraid he's definitely dead, Lucy; however this footage may provide clues as to who his killer might be. Also I would say, as you already suspected," turning to Lucy, "he spent the night with another woman." Miss Lang didn't say a word in response to what Celia Most had just said, this only finalised what she was already certain of.

"Let's adjourn to the conference room," Ronan announced, Lucy was last out the office; once she was certain she couldn't be seen she took the hair from its, clear, plastic envelope and held it, and looked at it – it was similar to her own hair – "Come on Lucy," called her superior.

"Coming," she called, putting the hair back in its envelope. Unfortunately, with handling the hair she had contaminated it, so if it was used in a trial it would reveal her fingerprints, and with it being so similar to her own hair colour it could be mistaken, quite easily now for Lucy's own hair; and so she may be seen as guilty of murdering her own fiancé.

Not realising this fact she walked into the conference room, head held high, and looked around the table. *Damn*, she thought, *that Celia bitch has got the seat next to our commander, which I wanted*. Reluctantly, she sat herself down next to Leon. "Right, now we're *all* here run the footage Ben," ordered acting commander Strobing.

A TV with Video, though these were mostly obsolete now, the video was combined with a DVD player; though mostly now only DVD recorders/players were available, had been set up at the head of the table. Ben operated the remote control handset and the picture, though a bit grainy, quite definitely, showed the hotel lobby; the time showed 18.00 hours, nothing of interest could, really, be seen; only the normal goings-on in any hotel lobby. "Fast Forward it Ben," the acting commander requested. Ben did as requested, and the picture speeded up, nothing of any importance happened until, according to the time display, 19.02, when a man walked into the hotel lobby, not a guest judging by his appearance, came into view.

Even though the picture was of a grainy nature Lucy, immediately, recognised the figure as that of her, now, dead fiancé, Mark Schnieder; as they watched he moved toward a large pair of double doors, above which was the sign *Restaurant*. "So," Ronan began, looking round at them all. "It would seem our friend, Mark, went into the restaurant, but what for?"

"I would have thought it was pretty obvious *sir*," Lucy called, from her place next to Leon. "It was to meet his tart!"

"Hmm, yes, well, I think we have learned what we can from that bit of footage, so if nobody has any objection might I suggest we move onto the next bit of footage? Ben, number 2 if you please." No one had any objections so the secretary complied with his commander's request. Footage DVD 2 was loaded and Mr Gillespe activated the *play* control; this DVD footage started at 19.05; they saw Mark approach a table with a blonde person at it, even though this person was not fully visible there was no mistaking the blonde hair that belonged to he, or she – as Lucy suspected, in fact they all now did.

They watched Mark approach and withdraw a chair, he, then, sat down revealing the face of the person with the blonde hair. A young woman, about 30 years of age, she had blonde, shoulder length hair, but Leon, who voiced his suspicions that her hair looked like as if it might be a wig, to mislead people; finally her eyes, what could be seen of them looked green, maybe a light green, in fact they seemed to shine. Nothing of the conversation could be heard as this was a surveillance camera only. They noted their fellow operative was wearing his communicator, however, didn't Lucy say when the body was found he hadn't been wearing it? Therefore, it had mysteriously disappeared.

By the time the two of them left, the display read 19.50. They watched as both people entered into view on their way to the elevators, they were holding hands. Leon had to restrain

Lucy before she went mad at what she was seeing. Ronan left the group and returned to the office; he returned a moment later with a thick folder/book, once the couple they were watching entered the elevator Ben pressed the *stop* button.

The final DVD was labelled *floor 3*. At the commander's request Mr Gillespie pressed the *play* button again. 19.55, the couple exited the elevator, and walked to a room midway down the corridor. Once they'd entered the room and were out of sight Ben pressed the *stop* button and ejected the disc.

The acting commander then started to flip through the book/folder, of known terrorists. "What are you looking for?" Celia asked him curiously.

"I'm sure that woman we saw is known to us, in a way, and with Leon saying her hair may have been a wig, I'm certain we know her." He flipped through the pages trying to find a likeness. Ben withdrew the DVDs from the table, and quietly left the room. The other team leaders were now crowded round their leader, watching as he flipped the pages, Lucy had her hands on his shoulders; he noticed she was still wearing her engagement ring, so why had she suggested they have more personal contact?

They studied every face in the book; eventually, on the last page, Celia pointed to Squeeze's profile and said, "Isn't that the woman, or a very good likeness?"

"It could be," murmured the commander, "but as you can see she has black hair However, the face shape is the same."

"Yes sir," said the man behind him, "however don't forget I said I thought the hair was a wig."

"You did indeed," remarked Ronan, starting to feel Lucy massage his shoulders – why was she doing that he wondered? "Apart from that she does look very similar, except as you will recall, she wasn't wearing glasses."

Lucy piped up, "She didn't need to; she may just have needed to wear the glasses for distant or close work, or perhaps she was wearing contact lenses."

"Agreed! Now we need to form a plan of further investigation." They all thought about what to do next.

"With your permission sir," said the other male member of the group, "I think someone should look at the hotel bookings for room 38 at the Hotel Tiffany, and I nominate myself."

"That's so simple, why didn't I think of it. You have my permission of course."

"Thank you sir," he announced and left the room.

"I shall be in my quarters, if anyone needs me!" announced Ronan, and also left the room. Celia and Lucy just looked at each other and followed the other two, one to go shopping in Geneva, and the other to do some practice at the shooting range. However, once the first was out of sight the second changed direction and walked towards her commander's, private, residence.

Once the work on the Admiral *Lazarev* had been completed the ship was powered up, and sailed out of it's dry dock into open waters; due to its great size it was steered, at a mere 5 knots, and was steered southwards, down the Persian Gulf, and then eastwards and out into the Arabian Sea. The vessel then sailed southwards again into the Indian Ocean; rounding the southern most tip of Africa it sailed northward up the Atlantic Ocean. Finally, once the ship became, more or less, level with the Gibraltar Strait, which led into the Mediterranean Sea the, huge, sea vessel moved to dock alongside Morocco The Africans, it was known, were very submissive and would give the *Proagnon* troops no trouble. However, some countries may notice, and maybe demand to know what a Russian battle cruiser was docked alongside Morocco. Still, they would all get their comeuppance soon. Plus anyone who did enquire was to be shot, no questions asked.

Back at *Proagnon* headquarters, Dr Q was planning the next attack; the troops who hadn't been needed aboard the Admiral *Lazarev*, just over 2000, had returned and a meeting had been called to inform them of their next mission.

Abdul, who had long since returned, and had been promoted to third in command, that was something special for him, as no one had, really, recognised his full potential before the July attack on the White House. He was indebted to Dr Q and always would be; however, secretly, he wanted to overthrow this Dr Q and become leader himself, as he felt he could produce better results and create more terror. However, at the moment, he was content to wait and bide his time.

Dr Q, the leader, outlined his plan; those men with the correct skills were to board their group of Russian bombers, no longer in use, and fly to different countries, and destroy that country's oil wells, one bomber though was to fly over to England and destroy their nuclear power stations, causing absolute carnage and fear; he had all the locations for the pilots. Abdul sat quietly, thinking that this operation should have been carried out before now; still he had to agree, it was an audacious plan.

The pilots were given their flight plans; a squadron of 7 of the aircraft were to fly north, and destroy the Middle East and then veering westwards into Africa destroying the oil and gas fields of Algeria, Angola, Bahrain, Eqypt, Iran, Iraq, Israel, Kuwait, Libya, Nigeria, Oman, Qatar, Saudi Arabia, South Africa, Turkey, and the UAE (United Arab Emirates). Abdul, as he was Iranian, started to feel anger as his leader read out the Middle East country of Iran, how dare this infidel think of attacking his third in command's own countrymen! The other countries he had no objection to, especially Iraq – who had been at war with Iran for the past 30 years, on and off. He knew his own countrymen of that time had done a few foolish things. "Dr Q," he began, "my fellow countrymen have never harmed you or us, in any way, so why attack them?"

"I never knew you cared so much," replied his leader, with a hint of menace in his voice. "I'll tell you what, if you care that much, you may leave if you like and rejoin your fellows."

Abdul thought about this, then said, panic in his voice, "But I'll be killed in the bombings."

"Exactly," snarled the leader. "So, Abdul, my dear fellow, make your mind up, is your allegiance to me or your country?"

He realised what his leader was saying, with a sudden realisation, "My allegiance, Dr Q, is to you, always."

"I'm glad to hear it. Now has anyone else got any other objections, or shall we move on?" The others shook their heads; "Good." Abdul was still seething though; he would have to act soon.

The second squadron was to fly further westwards and drop its bombs on: Argentina, Brazil, Chile, Colombia, Mexico, Peru, the U.S.A and Venezuela, and destroy their oil and gas fields.

A third squadron of aircraft was to fly eastwards and take out the oil and gas fields of the new western European, this included countries of the former eastern Bloc, countries of: Azarbaijan, Bulgaria, Croatia, the Czech Republic, Greece, Hungary, Kazakhstan, Poland, Romania, Russia, Slovakia and the Ukraine.

A fourth fleet of bombers were assigned to take out the fuel fields of, what was now eastern Europe. This region included the countries of: France, Germany, Italy, the Netherlands, Norway and Spain,

Finally, the fifth squadron of this type of aircraft were to be deployed to take out the oil and gas fields in the Asian, or the Far Eastern region. This region contained the countries of: Australia, China, India, Malaysia, Pakistan, the Philippines, South Korea, Thailand and Vietnam.

These attacks would harm the OPEC (Operation of Petroleum Exploring Countries) members, reduce the output of oil, for a while, and maybe kill a few thousand people in the process. As for the UK he was planning something special, which he'd outlined to his troops already. He decided, on afterthought, not to give the command to launch the bombers, yet.

He adjourned the meeting, and when he was safely in his office, he wondered how the three engineers/troops were getting on in France.

The three men in question were, at this moment, going through their training program, to enable them to be competent enough to work on the *Salark* cruise liner; the boat was, at this moment, being constructed in Germany's *Meyer Werft* shipyard.

The *Meyer Werft* was one of the remaining large German shipyards, headquartered in Papenburg. Since 1997 it had been part of the Meyer Neptun Group together with Neptun Werft in Rostock.

Founded in 1795 as a wharf for the construction of wooden ships, Josef Lambert Meyer started the construction of iron ships in 1874. Until 1920 there were more than 20 dockyards in the Papenburg area of Germany. Today, *Meyer Werft* was the only remaining shipyard in Papenburg. For more than six generations it had been a privately held and a family owned company. It had gained international recognition through the construction of roll on/roll off ferries, passenger ferries, gasoline tankers, container ships, livestock ferries and most recently luxury cruise ships.

Meyer was one of the largest and most modern shipyards in the world with 2300 employees, and it was home to some of the largest roofed dry docks in the world. The first covered dock had been inaugurated in 1987 and was 370 metres long, 101,5 metres wide and 60 metres high. In 1990/91 this dock had been extended by an additional 100 metres. In 2000 a second covered dock was built. The current cruise liner projects included *Celebrity Solstice* for Celebrity Cruises (owned by Royal Caribbean International), *Meyer Werft* was also constructing two new ships for the Disney Cruise Line and two *Salark* and *Solstice* for Crystal Cruises.

Due to its upstream location on the river Ems, the giant ships to be delivered had to make a 36km voyage to the Dollard bay and each time attracted thousands of spectators. Up until the completion of the Ems river barrier (Emssperrwerk) in 2002 the journeys were only possible at high tides.

Crystal Cruises, who were the owners of the *Salark* had been set up in the United States in 1988, and already had two liners, the *Symphony* – built in 1995, and able to hold 940 passengers, and the *Serenity* – buiilt in 2003, and able to hold 1050 passengers and 650 crew. Crystal had also had a liner named *Harmony* but this was retired in 2005.

The Crystal line had its main headquarters in Los Angeles, California, USA, but had opened a branch in the port town of Calais, in France – this was just to handle its Mediterranean cruises. Although the company had its main headquarters in America it was a wholly-owned subsidiairy of the large

Japanese shipping company Nippon Yusen Kaisha; the *Harmony* was transferred to the parent company where it underwent some alterations, and was renamed the *Auska II* and now catered to the Japanese cruise market, as part of Asuka Cruises.

The *Proagnon* agents had been asked, on their first day, by their instuctor, "Do you fellows want a job onboard ship or on shore?"

Each had looked at his companions, they had all nodded in agreement. "Onboard ship please," they had all answered.

The instructor, or whoever he was, had handed them each a list of the different departments onboard ship, for them to choose from. These included: the beauty salon, the casino, cruise staff, deck, engine, entertainment, food and drink, onboard auctioneers, galley, hotel operations, housekeeping, medical, photography, gift shop, or information technology positions. Each department contained many different and varying positions.

The three men, once they had indicated which department they required employment in they handed the lists back to the other man. "So," he said, "I see you all want employment in the engine department. Any particular reason you should all want to be in there?"

"We just want to be there to oversee the safe running of the vessel," which was a total lie. They wanted to be in the engine room as major accidents could happen in there, couldn't they? None of them said that, though.

"I'll see what is available," announced the instructor, and wandered off in the direction of the First Mate's office. The three agents smiled at each other, evilly; then went into a quiet bar from where they could still see the office, and sat down to wait. The man, instructor, returned from the office about half an hour later; as soon as they saw him the men went to receive what news he had for them. "I have consulted with the First Mate, and it turns out you gentleman are in luck. We still have vacancies for a fireman, you would be responsible for safety aboard plus any fire fighting that is required; we have vacancies for two of them, plus we have a vacancy for an electrician who would be responsible for the proper maintenance and repairs of the electrical systems on board ship, as directed by the Chief Electrician. There is only one of those positions available. I shall leave you to decide amongst yourselves which of you is the best qualified for which job."

"Finally I must ask, I probably should have done so before, to see your papers certifying you can do these jobs."

"Certainly," they each replied and handed their papers over, these were forgeries but looked authentic. This was getting better and better, once they'd heard there was a job as a firemen going they knew they would be able to sabotage things, but two firemen – it was like a dream come true, and now an electrician as well.

"For the duration of training," began the instructor, again, "you will be housed in the hotel *Emerald* next door; once your full 8 week courses are over you will be fully trained; the ship's maiden voyage is in 9 weeks." The men nodded and turned to walk out. "Once I have verified your papers, Mr King, Mr Smart and Mr Aman." The three merely shrugged their shoulders, as if to say *whatever* at this, and wandered out and into their new residence, for the time being, until their training was to begin. Mr Armitage, their instructor, merely thought the men a bit rude at just shrugging their shoulders, but said nothing.

Flying over the Atlantic Ocean, at the moment, was Mr Roberts, together with his companions, had caught a 767 flight from Birmingham International Airport, and were now at an altitude of 35,000 ft, and cruising at 500 miles per hour. They had allowed themselves to be seated in economy class with most of the other passengers; Roberts felt it would be too easy to have preferential treatment, and anyway, he wanted to see a, more normal, civilian life; he was due to retire in a few years.

Just then the pilot's voice came over the intercom, "Ladies and Gentlemen, we are approximately 20 miles from our destination of Washington Dulles Airport in central America and will be beginning our descent in the next few minutes. I would like to remind passengers to observe the *No Smoking* sign, and please extinguish all cigarettes; plus I would ask you to observe that when the *Fasten Belts* light is lit, to please fasten your safety belts. Thank you." Peter looked over at his companions; Gwyneth was fast asleep, while Hans was taking in every word "The time in Washington is now 12 noon, the temperature is a humid 24 degrees, and the weather is rainy."

The Boeing's 767 was an upgrade of the 757 aircraft. The plane was a wide bodied twin jet airliner, first produced in 1978, along with its sister, which had a narrower body; the 767 had a length of 61.37m, a total width of 5.03m, yet the interior cabin was 4.7m wide, the wingspan was 51.99m and a tail height of 16.8m. Performance wise its range was 10,370km, they were at cruising height but the aircraft could have gone another 30 miles per hour faster.

The engines under each wing had been supplied by Pratt & Whitney, but had the option of Rolls-Royce engines, they were PW4062s and each weighed 28,173kg, the electrics were supplied by General Electric, model CF6-80C2B8F and weighed a total of 28,804kg; he was surprised.

The aircraft, on this flight, was carrying a total of 325 passengers; though it could take a maximum of 375. The aircraft was built to replace the 727/737/757 and, of course, the 747.

The first 767, a –200, was rolled out on 4th August 1981 and first flew on 26 September 1981. Boeing planned to offer a shorter 767-100 with seating for 180 passengers, but it was never offered for sale as the capacity was too close to that of the 757's.

The 767 had been designed using engines used on the 747 with wings sized to match. The wings were larger and provided longer range than the initial customers wanted. However, the larger wings only increased fuel usage slightly and provided better takeoff and landing performance. Boeing had designed the 767 with enough range to fly across North America and across the northern Atlantic.

As the flight decks of the Boeing 757 and 767 are very similar and as a result, after a short conversion course, pilots rated in the 757 were also qualified to fly the 767 and vice versa. The 767 was approved for U.S. CAT IIIb operations in March 1984. This revision permitted operations with minimums as low as RVR 300 (Runway Visual Range 300 feet). It was the first aircraft certificated for CAT IIIb by the U.S.

In the late 1980s, Boeing proposed a stretched version of the 767, and then a partial double deck version with parts of a 757 fuselage built over the aft (rear) fuselage These concepts were never accepted though; Boeing later developed a stretched 767 version in the form of the 767-400ER, in the late 1990s.

The 767 sold very well from the late 1980s to the late 1990s, with a decrease during the recession in the early 1990s. After strong sales in 1997, sales declined significantly, due to the economic recession of the early 2000s and the increased competition from Airbus. In early 2007, United Parcel Service and DHL prolonged the 767's production with orders for 767-300 freighters of 27 and 6, respectively. In August 2008, Boeing received two orders for the 767-300ER, specifically to Japanese carriers All Nippon Airways & Japan Air Lines, who had been in serious talks for new build passenger airframes. Boeing also kept the line open in the hope of winning the US Air Force's competition for a tanker (the KC-767 tanker program, which used the 767 airframe. Renewed interest in the 767-300 freighter had Boeing considering enhanced versions of the 767-200 and 767-300 freighter, with increased gross weights and 767-400ER wing technology.. Boeing saw the advanced 767-200F and 767-300F complementing their new aircraft, the 777F, and allowed Boeing to compete more effectively against the A330-200F, which was larger than the proposed 767-200F and 767-300F, but smaller than the new 777F. In June 2008, the Boeing 767 had 1011 orders, with 965 of those delivered. Delta Air Lines was currently the world's largest 767 operator, at that time, with approximately 102 airplanes, including the 767-300, 767-300ER, and 767-400ER. Hartsfield-Jackson Atlanta International Airport, their hub had the highest number of Boeing 767 operations in the world. The Boeing 767 was a low-wing cantilever monoplane with a conventional tail unit that had a single fin and rudder. It had retractable tricycle landing gear and was powered by two wing mounted turbofan engines.

The 767 offered a twin aisle configuration of 2+3+2 in economy class with the most common business configuration of 2+2+2. It was possible to squeeze in an extra seat for a 2+4+2 configuration, as had been done by Skymark Airlines. However, the seats were very narrow and this was not common. The 767 had a seat-to-aisle ratio in economy class of an efficient 3.5 seats per aisle, allowing for quicker food service and quicker exit of the airplane than many other jetliners, which typically had four to six seats per aisle in economy class. It could carry freight in Unit Load Devices such as LD2s and LD8s. Its fuselage width did not allow larger ULDs such as LD6s, LD11s, and LD3s.

Newer 767-200s and 767-300s, as well as all 767-400ERs, featured the 777 style cabin interior, also known as the "Boeing Signature Interior". The 767-400ER also featured larger windows exactly like those found on the newer aircraft of the time. All new 767s built featured the Signature Interior, and this was also available as a retrofit for any of the older 767s. In addition to the Boeing Signature Interior retrofit option, a simpler model known as the "Boeing 767 Enhanced Interior" had also been available. This retrofit had borrowed styling elements from the Boeing Signature Interior; however, the outer section overhead bins were more traditional-style shelf bins rather than those on the 777-style pivot bins. There were three variants of the 767, which were launched on three separate occasions. Although there were a total of three variants, several versions have been produced.

The first model of the 767, and was launched in 1978 and entered service with United Airlines in 1982, and was the 767-200. This model was used mainly for continental routes such as New York City to Los Angeles. The 767-200 typically was outfitted with 181 seats in a 3-class layout or 224 in a 2-class layout. All -200 models had a capacity limit of 255 due to exit-door limitations. An additional exit door could be specified when the aircraft was ordered to allow for up to 290 seats in a high capacity all Coach (30 in pitch 2+4+2) layout. The 767-200ER extended-range variant was first delivered to El Al in 1984. It became the first 767 to complete a nonstop transatlantic journey, and broke the flying distance record for twinjet airliners several times.

The 767-300 was a lengthened 767 ordered by Japan Airlines in 1983. It first flew on January 14, 1986, and was delivered to JAL on September 25.

The 767-300ER was the extended-range version of the -300. It first flew in 1986 and received its first commercial orders when American Airlines purchased several of the aircraft in 1987. The aircraft entered service with AA in 1988. In 1995, EVA Air used a 767-300ER to inaugurate the first transpacific 767 service. The -300ER had a minimum takeoff run of around 6,000ft (1,825m), and a maximum of 7,900ft (2,400m). The 767-300ER could be retrofitted with blended winglets from Aviation Partners Boeing. These winglets were 11ft (3.4m) long and decreased fuel consumption by 6.5 % on the -300ER.

The 767-300F was the air freight version of the 767-300ER, this was first ordered by United Parcel Service in 1993 and was delivered in 1995. Due to its unique fuselage width of 15ft 6in, it was unable to carry ordinary Unit Load Devices, and instead had to use specially designed air freight containers and pallets. This model had three doors on the main deck plus two on the lower deck. Of the three doors on top, two were at the front, and one at the rear right side. The two lower doors comprised of one at the right front and one at the rear left.

In October 2007, All Nippon Airways (ANA) had sent one of its Boeing 767-300 (JA8286) to ST Aviation Services Co., in Paya Lebar, Singapore, to undergo the world's first 767 PTF (Passenger To Freighter) program. The conversion was completed, on schedule, in June 2008 and designated as a Boeing 767-300BCF, or "Boeing Converted Freighter".

The final variation was the 767-400 and was launched in 1997 on an order for Delta Air Lines and Continental Airlines to replace their aging Lockheed L-1011 and McDonnell Douglas DC-10 fleets. Orders were also placed by others including Kenya Airways and ILFC but these were eventually canceled. Kenya Airways and ILFC converted their orders to the newer Boeing 777. The -400ER was stretched 21.1ft from the -300 for a total of 201.4ft. It also saw a wingspan increase of 14.3 feet over the previous two variants and was the only 767 variant to also feature "raked" wingtips for increased fuel efficiency. Its first flight was on October 9, 1999 and it entered into service with Continental Airlines on September 14, 2000. This variant was only available as the 767-400ER, as there was no 767-400 variant. However it had less range than the other two ER variants. Boeing discussed extending the range further but the proposed 767-400ERX was never launched.

Interesting stuff, thought Peter, as he read the pamphlet and then replaced it; Dr Schaiffer helped Mrs Jones, who had now woken up, fasten her belt as the *Fasten Belts* light had come on, this meant their descent to America would begin at any moment. As the aircraft descended people started to cry out as their ears were hurting, children started crying as well, but, well, there was, basically, nothing anyone could do; the cabin was just de-pressurizing and everything would be okay once they were down. After a couple of minutes of pain, they all felt the bump as the rear wheels landed then the pilot, gently, brought the nose down and landed, the engines started screaming with reverse thrust as the pilot slowed the plane down. Once it had slowed enough, the pilot taxiied the aircraft to the main arrivals terminal; a mobile staircase was driven to the plane, and the main door opened. Every passenger departed, including the three members of HART. They were met, at the bottom, by several Marines, together with an ambassador, who ushered them into a Ford Taurus. Once they were all aboard, with their luggage, the driver drove off.

In France the three *Proagnon* troops had finished their, separate, courses, and were deemed ready to join the rest of the crew aboard the *Salark*. The cruise, as they all knew was just around the Mediteranean to prove the vessel was safe; however, Mr Aman and his colleagues knew they had to cause as much mayhem as possible, yes they would be martyrs but knew it would be justified, in the long run.

So the great day came, cloudy but relatively warm, the promise of some sunshine later, and the passengers started to arrive in their droves – there was to be 20,000 passengers on board for this, its maiden voyage – many young couples, some couples in the middle age range, and some couples in their twilight years – it'd be a shame to extinguish the younger ones lives, but this was just *Proagnon's* way. No-one would be safe.

The three man went below decks to begin their work The Chief Electrician requested his new understudy to check for any loose wiring; therefore the new Electrician, Mr Smart began to check, "What should I do if I find any?" he called.

"Try and find where it's come loose from and either put it back in place, or replace it."

"Will do, sir," he replied. His boss, satisfied, as this was only, really, a meneal task, left him to it. As soon as he'd left the room Mr Smart, after doing these checks for, roughly half an hour – several of the crew passed him but saw nothing amiss. Once he was sure nobody was in sight he produced, from his tool kit, a device similar to a welding torch, held it against a panel in the wooden walls and switched it on. A flame lit the wooden panel and, due to the heat being produced burst into flame. "Fire," called Mr Smart half heartedly, and retreated. The ship's computer, on the main bridge, registered this and responded, the overhead sprinkler system was activated. Everywhere Mr Smart went, below decks, and when it was safe to do so he would produce the welding type device and start fires. *Surely the computer couldn't deal with them all.*

The troops from the battle cruiser were all recalled, from wherever they were, to man their separate stations; once they were all aboard the cruiser, as big as it was, moved, slowly, out of port.

Back aboard the *Salark* the firemen had been called into action, as the sprinklers weren't holding the fires; however, just before he was called into action Mr King had been standing on deck, admiriring a pretty girl with long brown hair, she looked about 20, Mr King thought, and she was wearing a pink bikini, and had a pair of sunglasses on. The bikini top was undone so was loose around her ample sized breasts, but as she was laying on a sunbed Mr King couldn't see anything. Even though there were plenty of people on deck, sunbathing or having a swim in the cruiser's swimming pool, Mr King had been attracted to this one, particular, girl, he didn't know why. As she noticed the attention he was giving her she smiled, sweetly, at him

He smiled back, thinking to himself, *Why should this young woman, this totally innocent civilian, have to die?* Just then his radio crackled and he rushed below decks to help his comrade. As he was leaving the captain of the vessel issued an alert, over the loudspeakers, to both crew and passengers, informing them of what had happened. The voice carried on over the loudspeaker, "There is no danger to you, at present. Should things become more serious, or out of control, I shall sound the alarm and you are instructed to group together at your designated emergency posts; members of my crew will check all cabins, casino, bar, restaurant, and anywhere wherever a passenger may be, before helping you inside the life boats and, if it becomes necessary, launching them. As I say there is no danger to you, at present." Reassured, everyone went back to what they were doing.

In Geneva, at HART HQ, Ronan was happily watching TV, a can of beer in his hand, when his communicator bleeped; quickly he set the beer down and pressed the *receive* button. "Yes!" he snapped, angry at having his peace disturbed for the second time that day, but instantly regretting his flare of temper.

"Sorry sir," replied the receptionist who had taken over from Ben Gillespe, Lisa Bell. "It's just our satellite is showing two ships in th Meditarranean Sea. One, we know, is the new pleasure cruiser; the other matches the configuration of a Russian battle cruiser."

"What? I'll be over quick as I can. Have the men get their kits, and put them on yellow alert." The acting commander rushed out the house and up to the receptionist's office, in the main building. "What's the situation?"

"I have ordered the men to stand by," reported Lisa. "Now, as you can clearly see the battle cruiser seems to be keeping its distance, but, also, moving alongside the pleasure cruiser."

Damn, he thought, *this would have to happen while Peter is away.*

The captain of the *Salark* registered the new contact on radar; handing the binoculars to his second in command he ordered,

"It seems we have a visitor. Get on deck and see who it is." Also the instruments told him that most of the fires were now out. The second in command hurried up onto deck and looked over the starboard (right) side of the vessel; what he saw made him gasp in horror; he pulled, from his jacket, his radio, "Captain!" he said urgently, "The ship is a battle cruiser, named the Admiral *Lazarev*. Should we launch the lifeboats?" All he got back was static.

Aboard the Admiral *Lazarev* the weapons operator was on the command deck. "You know what must be done," announced his captain. "Destroy it!"

The operator operated his computer instruments, slowly the missile tubes lowered themselves into position, and the operator lined up the cruiser in its sights.

Oh shit! The second in command realised, *We're all gonna die!* With that he plunged overboard.

"Fire!" ordered the battle cruiser captain; the operator depressed a button and an SS-19-N was launched. It ripped into the cruiser, creating mayhem on deck. "Fire 2;" the second missile was launched, the trajectory had been altered, slightly, so it smashed into the boat's hull. "Fire 3," the third weapon, like the last, smashed into what remained of the hull. Quickly, the cruiser disappeared below the water line, leaving many people in the water. "Mow them down," he ordered his guncrew. Obediently, the guncrew manned the guns on deck and they shot everyone they could see on the deck of the other boat. What was meant to be a pleasure cruise had quickly turned into a nightmare from hell!

As the boat sank a pink bikini top floated to the surface. That was all that remained to show the *Salark* had once been there.

CHAPTER 6

Dilemmas & meltdown!

As soon as the acting commander, at HART, saw the first missile leave its tube he hit the red alert button on the wall, and spoke, nearly shouted, into the microphone, "This is acting commander Strobing; we have a situation in the Mediterranean. All troops are ordered to Go!" Then he realised his mistake. "Sorry, new orders, Air Squadron One into action. Main troops stand down."

He turned to Miss Bell, "Where did that ship come from?" he asked her.

"According to the data from our satellite it came from, roughly, here," she pointed to the map of the world, indicating the Gulf waters outside Iran and Iraq.

"So, the bastards are based in the Middle East."

"Could be," the receptionist agreed. "However, don't forget that Russian aircraft were used in the first attack, indicating they may be based in Russia, and then there's the fact the battle cruiser was situated alongside Morocco for two months, which may indicate an African base."

"Yes I admit it could be any of those three, we'll just have to check them all." Just then they heard the roar of aircraft engines, and turned, momentarily, to the window. Both saw the fleet of 6 refurbished, as they had all been withdrawn two years ago, F-14 TOMCAT fighter planes speed away followed by the slower E-3 Sentry airborne warning and control system (AWACS), plane, cumbersome in size but it had a look that was very majestic, with it's huge domed, rotating radar system, as it flew past the window; the AWACS was based on the old 707/320 commercial airliner.

The radar was 30ft in diameter, 1.83 metres (6ft) thick and was held at 3.35 metres (11ft); it had a range of 320 kilometres (200 miles) for low flying targets, or farther for aerospace vehicles flying at medium to high altitudes. Linked with a friend or foe subsystem the radar was able to detect, identify and track friendly or enemy low flying aircraft by eliminating any ground chatter returns that could confuse other radar systems. The system was jam resistant; this had been proved on many missions, in the past, while experiencing heavy electronic countermeasures.

The aircraft was powered by 4 Pratt and Whitney TF-33-100A turbofan engines, and could travel, on missions, for up to 8 hours before having to refuel. The crew aboard consisted of four with a specialist mission crew, depending on the mission – they varied, of 13–19, the specialist mission crew also varied in number, depending on the type of mission. The Sentry was sent there to monitor the situation, to relay information from the fighters back to headquarters and vice versa.

The squadron of 6 F-14's were all equipped with up to 4 AIM-7 Sparrow missiles, 6 of the AIM-9 Sidewinder missiles, and 4 AIM-54 Phoenix missiles; these were all air to air missiles. Also they carried many air to ground ordnance bombs; they included the MK-82 (500 lbs), 4 MK-83s (1,000 lbs each), 4 MK-84s (2,000 lbs each), the MK-20 cluster bomb, 4 GBU-10 LGBS (Laser Guided Bombs), a GBU-12 MK-82 LGB, 4 GBU-16 MK-83 LGBs and 4 GBU-24 MK-84 LGBs.

Finally, there was an MK-61A1 Vulcan 20mm cannon. Each plane contained a pilot and an intercept officer; and each was powered by 2 Pratt and Whitney TF-30P-41A1turbofan engines with afterburners.

The pilots of the Tomcat's contacted each other on their radio systems and grumbled to each other about having to attack a Russian built battle cruiser; but each of them had been fully trained to the, high, standards of a fighter pilot. What they were really grumbling about was the lack of support, either air support or an aircraft carrier; mainly because every aircraft carrier was in, a naval dry dock, in America, undergoing repairs or conversion to HART standards at the moment, whilst much of the air support vehicles were either away or undergoing repairs.

Finally as their target came into sight they readied their aircraft fighters for the attack, locking onto the ship with the lasers to aid the guidance of their bombs, and lowering the missile pods to the *attack* position.

Unfortunately for them the ship's radar had already detected the fighters when they were approximately 50 miles out. Control for how to deal with this threat had, now, been decided by the weapons computer and the operator. Slowly the missile tubes lined up with the oncoming fighters, each of the three tubes had a SA-N-8, Surface to Air, missile in it. The threat computer considered the correct trajectory and this was locked in "Ready sir," the systems operator called to his commanding officer.

"Fire," commanded the captain. "Blow them out the sky!" The first of the three missiles launched. The incoming jet's radar registered the oncoming missile, and the pilot tried to manoeuvre his aircraft out the way; however, all to no avail. The pilot managed to raise the fighter's nose, but the missile smashed into the F-14's undercarriage, and it exploded. The same fate befell two of the other jets, whilst the remaining three turned and fled. "This mission has been a successful one," announced the captain. "Now we contact Squeeze and inform her of our success, then head back to base." The large battle cruiser turned, slowly, and headed back through the Gibraltar Straits.

Squeeze, once she'd received the message from the *Admiral Lazarev's* communications officer, relayed it back to *Proagnon* headquarters, where Dr Q was eagerly waiting to hear the outcome. As he had predicted the operation had been a complete success, plus they had dealt a, small but, perhaps, significant, blow to the HART forces by destroying three of their F-14's.

Acting commander Strobing had watched the pictures with mounting horror, as they were beamed in *live* via the satellite; he looked at Lisa, crestfallen then said to her, downheartedly, "I'll be in my residence should anyone want me." He turned and slunk away, Lisa knew he was very unhappy, as it was him who had sent those men to their deaths. He paused and turned, in the doorway, and said, as an afterthought "Prepare the telegrams."

These telegrams were already prepared to inform loved ones, NOK (Next of Kin) that their son, daughter, husband, wife etc. had been killed in action; "I'll see to it at once sir, do we know who they were?"

"Their records should be in the file marked Air Squadron One, from the information we have you want records 2, 4 and 5. Oh, and I think we can recall the Sentry now."

"Okay sir," she saluted him. Lisa Bell may have been young, only in her early twenties – Ronan judged, but she had a good head on her and was liked by all the staff. He went out through the building's exit – the 2 security guards who were on duty as always, noted the acting commander with some satisfaction. As he wandered back to his residence he heard shooting in the distance, *The troops must be practicing their shooting skills, ready for the combat situations that await them.*

Acting commander Ronan Strobing walked inside and settled down to resume where he'd left off before he was called out, but he found he couldn't concentrate on the TV so switched it off and went upstairs for a rest; the faces of those, young, pilots were still haunting him. Several times he woke up, sweating profusely, and had to get up, bathe his face with cold water, then the acting commander looked in the bathroom mirror, the face that looked back at him looked awful. Eventually he managed to sleep for a couple of hours, felt better for it, and then went back downstairs to try and catch a programme on TV, he'd wanted to see it all the week, about famous authors; it might give him some ideas on how to improve his own writing techniques.

As the programme was just starting there came a knock at his door, more of a gentle tapping. *Who can this be?* he wondered. Reluctantly he dragged himself off the sofa and walked through to open the outer door. As the front door glass was frosted, and reinforced to stop bullets, he could only make out that the figure was reasonably tall, but under six foot.

He opened the door, "Oh it's you," he said. "And what do you want?"

His mind registered that the figure was carrying a bottle of wine. "Miss Bell told me you were feeling down after earlier, so I've come to help cheer you up," the person at the door replied. "I've come to join you for your evening meal."

Ronan looked up at his ornamental clock, it was a normal clock face but encased in a star shape, in the hallway; this device now read 5.35. Had time passed that quickly? Surely it hadn't but the clock read different. *Shit*, he thought with a start, *I'll never get my programme watched.* "Okay," he sighed resignedly, "come in."

"Thank you," replied the person and stepped inside. "Shall I prepare us a meal now, or what?"

"Yes, you can prepare the meal, the kitchen's just through there," he indicated the kitchen, as out of the five private residences, three had been built the same way round, whilst the other two had been built with slight differences. "I'm just going to finish off watching a programme on TV, it finishes at 6."

"That'll be fine as the food should be ready by then."

Reassured, but wondering why Lisa had told this particular person to come and cheer him up, he retired to the main room, and the comfort of the sofa, again. Unfortunately, the programme he'd wanted to watch was half over, but he still caught the last 20 minutes.

In the underground base the *Proagnon* technical crews had finished bringing one of the, old, bombers back up to standard. The crew contacted their leader, who sat back in satisfaction once he received the news. Now all he needed was to choose a target, give the flight plan to the crew and also inform them of which sort of bombs to use; he wanted to make this one dramatic. As he considered his options his mind drifted to the Russians, and the vehicles he'd ordered. Why hadn't they been delivered yet? In anger his gloved hand smashed down on the desk, sending the papers flying in all directions; in fact it was so loud a crash one of his, personal bodyguards, rushed in, afraid some serious mishap or illness had befallen his leader. "Are you alright sir?" he asked, his voice sounding concerned.

"Of course I'm bloody alright," the leader snapped. "Now pick those papers up, at once!" Reluctantly the bodyguard did as he was bid; once he had performed his task the guard nodded at his leader. "Thank you," Dr Q sneered at the man, "you may go." Once the bodyguard had left Dr Q then settled himself back in his chair.

Much calmer now he knew what he should do; contact that Russian fool of a foreign minister, Oleg Ayanseikov. After looking in his contacts book he powered up his personal computer, and accessed his email account: boss@Quantumexhibits.ir, or boss@Quantumexhibits.iq, both were just business addresses but they worked. He composed the email asking to know where the rest of his order was.

Knowing that Russia was approximately 1 hour and a half ahead the time he was working to, so he knew he'd receive a reply, at the earliest, that evening; having sent the message he could relax a little, and await the return of his second in command, plus the other troops. It was at that time his secure transceiver unit (STU), model 9, started to flash and make its usual warbling noise; he leaned, forward, over his desk, after screwing into his helmet a transmitter device; also he had to unscrew a panel level with his mouth. Once these were done he picked up the handset on the unit.

He could just have, easily, taken his helmet off, but none of the *Proagnon* troopers, except his second in command, knew what he looked like; nor who he really was.

When the STU-9 had unscrambled the signal for him, yet kept it scrambled should anyone else be listening in, he said "Yes?"

"Squeeze here sir. I have been in contact with the crew of the *Admiral Lazarev*; it appears the mission went well, they also *splashed* three HART fighters, F-14's to be precise, and we are all now returning to base. We should be back within the next few days, maybe earlier, maybe not, depending on the speed the vessel returns at."

"Thank you for your report, I shall await your return," and with that he replaced the handset. Once he had unscrewed the transmitter like device, and screwed up the panel in his faceplate he settled back to his report writing and writing out mission orders.

He thought for a moment or two, and then pressed a button, on his intercom keypad, that would connect him to the section where the bombers, together with their separate bombs, were stored. He looked over the list of *stolen* bombers at his disposal and selected the *Northrop Grunman* B2 *Spirit* (Stealth Bomber).

This air vehicle had been built in 1988, but hadn't seen service until 1997; and had been built in the USA to replace the aging *Rockwell* B-1B *Lancer*. As this mission was to be special the engineers were instructed to load the aircraft's full load of MK 82 bombs, its full load being 80; well, you never knew, plus it's full load of 16 MK 84 bombs. That should give them something to think about. He preferred not to use the nuclear arsenal, at the moment.

The senior engineer told him, "We shall do this as quick as we can, sir, and will get back to you as soon as the work is finished."

"That will be fine," the leader replied and cut the connection. Next Dr Q contacted Abdul's quarters, "Please come to my office," Dr Q announced, "I have a mission for you."

"At once my noble leader," answered Abdul, regretting his earlier actions. Once the connection was cut the leader smiled, cruelly – behind the faceplate of his helmet, to himself. Abdul Singh was a fool, and fools needed to be dealt with – although this one had his uses; Dr Q might deal with him once he returned, or he may decide to let him live, for another day. Suddenly, his mind turned to his missing agent, Sergey Satov; he had been a fool recruiting that Russian but, he was probably locked up now.

Abdul arrived at his commander's office, expecting the worst; ignoring the looks the bodyguards standing outside gave him he knocked on the door and his leader called, "Come in Abdul." Mr Singh was astonished, he'd never known his leader to be in such a cheerful mood; the third in command entered, now fearing that this cheerful reply was to make him feel at ease, yet once he entered he would find a pistol pointed at him.

Dr Q preferred to use AAA Leader Dynamics SAP, an Australian built semi automatic pistol – this had approval from NATO as it was a variation of the AAA Leader Dynamics SAC (Semi Automatic Carbine) – both were 5.56mm and mainly used by the Australian Automatic Arms. However, *Proagnon* had a few years ago, intercepted a shipment to their end destination and, subsequently, stolen the shipment.

Slowly, the door opened until the figure of Dr Q was revealed, seated behind the desk, "Come in Abdul Singh, there is nothing to fear." Of course, Abdul thought, the pistol may be held just below the top of the desk; yet both his leader's gloved hands were showing. "What is wrong comrade?" asked the voice behind the mask. "Do you fear me? I am no threat to you; please, sit down," a chair was indicated. Abdul, feeling slightly relieved now, but more on edge than ever, seated himself in the chair indicated, "Now Abdul, my *trusted* third in command, I should like you to lead a bombing mission."

"Will this be a suicide mission sir?" he asked. He was afraid, due to his outburst earlier, Dr Q may be planning to get rid of him sooner rather than later; yet he was scheming, in private, that one day he would lead an uprising and dispose of this, spineless infidel, bastard.

"It is not a suicide mission," replied his commander. "What do you take me for?"

Oh great! It is a suicide mission!

Both Celia Most and Leon Bigship had, by now, arrived back at the HART compound; Celia went off to her residence with the shopping she'd bought, from a family run store, whilst Leon went to the main building to find the acting commander. When he got there the duty officer, George Burnett, told him, "Mr Strobing seems to have disappeared sir, we've tried raising him on his communicator, we've tried phoning his residence, on the STU-8, and we've even been to his residence. His car's still in, so either he's inside his residence or he's simply walked out the compound; yet the guards on duty maintain they haven't seen him."

"Try his residence again, communicator and the STU!" Leon snapped at the man.

"Yes sir," replied Mr Burnett. "Lisa," he said to Miss Bell, "try the commander's residence again, both communication devices." Lisa Bell had not yet gone off shift, the fact was her relief, George Burnett, had arrived early.

"At once;" and she busied herself at some controls and dials that operated the communications devices. "It's no good sir, either someone is already talking to him, no idea who, or his communicator is broken." She looked up at the two men and they both shrugged their shoulders, defeated. "If his communicator is broken once he reports in I will have one of

158

our technical experts look at it;" she then moved to the STU and punched the button that would call his residence. She switched over to speakerphone instead of using the handset; the STU's electronic dialling came through loud and clear as the phone dialled and rang. Should anyone answer it the encryption code would be used and the message scrambled, enabling the user to talk to the other person without the fear of any hackers or enemy agents listening in. However, the machine just made its usual warbling sound; Lisa let this go on for at least a minute.

She then remembered and told her two comrades, "I remember now that when he left earlier he was in a dejected mood, as three crews from Air Squadron One, made up of F-14's, had been killed in action against a Russian battle cruiser – and he'd sent them out. Surely you don't think he's done anything stupid?"

"Poor guy," sympathised Leon, "it's a difficult call to make, especially when you're not used to commanding more than a squad of forty troops, at the most, at one time. No, I don't think he'll have done anything stupid, Lisa, he's too much of a trained professional; he's probably just a bit low at the moment, he'll come round once he's properly over the shock. Have you sent anyone round to see him?"

"No," she replied in defence, "he told me only to contact him in an emergency."

"Funny," he murmured, "I'm sure a guard said to me he'd seen someone else entering his residence. I could be wrong…"

At that moment Ronan Strobing, together with his dinner guest were sitting down to a meal. "What is it? he asked, not wishing to offend his guest's cooking skills, but curious at what he was eating.

"That my dear, is deep fried chicken, like me pappy used to make. A good cook he was, taught me everything I know."

"It's delicious," he announced, taking another mouthful. "I hate to say this but I'm not much of a cook, Mandy does most of the cooking in our house. Nearest I get to cooking is doing the washing up afterwards."

""Oh well," sighed his dinner guest, "I'm sure you have other talents." A, cheeky, grin followed that comment. They chatted, pleasantly, throughout, until they finished the food.

"Shall we leave these and retire to the sitting room for drinks?" he asked.

"Certainly, I shall follow through in a couple of moments," his guest answered then asked, "Would you like me to bring you a whisky through?"

"Yes please," he answered and made his way from the kitchen/dining room; once he'd gone his guest took a small phial from the pocket of their trousers; carefully they slipped two pills from the phial - the pills were a mild sedative/sleeping pill known as Diochemyze – and slipped them into his glass of whisky where they dissolved instantly. The guest poured themselves a glass of orange juice.

The person put the phial, containing the pills, away; and took the tray, with the drinks on it through to the sitting room; the tray was set down on the table in front of Ronan. He took his whisky, noticed a few granules in the bottom, "Have you put a spot of sugar or salt in this?"

"A little bit of sugar spilt out the bowl and I used a spoon to put it back in. Maybe I caught your glass with the spoon as I was spooning the sugar back in. That's all."

Ronan satisfied with this answer drunk a little of the whisky, it seemed to have a taste to it; it was probably just the traces of sugar. His guest drunk their orange juice and they chatted pleasantly. About five minutes after he'd finished his whisky the acting commander complained of feeling sleepy, even though it was early. "Will you help me to my bed please? I'm suddenly feeling a bit tired."

"Of course, my dear," replied the other person cheerfully, getting up to help him out of the room and upstairs. His movements were slow and sluggish as he half walked, and half staggered, upstairs; they entered the main bedroom and Ronan tried, unaided, to reach his bed; he managed four or five steps then collapsed on the carpeted floor. The other person watched him collapse, and then picked him up, laid him, gently, on the bed and undressed him, by this time he was unconscious.

He was put inside the bed. Ronan opened his eyes, or tried to, "You can go now," he said to his guest, "I'll be okay."

"I'm not leaving you like this," the other person replied; they undressed and got in beside him. He knew this was wrong but he couldn't do anything to prevent it, not at that moment. Did he want to?

If Commander Roberts ever found out about this both the other person, as well as Ronan would be, instantly, dismissed. Did they realise the implications their actions may cause? If so, did they care?

Slowly the battle cruiser returned, along the distance of approximately 28980 kilometres, 18,000 miles; its top speed – being what it was, at 59km/h, took two days to return. Squeeze allowed the combat troops a day's rest, to get over things, and then they returned to *Proagnon's* underground base where Dr Q was waiting to congratulate them, "Well done on your successful mission."

He turned to look at his second in command, "Squeeze, when you are ready would you come to my office please?" She knew it was more of an order than a request so she followed him as he left the room. Once they were seated in his office he told her, "I have sent our comrade, Mr Singh, on a special mission to England."

"Yes sir, but why send him?"

"I know he plans treachery against me, and am hoping he will use this time to think things through and realise his actions are futile."

"And if he doesn't?"

"Then he will be disposed of, when I feel the time is right," her leader answered. "Also, I am still troubled by thoughts of our missing agent, Sergey Satov; he should be locked up, I know that, but what would happen if he isn't?"

"Nothing," answered Squeeze, reassuring her leader. "Even if he is loose he can't find his way here, and even if he did he can't harm us."

"I wish I shared that view," replied Dr Q with a hint of doubt in his voice.

Dr Q was right to have his doubts because, at this moment, the Russian was running for his life; his only thought was to get his revenge on the bastard that had dumped him in this mess, Abdul Singh.

He had been on the run for days, having escaped on his transfer to prison, he had knocked his guard out – there should've been another guard but, as it happened, there had been an emergency, ironically just before the transfer.

He slowed to a walk, he didn't need to run. It had been felt by the authorities that as Sergey was a Russian national he would be making his way to one of the airports on the eastern side of the country and would be returning to the home of his birth. Therefore, they had alerted the police forces from the state of California and any other state he might try to make for. Also every airport and port had been alerted. Sadly, they were wrong in the assumption that the criminal would want to return home.

He had been arrested in Washington, after the attack on the White House, and had spent a couple of months at the Washington FBI field office, though it seemed like years. Sergey had allowed his moustache and beard to grow over that time, and he now walked with a limp; nothing harmful had happened to him throughout his stay. If people saw him now, with his matted hair, bushy eyebrows, moustache and beard, all were brown in colour they would, hopefully, mistake him for a man of 50 instead of his youthful 28.

Eventually it was decided that Sergey was deemed safe enough to transfer; however, the difficulty was finding a field office with a cell to accommodate him. Finally one was found at the Los Angeles field office and a transfer was arranged, where he escaped.

He usually robbed people, usually people on drugs, in back alleyways, usually he robbed them of any money they had but never the drugs. These drug addicts, he knew, couldn't report him to the, local, law authorities, in case it was found they'd committed a robbery, or were simply arrested for possessing drugs.

Once he had enough money Sergey Satov hitch-hiked his way from the eastern coast of the USA back to Washington DC. Usually he managed to get rides off truck drivers, taking their trailer units to specified destinations; most of the time they'd stop at a truck stop, most had a café, where the driver of the rig and Sergey would part company, because the criminal knew if he stayed with one tractor unit driver for too long he may be recognised, and that would never do; if, at the truck stop he couldn't get a lift he would sometimes climb up another trailer's back doors and perch on the roof, hoping they came to no low bridges, and also that no-one would spot him.

The Russian knew it was risky for him to be going to Washington lest somebody recognise and report him. If needs be he would hide out somewhere.

Eventually, after several days travelling the truck he had boarded arrived on the outskirts of Washington. The driver pulled over and let Sergey out. "There you go mate," the driver said, thankfully no-one had recognised him on his journey.

"My thanks to you," replied the criminal. "May your family prosper and have good fortune."

"Thanks," said the driver, a thickset man with square jaw, wild red hair and bushy moustache. The tractor unit then restarted and pulled away. Once it was out of sight Sergey, casually, walked into the main streets of America's capital, again hoping no-one would recognise him; putting some sunglasses on he walked into a tour operator's and purchased a one way ticket to Tehran. He figured with Mr Singh being Iranian he might as well start his search in Iran. After purchasing his airline ticket for the 11am Airbus flight from Washington *Dulles* International Airport to Tehran, capital of Iran, *Mehabad* International Airport, the next day.

Airbus was a European aerospace consortium that had its headquarters in Toulouse, France, but had significant activity across Europe; the company also produced around half of the world's jet airliners.

Airbus had begun life as a consortium of aerospace manufacturers. Consolidation of European defence and aerospace companies around the turn of the century. This allowed the establishment of a simplified joint stock company in 2001, owned by EADS (European Aerospace Defence Systems-80%) and BAE Systems (20%). After a protracted sale process BAE sold its shareholding to EADS in October 2006. Airbus employed around 57,000 people at sixteen sites in four European Union countries: Germany, France, the United Kingdom, and Spain. Final assembly production was at Toulouse (France) and Hamburg (Germany). Airbus had subsidiaries in the United States, Japan and China.

It had, in the past, developed planes such as the A300 – which was a 320 twin seated, twin engined airliner; the next airliner to be developed was the A300B, which was actually based on a proposal for a 300 seat airliner to be known as the A250.

Airbus Industrie was formally established as a *Groupement d'Interet Economique* (Economic Interest Group or GIE) on 18 December 1970. The name "Airbus" was taken from a non-proprietary term used by the airline industry in the 1960s to refer to a commercial aircraft of a certain size and range, this term was acceptable to the French linguistically. Aerospatiale and Deutsche Airbus each took a 36.5% share of production work, Hawker Siddeley 20% and Fokker-VFW 7%. Each company would deliver its sections as fully equipped, ready-to-fly items. In October 1971 the Spanish company CASA acquired a 4.2% share of Airbus Industrie, with Aerospatiale and Deutsche Airbus reducing their stakes to 47.9%. In January 1979 British Aerospace, which had absorbed Hawker Siddeley in 1977, acquired a 20% share of Airbus Industrie. The majority shareholders reduced their shares to 37.9%, while CASA retained its 4.2%.

In 1972, the A300 made its maiden flight and the first production model, the A300B2 entered service in 1974. Initially the success of the consortium was poor but by 1979 there were 81 aircraft in service. It was the launch of the A320 in 1981 that guaranteed the status of Airbus as a major player in the aircraft market - the aircraft had over 400 orders before it first flew, compared to 15 for the A300 in 1972.

The retention of production and engineering assets by the partner companies in effect made Airbus Industrie both a sales and marketing company. This arrangement led to inefficiencies due to the inherent conflicts of interest that the four partner companies faced; they were both GIE shareholders and subcontractors to the consortium. The companies collaborated on development of the Airbus range, but guarded the financial details of their own production activities and sought to maximise the transfer prices of their sub-assemblies.

In the early 1990s the then Airbus CEO Jean Pierson argued that the GIE should be abandoned and Airbus established as a conventional company. However, the difficulties of integrating and valuing the assets of four companies, as well as legal issues, delayed the initiative. In December 1998, when it was reported that British Aerospace and DASA were close to merging, Aérospatiale paralysed negotiations on the Airbus conversion; the French company feared the combined BAe/DASA, which would own 57.9% of Airbus, would dominate the company and it insisted on a 50/50 split. However, the issue was resolved in January 1999 when BAe abandoned talks with DASA in favour of merging with Marconi Electronic Systems to become BAE Systems. Then in 2000 three of the four partner companies (DaimlerChrysler Aerospace, successor to Deutsche Airbus; Aérospatiale-Matra, successor to Sud-Aviation; and CASA) merged to form EADS, simplifying the process. EADS now owned Airbus France, Airbus Deutschland and Airbus España, and thus 80% of Airbus Industrie. BAE Systems and EADS transferred their production assets to the new company, Airbus SAS, in return for shareholdings in that company.

Now all Sergey needed was a place to stay for the night, as it was said that the nights in America could get very cold, particularly now that snow had started to fall. He went round a few places, all as near to *Dulles* Airport as he dared, to see if he could rent anywhere, the owner of the third apartment block he visited, a rather greasy looking, rotund, sort of person, told Sergey that he could rent a room for the night for $200 and for an extra $50 dollars he would supply this criminal with the use of his daughter overnight.

As tempted as he was, after his months in incarceration, he declined telling the owner he only needed a room with a bed, so he could rest. The owner, Don Sanchez, reluctantly agreed to supply a roof over the Russian's head; Sergey paid him the money, and was directed where he should go and which apartment/room was his. Mr Sanchez smiled, at Sergey's retreating back, as if he knew something this other man didn't, and then he called for his daughter, Maria, whispered something in her ear, and then patted her backside.

The Russian reached the elevator, which he'd been directed to, and pressed the button that would call it, nothing happened; the panel was lit but he could hear nothing; he tried again and again, each time nothing. Finally, after ten minutes, he gave up; just for good measure he then hit the panel, this time something did happen – the backlight on the panel went out. The criminal shrugged and then trudged, wearily, back to the owner, who was standing in the corridor, "Your elevator is broken," he said matter-of-factly.

"Oh, it is temperamental, my friend. Best use the stairs," and he pointed to a set of stairs. Sergey thought he saw the hint of a smile creep across the man's face. Figuring it was his imagination the escapee began to climb the stairs; the staircase was dark and gloomy, yet he could see well enough. Reaching the third and top floor he made his way, down a gloomy, unlit corridor, toward room 3A, which was to be his room for the night.

He noticed that the door was, very, slightly ajar, it may be something or it could be nothing; thinking it was nothing he pushed the door open, and stopped in amazement. In the dim light, given out from the overhead, naked, bulb; was the figure of a young woman; the thing that had stopped him was the fact that she was naked. Fortunately, she only had her back to him; seeing this Sergey coughed, loudly, and this girl pulled a cloak like garment around her and turned round, and looked at Sergey, confusion in her face. "Sorry," she remarked, innocently, "but who are you?"

"My name is Sergey," the criminal began. "There is, obviously, some confusion here. Mr Sanchez told me this was to be my room for the night." Now he was inside he looked round, as best he could, in this light. The room was very drab, and contained only a single bed with moth eaten covers, a single, falling to bits, wardrobe and a chair. There were no washing or toilet facilities in evidence, but there was a, small – no, tiny, window, overlooking the street. *$200 for this dump*, he thought, *what was I thinking of?*

The girl approached him, walking in bare feet on the, bare, wooden floor boards. "Mr Sanchez told me I could have this room for another night," she told the Russian; she reached out to hold him but Sergey shied away, wary of what her intentions might be. "Come, sit down," she said to this man, he noticed she had a slight, Spanish accent. "I'm sure we can come to some sort of arrangement." He sat down – on the bed – beside her.

"I bet we could," he answered, a slight edge to his voice. "And you'd probably want to be sharing the bed with me." He, then, realised he hadn't yet asked her name, "What is your name, pray tell."

"Maria."

"Maria what?" he persisted.

"Maria Sangor."

"And how old are you Miss Sangor?"

"Old enough," was the reply

Sergey looked her over, she was a beauty, there was no doubting that, but he was nearly certain she was still only a schoolgirl – there was no doubting she was in her mid-late teens, but not yet the right age for that at least, so he was sure she was still only a schoolgirl. Even though he'd missed contact with women during his incarceration period he still had his principles. "Maria," the criminal began, "Even though I admire your beauty, and yes you have a nice body and are very attractive, it is better we part company now, as friends, instead of doing something we'll later regret."

Maria stood up, Sergey assumed she intended to leave, but then she turned to face him, "You say I have nice body, yet you do not ask me to your bed."

"No, Maria, I believe you are not the right age."

"Really," she announced, dropping her cloak. She had an even more attractive body than he'd first thought, with its pale, nubile, flesh. "If you refuse now I promise I will leave you in peace."

Yeah right, where have I heard that before? Sergey looked her over, pale flesh and young breasts; he wanted her but could he take the risk? "I'm sorry, Maria, but no."

"Okay," she sighed, resignedly, leant forward and kissed him. Then she gathered together her cloak and wrapped it round her. Sergey, seeing that to open the door she would need to let go of her cloak, politely, got up and opened it for her "Gracias," she said, politely, as she passed him. Once she had disappeared from view he closed the door; Sergey lay on the bed and thought he would have a good night's rest here; his only, real concern was the absence of a lock on the door – still when he decided to go to bed he would put the chair up against the door – slowly his eyes closed, he only intended to rest but soon fell sound asleep.

At HART the next day, in Ronan Strobing's residence, he awoke – with a clear head – and turned over. Then he saw her, Lucy Lang was in the bed with him, fearing the worst he looked under the bedclothes – both were naked. *Had he?* No, he couldn't have could he? If he had Mandy would kill him. Lucy's eyes, then, flickered open, "Good morning, darling," she said, giving him a kiss. "It sure was some night last night, I thought you'd never stop, Mark was good but you were definitely better."

Then she pulled the bedclothes back and got up, Ronan's eyes watching her every move.

Lucy, somehow, noticed his gaze, "Aw, does my baby want more?"

"No," he said, quickly, and she walked towards the bathroom. Once she'd gone Ronan got up, dressed in his combat fatigues, and went over to the bathroom door – not intentionally, and watched as Lucy pulled her underwear up. Even though he was watching her dress he felt nothing for her.

She could tell, by some sixth sense, he was watching and said, "Does my bum look big in this?"

"No," he replied, then instantly regretted it. Therefore, he moved away and walked downstairs; as he reached the bottom he heard it, his STU was making its chirping noise. He raced into the sitting room, found it – as it had been surrounded by books, probably by Lucy he realised, and picked it up; after the buzzing had finished he knew the signal was encrypted. "Hello," he said.

"Ah good morning commander," the, distinctly, male voice of Joshua Smith replied. "Lisa Bell was worried about you, sir, when you didn't answer last night."

"I was comforted by Lucy Lang, whom according to her, Lisa sent round."

"Lisa maintains she didn't send anyone round, as you wished not to be disturbed."

The bitch, Ronan realised, *seeing me at a low point, pretending to want to comfort me, and then taking advantage of me.*

"Thank you Josh, I'm fine now and will be in soon." With that he replaced the handset.

Lucy came into the room then, a spring in her step, "Breakfast's ready," she called. We missed morning exercise but, after last night, I doubt either of us needed it."

Ronan looked daggers at her. What now?" she asked, innocently.

The commander nearly shouted at her, "You, bloody well, trick your way in to this house, make me a meal and pretend to comfort me, drug me – I'm sure that's what you did, take me to bed, spend the night, and then say we had sex. However, the biggest insult is comparing me to Mark; yet the worst insult is lying to me."

"Would you have gone with me if I hadn't drugged you?"

"No," he replied, recovering his composure. "Lucy, I'll always see you as a very good friend, someone I can turn to if things are bad, but I just don't see you as a lover, no matter how you see things. Okay, I'll admit, we may, sometimes, be forced to share a bed, if things are really bad, but I can't share one with you willingly. I'm sorry."

Now it was her turn, "I admit I shouldn't have done what I did, and I'm sorry for it, but as you know I've always had feelings for you, and I think you do for me – deep down," he admitted she was right. "Anyway I'm sorry."

Now they'd each said their piece they walked from the sitting room to the kitchen; Lucy took the lead. "Does my bum look big in this?" she called back, in her American accent.

"No, of course not," came his reply.

"Cheeky!"

Once they were in the kitchen, they hugged to show there were no real hard feelings, and then they seated themselves at the table to enjoy a breakfast of porridge. Once both of them had finished eating they washed their dishes, got ready and went off to work.

Once Ronan was seated in the commander's office he began to think about Lucy, then his wife Mandy. He started to wonder, now, if Mandy was the right person for him, or could Lucy offer him more? They both had their individual, good points and bad points; Lucy could definitely cook, but so could Mandy. Yet he'd had two children with her, and how would they feel if Lucy took him away from them, he'd always be their father, but maybe Lucy would want a family someday. Then, supposing he did divorce his wife and go off with this American woman; and after a while she left him for someone else what would he do then?

He then began to wonder if he might get away with having a simple affair with his colleague, would that work? It may for a bit but then Lucy would want more from him, so he'd end up back to square one. Plus there was the fear Mandy might find out and divorce him anyway.

Finally, there was a third option, but he didn't like to think about it, unless he had to. The option was, it probably wouldn't work – or Lucy wouldn't agree to it, to lay down some ground rules, and then if Lucy agreed, and only if, he may give her the option of coming to his residence, every so often, and spending the night with him; why had she put him in this quandary?

However, it was then he thought that if they'd met years ago then, yes, something may have happened between them; yet she hadn't wanted to know and neither had he, so they'd both found other partners; but that was history.

Just then the intercom, on the desk buzzed, "Mr Bigship to see you commander."

"Send him in Josh," was the commander's cheery response. *What information has Leon got for me?*

The office door opened and Leon Bigship walked in. "Good morning commander."

"Good morning Leon. Please take a seat."

Leon seated himself, in the seat indicated. "Now what news do you bring me?"

"As you know sir, you sent me to look at the Hotel Tiffany's records, to see if there was any trace of that blonde killer. I went there and looked at the hotel's register. Room 38, where our killer stayed, was registered to have been booked by one Sarah Taylor."

Ronan got the terrorist ID book out the drawer where it was kept, and flipped to the T section, "Are you sure this is our main suspect?" he asked, handing his friend the book and indicating Squeeze's profile.

"I am a hundred percent certain she is the one," Leon confirmed. "Question is where is she now?"

"Yes indeed," murmured the acting commander, his mind still wondering what, exactly, had happened the previous night. Sensing his commander's mind was somewhere else Leon rose from his seat and, politely, dismissed himself.

Later that day the leader of *Proagnon* returned to his office, where he spent most of his days, retrieved his computer notebook from the drawer, in his desk, where he'd stored it, plugged it in and switched on. "You've got mail," the, female, voice of Squeeze reported as the back light lit the screen up. Once the, full, screen was lit Dr Q accessed his email account boss@Quantumexhibits.ir, he only used the iq address when he needed to. The email was a reply from Oleg@foreignministry.ru stating that he hadn't answered before because he had needed to consult his Defense Minister, Mikhail Suvorov, and had been told that the carrier and submarines were patrolling waters to East of the Russian coast line. The *Proagnon* leader was a bit put out by this, but was also assured that as soon as they were available they would be sent to Quantum Exhibits in Iran.

Satisfied Dr Q closed down the computer notebook, and then started to wonder how Abdul was getting on.

At that moment his third in command was 12,200 metres (40,000ft) up, above sea level in the double V shaped stealth bomber, along with the two crew members and the bombs, they were carrying, which he didn't like to think about; actually, he preferred not to think what might happen if one blew up, for whatever reason, and started a chain reaction, the fighter was flying at an average speed of 805 kilometres, 500 miles, per hour. The journey was only, approximately 7728 kilometres, 4800 miles, but as he would be crossing three time zones both he and the crew would be losing three hours of time. As the aircraft flew over the English Channel, the waters that separated Britain from Europe, the pilot brought the craft down to 6,100 metres (20,000ft), as low as he dared, and turned to his commander, this was meant to be a Stealth Bomber but you could never be too sure someone hadn't detected you, and asked, as they crossed the Dover Strait, "Which target shall we target first, do we go along the South coast or up the Eastern sea border first?"

"We shall do the job in this order: Dungeness, Oldbury; Berkeley; Wirfith; Wyfla; Heysham; Sellafield; Hartlepool; Hinkley Point - both reactors, Sizewell, again both reactors, and finally, the single reactor at Bradwell. Those are your orders!"

The pilot acknowledged his orders, once they were over the Dover Strait his co-pilot switched the aircraft over to the auto pilot, as it was difficult to fly the machine, and drop the bombs at the same time.

Dungeness A had been a legacy Magnox power station, and then in 1965 it was connected to the National Grid until it reached the end of its original life. The A station contained two reactors that each produced 223 megawatts (MW) of electrical power; combined producing 446 MW of power, the reactors had been built by The Nuclear Power Group (TNPG) and its turbines by C A Parsons & Company.

By the end of 2006 the 'A' station had ceased its power generation; however, due to the demand for electrical power

Dungeness A was reopened in 2010, employing approximately 150 people.

Dungeness B, nuclear, power station had been an Advanced Gs-cooled Reactor (AGR) power station; it had been built, originally, in 1965, and had been the first commercial scale station to be constructed. Unlike its sister station B station's reactors each of the two turbines, built by the same company that made station A's turbines, put out 600 MW each, combining to produce maximum capacity of 1200 MW, though standard output is only 1090 MW, and are turbo administrator sets.

Dungeness B station was due to close in 2018, but due to the demand for electric it has been decided to keep it open. The site employs, again, approximately 150 personnel.

"There she is," remarked the co-pilot. At this remark the pilot detected, on the instruments the reactors of station A and lined them up with the bomb guidance trajectory.

"Fire!" commanded Abdul. "That should give them something to think about."

The first Dumb Bomb, weighing 227 kilogram (500lbs), these were used for the majority of bombing operations where maximum blast and explosive effects were desired, was ejected from the B-2 Stealth Bomber, the crew of three watched it fall, each hoping it would fall correctly; the MK 82 bomb hit the reactor, with its M904 nose striking the reactor and shattering the top. "Another!" demanded the leader. Another of the MK 82 bombs was ejected from the bay of the aircraft; again the second device hit the reactor but this time it penetrated the top, but exploded too soon, in Abdul's opinion. However, it cleared any fragments from the top. "A third!" he almost shouted; again the bomb left its bay and this time fell, directly, into the reactor.

"A direct hit, sir," announced the pilot.

"Don't celebrate just yet," warned the commander. Although, even he had to agree the trajectory was perfect, and the MK 82 had fallen true. These bombs were General Purpose Bombs, also used for Blast Fragmentation.

As they watched the device exploded, this was more pronounced as it had exploded atop a nuclear reactor. Abdul knew there were usually safety features built into reactors; but as soon as the 500lb warhead exploded it, the reactor, completely seemed to blow apart; it was only an internal explosion and seemed to be contained within the outer casing that surrounded the reactor – Abdul's heart sank – however, as he watched the outer casing, slowly, began to crumble and fall apart.

As they watched the core of the reactor melted, the commander of the mission knew that once this had happened it would almost certainly destroy the fuel bundles and the internal structures of the reactor vessel. If the melted core dropped into a pool of water (for example, the coolant or moderator), a steam explosion called a Fuel-Coolant Interaction (FCI) was likely. If the air was available, any exposed flammable substances would probably burn fiercely, but the liquid nature of the molten core posed more special problems.

In a worst case scenario, the above-ground containment would fail at an early stage, (due to say an FCI within the reactor vessel, ejecting part of the vessel as a missile - this had been the 'alpha-mode' failure of the 1975 Rasmussen (WASH-1400 study), which Abdul Singh had read – probably in his college days, or there could be a large hydrogen explosion or another over-pressure event. Such an event could scatter urania-aerosol and volatile fission-products directly into the atmosphere. However, these events were considered essentially incredible in modern 'large-dry' containments. (The WASH-1400 report had been supplanted by the 1991 NUREG-1150 study.)

It had appeared to be an open question to what extent a molten mass can melt through a structure. The molten reactor core could penetrate the reactor vessel and the containment structure and burn down (core-concrete interaction) to groundwater.

With a fast reactor it was possible that the molten mass might mix with any material it melted, diluting itself down to a non-critical state. A water moderated reactor would go non-critical as soon as the water boiled away. However, if hot uranium dioxide had been combined with iron oxide a eutectic is formed which may cause the fuel to become more mobile than it would otherwise be.

Should all else fail the final three factors that would provide additional time to the plant operators in order to mitigate the result of the event were: Assuming that at the moment that the accident occurs the reactor will be scrammed (immediate and full insertion of all control rods), so reducing the thermal power input and further delaying the boiling.; After the water has boiled, then the time required for the fuel to reach its melting point will be dictated by the heat input due to decay of fission products, the heat capacity of the fuel and the melting point of the fuel; The time required for the molten metal of the core to breach the primary pressure boundary (in light water reactors this is the pressure vessel; in CANDU and RBMK reactors this is the array of pressurized fuel channels) will depend on temperatures and boundary materials. Whether or not the fuel remains critical in the conditions inside the damaged core or beyond will play a significant role.

When the reactor exploded the pilot had to move fast to prevent the aircraft being caught in the main blast of the explosion. Luckily, he managed to speed the bomber away, just in time.

They all knew that anyone, or anything, caught within the first one mile of the exploding device would be, completely, killed or destroyed. Anything within a one point two five mile radius suffered severe damage, whilst within a two mile radius suffered moderate damage, and finally within a three point five mile radius was lightly damaged.

The shock waves, on the human body – resulting from the immediate explosion, resulted in pressure waves through the tissues. These waves mostly damaged the junctions between tissues of different densities (bone and muscle) or the interface between tissue and air. The lungs and the abdominal cavity, which contain air, were particularly injured. The damage also resulted in severe hemorrhaging or air embolisms, either of which could be rapidly fatal. The overpressure estimated to damage lthe lungs was about 70 kPa. Some eardrums would probably rupture around 22 kPa (0.2 atm) and half would rupture between 90 and 130 kPa (0.9 to 1.2 atm). Workers at A station started running out the buildings, every one of them looked to be in agony. The radiation from the explosion would be carried in the air, for many days to come.

Satisfied with the outcome the Stealth bomber moved on. Slowly, but surely, the other three reactors at Dungeness were destroyed, the twin reactors at Oldbury, the next two at Berkeley, the reactor at Winfrith, though this had, actually been shut down since the late 1990s, the reactor at Wyfla, on the Isle of Anglesey; Heysham, Sellafield and Hartlepool – all single reactor stations, Hinkley Point and Sizewell – both twin reactor stations, last but not least was the single reactor station of Bradwell. Most of the stations had originally opened in the 1960s and closed between 2002 and 2007, but had reopened in 2010.

Thankfully, or not thankfully, depending on how people viewed things, Queen Charlotte, together with her consort, Gareth Andrews, had been advised to go to Balmoral Castle, her residence in Scotland – set in 7,000 acres, and stay there until the present crisis was over.

The destroyed nuclear power stations had taken a total of 54 MK 82 bombs, leaving a remainder of 26 MK 82 bombs for other use but still the full load of 16 MK 84's. "We shall use the remaining bombs on the oil fields, in the northern hemisphere, and cut offf oil supplies."

"Yes commander," his subordinates replied, and the aircraft flew off.

CHAPTER 7
Assets, tragedy, & a change of roles!

"Team leader Strobing," came Ben Gillespe's, formal, tones from team leader Ronan Strobing's wrist communicator, "we have a situation here. Commander Robert's has requested that you return to the main HQ building at once."

"On my way," he replied. "Get the other team leaders to rendezvous there as well." He set off at a run, to get there as quickly as possible.

"That has already been done."

Once he arrived, five minutes later, he immediately went up, in the elevator, to the fourth floor, and was shown into the commander's office, where he found the others waiting for him; however, he couldn't look Lucy in the face due to what had, allegedly, happened between them. He was sure she was lying though, but didn't want to show her up, so he kept quiet.

There was, now, a world map on the wall behind Peter Robert's desk; there were a multitude of red pins with flags attached to the map; and a multitude of them in the UK, two in the USA, one in the Mediterranean, and one in Russia, plus many others in countries throughout the world; these were probably to indicate which countries had been attacked by *Proagnon*. "Sit down please," said their commander, who had returned after the thirteen week world tour he'd been on – along with Dr Hans Schaiffer and Mrs Gwyneth Jones, neither were back at work yet. "Our satellite, last night, detected massive surges of power coming from the UK, once dawn had broken we saw what had been destroyed. We collated the data and this is the result," he handed a, hastily handwritten, list to each of them.

"Oh hell!" they exclaimed as they read the list their commander had given them; it seemed that *Proagnon* had destroyed all the power stations, be they coal, gas, oil, or, nuclear along with other storage facilities, in England,. The only member, in the office, that seemed, relatively – and maybe a little oddly, quiet, and maybe a bit subdued – for whatever reason, was Lucy Lang; still these power stations were in the UK, maybe that was why, probably.

There was a knock at the door, "Come in," called Roberts, as the others around the desk were still digesting the terrible information. Ben Gillespe entered the room and handed his commander a fax from Los Angeles, and a second fax from Washington. "Thank you," announced Peter, as he took the two sheets of paper. The, temporary, receptionist then left the room, noting how quiet everyone was.

The commander read the first fax, and murmured something under his breath, and then once he'd read the second fax he exclaimed, in clear, crisp tones, "Oh Jesus!"

Everyone assembled, in the room, looked up at this exclamation. "What's wrong sir?" asked Celia Most, hesitantly, afraid of the news and what implications it may have for HART, if any.

"It appears that our friend Sergey Satov has escaped from the FBI, whilst being transferred to their Los Angeles office, and now he appears to have disappeared."

"How the fuck did that happen?" said Lucy, in amazement. "They're meant to be one of the best law enforcement agencies left in the world."

"Apparently," began Peter, "he was due to be transferred, they'd got him settled into the police car when an emergency occurred. Therefore, the escort that had been due to travel with them, to ensure the Russian didn't try any funny business, was called away; but the transfer was made anyway because, as it happened, Sergey was perfectly calm, placid, and showed no signs of any violent behaviour at all; just to be sure the police doctor injected him with a sedative. Anyway, the transference went okay – doors were locked, handcuffs put on - however, at the other end Sergey had, basically, recovered by then, and so he managed to overcome the driver and escape."

"Weren't there any guards around to assist the police officer?" she asked quickly.

"There were, my dear Miss Lang, but by the time they got there to help, the Russian had vanished."

"So, basically, now he's on the loose, God knows where!" Peter finished. "Everyone is dismissed, for now."

Over the past few weeks they'd all noticed, at HART, different transporter aircraft arriving, depositing their cargoes, and then returning for further cargo. The transporter aircraft used were, all were now aged but still usable: the C-17 Globe-master III; the C-130 Hercules, the C-141 Starlifter, the C-5 Galaxy, and the MC-130 Combat Talon II.

The first to arrive, the Globe-master, possibly the only one left in existence – judging by the paint-work, had touched down, the rear ramp had been opened, once it was lowered to the ground, and a High Mobility Multipurpose Wheeled Vehicle (HMMWV) truck rolled out, with an *Avenger* (Pedestal Mounted Stinger) missile launcher system, on the back, followed by another HMMWV missile carrier – basically this one was an, enclosed, military attack vehicle, with the usual basic armour and a TOW launcher mounted on the roof, followed by another HMMWV truck – though this one was a 4 litter maxi-ambulance, with basic armour, and then another of the same sort of vehicles – this one, though, had a winch on, and could support anything from 2,500 – 4,400 pounds. In fact a total of 17 HMMWV's rolled out, as well as the missile launcher system, there were several different types of HMMWV vehicles – some with winches, ambulances, shelter vehicles, armament carriers, cargo/troop carriers, TOW missile carriers, and the M1069 tractor for the M119 105mm light gun.

The vehicles, once unloaded, were driven by some of the HART personnel, into one of the hangars. Once the aircraft had deposited its load the aircraft was refuelled, to its full capacity of 134,556 litres; while this was happening the 3 members of the crew, the 2 pilots and the loadmaster went and freshened themselves up for the journey back.

When everything was ready, the aircraft and the crew, the crew climbed back aboard the Globe-master, the rear door had already been raised, and one pilot started the 4 Pratt & Whitney F117-PW-100-turbofan engines, each weighed 40,440 pounds (180kN); the roar was very loud, slowly the C-17 speeded up and sped down the runway, and then the huge aircraft rose into the air. Once it had reached an altitude of 40,000ft it levelled off and began its journey home, this aircraft probably wouldn't be used again.

The next aircraft to arrive was the Hercules, however, the version arriving was the C-130J/J30, which deposited a total of 92 combat, reservist, troops. Again the crew complement, the standard six member crew complement, consisting of two pilots, one navigator, a flight engineer, and two loadmasters, and as the crew before, went and freshened up, and then re-boarded the, now, empty aircraft and started 4 Allison T-56-A-15 turboprop engines; each engine would produce a horsepower of 4,300 pounds. The assembled HART members watched as the big aircraft rose into the sky, the rear landing gear retracting vertically into the fuselage, whilst the nose gear folded away forward into the fuselage.

Next came the C-141B Starliftrer, which could carry a cargo of 30,600kg (68,000lbs) and, once it had landed, the tail section opened and two French produced Renault Vehicule de l'Avant Blinde (VAB) 4x4 APC/scout car's trundled down the ramp. The APC was also fully amphibious, and could mount a variety of different weapons systems as well as different turret mounts.

These vehicles could carry up to 24 personnel, two in the front and up to ten combat trained troops in the rear; the scout car, plus it could be fitted with the Euromissile Mephisto System; this Mistral air defence system, mounted on top, featured four Mistral air to air missiles, other variants of the vehicle included a formidable anti-tank system. Other air defence variants included the twin-mounted 20mm cannon system. This vehicle was also available in several other variations.

Following the second VAB came, approximately, 150, M-151 jeeps, a third contained the Internally Transportable Vehicle (ITV), another third contained the Light Strike Vehicle (LSV), and the final fifty contained the Reconnaissance, Surveillance and Targeting Vehicle (RST-V). Some of the Jeeps were Fast Attack Vehicles (FAVs).

The six crew members from the aircraft: the pilot, co-pilot, two loadmasters, and both flight engineers, once all the cargo was offloaded, exited the large plane, the pilot set up the aircraft for refuelling, and then went and joined them. They went inside the crew quarters, showered, rested, and readied themselves for the flight back

At the moment the huge, military transport aircraft was sat on the runway, refuelling; it could carry a maximum fuel load of 23,592 gallons (89,642.6 litres). Once the refuelling was complete, a simple matter that took less than half an hour. A mere one and a half hours later, once all pre-flight checks had been completed, the plane's 4 Pratt & Whitney TF33-P-7 turbofan engines roared into life; and the vehicle began to roll forward, on its landing gear of three dual wheel sets, as usual two at the rear and the third under the nose of the aircraft. Once the vehicle had reached maximum thrust it roared along the runway and lifted off.

The last of the big four, as the HART troopers affectionately referred to them, wasn't due for another hour so everyone busied themselves by taking the deposited vehicles into the four free hangars, ready for use, there were actually ten hangars, four were kept vacant, so they could house the four transport aircraft; one already contained the F-14 Tomcats, together with some F-15 Eagles and a few F-16 Falcons. The final hangar was also kept vacant for the military helicopters: the Apaches and the Pave Low IV's, once they arrived.

When the personnel had finished putting their, military, assets away; the blue sky was suddenly dominated by the, massive, silhouette of the C-5B Galaxy, bringing their main asset, the M1A2 Abrams Battle Tank (MBT), all 68.7 tons of it. As with many other military vehicles the Abrams was available in different models; there was the M1, the basic model, the IPM1, the M1A1 and the M1A1D, all were amphibious. Each tank contained four crew members, the tank commander, the gunner who, obviously, fired the main 120mm tank gun (its main armament), the loader who was responsible for loading the armament manually, in case the automatic loading system failed, and the driver who drove the giant rumbling vehicle at speeds up to forty one and a half miles per hour. The tank commander could override the gunner when it comes to firing the main gun. Also, he has his own weapon in the form of a

.50 calibre M2 machine gun; there is a .762 M240 machine gun; this is the vehicle's coaxial weapon, mounted on a skate mount – which was fixed and aligned with the main weapon, and fired by the loader. This gun was used to suppress any enemy forces.

The Abrams also had two secondary armaments, in the form of two six barrelled M250 smoke grenade launchers – one located on each side of the main gun; The machine, heavily armoured, was like a small fortress.

There were seven wheels in each track on the vehicle; six were wholly visible whilst the other one was only half visible. As this machinery rumbled away, the Galaxy's six crew members took the time to lean back in their seats, and relax. As with the Starlifter before it the Galaxy had a pilot, co-pilot, two loadmasters, and two flight engineers. Plus in this huge, gigantic, transport aircraft; almost the length of a football pitch and as high as a six storey building, plus the cargo compartment was the size of an eight lane bowling alley. The C-5 was the main transport aircraft that could help transport much of HART's combat equipment, this included the 74-ton (66,600-kilogram) mobile scissors bridge, tanks and helicopters; also inside were accommodations for a relief crew of seven, and eight mail couriers, all on the upper decks forward and rear compartments have galleys for food preparation, as well as lavatories.

This plane also had a roll on/off effect, in which the tail door of the plane dropping to become a ramp, also the nose section of the aircraft could be raised to enable the roll on and off effect.

The aircraft, as well as being able to transport vehicles, in its cargo compartment could also, instead, have 267 airline seats fitted, and together with the 73 available passenger seats, on the upper deck, could be used to transport combat troops; however, the maximum combined total was 329 troops, over water.

As before, but this time on board the aircraft, the crew freshened up while their vehicle was being refuelled. to its capacity of 51,150 gallons (194,370 litres). Once refuelling was finished and the pilot was given the 'all clear' he started up the plane's four General Electric TF39-GE-1C turbofan engines;

these put out, separately, 41,000 pounds of thrust, the Galaxy needed it as it was such a huge aircraft. The 28, flotation landing gear, wheels started to roll; the aircraft's power built up, and then slowly at first, then faster, the *monster* plane whizzed down the HART runway and took off into the sky. The wheels retracted and, when high enough, the plane levelled off to continue its journey back to fetch some more assets.

As the Globe master III would not be returning, yet the other three would, it had been decided to use the hangar that the Globe master would have used for the MC-130H Combat Talon II and the Euro fighter jet fighters. The MC-130 also acted as an air to air refuelling aircraft, and would assist it's earlier sister aircraft, the Hercules, in performing air drops, of either troops or equipment.

As soon as the Combat Talon aircraft landed it was directed, using the orange paddle system, by the ground staff, to the hangar reserved for the machine. All the hangars were at least 80m (262.4ft) in length, 25m in height (82ft) – but 20m (65.6ft) at the doorway, and 80m (262.4) in width; the doors, all double were 70m (229.6ft) wide, enabling the widest of military vehicles to get out. Although this was slightly tricky for the pilot of the Galaxy, as its wingspan was a total of 67.9m (222 feet, 9 inches) and a height, at its tail of 19.8m (65 feet, 1 inch).

Luckily the MC-130 and the C-130 were only of a combined length of 59.7m (195,816ft), so could be stored, nose to tail, in one hangar. However, the C-5B and the C-141B had a combined length of 126.3m (514,262ft), so had to be stored in separate hangars. Each hangar had a set of double doors, same height and width, at front and rear; therefore, the pilots would land their aircraft, and, carefully, drive it in, using whichever doors were open, and then once it was needed to do an airlift, of some sort, it could be driven out the other doors and onto the runway.

The Hercules reappeared, landed, then joined its sister craft in the same hangar, ready to perform airlifts. The pilot throttled down the machine, applied the brakes, and brought it to a standstill. With everything done the crew left the craft and went to the quarters designated for the pilots of all the planes, leaving the engineers to check over the vehicle.

In the early evening the Starlifter returned, this time with anti-aircraft weapons that could be mounted on trailers, some that could be towed, and others that could be mounted on the rear truck trailers; also the C-141B brought a few anti-tank weapons, along with the anti-tank guided missiles. Once everything had been unloaded, satisfactorily, a mobile tug truck was brought forward – painted in camouflage colours – and attached to the front of the aircraft; the tug pulled the air transport vehicle to its designated hangar, to await further instructions from the commander of the soldiers within the compound. Again once the pilot had shut down all the systems, on board, the rest of the crew, as well as himself, left the aircraft to be checked over by the engineers, and went to the quarters to join the crews of the previous two aircraft.

Finally, the C-5B Galaxy returned; once it had landed the soldiers were amazed, though it was no 'real' surprise due to the transport aircraft's size, to see that it contained:, when the nose entrance opened, five Apache AH-64D attack helicopters – complete with its armaments of: Air to Air Missiles (ATAMs), its Hellfire missile system – including the total of 114 Folding Fin Aerial Rockets (FFAR), whatever its mission, plus the 30mm cannon; and two M2A2, but only one M3A3 Bradley Fighting Vehicle System (BFVS) vehicles, these were other tanks but shorter in length and width to the Abrams; the only points it was better in was it was about 61cm (2ft) taller, plus it had a top speed of 45mph whereas the Abrams was three and a half mph slower. The Bradley was equipped with a main armament of a M242 25mm 'Bushmaster' chain gun – this had a single barrel with an integrated dual feed mechanism and remote ammunition selecting; the barrel could fire either armour piercing (AP) or high explosive (HE) ammunition at the flick of a switch, a 7.62 coaxial mounted machine gun and a TOW missile launcher with twin tubes.

The Galaxy was taken to its hangar, once its cargo had been removed, and the crew left their plane to go and join the other aircraft crews. Looking out of the conference room, which adjoined the commander's office, window Ronan Strobing watched all the activity, and smiled to himself. *Thanks to Peter's negotiations with the acting world leaders, HART were, now, ready for anything.*

In the conference room overlooking the compound, Peter Roberts, together with Hans Schaiffer, who had returned to work that morning, were looking out the big glass window, at the new, if somewhat old, vehicles. "Yes, a lick of paint or two should make them look brighter, and more ready for action," observed Peter. Just then they both heard the STU-8 chirping and warbling. "Oh well," he murmured, "no peace for the wicked, to coin a phrase." He walked back to the office, followed by Dr Schaiffer, and picked the receiver up "Yes," he said, and listened. Evidently, somebody; overseas was trying to contact him, as Hans noticed him press a button, on the keypad, to enable him to take the call.

Every incoming call to HART went to the receptionist first, and then – if needed – was put through to the commander's office, if necessary; all calls were monitored, though.

He listened, intently, to the person at the other end, and then once he'd replaced the handset he looked up at Hans, his face was now a ghastly white.

"What is it sir?" asked his, old, friend in concern.

"We must contact Ronan straight away, as his wife and daughter are in hospital." He buzzed through to reception, "Get me team leader Strobing, quick as you can."

"Yes sir," answered the voice of Lisa Bell, who was working reception early tonight.

Next he turned to Dr Schaiffer, "Please wait."

"Yes Commander," he answered, in his German accent, "but what do you need me for?"

"To make sure he doesn't fly off the handle or do anything stupid." A moment later Ronan Strobing knocked on the door, and then, as he'd been sent for, entered the office without waiting to be asked, "You sent for me sir?"

"Yes, please sit down." Ronan seated himself in the seat offered to him by Dr Schaiffer. "Now I'm afraid there's no easy way to say this but your wife's in Hull hospital."

"What?" He almost shouted, "Why?"

"They wouldn't tell me everything, but, from what I can gather, she's been involved in some sort of accident. Your daughter is hurt too."

"I must go to them, is there a *Gulfstream* jet available at the airport?" He asked the commander, hurriedly.

"Yes," replied his superior. "It is fuelled and ready to leave, as soon as you're on board."

"Thank you Mr Roberts, Mr Schaiffer," he nodded at the other man, and then rushed from the office, and out the building.

"Poor Ronan," muttered Dr Schaiffer. "I wish I could help."

In his haste team leader Strobing almost collided with Miss Lang, "Hey watch it," Lucy said, "where's the fire?"

"Sorry Lucy," he apologised hastily. "My wife and daughter are in hospital, back home, I'm going to see if they're both okay." He hurried on, towards his own residence to pack, but if he'd looked back he would have seen a smile cross her face, but it wasn't a smile of malice or of triumph.

He reached his residence, packed what he thought he would need, and then drove off, in his official HART car, towards *Cointrin* Airport. As he got there he assumed the *Gulfstream* he would be flying aboard would be the basic G-150.

He showed his pass, and was rushed through the airport and out to the waiting aircraft, suitcase in hand, he was surprised to see the plane was a G-650 – a recent addition to the fleet, and climbed the motorized staircase to board the jet. As he boarded the G-650 he was greeted by two stewardesses – one was Asian, according to her name badge she was known as Ming Hassan, the other looked African and according to her name badge she was known as Tai Roberts – between them stood the captain, Sam James, together with his co-pilot, Jeff Anles; they both saluted Mr Stobing, Ronan saluted back, "We'll be going as soon as you're strapped in, sir."

"Thanks," Ronan replied and quickly made his way to the seat designated for him. The aircraft's engines stirred into life, a minute after he was seated, and they started taxiing towards the runway; once ready the twin Rolls-Royce Deutschland engines built up speed and the jet lurched forward.

As soon as the aircraft was in the sky, and they'd levelled off the pilot's voice came over the intercom, "We have now reached our cruising altitude of thirty-five thousand feet, our speed is an average of 700km/h (435mph), therefore we will be landing at Doncaster-Robin Hood-Airport in, approximately, four and a quarter hours, varying on the wind which is a north-westerly at the moment, speed 8." The captain's voice then cut off, and Ronan sat back in his seat to view his surroundings.

The G-650 was a totally different aircraft from the G-150 that HART generally used for conveying their operatives to where they needed to be.

This model of the jet, he knew, was similar to its predecessor, the G-550, in the respect that it had a "PlaneView" cockpit (which consisted of 4 Honeywell DU-1310 EFIS screens, and a Gulfstream-designed cursor control system), and an "Enhanced Vision System" (EVS), an infrared camera that would display an image of the view in front of the camera on a heads up display. The EVS system permited the aircraft to land in lower-visibility instrument meteorological conditions other than a non-EVS-equipped aircraft. This aircraft could be distinguished from the other *Gulfstream* jets by as having oval passenger window on both sides of the aircraft – all 28 inches (71cm) wide, also it was of metal construction (a composite construction was used in the empennage, winglets, the rear pressure bulkhead, the engine cowlings, cabin floor structure and nany other of its fairrings.

The jet had been extended 13.11 metres, heightened by 1.90 metres, plus the wingspan had gone from 16.94 to 30.36 metres – the wing's sweep was now greater than its immediate predecessor, the G-500, and earlier planes; this was now 37 degrees, whereas earlier products had wing sweeps of 27 degrees or less.

The maximum cruising speed had been raised from 850km/h to 982m/h; and its mazimum range of flight had improved from 5476km to 102,960 metres (at cruise speed). Plus the jet's maximum service ceiling (altitude) had increased from 45,000ft to 51,000ft.

Internally, the cabin had been heightened by .16 metres, and widened by .85 metres, but the passenger capacity was, basically the same. The jet came, now, with a fully equipped kitchen – so no stewardesses were, really, needed, but as the G-650 hadn't been in service long people still felt better if, at least, a couple of them were aboard – though they would be phased out gradually, fully by 2018. Also it contained many entertainment features, including a satellite phone (in case he needed to contact HART urgently (for any reason) and an internet terminal, plus the usual goodies.

The flight aboard this, vastly, improved airliner passed uneventfully, thankfully; once they'd landed, the motorized staircase was brought to the aircraft, and the door was opened; Ronan Strobing, quickly, thanked the pilots, and then bolted down the stairs, suitcase in hand; and practically ran into the airport. "Strange person," remarked Jeff, returning to the cockpit, to taxi the aircraft to the hangar designated for the plane.

The Hyundai 4x4 had been rolled out its garage, by an airport official – who now stood beside the vehicle, keys in hand. As Ronan reached him he handed over the keys, "Here you go sir."

"Thanks," he replied, taking the keys; he opened the vehicle, practically threw the case inside, started up and gunned the engine. He kept to the speed limits round the local roads; once he got onto the M18 motorway he, really, gunned the engine, speed rising to nearly 100mph in his haste, it was the same on the M62 as on the M18, as the red Hyundai flashed past drivers in the other vehicles simply stared at the quickly disappearing 4x4.

Once the vehicle was back on local roads he dropped to the speed limit, or as fast as he felt comfortable with, and continued his journey (eastwards) to Hull Royal Infirmary. He found the hospital, parked up, and went inside the building; the nurse on duty told him, after he'd explained who he was and shown her his HART identity card, Mandy was in ward G2, on the second floor, she direected him to where the lifts were and then to the right ward. Ronan followed her directions and found the ward, G2; he again enquired at the main desk, and was directed to a private room with its door partly open.

Ronan entered, fearing the worst; but there was his wife, in bed – however, she was attached to, many, different hospital machines. "Mandy," he cried upon seeing her, "where's Zoe? I was told she was with you." He sat in the chair beside her bed.

"Oh Ronan, darling, I'm pleased to see you," he kissed her on the forehead, "I don't know where Zoe is, they won't tell me. As for what happened," her voice was croaky. "I remember, walking in a park with our daughter, near KillingHolme; next thing I know there's this loud bang, I call for Zoe, who comes running towards me. Then I see something flying towards her, from the back, so I make a dive to save her – push her out the way, anyway, I manage it, only thing is, was I in time? Then I feel a terrible pain coming from my side. I dialled for an ambulance from my mobile, then I can't remember anything else, until I woke up here. Where's our daughter, Ronan?"

"I don't know," he replied honestly. "But I'll find out." With that he said to his wife, "I'm going to see the nurses about this, don't you go anywhere," she laughed at that as he strode from the room. She had such a great sense of humour.

The team leader of HART enquired of his daughter at the desk. "I'll have Dr Matthews come down and see you;" a nurse, at the desk, told him and she lifted a telephone handset. *Why do that?* Ronan thought, *surely you know unless there's something else. Something terribly wrong with her.*

"Thanks," he said and, suddenly, remembering Simon, he rushed back to where Mandy was. "Where's Simon," he blurted out.

"It's okay, he's with my parents. I had a nurse phone Simon's school, and then my parents." Ronan sat by her again, happier now, and held her hand – it was difficult with all the tubes in her arm – but they managed it.

A few minutes passed then a man dressed in a white coat entered the room, Dr Ernest Matthews; he pulled up another of the plastic chairs and sat down, "Hello Mr and Mrs Strobing," he said in greeting, "I believe you asked for news on your daughter, I'm afraid it isn't good news."

The couple looked at each other, "Please tell us," Ronan said, his voice tinged with fear. "If she requires an operation please do it, make our little girl better, if you require money for specialist machines and experts we'll pay, anything." He looked to his wife for confirmation, and she nodded.

"I'm afraid it isn't as simple as that, I wish it was," came the reply. The couple noted now that he looked crestfallen, and now started to show the emotions he felt; his voice started to crack as he told them, "Mr and Mrs Strobing, we did all we could for her but she died on the operating table. We found many shards of glass in her body, and so she'd suffered massive internal bleeding. I'm so sorry."

"That must be what I tried to save her from, the glass, though now it's obvious I wasn't quick enough."

"Never mind, babes," Ronan seemed to be taking this all very calmly, still he was probably used to it, due to his job, Mandy realised. She knew a little about his job but he'd never fully explained it to her, probably he couldn't fearing this may compromise the people he worked for.

"I'm sorry to ask this," Dr Matthews responded solemnly, "but I must ask one of you to identify her body, we assume it's her but we need one of you to confirm it."

"I'll do it," announced the father. "Well I'm the obvious choice, at the moment." Then seeing the look on his wife's face he added, for her benefit, "I'll be as quick as I can."

"Before we leave," the medical man announced, "I have something else to tell you both."

"Oh," the couple looked at each other, in puzzlement. "What is that?"

"Your injuries Mrs Strobing; it seems, we ran tests when you came in, that some of the shards of glass may have penetrated your inner body linings. We performed emergency surgery to remove these and were very successful, but…"

"But what?" her husband demanded, wanting to know the truth.

"…on further examination it appears one of these shards has embedded itself deeper and further in your body than at first thought; and we were reluctant to remove this piece, in case you died. So I'm afraid it's still in you."

"What?"

"It should do you no harm, in the long run," he assured them both. "Now Mr Strobing." The doctor got up and led Ronan from the room, and then they left the ward, passing the nurses, on duty, and boarded a lift. Dr Matthews pressed the basement button and they began their descent to the floor wher the hospital morgue was situated.

As they were descending, into the bowels of the building, Ronan asked the doctor, "She will be alright won't she?"

The doctor looked him full in the face and apologised, "I'm sorry, but we also found she'd bled, internally, so I think the glass may have done more damage than first thought. I'm very sorry. You must prepare yourself for the worst."

"So I'm going to lose Mandy as well. What can I do doctor?"

"Mr Strobing," the doctor replied, "I'm afraid there is nothing you can do, she may have a few hours or a few days left, maybe more, all you can do is make sure she lives out the rest of her days in comfort."

The lift arrived at the floor they wanted, and came to a halt. "Here we are," announced Dr Matthews and stepped out, Ronan followed him. The corridor they were in was very gloomy, and poorly lit; however, at the end was a, reasonably, well lit room. The two of them walked towards it; when they got closer, Ronan looked up – he wasn't sure why, the sign above the door revealed the place was the hospital morgue.

The two men walked inside and over to the small cubicle marked C. Once Mr Strobing had identified his, dead, daughter's body, they left without a word. Dr Matthews escorted him back up, in the lift as they re-ascended into the main hospital building. Ronan entered ward G2 again, and found Mandy's room. Once he'd sat down she looked at him, "Is it?" she asked her husband, desperately wanting him to say it wasn't, but he just solemnly nodded.

She started weeping then, and he tried his best to comfort her but he knew he couldn't. He'd lost his daughter, and he was going to lose her soon – he didn't know when. Why was the world so cruel? However, the doctor had advised him not to tell her, in case she panicked or did something stupid.

For the next couple of nights, and days, he kept a bedside vigil; on the fourth day Mandy turned, looked at him and said, "Go home! Get some rest! You look bloody awful."

"But," he protested, "I'd have to leave you and I don't want to."

"Never mind me," she told him, sharply, "you can't function, properly, without sleep!" Reluctantly, and in the knowledge he may never see his wife again, at least not alive, he stood and walked away. Upon reaching his vehicle he got in and left; he was feeling so sad and tired; he arrived home about an hour later, went in and went straight to bed.

Within five minutes he was fast asleep and didn't wake again until three that afternoon, he'd been asleep nearly five and a half hours; he got up, shaved, showered and dressed, then went downstairs and prepared a, light, meal for himself. At around four thirty the phone rang, he duly answered it, "Hello."

"Mr Strobing?"

"Yes."

"It's about your wife," the voice said, "I'm sorry to inform you that your wife had to be operated on earlier; however, unfortunately, she didn't make it. If you want to talk to Dr Mathews then you are welcome to come in."

"No, I don't!" he responded, forcefully, and put the handset down; then he rushed upstairs, and vomitted in the toilet. *Why?* As he stood again, once he'd finished, he decided there and then he would get revenge on these terrorists, whatever it took. Once he got back to HART Lucy would want to get more involved with him now, once she'd heard the news. Maybe he'd let her, maybe he wouldn't – not straightaway.

Once he'd more or less got over the, initial, shock, he rang the hospital back and apologised to the nurse who'd rung him; she was only doing her job.

Sergey Satov awoke, in the morning, in the room he'd rented; once dressed and everything he hired a cab, there were plenty around, to take him to *Dulles* Airport. As the, yellow, taxi journeyed towards the airport, there was much traffic on the road this morning, the driver turned and asked, in an American drawl, "Going somewhere nice, mate?"

"Yes," answered the Russian from the back seat, "I am going on holiday," then added hastily, if the driver realised he had no luggage, "to my friend's villa, in Spain."

"Lucky you," remarked the man in the front seat. The cab reached the airport, at last, "That'll be $20 please."

The Russian handed the cash over, "Here you are." He also passed over a $5 tip; then he got out the rear door, and onto the sidewalk. This would be a long journey, but it would be worth it, hopefully.

The passengers for *Airbus* flight 709 to Doha Airport, in Qatar boarded the A320 jet liner, at just gone midday. Qatar Airlines had purchased the model in 2005, it was a single aisle aircraft, of the old two engined variety. He found his seat, 4H, and sat down, most of the others on the flight were of Middle Eastern origin; therefore, he stood out among these people, but, after all that'd happened to him, he didn't really care.

Luckily he was sat in a seat by a window; there was a boy sat in the next seat, and in the furthest of the three seats, or the aisle seat, was the boy's mother. He had listened to the in-flight safety brief's so he got a book out and proceeded to read.

The captain's voice came over the intercom, "This is Qatar Airlines flight Delta Lima to Doha. Our flight is 6909 miles, we will be flying at our cruising speed of 533mph, therefore our journey should take us roughly 13 hours; we shall be flying at an altitude of 33,000ft. As we shall be crossing several time zones we should land at Doha Airport at approximately 01.30 (local time) tomorrow morning."

Sergey listened to this with interest, such short a flight, theoretically, but so long in practice; the Russian decided to have his meal (whatever it was) and then go to sleep; as it turned out the meal was a chicken dish, which he enjoyed. The boy in seat 5H started to pester him by fidgeting; the boy then muttered something to his mother, it was in an native, arabic, language. Nodding, the woman looked over at Sergey and said, in as good English as she could manage, "My son would like to sit near the window. Would you be prepared to swap seats with him please, sir?"

He didn't really want to move, but found himself agreeing. Sergey and the boy swapped seats, so now he was sitting in between mother and child. Reclining his seat, as best he could, the Russian went to sleep. Sergey awoke, several hours later to find the woman and her son asleep, and the cabin in semi-darkness. Peering out the window, he saw they were over water, which part of the globe was it?

Eventually, after the long flight, they touched down at Doha Airport, in Qatar.

Doha was the largest city in Qatar, with a population of over 500,000 people. Located in the Ad Dawhah municipality of the Persian Gulf, 80% of Qatar's citizens live in the main city of Doha, or its surrounding suburbs, and it was also the economic centre of the country. The main city was also home to the Education City, in Qatar, an area devoted to research and education. Plus Doha had been the site of the first ministerial-level meeting of the Doha Development Round of the World Trade Organisation (WTO) .

Doha was founded, in 1850, under the name Al-Bida; the name Doha came from the arabic *ad-adwha* meaning the big tree, this reference must be to the position of a prominent tree that had once stood where the original fishing village was, on the eastern side of the Qatar peninsula.

Over the years came many wars and, subsequently, many changes. Qatar had many oil and gas sites, and the wealth from these products has been, clearly, visible in Doha; however, in recent years Doha's economy had been moving away from the oil and natural gas industries, although Doha's main focus was still not tourism. However, Doha's real boom came in the form of real estate. This rate of growth led to projects such as the Lusail City project, which was constructed north of Doha and eventually housed 200,000 people. Construction had also boomed in Doha, a result of increasing corporate and commercial activity in Doha; this became most visible with the changing skyline of the city, as Doha now had over 50 towers, the largest of these was the Dubai Towers. A further 39 new hotels had joined Qatar's booming tourism market, this added about 9,000 new rooms. Some of the key projects in Qatar, over the years, had been; the Aspire Tower, the Education City, the museum of Islamic art, The Pearl, the Lusail, Al Waab City, and the Dubai Towers.

There were six main universities/colleges in the Education City, whilst other universities and colleges could be found around the city. Also, there were several sports venues situated within Doha, and in its surrounding suburbs and only the year before Doha had played host to the Asian Cup.

Doha was situated on the Arabian Peninsula, and as such the climate could get very hot. The temperatures could average over 40 degrees Celsius (104 °F) from May to September, and the humidity was variable. Dewpoints could reach above 25 degrees Celsius in the summer. During the summer months, the city averaged almost no precipitation (rain), and less than an inch (25 mm) during the other months. Rainfall could be very scarce (the average was 70 mm per year), falling on isolated days mostly between October and March. During cool winter nights the temperature could rarely drop below 7 degrees Celsius.

Sergey could feel the heat, even though it was night/early morning, before he stepped off the plane and onto the mobile staircase, even though it was very early in the year the temperature was roughly 19 degrees outside, not really hot but there was the humidity to add on. However, the Russian had experienced these sorts of temperatures before, not many times, but he had; therefore, he could withstand the heat.

As he ventured, from the tarmac of the runway, into the main terminal of the airport he looked around in surprise, the lighting was on and he could see clearly the airport had, practically, doubled in size, from when he was last here, taking a holiday, before *Proagnon* had recruited him in 2007. It was said then that this place was due to be expanded, but now, in 2012, it looked like the work was progressing, at a steady pace. Several of the areas of work had been completed; these were: the site mobilization; the excavation & removal of the rubbish tip; reclamation of further land; the engineered landfill; and the passenger terminal Foundation, so the sign, on the wall, said. Many of these had been nearing completion upon his last visit.

Also there had been built a new passenger terminal complex; and a Emiri terminal parking structure, together with a mosque. Plus there was a new airfield paving & road tunnel; a landscaping & irrigation; a new utility system; many airside/landside roadways; and many other airport operation facilities. A fuel system had been installed as well; also there were now, of course, air traffic control & support facilities; plus airline engineering & operation facilities.

Bechtel had been the main contactors for this project, they had implemented a stringent management style at the site to ensure the success of the project, from the appointment of subcontractors' key personnel down to the vehicle moving speed at the site. Subcontractors maybe removed from the site due to nonperformance or noncooperation, exceeding the speed limit, etc.

Sergey looked up, expecting to see the usual, basic, roof of an airport building, but to his surprise he saw a waved roof, obviously there was a water theme to this complex, as there were also many plants, usually, found in the desert being grown here. He decided that Bechtel, the company behind the transformation, had done a really good job, a job to make Qatar proud.

Sergey Satov wandered through the place, there were plenty of people still making their way here and there, and to the exit doors. Upon reaching the outside he bumped into one of the airport staff, who looked to be just coming on duty. "Excuse me," said Sergey, "you don't know of anywhere I can stay till later today? Until my connecting flight to Tehran?"

"Why yes sir," replied the airport worker, he was reasonably young, Segey thought. "The Al Bustan, just a mile east would be your best bet," and he pointed this Russian visitor in the quickest direction.

"Thanks," the Russian answered, and set off. *Strange*, thought the member of staff, the man had no lugguage with him and he'd set off – walking, whereas most passengers, who had just got off inbound flights, and, usually, suffering from jet-lag, would have hailed a taxi. Maybe the man didn't have much money, yet why had he asked for directions to a hotel?

196

The young man ignored these thoughts and went inside the terminal, to begin his shift.

At *Proagnon's* underground headquarters Dr Q had received a message from one of his subordinates that the three makes of Russian tank he'd ordered, the T-72, T-80 and T-90 had arrived, the armoured personnel carriers, APCs, were expected to follow shortly.

The three tanks, each contained 3 crew members; gunner, driver and commander. These, upon leaving their vehicles, were shot dead by the *Proagnon* troops who were to replace them. Each one weighed over forty tonnes, forty-one for the T-72, the T-80 weighed forty-six, and forty-six and a half for the T-90; each had been developed from an earlier model, the T-72 from the T-62, the T-80 from the T-64, and the T-90 was derived from the T-72.

They each contained two armaments, the main gun barrel – that fired Ant Tank Guided Missiles (ATGMs), plus, as with many tanks, a secondary armament – a 7.62mm coaxial machine gun, plus a 12.7mm antiaircraft machine gun. "Now we have power," he announced to his troops. "We can begin our conquest."

"Shouldn't we wait until the APCs arrive?" Squeeze asked him.

"Hm, oh yes, perhaps we should," he agreed after a moments thought. "After all the tanks can only carry three crew each, even though we've left 727 troops on board the *Admiral Lazarev* that still leaves us with 2273 troops, many combat trained and will therefore use our aerial vehicles, and some our nautical vehicles – once they arrive. Therefore, we should have enough troops for the land, air, and sea, assaults, and no-one can stop us," he laughed, evily, then stopped. "Of course, we may get some resistance from HART, but even that is futile."

At HART HQ Peter Roberts was doing a re-evaluation of the current situation, when his STU-8 started to chirp and warble; *Funny*, thought Peter, not many people knew the extension number that would bypass main reception. He answered it anyway, thinking it might be important, "Hello."

There was a lapse of around 30 seconds while the incoming signal was encrypted and scrambled, "Hello sir," announced the weak voice, even though the voice sounded weak – there was no mistaking it.

"Ronan," his commanding officer said. "How are your wife and daughter?"

"They're both dead!" the team leader replied, with as much force in his voice as he could muster. Peter knew the hardest time for the young man would come on the day of their funerals, he'd found it hard when his, own, wife had died.

The killing had been the result of a grudge from the son of a killer Peter had helped to capture, and imprison. The father had spent a couple of months in prison, and then he'd died. The son had blamed Roberts and had managed to track Peter down; however, when he'd broken in, intending to kill the army man, he had found Peter's wife, Nicola, alone at home as her husband was away at a formal dinner function. The killer, named Adam Barker, had simply, it was thought, killed Nicola, in revenge, and then blown up the apartment. Once Peter had got home he had found the still burning fire, and had guessed, instantly, who'd done the killing; as he'd sworn revenge on Mr Roberts at the time of his father's trial. However, the last he'd heard Mr Barker had been caught and imprisoned in HMP Belmarsh.

"I am sorry," said Peter, "you have our condolenses. I shall, fully, understand if you wish to leave us."

"I do not wish to resign, or leave," announced the younger man. "I want to hunt every last one of these terrorists down and kill them, crushing their spirits and their feeble existence!"

"Okay Mr Strobing, I hear and understand that sentiment. Return as soon as you wish to, after the funerals."

"Thank you sir, bye for now."

"Bye for now." The commander sat back, thinking, when he'd reached his decision he pressed the button, on the keypad, and contacted reception. Gwyneth Jones had returned after a few days extra leave. "Gwyneth," said Peter, "I believe the time has come for us to use the Unmanned Aerial Vehicles

(UAVs) to gather information as well as the satellite and the AWACS, you have my, full, authorisation to activate several of the GlobalHawk UAVs. Please key in the activation codes."

"Yes sir." Roberts knew that Mrs Jones was a quick typist, after a minute her voice announced, in its Welsh accent, "UAVs have been launched sir. Was there anythiing else?"

"Not at this present moment, and thank you Mrs Jones." He replaced the receiver. Ronan Strobing, once he'd overcome the shock of his wife's and daughter's deaths, drove round to his mother- and father-in laws house, and politely knocked on the door. His son, Simon, answered it, "Dad," he cried joyfully, hugging his father fiercely.

"Hello Simon," replied his father. "Are Gran and Granpa in?" he asked.

"They're in the front room, why?" his son asked seeing the upset look on his Dad's face.

"I have something I need to tell them, and you," he muttered. Ronan followed his son into the main room of the house to see Arnold and Elle Stevens, his in-laws. Mrs Stevens offered him a seat to sit in, after pleasantries had been exchanged, so the younger man seated himself. "Mr, Mrs Stevens," he'd never, really, felt comfortable calling them by their first names, "I have some news for you, and I'm afraid it isn't good news."

"Well, what is it this time!" Arnold Stevens demanded, he'd never got on with his daughter's husband. As far as he was concerned Ronan wasn't good enough for, his precious, Mandy. Ronan knew he was right and he was about to admit he'd failed her.

"Patience Arnold, let the boy speak," Elle Stevens retorted. She had a different view of her son-in-law than her husband. When Mandy had gone on that date with him years ago, unfortunately they'd had to cut the date short, but Ronan had walked her home Mrs Stevens had immediately taken a liking to her future son-in-law, reasoning if he made her daughter happy, which Ronan evidently did, no one should object to Mandy's happiness. What would she think of him now?

"There was an accident," Ronan began, "and Mandy, as well as Zoe, was hurt. They were both rushed to Hull's Royal Infirmary, but, unfortunately, Zoe died as soon as they got them there."

"You poor love," soothed Elle.

"And why weren't you here to look after them?" Arnold asked, angrily. "Don't people take their marriage vows seriously anymore?"

"Is Mandy okay?" asked Mrs Stevens pleasantly. However, the look on Ronan's face, practically, said it all.

"The surgeons perfomed an operation on her, after Zoe had passed, which was successful. As soon as I heard, as I've been away on business, I came straight back home and went to see her. I stayed with her for three whole days, without sleep. Anyway, eventually, Mandy told me to go home and get some rest, which I did feeling she would be okay, in the short term. I got a phone call from the hospital about two hours ago, saying that complications had arisen and they'd taken her into theatre again, but, again, unfortunately, she died as well. I'm sorry."

"You bloody well ought to be as well, first a grandaughter, and now our daughter. You should've been here to look after them. I always said you were no good for her and I was right!" Arnold stormed at him.

"And where were you while all this was happening. Sat on your backside counting the money you made from stocks and shares," ccuntered the younger man, just as loudly. It was this point when Simon started crying.

"Shut up, both of you!" snapped Mrs Stevens; both men looked a her, she was normally the quiet one. "Simon's just lost his mother and sister, and all you two can do is bicker and hurl accusations at each other."

"Yes quite my dear," muttered Arnold, apologetically. "I'm sorry Ronan."

That's a first, he thought, *An apology from Arnold.* "I'm sorry too Arnold," Ronan replied.

"Can we do anything to help dear?" Mrs Stevens asked, quieter now.

"I hate to ask, but could you look after Simon a while longer, as I feel I must return abroad to complete my business? Of course, though, I'll be here until the funerals are over."

"Of course we'll look after Simon, for however long it takes for you to complete your business, won't we Arnold?"

"What? Oh yes dear," he answered, he seemed more relaxed now.

About a week later the funerals of Mandy and Zoe Strobing took place at Lincoln, Roman Catholic, church, where Mandy had been born. Everyone had turned up, both Ronan's and Mandy's relatives, and, close friends of theirs – about forty people in all.

The service went off without a hitch: afterwards, Ronan told Arnold, Elle and Simon, that he was leaving to catch his flight, and would, hopefully, return as soon as could. As he drove away from the church he realised tnat now the terrorists had made this a personal matter now, for him at least.

The three designs of Russian APCs, the BTR-60P, -70, and -80, had arrived at *Proagnon's* land based holding area. Combined they could carry 28 crew and passengers, they were all heavily armoured – an array of machine guns helped in the defence of the vehicle. All were amphibious, and each had a speed of 80km/h (50mph) on the road, while a speed of 10km/h in water.

The head of *Proagnon* looked them over, he had been transferred from the bunker to inspect the fighting vehicles. Now he needed some airpower, okay, he had the MiGs and the Hinds, plus the bombers, but he felt they needed more, so he had placed an order at the Chinese Defence Ministry for a number of jet fighters.(interceptors). These included: the J12, J11 Flanker, J10, J9/FC1, J8 finback, J7 Fishbed, J6 Farmer, J5 Fresco, and the J4 Fagot – all were Jianjiji series. Satisfied with the military aspect of things Dr Q was transported back to the bunker by helicopter.

Sergey Satov arrived at the Al-Bustan hotel at about 6am. As his flight wasn't until 21.00 hours he decided to have a rest, and get some food inside him. He staggered inside the five storey building, and walked drunkenly over to the reception, the Russian looked disorientated. "I want a room," he said to the Middle Eastern looking man behind the desk, since Abdul had left him to be caught in America he detested these people, but he had to do business with them.

"We have a room spare on the second floor, it has just been vacated so the maid hasn't had chance to clean it up," replied the receptionist, checking the computer records as he was talking.

"I'll take it!"

The man behind reception passed a key over, "Here you are sir, room twenty-three. Now there is the small matter of payment."

"How much?" he demanded.

The receptionist, taken aback by this man's ferocity answered in a calm voice, "How much do you have on you?"

"One hundred and fifty American dollars." This was a lie but how would the receptionist know.

"Okay 150 dollars it is." The Russian handed the cash over, then went up and found room twenty-three; he walked inside, the room was a double with en-suite bathroom, television, all the usual things found in a hotel; it was well worth $150. Sergey immediately changed the door sign to the *Do Not Disturb* position, wandered over to the bed, and, promptly, flopped onto it, not bothering to undress, and fell asleep; he was worn out, but his sleep was very fitful. The Russian awoke, properly, at around 13.00 hours – as soon as he woke up he couldn't remember where he was, for a start, then everything came back to him.

He got up, albeit shakily, and left the room, making sure he closed the door, and took the elevator downstairs – even though he was only on the 2nd floor. Leaving the elevator Sergey walked around the hotel, trying to get his bearings, as he was still a bit dizzy. The Russian wandered first into the restaurant and looked at the food on the buffet tables; he felt hungry but when he looked at the food he felt nauseas, and suddenly lost his appetite.

Sergey left the restaurant and found the hotel bar, he wandered inside thinking a drink might make him feel better. However, before he got as far as the bar he, suddenly, felt the urge to use the toilet, so he had to rush out, rather quickly. Afterwards he felt fine and ready for something to eat and drink.

Later on, about 18.30, he hailed a cab and instructed the driver to take him to the Airport. The Russian terrorist, he no longer thought himself a criminal, paid the driver, in dollars of course, when they arrived at the complex. "Have a nice flight," said the driver, jovially, once he had taken the money.

"Don't worry, I will," replied Sergey cheerfully. *Anything to get away from you people.* Sergey entered the main terminal and handed his ticket over.

"Thank you sir," remarked the young lady at the check-in desk. "I see you're travelling light," she added, noting the absence of suitcases, all he had was a shoulder bag. The Russian mumbled something in response and walked away. "This way sir," called the check in operator as he began walking in the wrong direction.

"Thank you," he replied, as he passed her. He went through to departure lounge C, and joined all the other passengers, to await the flight. This flight would be taken on a Boeing 787-9 – which was a new variant of the 787, instead of an Airbus, he didn't mind though. At 21.02 the passengers were called to board the aircraft that would take them to Tehran's *Mehrabad* Airport. The plane, which was a wide bodied jet airliner, with the capacity to carry up to 290 passengers in its three classes – business, first and economy. Once every one of the 270 passengers were seated, and internal checks were complete, the two General Electric Gnex engines started, and the plane taxiied to the runway. When the pilot gained clearance, from the control tower, he throttled the engines up to their maximum thrust, and the airliner hurtled along the runway; it rose into the air to start on its 721 mile journey. According to the pilot they should be in Tehran in, approximately, 1 hour 20 minutes.

Sergey relaxed in his seat. *Not long now until we meet again Mr Singh.*

Over in England a *Gulfstream* G-150 took off from Doncaster-Sheffield airport, carrying Ronan Strobing back to HART HQ.

The plane landed at *Cointrin* Airport, just outside Geneva. Ronan was collected by an official HART car, driven by Lucy Lang, "How was the trip?" she asked, assuming it'd been a short break, of some sort.

"Terrible!" he answered bluntly. "I watched my wife as she lay dying. In fact I sat with her, and then, after three days, she ordered me to go home and rest; I did, and later on I got a phone call from the hospital informing me my wife had died; that's on top of my daughter being killed."

"I am sorry," his fellow team leader responded in a gentle voice.

"Are you? Are you really?" he asked, slightly angry. "As soon as you find out your fiance's dead, you turn your attentions to me. I refused you then, and I would, probably, still refuse you now."

"Only probably, my darling?" she enquired teasingly. "Don't forget, I'm always available if you need a shoulder to cry on."

"I do still have my son to consider." They reached the compound, and were let inside by the security guards at the main gate. Lucy drove the car, slowly, up to Ronan's private residence.

"Here we are," she said cheerfully, "home sweet home."

She parked alongside, and then helped him in with his luggage. Before she left Lucy said to him, in a sweet voice, "If you need comforting anytime, you know where I am." She smiled sweetly at him, and then left. He unpacked his suitcases, and then went to switch the television on.

No sooner had he got sat down than his wrist communicator buzzed. *What now?* He thought, "Team leader Strobing to the commander's office."

Ronan got up, switched the television off, angrily, then hurried to Mr Roberts office, in the main building. When he arrived he found the other three team leaders, Peter Roberts, together with Dr Schaffer waiting for him. As he arrived he saluted, and then sat in the chair offered him. "Thank you for comig," their commanding officer said, "I'm sure you're all wondering why I called you here."

"I think that thought has crossed our minds," Celia Most remarked. "But I'm sure there's a good reason for it."

The commander looked at each of them in turn, "There is a good reason Mrs Most," he said then added, "from now on you're not going to just be team leaders, though that is still one of your duties, you will be Departmental and Operational Commanders. You will each, also, have a separate department to run." He looked over at Leon Bigship, "Leon you will run the department for sea warfare; Ronan you will run the department for land warfare; while Celia you have the air warfare department. Are there any questions?"

"Just one sir," Lucy said. "Which department do I get?"

"Ah Lucy," Peter replied, "you may help out with any of the other departments, or you can choose not to have a department to run. Which would you prefer?"

"Well sir," she replied, thinking it over. "I think I would like to help and assist Department leader Strobing run the land warfare department."

"That will be fine Miss Lang, if Ronan has no objections."

"No sir," said Ronan. *Why me?* he wondered.

"Right, that's that decided. Onto the Operational Commander bit. You will be termed this when you are out performing operations, in the field. Dismissed and I'll see you in the morning. "Ronan," Peter said, "it's good to have you back. Shame it couldn't be under happier circumstances." His junior officer nodded, then left.

As he stepped outside, into the cool air, he met Lucy and she linked arms with him, and then they walked off together.

CHAPTER 8

Strange bedfellows & the big bang!

The airliner, carrying Sergey Satov, arrived in Tehran, at its destination of *Mehrabad* Airport, at roughly 22.30; luckily for the Russian both Doha and Tehran were in the same time zone, so he escaped any form of jet-lag. The passengers aboard all pushed and shoved to get out, but Sergey remained patient and waited until all the other passengers had passed him by, and then he got up, from his seat, and followed them all out into cooler evening air than that at Doha.

He walked through the airport (Terminal 6) admiring the terminal walls and ceiling; they were very different from the terminal he'd walked through at Doha's airport. He was looking around and not looking where he was going when he bumped into someone, it was a young woman; she looked at him with her dark, brown eyes. "Sorry," he apologised, staring down at her with his icy, blue eyes.

"That's perfectly alright," she replied, looking up into his face. "No harm done," and she, casually, moved away from him. However, the Russian noted she never moved too far away from him. Was she waiting for him for some reason, or, was she waiting for someone else? He couldn't make up his mind which it was, he still had $1000 on him.

The woman kept an even pace with Sergey, keeping him in her sight, as he walked through the main hall and on towards the exit of the building. Was she really, an assassin, sent to kill him? Had Dr Q learnt of the Russian's escape, and realised that he may be able to threaten the terrorist organisation, in some way? No, he reasoned, no one except the FBI knew and that organisation had no contacts with *Proagnon*.

He met her again outside the terminal; she was trying desperately hard to pretend that she hadn't noticed him, let alone followed him. "Oh hello again," she said as she saw him. "Are you on holiday here?" she asked him, casually.

"No," responded the Russian matter-of-factly. "I am here to, hopefully, meet someone." He quickly added, before she asked, "His name's Abdul Singh."

Sergey could see her thinking, or pretending to, "I don't know anyone by that name, I hope you find him." She was evidently, lying but he said nothing, she may be of some use – somehow. *So do I*, the Russian thought darkly.

"Anyway," she continued, "have you anywhere to stay?"

"No," was the simple reply. He was sure she already knew that fact so why had she asked him?

"I run a type of boarding house, in the small town of Qom – which is south of here, I can't offer all the facilities of a hotel but if you want to stay with me you can. My name's Miranda Ochas." *She could be of use*, the Russian thought.

"Sergey," he responded, "and yes, I think I would like to stay with you. How much do you charge?"

"We'll decide on the journey there." She then moved through the crowd that was leaving the airport – taking Sergey's hand and leading him along behind her. She then hailed a taxi that was just pulling in by the airport building. Sergey helped the driver load Miranda's luggage aboard. Remarkably enough it felt quite light, as if each suitcase had nothing in it. Once the Russian, together with the driver, had climbed inside she gave the driver her address in Qom. Sergey sat in the back with Miranda, and the driver pulled away. "So Sergey;" she began, "how much do you think is a fair price for the room?" He couldn't help but notice that she was looking strangely at him; an unnerving feeling crept into him.

"I'll let you know once I see the room," he answered. He leant back in the rear seat and closed his eyes, he'd had a very long couple of days; admittedly, he'd rested at the hotel, in Doha, to relieve his jet-lag, but for some reason he didn't feel properly rested yet. Maybe the Russian would feel better tomorrow.

The journey was just under 50 miles, but the driver wasn't exactly driving fast, he would have to drive faster in Russia, and have the vehicle to.

As he settled back further he thought he felt a movement of some sort, Sergey opened his eyes briefly, and saw Miss

Ochas touching his trousers, near his pocket. The Russian pretended he hadn't noticed, Miranda hadn't seen his eyes open, and so he closed them again; however, he started to move his left arm, as if he was having a dream.

Sergey planted his hand, firmly-but not too tightly, around her wrist and lower arm, it was thinner than her sleeves had led him to believe. "And what the fuck are you up to?" he demanded crossly, not opening his eyes but he could imagine the look on her face at being caught; luckily, there was a glass partition between them and the driver.

"I am sorry sir, I meant no harm. I was merely making sure you could pay, or I would have had to ask for payment some other way."

"More like you were going to rob me, and then, conveniently, disappear."

"Oh no sir, I would never do that," she stammered, "and leave my guests." *I bet you would if you could*, he thought, opening his eyes, and fixing her with an icy stare. "Please sir, don't hurt me," Miranda pleaded with him.

"I'm not going to hurt you. I just want you to realise I'm not as foolish as some of your other guests might have been, in the past."

At about 23.45 the taxi cab pulled up outside, what Sergey considered a ramshackle building that might have, once, resembled a house; Sergey did think about just getting out and walking away, but it was late for that; plus he doubted he'd find anywhere else – at this time. "That'll be 983,872.77 Rials if you please."

"I'm sorry," said the Russian. "I only have American dollars on me. I forgot to get my money changed." He glanced at his companion, hoping she might offer to help him out but she didn't, or just didn't want to.

The driver was glaring at him now, "American dollars aren't much good to me, I ought to charge you extra for wasting my time, but considering this is your first time in our country I will give you the benefit of the doubt; if you can produce 100 dollars for the ride I will call it quits." Sergey, quickly, extracted $120 from his inside pocket and paid the driver.

"The extra 20 dollars is a tip, and I am sorry I was foolish enough to forget to change my money," he said to the driver, who was a, rotund, greasy looking man; Sergey exited the taxi followed by Miranda, he got her luggage out the boot. As her cases felt so light he began to wonder if there was anything in them at all; once he'd shut the boot the taxi started up and roared off, Sergey thought this rude as the driver could've offered to assist them.

Miranda unlocked the front door of her house and they went inside the building; it was a mess, bits falling off here and there, chipped paint, cracks in the walls, and the stairs didn't look safe at all; how someone could live here was beyond him. "The bedrooms are upstairs," the owner of the house called, "if you want to inspect them." He started to ascend the steps, trying to tread carefully, when one of the boards gave way and his leg went through it, Sergey gave a yelp of pain. Miranda's voice came from the kitchen, "Mind the staircase, some of the boards are a bit rotten."

"I think I've just found that out," the Russian called back, a trace of sarcasm in his voice. Miranda came through from the kitchen and laughed at him, when she saw his predicament.

"I'm sorry, I shouldn't laugh, but you look so funny," she remarked.

"Don't just stand there gawping, do something," Sergey shouted at her. As quick as a flash she bounded up the steps, sometimes taking them two at a time; once she was on the step above him she put her arms under his, Sergey was surprised at how strong she appeared to be.

Due to Miranda's small size he'd expected her to struggle but she didn't, "Try and push, as much as you can on your good leg, and we'll soon have you free." Sergey pushed, as much as he dared, on his other leg, and, as she had told him; eventually, he was able to get free.

As his other leg became free again he fell backwards. Miranda gave a gasp as he fell back onto her; as soon as the Russian realised she was underneath him he got up and thanked her, "No problem," the Middle Eastern woman told him, and then he apologised for falling back onto her. "No problem," she told him again, "actually I quite enjoyed it."

What a strange woman, he thought, and then continued up the stairs, being very careful. "I'll be downstairs, in the lounge," Miranda said as she walked back down the stairs.

About five minutes later he returned downstairs to find Miranda, in the lounge with a cup of, what looked like, tea for him. He sipped at the drink, and then looked up at the clock; it was 00.30. "I think I'll take the smaller of the two bedrooms, as I am travelling light," he said and smiled at her, a big grin of a smile.

"Okay," she replied, "we'll discuss tomorrow, sorry later today, how long you wish to stay and how much you are prepared to pay per night. Is that okay with you?"

"That's fine by me," Sergey responded, draining the last of his tea. "And thank you Miranda."

"What for?" she asked him.

"For letting me stay here, instead of having to pay for a hotel, and for helping pull me free."

"That's no problem. Shall we go up now?"

"Yes," he answered, following her from the room. As they reached the top of the stairs Sergey turned to her, "Goodnight then."

Miranda turned, "Goodnight Sergey," and she went into her bedroom, and closed the door. Sergey went into his bedroom, undressed, and then got into bed. Was it his imagination or had he seen a big cheesy, grin on her face?

Sergey awoke next morning, in his host's house, at around 08.00; he was unsure where he was at first but then memories of last night and this morning came back to him. Quickly, he dressed and bounded down the stairs, carefully avoiding the hole he'd made the previous night, he found Miranda Ochas preparing a typical, Iranian, breakfast of Nan-e gisu bread; which the Russian learnt was a sweet Armenian bread, and could be eaten in the morning or with tea later in the day. This was followed by some dates and then washed down by a cup of coffee. *What a diet*, thought Sergey, but if these people wanted to live in this way that was fine by him.

"How much for the room?" he enquired; after breakfast was over.

"How much do you think you want to pay me?" Miranda asked her guest. "I know you only have American dollars, but that is fine with me."

Sergey produced 100 dollars and passed it across the table, "Is that okay?" he enquired, thinking $100 was more than generous enough.

"A little on the low side from what people usually pay me but it will suffice," she replied sounding a little downhearted. "Anyway, may I enquire now how long you wish to stay?"

"Actually, I hadn't, really, given that much thought," Sergey confessed. "A week, perhaps ten days," he told her. The Russian knew he couldn't pay for more than 7 days, but if he offered to fix the step he'd broken, on the stairs, she may let him off the excess money. However, if not she'd probably think of some way he could pay, he shuddered at that thought.

In Geneva, inside Ronan Sttrobing's residence he awoke, and rolled over; his companion was had her back to him. He traced his finger down her spine to the top of her buttocks; a moan came from the body next to him, and she rolled to face him. "Morning Ronan," came her reply, in her silky, smooth voice, and she leaned over and kissed him. "Thank you for letting me stay here the night," and then she got up and went into the bathroom, to shower and dress in her combat uniform.

The, new, land warfare department head admired her body as she strode across the room; then he lay back wondering if he'd done the right thing by letting her stay the night, what with his wife having only been buried a few days earlier. Yet here he was, already bedding another woman – what would people say, and then there were Simon's feelings to consider; how would he feel about his father bringing another woman home?

He'd cross that bridge when, and if, he came to it, for now he'd just enjoy her company, and, maybe, anything else that may happen. Putting those thoughts to the back of his mind he got up and dressed, in the usual HART battle dress uniform (BDU) of: beige coloured combat trousers and button down tunic, regulation lace up boots, up to the shin, and then Ronan put his firearm, a Beretta 92, semi-automatic pistol, in his gun belt. Once he was, more or less, ready he sat on the bed to await his companion's return.

His fellow HART officer returned, kitted out in similar clothes to what he wore, except she carried through, in her gun belt, a Beretta 9000 – which was slightly shorter than his 92, having a length of only 168mm (6.6 inches). "Are we ready?" she asked him, knowing the answer already.

"Yes, I'm ready if you are," was his reply. They walked down the stairs, one after another, grabbed a quick piece of toast, and a cup of tea, and then left his residence.

"Good morning Mr Strobing, Miss Lang," called one of the, patrolling, HART troopers, dressed in similar clothing to theirs.

Ronan felt slightly worried in case this trooper, Mark Andrews – a Frenchman, put two and two together and guessed the land warfare departmental head, and his assistant were having an affair. If he did he might let this information slip in front off his line sergeant who would then feel it his duty to report this to his group captain.

He may inform his team leader, Celia Most, in which case she might then feel it her duty to inform Peter Roberts, though as she and Ronan had known each other a long time he felt she wouldn't; or perhaps the group captain might decide to go over his team leader's head and inform Roberts himself. Either way if Roberts found out about both Lucy and himself they faced instant dismissal. Relationships, sexual or otherwise, between colleagues were frowned upon, and not encouraged; and may also affect a soldier's reaction time, in a battle zone.

"Good morning Andrews," responded the American woman. "Please excuse Mr Strobing, he just had a bad night." She gave Ronan a crafty wink, and a smile.

"Thank you for handling that," said the Englishman once they'd moved away, "I don't think I could have." It was at that moment Leon Bigship spotted them and came over.

"Hello you two, ready for the new day's excitement?" he asked, acting as though he saw nothing with two friends walking together, and didn't suspect a thing.

"Oh yes," answered Ronan, "we're ready for what the day has in store for us, aren't we Lucy?" She just nodded in agreement.

"Good, good. With our new promotion we might get the chance to see more action."

The other two exchanged a quick look. Oh yes, more action than you think, they thought. "But we mustn't forget our other duties," Lucy said to him, as if trying to allay any suspicions he might have.

"You're right there," replied the new sea warfare departmental head, "I'm just heading over to the main building. Y'know, see if anything needs doing."

"So are we," answered department head, Operational Commander, and team leader, Strobing quickly, "we'll walk with you." He knew Lucy had probably had other ideas, but those could wait. Arriving at the main building all three of them took the elevator up to the fourth floor, and entered the conference room, to find Commander Roberts along with Dr Hans Schaiffer, and Celia Most, waiting for them.

The other three seated themselves around the table, in the chairs provided; on the table was another map of the world. "Now we're all here," announced Roberts, from the head of the table, "we shall begin."

""Ronan," he said, turning the male member of his land warfare department. "Whereabouts do you believe *Proagnon* is based?"

"Well sir, if I remember rightly, I guessed – this is purely guesswork – they are either in Russia, somewhere along the northern coast of Africa, or somewhere in the Middle East."

"And this was while I was away?" his commander asked.

"Yes, that is correct sir."

"And yet you did nothing about it?"

"No sir, the simple reason was I didn't want to send all four groups of, our soldiers out and only three, or less, come back. In short, I felt I needed more information, together with your advice."

"That is very commendable Mr Strobing, you did the right thing. I'm sure we all agree it is senseless to just throw troops away needlessly." Everyone around the table nodded.

"Anyway, as I feel we have the military might now, I will be authorising airlifts into these areas soon, and I may call upon each of you to lead one of these groups."

"Understood sir," each of them said in turn.

"We shall use several of the M-151 jeeps, and perhaps two groups will get an armoured VAB, whereas the other two groups will get a HMMWV. Each group will be supplied with a helicopter, should the helicopters be redesigned and ready for use, and I shall be coming on one of the missions later, probably to Africa. Is that all understood?"

"Yes sir," they answered as one.

"In that case you are dismissed, and are asked to report to the shooting range, at 13.00 for target practice." They all filed out the office, except Dr Schaiffer, and got into the elevator.

As they descended Miss Lang piped up, "I wonder who'll get which mission?"

"Yes, I wonder," replied Celia, somewhat mysteriously. "Still, I think we ought to go and put our bullet-proof vests on, just in case."

"Good idea," responded Leon, as the others murmured their agreement. When the elevator had reached its destination they all stepped out, left the building, and walked back to their own residences, to put their bullet-proof vests on.

Back in the office Hans Schaiffer looked at his leader expectantly. Peter looked up at him, "I may need you to take command of the compound in my absence, but for now you may carry on attending to your normal duties. I shall summon you when I am ready to depart, and give you instructions."

"Yes sir," he answered, saluted, and left the office to return to the medical wing.

Each team leader's vest was augmented with metal (steel or titanium), ceramic or polyethylene plates that provided extra protection to the vital organs. These hard armour plates had been proven effective against all handgun bullets and a range of rifles. These upgraded baullet proof vests had become standard in military use – but now the vests had been transferred to HART for their use – as there was now no, real, military forces to speak of, as soft body armour vests were ineffective against military rifle rounds. The layers of very strong fibre in these vests can catch and deform all soft bullets and spread its force over a larger portion of the vest fibre. The vest could absorb the energy from the bullet, bringing it to a stop before it could penetrate beyond the vest. A deformable handgun bullet mushroomed into a dished plate on impact with a well designed textile vest. Some layers may be penetrated but as the bullet deforms the energy is absorbed by a larger and larger fibre area. While a vest can prevent bullet penetration, the vest and wearer still absorb the bullet's energy. Even without penetration, modern pistol bullets contain enough energy to cause blunt force trauma under the impact point. Vests' specifications include both penetration resistance requirements and limits on the amount of impact energy that is delivered to the body. Vests designed for bullets offer little protection against blows from sharp implements, such as knives, arrows or ice picks, or from bullets manufactured of non-deformable materials i.e. steel core instead of lead. The force of the impact of these objects is concentrated in a relatively small area, allowing them to puncture the fibre layers of most bullet-resistant fabrics.

There were six different types of vest for each member to choose from; from protection against stab wounds to multipurpose vests, providing protection from gunfire and sharp objects, knives, arrows and ice-picks; although there was one, recently modified, that protected the wearer from gunfire, stab wounds and explosive devices. All armour included a protective vest, ballistic shoulder protection, as well as protective side armour; occasionally, a helmet was worn, depending on the wearer.

Each of them chose the vest that would more or less, protect them from everything; and was deemed the most appropriate for their mission; once kitted out, in these, all four had a meal, or whatever, and then waited until 12.45. At this time all four of them, now in their capacity as Operational Commanders, walked over to the shooting range for target practice; the officer overseeing things was Sergeant Mike LaBelle. Sergeant LaBelle was around forty years old, 5'10", and had served in both Gulf Wars. He had been recruited by Peter Roberts in 2008 when his tour of duty was ended.

A few minutes after the Operational Commanders arrived, both Commander Roberts and Dr Schaffer joined them. Both were similarly kitted out "Bring up the targets Mike," requested the overall commander.

"Will do sir," the sergeant answered. He turned to a control box, on the wall behind him, opened it, and operated some controls inside; six lanes, out of a maximum of ten, lit up. Each had a fresh target at the end, "Choose your weapon."

Before them was an assortment of weapons: assault rifles, rifles, machine guns, sub-machine guns, pistols, and shotguns. They each tested the different sorts of weapons – gauging them for weight and ease of use. In the end most of them settled for the Brugger & Thornet MP5 sub-machine gun, while Roberts and Schaffer settled for the Beretta 9000 pistol.

This done; and the weapons tested all six of them walked back to the main headquarters and went up to the commander's office to receive their final instructions. "All four of you have been designated a Chinook to transport your soldiers, plus yourself to each of your destinations."

"The Chinooks have been readied for use commander," the voice of Mrs Jones came from the intercom that was situated on the desk.

"Thank you Mrs Jones," responded Mr Roberts. "Okay gentleman, ladies, report to your team barracks and collect what you need, and then report to one of the Chinooks and let's get this show on the road, or in the air. All the pilots have their individual, flight plans, Once you arrive at your, specified, destinations you are requested to use the SAT-phone to contact headquarters to let us know you've arrived. Dr Schaffer and I will follow later, in a Blackhawk. Good luck."

"Dismissed!" The four team leaders then left the building, ran to their, individual team barracks and selected the soldiers best suited for the operation, they did prefer not to leave anybody out, but sometimes it couldn't be helped.

However, one of them only had to choose two officers to assist in their mission; yet every soldier was readied, in case.

The fourth Chinook would take the team, on board – whichever it was, to *Cointrin* airport, the three operatives would then board a Boeing 787-8, along with regular passengers, for their journey to Russia. The other soldiers would be taken onto the HART military compound outside Zurich, and then they would be returned to the main compound, in due course.

The four team leaders, whether it was Ronan, Celia, Lucy or Leon then selected the kit they would take: an assortment of M14, M15 and M-16 rifles, a TAC SAT telephone that would send a signal up to the satellite which would then be transmitted back to HQ, so the base crew knew if any of their teams was in trouble and be able to organise a prompt rescue mission; plus all Operational Commanders had been requested to contact headquarters to confirm they'd arrived at their, specified, destinations. Finally, they selected the rations for the trip, most were canned foods that were easy to open and didn't always need cooking; however, a, camping stove was to be taken along as well. Plus various types of clothing, tents, and flares. The men were also allowed to take their M9 9mm pistols; for close kills. Several general purpose machine guns, including the M240; and a heavy machine gun, the M1917, were included. Finally, hand grenades were packed into the soldier's kit as well. The Operational Commanders were now satisfied that their squad of soldiers were ready. Since the death of Mark Schneider his squad of forty soldiers had had to be distributed among the others; it would have been simpler to promote someone else to team leader, but if this was the way Commander Roberts wanted to do things so be it. Therefore now there were now 50 soldiers in each squad, compared to 40 in each squad when there had been five team leaders. The soldiers, together with their squad leaders exited their barracks and ran to where the Chinooks waited, rotor blades turning.

They were to be flown out on the twin rotored, twin bladed CH-47D helicopters, the Chinook had first been flown by the U.S. Army on September 21st 1961, however, the model then had been the CH-47A; though over the years it had changed little, except in its engine power, and sometimes its capacity. Two Lycoming T55-GA-72 turboshaft engines powered the machine; each putting out 3,750 horsepower.

The soldiers would also be taking several M-151 jeeps with them, to act as scout vehicles. The soldiers would be airlifted to their designated areas. Once there the HART soldiers, together with their squad commanders, would find somewhere to set up a camp and, maybe, a main base, but away from any prying eyes.

The men all boarded the waiting Chinooks; once they were all aboard and strapped in, all 50 of them, the Chinooks would lift off.

In Lucy Lang's case the 50 soldiers, as well as herself, boarded the helicopter that was designated 'B'. Once everyone was aboard, and strapped in, the pilot – Colonel Sebastian 'Seb' Mcintyre pushed the switch to bring the engines up to full power; once the engines, the Colonel judged, had reached their full power he and his co-pilot, Lieutenant Alice 'Ali' Havers – a woman no less, pulled back on their control columns and the giant aircraft rose steadily into the air. Once the CH-47's turboshaft engines had a rhythm to them, and the aircraft was put on auto-pilot. Mcintyre turned, in his seat, to his passengers, "How is everyone?"

"Well," answered Miss Lang, whose team the helicopter was carrying, "no-one's been sick, so far, so everything seems to be going fine Colonel. By the way, where are we bound for?"

"Y'mean they didn't tell you Missy," there were only a few people who could get away with calling Lucy 'Missy' and Colonel Mcintyre was one of them. "We're headed for northern Africa."

Lucy looked crestfallen; she had hoped both Ronan and herself would have been assigned to the Middle East. "Hey, cheer up Missy; it isn't the end of the world."

"It could be," she murmured to herself. Luckily neither Mcintyre nor anyone else seemed to hear her. The Colonel then went back to his pilot's seat, and resumed command of the machine which was flying at a speed of 150mph (241.5km/h), in a southerly direction, towards its destination of the northern region of Africa. "We shall be hovering, not landing, just south of the Chott Djerid, which is a lake south to the main town of Annaba – in Algeria. We shall be landing, hopefully, in a densely wooded area."

"However, as this journey is more than 400 miles, which is this aircraft's range, we shall be refuelling in mid flight; this will be performed by the KC-135 tanker aircraft which will be shadowing this aircraft. There is an unused air-strip in the area we are travelling to; therefore, what I propose to do is get the helicopter as close as I can to the ground, without damaging it, then I shall lower the exit ramp and let you out that way," Mcintyre said. "Don't worry, it's quite safe," he added to reassure them all.

All the HART soldiers, all combat trained, were looking forward to this; after months of inactivity here they were, doing something they were properly trained for. The total journey distance was 1100 miles; so the journey would take, at their present speed, just under, or over, seven and a half 8 hours, so as they'd set off from headquarters at roughly 14.00 they should arrive at around 21.30, probably the vehicles would arrive tomorrow. Tonight was just a scouting mission to build up a command post.

Once they'd been in the air 2 hours Sebastian's voice came over the intercom, "Time to get feet wet," an old military saying that, literally, meant they were about to cross a stretch of water, in this case the Mediterranean Sea. Another couple of hours later – it might have been sooner – a clunk was heard through the cabin as the tanker's fuel nozzle locked onto the forward probe deployed by the Chinook. This sound unnerved a few of the young soldiers, who had never been on an aircraft that was capable of mid air refuelling, and they looked around in alarm. Noting their comrades had not really, reacted to this – in the same way they had – the soldiers settled back down.

Lucy noted the reactions, but knew once they'd been on a few missions, similar to this, they would learn – as the others had – to become accustomed to mid air refuelling.

Once the helicopter was fuelled up the tanker aircraft unhooked the fuel line from the CH-47 and flew up into the clouds to await the next radio contact from Colonel Mcintyre.

Eventually, after seven and three quarter hours, plus needing to be refuelled twice, the helicopter started to descend slowly, and then it was that Mcintyre said to them, "Ladies and gentleman, we have arrived at our destination. You will find parachutes under your seats; please affix them and then when Missy gives the clear signal, I will lower the exit ramp. "

Every one of the combat soldiers slipped their parachutes on; then, once they all had their 'chutes' on – and they were fastened correctly, their squad leader banged three times on the wall between the cabin and the pilot's area, on cue Sebastian Mcintyre lowered the exit ramp and the troops jumped out, followed by their commander. It wasn't far to the, jungle, floor; thanks to Mcintyre's and Havers's, careful, maneuvering.

When every trooper was out the ramp was raised; and the Chinook helicopter rose into the air and flew away. When everyone had more or less, landed they gathered in a semi-circle around their leader. "Break out the TAC-SAT phone," she ordered. Once the TAC-SAT phone was produced Lucy set it up, hopefully the satellite would receive the transmission and relay the signal to HART headquarters, the system was fully encrypted so no-one could listen in – at least that was the theory. As soon as she was put through to headquarters, she said, "Lucy Lang reporting in, from Africa, all the soldiers are down and are ready for further orders."

There were no specific orders at that time, so Miss Lang replaced the receiver and looked up at the squad of soldiers "As there are no specific orders, yet, I think we should scout these woods out, find a clearing and set up a camp, and a command post. But, remember, be silent and be careful. We'll meet back here at 22.30 to set up the tents, and then get some rest, and sleep. Remember to wear your night vision goggles."

Each soldier was kitted out in, camouflage, combat wear of green clothing and black rubber boots with holes in, so the boots didn't get overheated. Each wore helmets with a, very, thin layer of steel inside to act as protection for the head, they'd also brought wide brimmed hats with them, because they all knew temperatures could get very hot in the daytime After sunset, however, the clear, dry air permitted rapid loss of heat therefore the nights were usually, cool to chilly. All of them also had green and black make-up on their faces to enable them to blend in to the jungle surroundings.

Each of them were also wearing utility belts that contained extra ammo clips for their M-16s, plus grenades and anything else they may need. Anything extra they may need could be found in their rucksacks.

The troops wandered off in different directions, as quiet as soldiers with hob-nailed boots on could be; Lucy watched them go, a fine bunch of men and women – though she did have reservations about one or two of the younger members – but they would come through, in the end. Then she heard a twig snap, the sound was faint but it came from an easterly direction; fearing one of her troopers had made the noise she followed, being as quiet as she could, now some leaves rustled and there was a quick burst of gunfire, an AK-47 if her hearing didn't deceive her; quickly, she produced her own M-16 Carbine. Dropping to the ground, when she had to, Lucy crawled along the jungle floor. Reaching into her backpack, and fiddling about for a few moments, the American produced her goggles and put them on. The glasses were infra-red so they enabled the wearer to see perfectly, in the dark.

Eventually she crawled into a wooded area that overlooked a valley – just over the border with Tunisia, this was like a crater surrounded by trees; not crawling too far forward, so as to reveal herself to the occupants below and peered into the area. Suddenly, the wind whipped about her and she looked up, the American watched, in surprise, as a Mi-24 HIND D class helicopter began its descent into the crater. She tapped a button on her communicator that would log the area's co-ordinates. However, she watched on – intrigued – as the rear exit ramp was lowered; eight *Proagnon* troops marched out, and formed two lines of four at the rear of the aircraft, as she continued to watch another man followed, he seemed to be in charge as the others all knelt before him.

She couldn't identify the man but the soldiers, she thought were definitely *Proagnon*, so this must be a type of secondary command centre, or training camp, as there were many huts in the background; but towering above them all was a large grey building, this was probably the command post of some sort;

there was a set of wooden, double, doors which gave onto a grey building behind; all in all the building was of a similar shape to a church.

Committing all she'd seen to memory, the American, slowly, withdrew from her hiding place and made her way back to the HART encampment. A twig snapped; however, Lucy reasoned, she should be far enough away to avoid being heard by the enemy agents. She just needed to watch out for snakes or any other wildlife that might roam the area, luckily she saw none.

When all the soldiers had returned to camp their commander informed them of everything she'd seen. She produced the telephone and contacted HART HQ, once Gwyneth was on the line Lucy informed her of what she'd seen. Mrs Jones told Miss Lang that she would let Mr Roberts know; Lucy thanked her and cut the connection, which had been encrypted.

Gwyneth Jones, after she'd informed Peter Roberts, wondered why the satellite they used, or the UAVs, that had been launched and were over the area, hadn't picked this activity up, it was probably due to the dense foliage. Roberts told Miss Lang on the satellite phone, "I'll get back to you, in the morning with orders for your troops and yourself." He replaced the receiver, *How could this have happened without any prior knowledge?*

They met at one of Iran's best restaurants, the Golestan Palace, in Tehran; it was an open air place, but with a, small, indoor area for tourists who preferred not to sit in the heat. The two men moved to a table in the far corner, so they could speak in, relative, privacy. They both ordered Ash-e-anar – an *aash* to start with, which was a thick soup. "So, said the elder one – who was a Korean named Lon Hwan. "What information do you require?"

"Simple," answered his Russian lunch companion, lowering his voice as the waitress took their dishes. "I require the location of the *Proagnon* stronghold. I know it's near here, and you know where it is."

"*Proagnon* now have three, or is it four, strongholds. I am afraid Dr Q would kill me if he knew I was here now, meeting you of all people."

"Comrade, do you not remember our homeland?" asked the Russian. Even though Hwan was Korean, his family lived in Russia, and he had been born in that country. However, he looked more Korean than Russian.

"Indeed I do my friend; and it was your family that helped mine in times of hardship, such as the cold winter of 1990, but those are times in the past my friend. Now we work for a greater cause." The main meal arrived then, a sumptuous helping of *koresht,* a stew that was served with Iranian rice, together with, as requested, the eggplant, aubergine, or *the potato of Iran*, each got two. As they ate their main meal the elder one looked across at his companion, again, and asked, "Why do you want such information?"

"You will recall," replied Sergey, conversationally yet keeping his voice low, "the attack on the American White House, their principal's stronghold, I was part of the group and was caught; however, my commander, Abdul Singh, instead of mounting a rescue mission left me to rot whilst he escaped a free man. Therefore, I want to find him."

"Ah, I see your problem," said Lon, "to find a man that doesn't want to be found, because he knows he's done you wrong. That is a most perplexing puzzle."

"Unfortunately, I cannot help you my friend," said the Korean. "Here comes desert," he said looking up. They were served two bowls of Goosh-e Fil (Elephant's ear), which was a deep-fried dough, fried in the shape of a flat elephant's ear and then covered with sugar powder. This was topped by traditionally prepared Iranian ice cream. "Ah," noted the Korean, "A pleasant dish to finish our meal, plus as it is warm outside, an excellent dessert to cool us both down."

"My thoughts exactly," observed Sergey. *If this fool will not tell me the information I require I must deal with him, and find another source that will tell me.*

The two men finished their ice cream dishes, and were asked if they'd like anything to follow. "Yes, we would," replied the Russian, looking at his friend. Two cups of Doogh followed the desserts. Doogh was the standard drink for accompanying Iranian dishes. It was a drink, which combined yoghurt with water, or soda, and dried mint.

When they'd finished their drinks both of them got up from their seats, Lon paid the owner and both men left the restaurant. They set off and crossed the road, Kayyam Street, and started to walk through Park-e Shahr.

Lon saw his friend was wearing a pair of white, cotton gloves; he'd been wearing these all through the meal at the Golestan Palace. The Korean was curious, "Why are you wearing gloves?"

"An accident," replied Sergey bluntly, "I burnt myself." The two men walked on, through the park; once Sergey deemed they were far enough in, there were not many people about to see him, he pushed his friend. "Hey what gives?" demanded Lon Hwan indignantly; as he gazed up at the Russian, he was only 5'8" whereas Sergey was 6'4", he noticed a sudden change in his friend's face. "S-S-Sergey?" he stammered, then he noticed the switchblade that had, somehow, appeared in the Russian's hand. "Don't be a fool."

The Russian then grabbed his Korean counterpart, in a vice like grip; slowly he drew the other man forward and pushed the blade into Lon who screamed as Sergey pushed the knife in deeper, then all of a sudden his body sagged. The Russian withdrew the knife and let Hwan's body fall to the floor; Sergey kicked him to make sure he was dead, but judging by the blood leaking from his body the Korean was, definitely, dead. Quickly the Russian knelt over him, so if anyone passed he would look like he was helping the man, and strarted searching inside his jacket; he found, more or less, what he was looking for at once, he removed the man's Fox 17 9mm pistol, along with all the papers that could identify Lon Hwan, and then lifted the body, careful not to get blood on himself, and dumped the Korean's body in the undergrowth. Satisfied the Russian took his cotton gloves off, dropped them in a waste bin along with most of Lon's papers, got a cigarette lighter from his inside pocket and lit the corner of the Korean's passport; dropped it on top of the other documents and casually walked away, whistling as he went.

Hopefully no-one would notice the fire, or the dead man, too soon; and hopefully the incident would be blamed on one of the numerous youth's that occupied Tehran.

The switchblade was Miranda's; he'd found it on the top shelf of her wardrobe, as he was exploring her room, and had decided it might come in useful so he'd taken it. It had been concealed, up his shirt sleeve, while he and his companion had been eating, and now he was going back to her house, in Qom, to replace it in its original place.

The squad of 50 HART troopers had a restful night; they had all set up their tents and put protective nets around them, their American commander didn't though; she kept on wondering why the *Proagnon* troops – she'd recognise those blue uniforms anywhere – hadn't heard the Chinook as it had brought them in; maybe they had but, as the HIND was approaching as well, they had assumed it was the other helicopter, yet there was no mistaking the difference of the engine noise, or the size; the Chinook was louder as its engines were more powerful due to its size.

However, no enemy troops had thundered into this clearing, with AK-47's blazing, so the HART soldiers were safe, for now. Putting this problem to the back of her mind, for now, she settled back and tried to get some sleep.

Celia Most and Leon Bigship, together with their combined total of one hundred soldiers had arrived in the Middle East, at the old army complex east of the town of Jedda.

Jedda was located at a spot that was roughly halfway between the two mountain regions of Al-Hejaz, in the north and the Asir mountain region in the south.

All the soldiers were wearing beige, coloured, uniforms, ideal for desert warfare, and all were equipped with water bottles. Once everyone was out the helicopter both Operational Commanders had reported into headquarters, as they were in the same region it was deemed silly to bring two of the TAC-SAT phones – even though none of the Operational Commanders knew where they would end up.

However, Peter Roberts had instructed each flight crew, via Gwyneth Jones, which squad to take; therefore, the colonel on the flight crew, who also doubled as co pilot, had watched out for whichever team they'd been instructed to take and persuade them to board the, correct, aircraft. It was wrong and Roberts knew it, but he wanted to see how well Celia and Leon worked together.

Thanks to the computer 'Memory Stick' Leon had used in Russia, they now knew who two of the *Proagnon* contacts over there were, Oleg Ayanseikov (the foreign minister) and Mikhail Suvorov (the defence minister), but were there any more; that was what Peter had sent Ronan, together with two of his team; Harry Danto and Tammy Smith, to find out. They had flown out with their team to Zurich, then Ronan had selected the two agents to accompany him to Russia. The three of them had then boarded a Boeing 787-8, along with about 224 other passengers, for the flight from Zurich airport to *Sheremetyevo* airport, the journey was due to take nearly 15 hours and where they were headed was two and a half hours ahead of Geneva time; therefore, they took off at three in the afternoon, and arrived in Russia at, roughly, half past eight next morning.

The passengers, all 227, got up, all were a bit weary, and exited the aircraft followed by the three HART agents, and then two crew and the three stewardesses; it was raining, not hard, and there was a cool breeze blowing, so everyone, quickly, hurried into the main building (Terminal B). Thankfully, the air was warmer in here.

The three agents lined up with the other passengers, at the luggage carousel, to await their luggage; about half an hour later they had their suitcases, and left the main building to find a taxi.

The rain had eased slightly since they'd landed, which was good, and an unoccopied taxi pulled into the kerb; the driver, a rather overweight Russian, hurried out and helped them with their luggage. "Don't mind the weather," he said to them, in a rather gravelly voice. "It always rains in Russia. Tourists are you?"

"We are," replied Tammy, in her light, airy voice, "just arrived."

"Old Andreyi'll look after you, find you a good hotel." The two men looked at each other in surprise, here was a Russian being friendly, and helpful, to them. They all got in the cab, or mushkrutkas as they were sometimes known and it pulled away; As they turned onto Leningradskoe Highway, south into Moscow their problems began; there was, practically, bumper to bumper traffic heading all the way into Russia's capital, they were crawling along at 5mph (sometimes just coming to a grinding halt. Andreyi hooted the horn, on quite a few occassions, and muttered a few choice words to himself; even though none of the HART agents knew any Russian they could tell he was cursing). Ronan almost wished they'd taken the metro, or even the express from the airport to the Belorussky Rail Terminal. However, he reasoned, these trains would all be full of commuters.

An hour and half later, of horn-honking and cursing, they pulled up outside the Rossiya Hotel, in Moscow, a magnificent building with twenty-one floors, and it also overlooked the Kremlin. The hotel had been built in 1967, and had been partly destroyed by fire ten years later. Eventually, the building had been demolished in 2006, but, after many protests, it had been rebuilt on the same site.

The three agents got out and looked at the building in awe, even though the hotel was only located within easy driving distance of the airport's main terminal building except in rush hours, the three agents had decided to take a taxi, they did have heavy suitcases, and had paid the price. "That'll be 25 Euros please," Andreyi told them. Ronan paid him, and then they got out the cab; Andreyi unloaded their lugguage for them. "Magnificent building isn't it?"

"It is sir," replied Mr Danto politely.

"Since Russia joined in the EU, we've made good use of the trade agreements. Now we build things to last." Even though the hotel had originally been built in the sixties, when Russia wasn't in the EU, it had been completely rebuilt, to it's former glory, in 2008. Once the Russian cab driver had unloaded the suitcases, he bid them farewell, and to have a good stay, then got back in his car and drove off.

The other three people turned and walked into the, main, foyer of the hotel. As they entered they passed the two doormen standing outside on duty, dressed in their, red, uniforms with a shade darker red overcoats on, white gloves, black boots, and dark red peaked cap; both were a good six foot tall, neither smiled at the three people. The foyer was full of people milling about, pushing past each other; eventually, they reached the reception desk, a wooden construction with two telephones, and a computer, on it. The receptionist, a young man in uniform, looked up as they approached; "Greetings, may I help you?"

Harry Danto looked at him, straight in the face, and simply said, "HART," then each of the three showed their ID cards.

"Ah," muttered the receptionist, "you must be our guests from Geneva." Turning to the computer he said to them, "You're in rooms two-fifty-five, -six, and -seven."

"Thank you," replied Ronan, who was the team's Operational Commander. "We hope we enjoy our stay here. Tell me, where is the Foreign Ministry?"

"In Moscow, along with all our other main buildings of power," replied the young man helpfully. "Will that be all sirs, madam."

"For now," muttered Mr Strobing. With that the receptionist handed three keys over, and directed them toward the elevators.

Once they were in the elevator, going up to the second floor, agent Danto said, casually, to the others, "He seemed a helpful chap." The others agreed.

"Which room do you want Tammy?" asked Ronan, who had the keys to the three rooms in his hand.

"Room two-five-six I think."

He handed the key over, "Now you Harry."

"Room two-five-seven."

"That leaves me with two-five-five," their Operational Commander said, as the elevator doors opened, They walked down the well lit corridor to their, respective, rooms and went inside. Once Ronan was in his room he produced the TAC-SAT phone from his suitcase and contacted HART. "Operational Commander Strobing here, my team is in place."

"Thank you commander Strobing," replied the HART receptionist's strong welsh tones. "Keep the phone near you at all times; will be contacting you with mission details shortly."

"Understood. Out," and he replaced the receiver. He then laid out on the bed to rest, he assumed the others were doing the same, as it had been a long flight and none of them had tried to rest on the journey over; all three wishing to stay alert in case an emergncy, of some sort occurred and they had to intervene.

The nine *Proagnon* agents who had been training for the past sixteen weeks for their new jobs: a group of three to be waiters aboard an American airliner, the second group of three to work aboard a Metro train, and the final group of three to work aboard a new supertanker; each group had a bomb to plant aboard their vehicles; however, no-one knew which team's bomb would be detonated, as Dr Q would be detonating the bomb from the underground bunker, patching the signal into a radio transmitter. Would one bomb explode, none, or all three?

At HART HQ Peter Roberts had discussed the night before's call from Operational Commander Lang with his number two, Hans Schaiffer. "What would you suggest my old and trusted friend?" Roberts asked the man standing before his desk.

"I would suggest you order her to keep an eye on things for the moment, because if it's just a training camp we needn't go in just now, all guns blazing"

"That may be appropriate for now, yes, and, let me guess, if they do start to mobilize forces, then we go in."

"Quite correct," answered Dr Schaiffer.

"Thank you," said Peter. He buzzed through to Gwyneth, "Gwyneth, contact Miss Lang and inform her that she and her troops are to observe the camp, but take no action unless hostile action is taken towards them."

"Yes sir," replied Gwyneth through the intercom. She contacted the team in Africa and informed the Operational

Commander of the overall commander's decision. Of course, as she had guessed, Lucy didn't take kindly to the decision, but still orders were orders.

It was then she heard the distinct sound of the CH-47 Chinook's twin turboshaft engines; praying that no-one at the *Proagnon* camp could identify the sound she looked up. There it was, just hovering – although Lucy knew it wouldn't hover for long; she quickly gathered the squad together, the ramp lowered, on the underbelly of the Chinook and the two male members of the crew: pilot and flight engineer pushed out several vehicles, attached to parachutes. Once all the vehicles had been deployed the ramp was raised back up and the transport helicopter flew away, on its journey back to headquarters.

Lucy, together with some of the soldiers, found the vehicles the helicopter had dropped and cut the parachutes of; there were 4 M-151 jeeps and three HMMWV vehicles.

Sergey Satov had returned to Qom and put Miranda's switchblade back where it had originally been; of course as he'd used cotton gloves for the day, even though his hands were now sweaty, from the heat, he hadn't left any fingerprints, hopefully. He exited her room and descended the stairs; he'd just reached the foot of the stairs when the lady, if you could call her that, of the house came in, a big smile on her face, "Sergey my friend," she said cheerfully, and beamed up at him. "Did you manage to meet with your friend?"

"Yes," the, big, Russian replied darkly, "alas, he couldn't help me, so my search for Abdul Singh goes on."

"Oh well," she muttered, "I'm sure you'll find him, in the end."

"I hope I will," the Russian said, wallking through to the main sitting room and seating himself on the blue sofa. "Miranda," he called, "have you any beer?"

"Yes I have," she called back, "I bought some more in earlier, I'll just get you one." Sergey heard a door open, he assumed it was a fridge, and a few moments later Miranda reappeared, came into the room, and handed him his can of beer. "I'm just going upstairs for a bath," the owner of the house said, "feel free to watch the TV."

She then left the room; the Russian switched the TV on and picked up the remote control and started to flick through the channels aimlessly. There were many channels on this network; he came across soaps (he assumed them to be soaps), dramas, news channels, intellectual programmes, religious channels, kids programmes, exercise channels, and, he was surprised to find – especially running at the same time as kids channels – porn channels. Settling on one of those, well actions speak louder than words, he settled back with his beer; it was a basic story of a warrior conquering an evil king, the warrior was a female and was very, scantily dressed.

As soon as the programme was over, he'd enjoyed it – there wasn't much like that in Russia, some half an hour later, he heard the Iranian's, light, footfalls coming down the stairs so he, quickly, changed channel to one of the news channels. When Miranda appeared in view he saw she was wearing a, light, pink robe around her; she walked across to the kitchen, and reappeared, moments later, with a second can of beer. Holding it in her hand, she came into the sitting room and sat by him. "Been enjoying the TV have you?"

"Yes," answered the Russian hesitantly, "your news is most fascinating."

"Come off it Sergey I know what you've been watching; every man does it, I have no objections, it's there for people to watch and if they want to watch it that's up to them; y'know I sometimes watch that channel if I'm feeling very lonely."

Sergey now understood – in a way, these Middle-Easterns, especially Miranda – it seemed weren't exactly that way inclined, but if the opportunity presented itself they wouldn't always say 'No'. Even his landlady wouldn't refuse, if that what she was?

Suddenly a news item caught Sergey's attention. "Earlier today," the newscaster started by saying; "A body was found in the Park-e Shahr, hidden in undergrowth; he was killed, it appears, by a single stab wound, he had no identifying papers on him so police have no idea who he was. All they will say, for certain, is he was of Korean background, and of a height of around five-foot-eight-inches, also he looked to be in his late thirties or early forties. Whatever this newscaster has said is pure speculation, at the moment."

Miranda looked over at Sergey from her seat, he was sat, bolt, upright, as if in some sort of shock. "Was he your friend?" she asked her Russian guest, both quietly and innocently.

"Yes," he answered, equally as quiet. "He introduced me to Mr Singh. Please excuse me," and he, suddenly, walked from the room and rushed upstairs. She heard him as he vomitted into the toilet. *Poor baby*, she thought, and, secretly, smiled to herself.

Once she'd finished her can of beer she took the two, now empty, cans out to a container in the rear yard, it was still warm and humid, the temperature had become cooler of late, and was now about 11 degrees Celsius (51 degrees Farenheit) but the air still had a humidity of about 76%, however that would drop, overnight to about 1 degree Celsius (33 degrees Farenheit) with a humidity of 75%; plus there was a medium risk of rain, even though it was starting to drizzle now.

She finished her task, and went back inside to prepare some food, if her guest felt up to it. Not finding him downstairs she thought that he must be taking a bath to revive his body, maybe easing any aches and strains he'd picked up that day. Figuring he may not feel that hungry Miranda brought out, from a cupboard some Tah-chin, which was a rice cake that she'd made a day earlier.

As she was leaning forward Sergey came into the room and coughed, to grab her attention. Miranda, visibly, jumped; she hadn't heard him come down. Turning round she put the cake, which she'd managed to keep hold of, on the table. "Sorry Sergey, I didn't hear you come downstairs."

"That looks good," he said, gesturing to the cake. "What iss it?"

"Tah-chin, a rice cake, would you like some?"

"Yes please," answered the Russian, helping her to set the plates out; when that was done he seated himself in one of the, wooden, dining chairs, Miranda placed the cake, on the table, between them, and then found a knife to cut it, and sat opposite him. She cut them both a slice each, she wasn't sure if her guest would enjoy the cake, but he wolfed it down hungrily.

"Can I have another slice?" he asked his host, politely.

"Oh yes, please help yourself," his landlady answered, passing him the knife.

He cut another piece and started eating, more steadily this time. Miranda noticed he was staring at her, across the table, for some reason. "Is something the matter?" she enquired.

"Not at all," the Russian replied. "May I ask you a question?"

"But of course," was the reply. "You may ask me anything you like."

"Well," he began hesitantly, "you've admitted to watching porn programmes, occasionally. I was wondering, not for my benefit you understand, obviously, if you'd be prepared to do some of the things those women do?"

"If I'm truthful it would depend on who I was with, and the circumstances," was the answer he got. Sergey never batted an eyelid at this response. The time he saw, looking up at the clock, was about half past nine. Where had the time gone?

Deep down Sergey was beginning to like Miranda – though he wouldn't admit it, due to his hatred of the Iranians, in particular Abdul Singh.

At the Rossiya hotel, earlier that same day, Ronan Strobing had looked out his room window, using binoculars, and noticed the hotel, actually, overlooked the Russian Kremlin, in which Vladimir Krushkev (Russia's President) had offices. General secretaries, Premiers, Ministers, and Commissars all had offices in the, main, building as well, along with many other members of Russia's government; once a week the government, along with the President, would meet to discuss the business of the country.

There were many other buildings within the Kremlin walls; there was the, main, building, four palaces, four cathedrals; and the Kremlin towers there were 24 of these now. This historic complex, at the heart of Moscow, overlooked the Moskva River (to the south), Saint Basil's Cathedral and Red Square (to the east), and Alexander Garden (to the west).

The HART complex was a lot larger, thought agent Strobing, about six of the Kremlin complex's could be fitted into the military complex. He wondered about the rest of the team, those he'd had to leave behind. Still, he'd left them in the, competent, hands of Sergeant Daniel Davis, and if he needed assistance there was always Commander Roberts, and his experience, to call upon. The TAC-SAT phone, at his side, started chirping, Ronan answered it, knowing the call would be from headquarters, in Geneva. "Yes," he said simply.

"Your orders are as follows. You are to keep a close watch on the Kremlin, Mr Roberts has organised transport – which should be with you shortly, and photograph everyone you see going in and out the building. Once you have done this return the camera films, we will develop the prints, and then study them – blow them up if necessary. Harry has the surveillance camera."

"That is all understood. Thank you. Out," and he replaced the receiver.

The door handle to his room rattled and he turned, startled by the sudden noise. "Hello," he called, rushing across the room, but making sure he had his pistol tucked in the back of his waistband.

"Sir, it's Tammy Smith, the car's here."

"Password," he snapped authoritively.

"Roberts," replied the female voice, from outside. Satisfied the Operational Commander opened the room door and left the room to join his two, fellow officers. He'd just been told Peter Roberts had arranged transport for them, evidently he'd made arrangements for a *Fiat* Panda to be ready upon their arrival.

The car may have been a couple of hours late, the Operational Commander had wanted to clear this business up earlier, but at least it had arrived. Harry had the camera bag, with a Nikon camera in it – the camera had an extended lens, so it was good for these sorts of missions. "Are you both ready?" Ronan asked, not saying but meaning had they got their guns, and listening devices with them. Plus they were takiing the uniforms of three Russian soldiers with them, in case they were caught.

"We are sir," was the reply. They turned and walked back towards the elevator; one inside Miss Smith pressed the 'down' arrow, and the elevator descended to the ground floor. The three agents handed their keys in to the receptionist, and left the building.

Three of the nine *Proagnon* agents that had boarded the plane that would either end their lives or not, no-one knew. This was only a shuttle flight between JFK airport, in New York, and Newark airport; these three were employed as stewards, as the shuttle flights didn't have stewardesses on board Once on board the leader of the group, Kismet Andon placed their explosive device inside the toilet's cistern, and primed it. Satisfied he returned to the main cabin area to start the job of serving passengers with drinks, papers etc, along with his fellow agents.

The second group of three was again, employed as waiters on board the train that ran from Sacramento to Kansas City. Again once aboard the group leader, Arthur Manto, placed their explosive device, again, in one of the toilet cistern's, and primed it.

Finally, the third group, who were employed as firemen, boarded the USA's newest, oil carrying, supertanker, *Megatonia*, which was capable of carrying, at full capacity, 650 million tonnes of crude oil. The vessel would come to a halt and drop anchor in the Arabian Sea, and then small tugs would be deployed to traverse the Persian Gulf, they would collect about 1000 tonnes of oil, and then return and unload their cargo aboard the supertanker; this process would be slow but as the main vessel couldn't fit up the Gulf this was the only way to get round this. This groups leader, George Sanders, placed the group's explosive device in a locker, primed it, and then covered it with a dirty overall. The ship set out on its journey, retrieved a good percentage of the oil, and then resumed its journey homeward.

The aircraft filled with passengers on the return journey from work the evening the ship was due to dock. Passengers boarded the train from Sacramento on the journey to Kansas City. One of the journeys was ill-fated but which one?

In *Proagnon's* underground bunker Dr Q looked up, at his wall clock. It was nearly time; best give it a few more minutes, in case one was late, or slow moving. Squeeze and himself had devised this plan about four months back, measuring distances, comparing each vehicle's speed, thus enabling them to approximate the times as to where each of the three vehicles should be. If he detonated the device, whichever he chose, at the right time he could wipe out millions, well maybe not millions but it was a nice thought.

After the few minutes were up he got up and took the detonator from his office drawer, turned the dial and pressed the button on top. In the USA the bomb went off, and there was blackness.

CHAPTER 9

Casualties!

The tremendous explosion rocked the USA; the ball of fire that was created could be seen many miles away, citizens panicked thinking it was an earthquake of some sort, resulting in a fireball; this explosion was quickly followed by a great, black, mushroom cloud. The HART satellite, which was still in operation despite the deployment of the UAVs, captured the explosion as it happened and relayed the pictures back to headquarters, in Geneva. When the explosion occurred the satellite seemed to jump.

Once things had died down the caretaker President of the USA, Arnold Smee, was soon on the telephone, to call an emergency meeting of all the defense personnel. A fleet of Chevy Suburbans with Secret Service agents aboard, ferried the required men to Camp David; as soon as every minister, that was available, had arrived, and were sat down; two Secret Service agents remained by the door in case of an assassination attempt, Arnold looked around the table, at his ministers. "What the hell happened?" he demanded to know.

"It would appear, sir," replied a, new, junior minister, "that an explosive device was, somehow, concealed aboard the new *Megatonia*. As it was only carrying 600 million tonnes of oil, and travelling at a speed of only 18mph, I know that isn't fast but, what you have to remember is, it was an Ultra Large Crude Carrier (ULCC), it was new and don't forget if it had done the crash stop maneuver (from full ahead to full stop) that would've taken a further seven kilometres, and would've taken, approximately, 20 minutes. Therefore, I don't think, sir, even if we'd known, we'd have stood a chance, in hell, of preventing this."

"Thank you for explaining that which we already knew," thundered the man at the head of the table.

"You did ask, sir," shot back the minister.

"What I meant was has anyone got any ideas on how to deal with this? I shall, of course, be making a public announcement shortly, to try and reassure the American citizens."

"We could contact HART," replied another minister, Liam Reynolds, he was minister for foreign affairs. "This would seem to be an act of terrorism," several heads nodded.

"Contact HART," Arnold snapped, "it was them that involved us in the first place."

"Maybe so," said the other man, "but, if you think about it, they're the only, real, ones who can assist us."

"I will consider it, in fact that's what I'll probably end up doing. Thank you for coming gentlemen."

Arnold looked up at the Press Officer, as the men in the room filed out, who'd been hovering in the corner – nervously, "Tell the media I'm organising a press conference for two hours time."

"Right away sir," replied the man, walking to an ante-room in the far corner, which also served as his office, from which he could contact all the media companies: Fox, ABC, KBIA – a recent addition, CNN, Sky News, and the newspapers that were delivered to the citizens doors, or were able to purchase in shops.

The caretaker President was whisked away so make-up could be applied. His speechwriter came to him, as he was getting ready, "Sir, what exactly are you going to say?"

"I don't know yet, Graham, I'm just going to let it come from inside. Basically I'm going to say this has been a terrible blow, condemn such acts as those of cowards, I might rebuke HART for not acting quicker. Do we have the number of lives lost yet?"

"Over two thousand, sir, though we have no actual figure yet."

"That'll do," the Commander-in-Chief snapped at the press officer, while make-up artist, Mandy Simmons, finished applying the make-up for his television appearance.

"Okay, you say so Mr President," and the speechwriter left the room. The President, his hair was still, slightly, ruffled as he entered the conference room, and took his seat at the head of the table; the reporters and newscrews all fell silent. "Are we ready yet," the man demanded.

"Nearly sir," the cameramen responded, hooking the last cables up – there was only the CNN camera crew, but the other networks would take their footage from this network. "Right. We are live in five, four, three, two, one, zero," and the light above the lens went out.

"Fellow citizens," began the caretaker President. "As you cannot have failed to notice, an explosion took place earlier today completely destroying the new supertanker, the *Megatonia*, this new supertanker was on it's maiden voyage when it was destroyed, and it was carrying 600 million tonnes of crude oil from Saudi Arabia to harbour. From there it would've been taken to our refining rigs in Dallas. Unfortunately, the explosion, as big as it was, also killed many people; the estimate which was handed to me a few minutes ago, was in the region of two thousand," Arnold took a sip of water from a cup handed to him, by someone off screen.

"This event, we believe – after consultation with the interim government, was a covert operation and the work of the terrorist group *Proagnon*. Why they made this attack on the USA we cannot comprehend. Was it because we supplied military resources to the Human Alliance for the Retaliation against Terrorism (HART)? No one knows, or if they do they haven't told me yet. We, in the United States of America condemn terrorism, and will do everything to stamp it out."

"I feel the sorrow of all American people, when such events happen. As some of you, those who have worked with me – and those that still do, know my life has not been without sadness; I was a pickpocket in my, very, young days, my mother a beggar, and my father was a thief. Before I go on some of you may think I should not be in this job, but as you will hear I, quite suddenly, became a changed person. Anyway, one day my father and I were in a shop, he was carefully concealing items about his person whilst I was distracting the shop owner; when a man came in with a gun, and demanded all the money in the cash register."

"I hid, I was only small, down the end of a long aisle, and I watched as my father, being a brave man, tried to surprise the robber from behind. Sensing he was behind him the robber swung round and fired at point blank range; my father fell,

239

bursting the milk cartons he was hiding. The police arrived a few minutes later, as the cashier had sounded an alarm, and shot the robber after a shoot out. I resolved then not to become a thief like my father, and to give up pick pocketing."

"My mother, on the other hand, was frail and weak; when I got home from the shop, I ran as fast as I could, not daring to look back in case the robber had, suddenly, come to life again and was chasing me, I told my mother what had happened; she turned, deathly, white and simply collapsed – I started crying and willed her to get up again. When she did not get up after five, long, minutes, I ran to my father's friend's house and told him that my mother wouldn't get up. A look of concern crossed his face; and he hurried back with me; when we got there mother was still laid out on the floor, he checked her arm, and then her chest; when he turned back to face me it seemed like he had grown old, all of a sudden. What he said to me was, "I'm sorry Arnold, your mother's dead!""

"He took me back to his house that night That day is one I'll never forget. So, citizens, when you judge me don't judge me on what I once was and what I did, judge me on what I've become."

"Finally, I wish to say that some blame must rest on the commander of HART's shoulders. If he had not asked us to provide them with, certain, military vehicles and armaments we may not have been targeted. There again maybe we would anyway, who knows?"

"Thank you for listening and have a good night."

"Jumped up little turd," said Roberts angrily. "Trying to blame us; he offered that millitary, help."

"Yes, yes," Schaiffer said, he was standing behind his superior as they watched the broadcast, "but did you hear what he said about his background."

"I did," Peter replied testily, "how does that help us?"

"Next year's election year."

"And your point is?" replied the commander of HART.

"Think my dear Peter, think. This could benefit us because think back to 1998."

"I'm sorry I'm not up on politics."

"The Clinton scandal. He was found to be a liar over his affair with Monica Lewinsky, and he was impeached, but was still allowed to serve his, full, second term. Now, this one, Arnold Smee, okay he's only the caretaker President, who claimed he was always so upstanding; now we find out about his true beginnings on live television as well. It couldn't have been better timed."

"You're right Hans. Y'know, sometimes I could kiss you, but I won't," Roberts said, realisation finally dawning.

"Much appreciated sir," was the reply he got. Roberts then asked for a call to be put to through to the, main, switchboard of the Russian Kremlin; not many people had this number, just heads of different countries, and HART. "Which office do you require?" asked the female operator, she sounded too young to be in that job Roberts thought.

"President Krushkev's office please," replied Peter reasonably, but giving Hans a look that told him his commander thought this operator was absolutely useless.

"Just putting you through to his secretary," replied the operator, the line went, more or less, dead; about ten minutes later Peter was about to give up and replace the receiver, when another female voice, this one belonged to an older woman, said, "President Krushkev's office. What do you want?"

Even though the woman sounded a bit cross at being disturbed, well it was 10.30pm (local time) in Russia, only 9pm in Geneva; Peter asked, in a friendly tone, "Is President Krushkev available please?"

"I don't know," answered the voice bluntly. "I suppose you want me to find out?"

"If you would please," replied the commander of HART, still in a friendly voice even though he would have, gladly, throttled the Russian woman.

"Well, who are you, and what do you want of Mr Krushkev?"

"My name is Peter Roberts, I run an organisation called HART, and I wish to arrange a meeting with him." *Was this bloody necessary every time?*

"I will see what I can do," his secretary said, seeming to thaw a bit. "Please hang on." *What to?* Roberts thought.

After about thirty seconds a brusque, no nonsense, male voice came on the line, "Roberts! So you decide to call me. Don't you know what time it is? What's with this meeting?"

"Greetings President Krushkev," Roberts said, "I'm sorry for calling at this hour and not earlier; I hear someone tried to assassinate you, it was a good job they failed as Russia has never had such a finer President," he looked up at Dr Schaiffer, and his expression read *pity they didn't succeed.* "Anyway Mr President," he continued, "I would like one of my agents to meet with you if you would allow them to. Would that be a possibility sir, as he may have some information for you?"

"I see no reason why not," the Russian President said. "Just let me consult my diary – all Presidents and Ministers kept the diary – as did their secretaries," Roberts heard the rustling of pages, "what about Monday at 4pm?

"I think that should be fine sir, I will relay orders to him tomorrow, and thank you sir. Again, I'm sorry about the timing of this call."

"I look forward to meeting your agent," replied Krushkev bluntly, and put the receiver down.

Son of a bitch!, thought the commander of HART, but said nothing. "Well Hans, that was productive."

"It was sir," his number two answered. "And you never lost your temper once," he added, with a hint of sarcasm. It was then Peter realised that Dr Schaiffer had been analysing him on the phone; facial expressions and body language. Not that he minded, it was, after all, part of Dr Schaiffer's job.

Peter Roberts looked down at the forms, on his desk, and said, "We'd better get this paperwork filled in and up to date, and then we can send it to all the countries who have promised us help."

"Yes sir," replied Hans Schaiffer, and sat at his superior's desk. After the paperwork was finished he left to return to his own office.

In Saudi Arabia both Leon and Celia were in their beds, as were the rest of their troopers, after their 4,600km (2857 mile) journey; both had set up their command centre in the highlands of Al Hejaz, the mountain range that was in the north and ran alongside the western coast of Saudi Arabia.

The mountains in the nortern area, they knew, were between 600 and 900m tall (2,000 to 3,000ft), occasionally some of the mountains exceeded 2,000m (6,500ft). The rainfall, in this region, wasn't very frequent, but there were streams flowing down the west side of the highlands allowing for some limited agriculture in the surrounding valleys and, also, on the narrow coastal plain.

On the eastern slopes of these highlands were channels where prehistoric lava had flowed which had solidified to form vast barren fields of dark coloured broken basaltic stone that was known as harras. South of Al Hejaz the highlands countinued into the southern highland region known as Asir. The highlands in this region were more rugged and were higher than in its northern counterpart.

Many of the Asir highlands were between 1,500 and 2,000m tall (5,000 to 7,000ft). The highest point, in this region was known as Jabal Sawda, which was 3,207m (10,522ft) and was located near the border between the countries of Saudi Arabia and Yemen. The Asir region received more rainfall than the northern highlands; therefore, allowing for more widespread farming.

The HART soldiers, together with their Operational Commanders, had been exploring the southern region in the hope of finding a place for a secondary command centre; but decided that the mountains in this region were far too tall, and it would be easier for an enemy helicopter gunship, or jet, to pick them off; plus as they would need to light a fire, for cooking purposes and to keep them warm, the flames may be seen. Finally, there was the added danger that a farmer may spot them and mistake them for terrorists, that was one thing they didn't want. No, the Operational Commanders decided between themselves, they would stick to their, primary, command centre in the northern region of Al Hejaz.

However, once they had decided to have the main command centre in the northern region, and have no secondary command centre they needed to transport the 100 soldiers through Saudi Arabia; they could have gone a couple of ways; they could climb the mountains, but would risk been seen from the towns of Al Ta'if, and Makkah (Mecca); or they could go down to the south-west and hoped to scale the highlands in the south, then attempted to cross into the Al Hejaz region, but this way could prove extremely dangerous, plus they risked being seen from the towns of Nijran and Jizan. Finally, they could just throw caution to the wind, and cross through the centre of the country, although the centre was mainly desert and the weather could get extremely hot; and then there was the added danger of cutthroat thieves and the nomadic Bedouin tribes.

So it looked like either going through the towns where it may be less hot, or not; there again it could be a journey through the highland passes, in which they may lose a trooper or several, most of the men had removed their tunics as it was getting hot. Eventually, it was Leon who decided, as he had been to one of the nearby farms and came back driving a, large, cattle truck. As soon as he'd killed the engine he hopped out and said, to the amazed look on Celia's face, "I borrowed this from a farm back there. It would suit our purposes most adequately, I think." Next he added, "It's a bit smelly in the back, but, I think, twenty troopers can fit in the back, then I shall drive the cattle truck northwards along the highway, to the Al Hejaz region, deposit the soldiers and then return for the next twenty, and so on. Shall we try it?"

"Might as well," Celia replied. "I haven't got any better ideas." The tailgate was lowered and the men, and women, slowly, and hesitantly, climbed inside; the smell that hit them was terrible, "It's worse than one of your farts Jonesy."

"Shut up Glendel, my farts aren't this bad."

"Wanna bet," said Tommy Glendel, one of HART's explosive experts.

"Shut up you two and keep moving," ordered Celia, angry that they were arguing over a little smell. Leon had warned them.

"Yes boss," they replied, and walked further inside. More soldiers followed them into the back of the truuck. It was evident, by the smell, that the truck had never, thoroughly, been cleaned out, as they were still patches of mud, at least everyone hoped it was mud, on the floor.

When all of the twenty soldiers were in and seated, as best they could, Leon climbed in the driver's seat – the tailgate was closed and a sheet of, green, tarpaulin fell over the back, blocking anyone's view of the cargo, and Celia went round to the driver's window. "Take the rest of the soldiers," Commander Leon Bigship whispered to her, "into the lower region of the Aris region and wait there."

"Okay, will do," she answered then added, "you are free to depart." The truck grumbled into life and Leon drove it northwards, Celia smiled at his intuition as the rest of the HART personnel followed her into the scrubland and lower regions of the mountainous area. Luckily the area where they were had a good view of the road, so they could see the truck when it returned.

About an hour later the automobile did return; Leon drove it into a small valley that had mountains on both sides, "Next twenty," he called as the truck came to a halt. Celia selected the next twenty – she lowered the tailgate and they climbed aboard, again complaining of the smell.

Once they'd, all, settled down the female operations commander fastened the tailgate back in place, lowered the tarpaulin, then went to the driver's window; after a word the truck was off again, bouncing along the uneven roads. Several times the vehicle would hit potholes or bumps, which would result in a few choice words from his passengers, but Leon ignored them.

He drove the truck along the same route a further three times. The last time was a bit hairy though, as the cattle truck hit a pothole; Leon braked, but before he could regain control the vehicle started to slide towards a ditch.

As the vehicle slid ever nearer Celia reacted fast, "Engage the engine, full braking," she shouted at the other operations commander. She grabbed hold of the steering wheel and spun it to full lock. As Leon pressed the accelarator, right to the floor, they heard the rear wheels spinning, as they tried to regain purchase on the road.

Slowly, very slowly, the vehicle stopped sliding, and the truck lurched forward, then stopped, much to the annoyance of drivers of other traffic on the road. Leon restarted the cattle truck, and they carried on, northwards, to their destination, to join the other eighty soldiers, that had already been transported there. Once everyone was at the base of the mountains every soldier, together with the two Operational Commanders started to climb the rock face using any handholds they could find – luckily they'd all been trained well and none of them fell - and then they began to explore the network of caves in search of suitable sleeping quarters, and a suitable place to set up a central command centre, with none, or very little obstruction, of the TAC-SAT signal.

In Algeria, Africa, Lucy was observing the *Proagnon* encampment in Tunisia. Soldiers, mainly young ones, kept arriving by transport helicopters, mainly HINDs. Of the man she'd seen arrive, who seemed important, there was no sign. The HART soldiers, as well as herself, had also explored several other surrounding areas and had journeyed westwards once the vehicles arrived. They had discovered a narrow gorge running alongside the Atlas mountains. All of them felt it would make a good command post although Lucy feared it may interfere with some of the communications equipment they'd brought.

However, even she had to admit it looked an ideal place, and as the slope was only gradual it would also make an ideal storage place as well; and if need be there were caves and outcrops of rock along the lower levels. So all the vehicles that had been flown in, for the squad's use were driven into the valley; a squad of troops were left on guard duty, whilst the others bedded down, in the caves, for the night.

At the Rossiya hotel Sunday morning dawned reasonably warm, in fact it was a freak occasion in Russia; when the three agents had arrived Friday morning it had been raining, in the afternoon it had cleared up but was still cool, with a light breeze; Saturday had turned out to be similar weather to the previous afternoon.

The Operational Commander awoke to the warbling sound of the TAC-SAT phone, he picked up the receiver, "Commander Strobing."

Peter Roberts voice came through loud and clear, "Ronan, I have arranged for you to meet President Vladimir Krushkev, at the Kremlin's main building, at 4pm tomorrow. Take with you the Memory stick and, above all, don't forget. Is that understood?"

"Yes sir," came the, somewhat, sleepy reply.

"HART out," Peter said, and replaced the receiver. *Great,* thought commander Strobing, looking over at the clock which read 7.30. *I have to meet Krushkev tomorrow, and Peter informs me at 7.30 Sunday morning, when I'm trying to have a lie in.* Since he'd been disturbed he got up and proceeded to the bathroom, to get a shower; he still missed her, but perhaps it was for the best.

One person who wasn't having a lie in was Tammy Smith, who was a keen jogger; she had got up at 6am, dressed in jogging gear; shorts – she didn't mind the weather over here, trainer socks, together with her trainers, purple coloured T-shirt, her sweatband – an orange colour – around her head, plus her CD walkman so she had some music to listen to on her way round. Finally, she grabbed a water bottle, stuck it in her waistband, and took the elevator down to the lobby.

As Tammy exited the elevator she received many admiring glances from some of the, younger, Russian men, which she ignored as she walked out of the hotel.

Tammy started to jog, up the street, away from the Rossiya; building up a sweat she had to stop several times to drink from the water bottle; once it was empty she dropped it into one of the many bins that were dotted around the streets.

As she carried on pounding the streets of Moscow she came across a man out, walking his dog. *Strange,* Tammy thoughht, *It's only about 7.30,* plus the man was wearing sunglasses and a long raincoat, and for some reason he seemed to be carrying a water bottle. "Morning," she called upon reaching him; she stopped by him, the dog, a small spaniel, seemed very placid, as she rubbed its ears.

"Ah good morning to you," was the reply. "I see you are out early, enjoying the sunshine, got to keep the muscles going. Yes?"

"Oh yes," Tammy responded, thinking this man was just another friendly Russian, and therefore harmless. They were standing in the middle of a park and there weren't many people around, at that time in the morning, to hear him. Suddenly, the dog, who had been so friendly before, bit into Tammy's calves, and tried to jump up at her; the teeth were barred, and he was growling ferociously.

"Come away Trotski," the man called to the dog; Tammy's calves were bleeding, not profusely – just thin rivulets of blood. "I am sorry," the man said, unscrewing the water bottle.

"It's okay," replied agent Smith, "I haven't got far to go."

"Please let me help, in fact I insist," Trotski's owner said, emptying the water bottle on her lower legs. The water really stung; he, then, turned the bottle in his hand so Tammy could see the label. Even with her eyesight starting to fade, and her legs, those long muscular legs, starting to feel like jelly, she could make out the shapes of two letters on the bottle, VX – a nerve agent, which had been banned from use years ago, but traces of it still turned up now and then. Slowly her legs buckled under her and she collapsed; leaning over her the man felt for a pulse – first in the neck, then her wrist – there was none, she was dead! Smiling to himself he took the cellular phone out the inside pocket of his jaclet, and dialled a number, when it was answered he simply said, "Job done."

"Very good, your services may be called upon again."

"Understood," and he thumbed the 'end call' button. Whistling to himself he carried on walking his dog.

In Miranda's house, in Qom, Sergey was asleep, but awoke, quite suddenly, shivering; there was very little breeze so why was he cold; deciding to go and make himself a hot drink, and maybe watch another porn programme – if he felt like it - whilst the owner of the house was asleep, the Russian climbed out of bed, slipped some underwear and a T-shirt on, and then, stealthily made his way downstairs.

Reaching the bottom of the staircase he saw that the sitting room door was slightly ajar – that wasn't unusual; however, then he thought he saw a flicker of light through the gap. Assuming it was nothing the Russian walked into the kitchen, made himself a cup of tea, and then carried it into the sitting room; he was most surprised to see the owner of the house seated on the sofa, in fact he was so surprised he nearly dropped his drink, "Miranda," he stammered, "what are you doing here?" He noticed the volume, on the TV, was down low.

"Probably the same thing you are," she answered. "I felt a sudden cold feeling and started shivering; not wanting to disturb you I came down, made myself a hot drink, and then came in here to watch TV."

"When I turned the TV on I first lowered the volume – so as not to disturb you – then I flicked to one of the porn channels; just for something to watch."

"I see," Sergey said, sitting himself beside her; he noticed she was wearing her pink robe, as he looked closer he was, practically, certain she was wearing nothing underneath, was that accidental or on purpose? Did she, secretly, harbour feelings for her Russian house guest? He hoped not. Sipping at his drink he looked over at the TV screen.

The programme on screen ended, and the TV programme announcer – a scantily clad female – appeared on screen, and announced what the next programme would be; Sergey didn't take much notice of what she said, as he was having a drink of tea; the titles started and he looked up, the programme was called 'The Music Box of Delights', a simple title for a simple show; basically a music box was opened – and played a tune, plus there was a dancer, as found in many music boxes – the only difference was the dancer that was revealed was real.

"How can you watch this," muttered the Russian, "it makes a mockery of the female figure. It's totally obscene."

"It may be," replied Miss Ochas. "But I bet you wouldn't say 'No' if someone was to do that for you."

"Possibly not," murmured Sergey, maybe it was the way he'd been brought up in Russia. Before he could stop her

Miranda had turned the lights on, but turned them down 'low'; she switched the TV off and set up a CD player.

She moved into the middle of the room, "Are you ready?"

He looked toward the woman in the middle of the room, and realised, with a start, what she was up to; she was going to prove she was right, in her observation of him. He may object to that programme, but she was correct in what she had said to him. "Okay," Sergey replied reluctantly, thinking, and hoping, she was bluffing. However, he had the awful feeling she wasn't.

She pressed the remote control, in her hand, and the CD player lit up, Miss Ochas moved over toward a chair and flicked the remote control again, a whirring came from the machine. Miranda placed the remote control, quickly, on a chair and straightened back up; as the music started to play the Iranian woman undid the pink robe, and threw it to one side. Then she started to dance – this went on for about ten minutes, sometimes she would try and encourage the Russian to dance with her but he refused every time.

She stopped and slipped her robe back on, all through her dancing Sergey hadn't even cracked a smile – was his face set in stone or something? Miranda had expected some reaction, she didn't know what, but there had been nothing. She came back over to where he was sitting – to collect the empty cups – and she bent right over so he could see straight down the front of her robe, still there was nothing. She straightened up and walked out the room, calling after her, "Please turn the lights off when you come up."

"Will do," was the reply, and then came something Miranda wasn't expecting to hear. "Your dancing was very good."

"Thank you," she said. "I'll see you in the morning. Strangely Miss Ochas had developed feelings for her guest, and she, desperately, wanted to share a bed with him, but did he feel the same way?

Probably not, she decided, and continued on her journey to bed, after placing the cups in the kitchen sink.

Sergey could tell she had feelings for him, but if he got involved with her, now, it would compromise his mission; he might reconsider things differently afterwards, if the outcome of his mission was a successful one. Turning off the lights, in the sitting room, he went up to bed.

At *Proagnon* headquarters, Dr Q had watched as the ULCC supertanker, complete with it's 600 million tonnes of crude oil aboard, had smashed into America's southern coastal region, with the timing of the explosive device to explode when it did the supertanker had not only exploded but had killed thousands, and started an oil slick, the likes of which had never been seen before. Still, the clean-up was their problem, not his. Plus he had watched, with interest, their caretaker President's speech, about his background, and his condemning of HART. *Good*, the man thought, *if this goes on no-one will trust HART*.

He had also received a call on the STU-9 informing him that their agent, in Russia, had managed to eliminate one of the HART group. He was going to try and eliminate a second member after, the contact had told him, his meeting with President Krushkev.

It also seemed that the training camp, in Tunisia – in Africa, monitored by Abdul Singh, was running smoothly, as he had heard no reports to the contrary.

He summoned *Squeeze* to his office; once she was sitting on the opposite side of his desk her leader brought her up to date with everything that had occurred. "Everything goes well, don't you think?"

"It does sir," his second in command replied. Then she asked him, "But what has happened to our naval forces from Russia, and our fighters from China?"

"I do not know," he responded honestly, "I shall chase them up." He produced a second STU-9 and punched a number into it; several seconds later, though it seemed like a lifetime the receiver was picked up.

"Yes," said Mikhail Suvorov's strong Russia voice, heavily accented.

"Dr Quantum, of Quantum Exhibitions. When will the other sea vessels be with us?"

"No-one, from my ministry, has inormed you. The submarines were scrapped a week ago. The Admiral *Kuznetsov* aircraft carrier, however, is still operational but is undergoing

251

massive repairs as her, main, reactor has been damaged; I don't know when these repairs will be finished as the new reactor is being specially built in Alaska. Once the reactor is installed we will send it"

Dr Q thundered down the phone, "So we get no submarines, no-one did inform us, so therefore, we are not very happy. Get better trained staff," and he slammed the receiver down. Turning to Squeeze he said, "Now we try China."

He picked up the receiver, again, dialled a different number and waited patiently. "Why does nothing run smoothly?"

Before she could answer him someone must have answered, as he said, "This is Dr Quantum of Quantum Ehibitions. What has happened to the air fighters we ordered a few weeks back?"

"Regrettably I have to inform you that many fighters have been destroyed, in conflicts, plus we have needed to completely rebuild most of our fleet of SU-27s due to a fault in the fuel tanks. As soon as they are ready we shall deploy them to you."

"Thank you," replied Dr Q evenly. He replaced the receiver and turned to face Squeeze. "Bloody Russian fools, scrapping the submarines. Still, some of them have provided good service for us. Our agent, over there, has managed to dispose of one of the three HART operatives, and is, hopefully, going to try to dispose of another after he has met with their President Vladimir Krushkev."

"That is good news sir," responded Squeeze. "Now I have been in contact with agent Singh, he reports that one of the look-outs, at the training camp, spotted a Chinook helicopter flying in the day Abdul arrived, then a second one, or it could've been the same one, flying in the next day and distributing several large shapes. Even though he wasn't close enough he recognised the Chinook's twin turbine engines; the objects that were dropped the next day, he assumed, were vehicles. Yet no action was taken."

"It may only be a reconnaissance mission. Order them to take no action, yet."

"Will do sir. Are there any further orders?"

"Not as yet," responded her superior. "You are dismissed for now, but please keep me informed of progress." Squeeze left the office thinking, if she'd been in command she would have ordered an all out attack on this reconnaissance mission. It was clear, to her anyway, that it was more than a reconnaisance mission.

Well Dr Q knew best didn't he? Or was it time for a change of leadership? She knew Abdul Singh was plotting to lead a revolt against him; Abdul hadn't told her but she had her spies.

In Russia none of the team that had been deployed, Ronan Strobing and Harry Danto, had noticed their companion's absence. They just put it down to, either she'd taken a different route – which was longer, or Tammy'd met a man and gone off with him, however she knew she was meant to stick within the team, as much as possible.

After he'd had breakfast, in the restaurant, Harry returned to his room, and switched the TV on; then he went to the bathroom – to get himself ready for the day's happenings – but left the TV on, it was tuned to one of Moscow's numerous news channels, some were legal whilst others were not – though if the police closed down one illegal channel another would soon start broadcasting in its place, when he heard a news headline, Woman's body found in local park, and rushed back into the bedroom to see the broadcast in its entirety.

"About half an hour ago a young woman's body was discovered in a park near to the Rossiya hotel; police say that it looked as though she'd been out jogging, and had fallen foul of one of the city's many street hoodlums, who killed her for whatever reason. Strangely enough, the only marks found on the body were, what look like, teethmarks around the lower legs. She had nothing on her to identify her."

Harry looked at the pictures rolling by, of the grim discovery, and knew, straightaway, that it was Tammy Smith; evidently someone wanted them all dead. Immediately that set alarm bells ringing, in his head. Would Ronan be safe in his meeting with the Russian President? Or was the young Russian HART agent simply worrying unnecessarily?

He switched the TV off and resumed in his preparations for the day ahead; he'd liked Tammy, even fancied her at one point, who was doing this and why? It had to have some connection to *Proagnon* but who knew they were in Russia? Peter Roberts, Dr Hans Schaiffer, and Gwyneth Jones; was one of them a traitor? No, he couldn't even possibly contemplate that thought.

His preparations complete, he left room 257 and walked down the hallway to room 255, where he knocked on the door, the usual three times, "Ronan, it's me, Harry, let me in."

"Password."

"Jones, Harry said, and the door was opened to admit him. The HART password for all agents, on foreign soil, changed every day; it was usually one of their headquarters staff's surnames, but occasionally it would be a piece of equipment they used, or had with them.

Harry almost flew inside the room, "Did you see it? Did you see it? Did you see it?" he asked rapidly.

"Calm down. Did I see what?" Ronan asked. It was then that agent Danto saw the towel wrapped around his Operational Commander's lower region, Harry realised Ronan had just got out the shower.

"I'm sorry sir, I didn't know you weren't dressed," the young HART agent apologised, "I'll go if you want."

"Bollocks! You'll stay right there and tell me what this is about, I'll dress when you've gone." The Operational Commander then went over and sat opposite the young agent, crossing his legs in case Harry got any funny ideas about him.

"Well sir, I'd just gone into the bathroom, to have a quick wash etc, leaving the TV on; it was tuned to one of the Russian news channels, when a news item came on – it was the headline that caught my attention."

"Which was," Ronan prompted.

Woman's body found in local park," agent Danto replied. "I wouldn't have given it much thought except for the fact Tammy's not been in contact with us for a couple of hours; I'm assuming you haven't heard from her."

"No, no I haven't," the Operational Commander replied.

"Anyway, I dashed back into the bedroom to watch the item. I watched, and listened to the full item, and it turns out it was our fellow agent. According to the report she was killed by a street hoodlum, but I think she was targeted. Now I am worried about your meeting with President Krushkev; should I come in with you to give added protection? Or do you think I am worrying unnecessarily?"

"Just drive me there," replied Mr Strobing, "and escort me to the entry doors. However, I do appreciate your concern."

"One other thing commander," said Harry, "I think someone in HART may be a traitor; as only three people knew we were coming here: the commander, the doctor, and, our receptionist."

"Even if someone is targeting us, and assuming your theory about a traitor is right I am in charge of this mission, and I, still, fully intend to meet Krushkev." With that Ronan got up from his seat, and walked back to the bathroom, "You can see yourself out," he was annoyed, not by the mission, but by this young fool and the influence this had had on him.

"Understood sir," agent Harry Danto said, and followed his commander, for this mission, along the corridor towards the door. Somehow Ronan must have stepped on the towel, as it suddenly fell in a heap on the floor, and Harry was greeted to a rear view of his commander.

"Wait," Mr Strobing said as he pulled the towel back up. "And don't you dare tell anyone about this"

"No sir, of course not sir," the younger man assured his immediate superior. "I'll meet you in the hotel lobby when you come down," Ronan nodded and Harry left to make his way towards the elevator. Once inside he chuckled to himself, uncontrollably; he'd seen a different side to his commander, when they returned to barracks, in Geneva, he'd waste no time in telling the rest of his fellow soldiers what he'd witnessed. That's if they got back to Geneva.

The elevator arrived, in the lobby, and Harry got out and sat in an unoccupied chair; was it his imagination or was the man seated opposite, in raincoat and sunglasses watching him? Plus why, if he was, did the Russian have sunglasses on? There was a layer of snow on the ground, as there'd been a heavy snowfall during the night. Agent Danto decided he'd never understand Russians and their behaviour. He'd, maybe, been away too long.

Harry Danto had been born in 1990, hence he was 22, in one of the outskirts of St. Petersburg, in Russia, and in fact not a million miles away; he was one of three sons to his mother and father. His mother was a shop assistant, while his father had been an office worker; his brothers, as far as he knew, were both junior office clerks, and they were both a bit younger; Yusef was 20, whilst Igor was 17.

He was still smiling to himself about the unfortunate incident that had happened upstairs; he knew Yusef was gay, but what he did, behind closed doors, was of no interest to the other two brothers, plus however Yusef chose to live his life was of no concern anymore. Harry was starting to feel more than a little unnerved by this man; he was certain now the other man was watching him but why?

Taking the initiative Harry spoke to the man, "Excuse me sir, may I ask why you seem to be staring at me?"

"I'm sorry for staring," muttered the Russian. "I thought I knew you." At that moment commander Strobing came into the lobby, carrying a briefcase, and said to his subordinate, "Come along Harry, I tthought we were visiting the Moscow 'Revolution' Musuem today until my meeting with Krushkev."

"We are sir, sorry sir, I'll just fetch the car," and he scampered away towards the entrance foyer. Ronan had brought this young agent, as he had felt if the man came on this mission he might mature. Evidently, this was not the case; the sooner Harry was removed from his squad the better.

The man in the sunglasses got up, out his chair, and ambled off in the same direction as agent Danto; he was probably a tramp, of some sort, who had come in out of the cold, Ronan thought, but if he was where were his belongings? Then it struck him, of course, they'd be at the Hermitage, a hostel a few streets away. There had been a bit of trouble there a few years ago, but that had been resolved.

From the doorway Harry summoned his superior to the, blue, Fiat Panda;, discarding the magazine he was looking at commander Strobing stood up, straightened his suit, and walked towards the hotel entrance.

In Africa, the squad led by Lucy Lang were making preparations for their commander-in-chief's arrival. Although he wasn't due for another couple of days they wanted to get things ready and properly set up. They made a landing strip, to the south of the Atlas mountains, for the BlackHawk helicopter that would be carrying both Commander Peter Roberts and Dr Hans Schaiffer.

In the Al Hejaz mountain range there was not that much to do, at the moment, for the HART soldiers, or their commanders; but they were both sure the action would soon hot up, the only thing that was hot, at the moment, was the weather, therefore every male soldier was stripped to the waist.

The female soldiers, there were only a couple beside Operational Commander Celia Most, wore shorter cut trousers and were allowed to undo the top couple of buttons on their tunic; thus earning them a few admiring glances, as well as a few whistles, from their male counterparts.

In Russia, though, the time was approaching for Ronan Strobing's meeting with the president. Harry was still trying to convince his commander to let him go along, but the Operational Commander still refused, once back in the Fiat after their tour of the museum, it was so large it had taken them five hours to get round, Ronan checked, in his briefcase, that he had everything he'd need. Memory stick, laptop, some papers, and, of course, his trusty Beretta 92 – it was fully loaded – just in case of trouble.

The car was driven through the streets and admitted, after the two agents had shown their passes, into the Kremlin courtyard. Ronan, before he went inside, transferred his pistol into a shoulder holster he was wearing. He was escorted to the doors by Harry but went inside alone, much to agent Danto's displeasure, who returned and waited in the little Fiat. About an hour and a half later Ronan appeared at the entrance doors, totally unharmed; the younger agent went to meet him, "What happened sir?"

"I'll tell you back at the hotel," growled the commander. "Let's go."

"Right-o sir," Harry replied, walking behind his commander. Although there was snow about, it was reasonably sunny. A glint of light, like light reflecting off glass, caught agent Danto's eye, and he looked up. There, on top of one of the buildings, was, what looked like, the shape of a man with something in his hands.

With the sudden realisation of what the man shape was holding, a sniper rifle, the younger agent shouted, "Down sir." Just for good measure he gave his superior a push forward, just as the barrel flashed, and the shot rang out.

"What the hell do you think you're up to agent Danto?" When no reply came back Ronan, slowly, turned round; the young man was laid on the ground, staring sightlessly upward, a small hole in his forehead the evidence he'd been shot, blood started to smear his face. Ronan felt for a pulse, there was none; he started weeping as Kremlin guards came running up.

Okay, the man had been a pain in the ass, most of the time, but given the right training he would've made a good agent; yet his life had been cut tragically short; so now three were down to one. "Thank you Harry, and God Bless You," the commander said as he closed Harry's, now, sightless eyes.

"Are you okay sir?" asked the chief guard coming to a halt by the two men. "Did you see what happened?"

"I'm okay," answered Ronan, tearfully, "this man isn't though. As for what happened, I would've thought it was obvious, someone went and bloody shot at us." He didn't wait for a response, just got up made his way to the Fiat. He was angry that the security seemed to have been downgraded.

"Wait a minute sir," called the chief guard; Ronan ignored him, got into the little blue car and tore off. As the car skidded to a halt outside the Rossiya, the remaining HART member got out, slammed the door, and handed the keys to a doorman, saying, "See to it," indicating the car.

As they were standing there came an explosion - from underneath – which blew the car apart. "I guess you won't be needing these anymore," Ronan said, taking the keys back from the startled doorman. He walked off and threw the keys in the Moskva river. "There," he said as he returned. "No keys, no car, no problem."

He walked past the, astonished, looks on the faces of the two doormen; went inside and up to his room, to report the deaths of his two comrades to HART headquarters.

At HART headquarters, next day, Peter Roberts and Dr Hans Schaiffer boarded the UH-60L BlackHawk helicopter; the aircraft would fly them to the northern area of Africa.

Once its passengers were aboard, and strapped in, the BlackHawk's pilot started the aircraft's two General Electric T700-GE-701C free turbine turboshaft engines, each one was situated either side of the helicopter's fuselage, and its four bladed rotor, together with the four bladed tail rotor started turning; once the machine had built up speed the pilot and co-pilot pulled back on their collective colums, and the UH-60L rose into the air.

Unlike the Chinook transport helicopter, which had been used to transport the squad of HART soldiers, and then their vehicles, to this area, the Black Hawk could reach the destination on a single tank of fuel, whereas the other helicopter had needed refuelling twice.

The helicopter passed over the Meditarranean Sea and over the northern coast of Africa. The pilots saw that a landing strip had been prepared for the smaller helicopter, The BlackHawk maneuvered into position, and switched its landing lights on. To avoid detection the lights had been dimmed, right down. The two pilots lowered the aircraft, slowly and carefully, in its vertical landing maneuver. Once the UH-60L was on the ground, and the engines had stopped, its two passengers got out.

"Welcome commander, Dr Schaiffer," said Miss Lang, in her American accent.

"Thank you," Peter replied, "this *Proagnon* training camp you've found, where is it?" The commander, Lucy knew, had always been, and still was, a man of action. Probably a result of his military background.

"It is just over the border, in Tunisia. As you know, sir, some more soldiers arrived a few nights ago in a HIND D class helicopter, along with another man who seemed very important."

Roberts was immediately more interested, at that piece of news, "What did he look like? Can you remember?"

Lucy thought back, and then responded, "He was dressed in similar clothing, but his uniform may have been a slightly different colour from the others. I think he had a helmet on, but hadn't any covering over his nose and mouth. He may have been of Middle-Eastern origin with a thin, pencil like, moustache. However, sir, you must remember I had my NVS on, so some details may be wrong."

"Even if they are wrong you did well. We shall organise a raiding party in the morning, and once we are fully prepared and ready we shall go and attack them. Now we must all get fully rested." Peter found a comfortable spot, well as comfortable as possible, produced his sleeping bag, unfurled it, and climbed in. Every soldier followed suit, some didn't have, or like, the comodity of sleeping bags, and curled up on the bare earth underneath them, yet they all had small, one man, tents.

Next day, after breakfast, if you could call it that, Peter Roberts called all the soldiers together, along with their Operational Commander, and said to them, "Right let's get suited and booted," all the HART soldiers, plus their Operational Commander, and their overall commander, dressed in their jungle warfare uniforms, these were of green with black patches; they then rubbed into their faces some green and black make-up to help disguise them further. The soldiers, all 50 of them, selected an M14, M15 or M-16 to use in the attack, as did their Operational Commander. Peter Roberts, as they knew, preferred his Beretta 92 pistol, as did Ronan. Lucy Lang took an M-16, plus she had her Beretta 9000 on her, as well.

Roberts instructed Dr Schaiffer to stay behind, with the pilots, as it was felt he was irreplaceable, on the medical side. Although Schaiffer would have liked to have gone, he knew his superior was right.

As soon as everyone was ready the, overall, commander led them out to the M1097 HMMWV, which was a soft top troop carrier; it was slightly larger than a normal troop carrier carrying two crew, and eight personnel and/or equipment/materials. It also had amphibious capabilities and could ford hard bottom water crossings up to 30 inches deep without a deep water fording kit and up to 60 inches with the kit. The vehicle could also be used, a variation – the M1035 – as an ambulance. Both vehicles would be attending; the ambulance in case of casualties.

"Sir," said Miss Lang, hurriedly. "Don't you think we should go on foot to be quieter, element of surprise and all that."

"Maybe you're right," he conceeded. "Everyone, follow your Operational Commander and follow everything she does. These vehicles, however, will attend, in case we require their assistance." The American woman moved off, trying to keep as silent as she could; her troops following in her wake, the equipment and whatever else they would need were loaded aboard the M1097 and Roberts climbed in the passenger seat. Once an hour had passed – the time allowed to get there – the M1035 and the M1097 started their V8, 6.2 litre diesel, engines, engaged the turbo-hydramatic transmission and moved off into the jungle.

The HART soldiers, together with their two commanders; Dr Schaiffer had been ordered by Peter Roberts to stay behind, if they needed medical assistance he would be contacted, moved off – crawling along flat where they had to – and walking, albeit in a crouch, where it was safe. After a good two hours crawling and crouching they reached the rocky outcrop that overlooked the camp. "There it is sir," Lucy whispered.

"Yes, very impressive, you've done good work," was the whispered reply. "Now how do we get down there without being detected?"

"We could just go for an all out attack sir."

"And lose the element of surprise, I don't think so Miss Lang."

"If it's of any help," said Lucy, "there are only the four guards on patrol, and they rotate every two hours – regular as clockwork; so what about launching the attack as the new guards are coming on duty?"

"It may work," replied her commander, he fingered his communicator and twisted the dial to general. "All ttroops, be ready to follow us in."

"Acknowledged," they each replied.

"Are they all wearing armour?" Peter asked Lucy.

"Of course sir," Lucy assured her commander.

They waited, watching, as the guards continued their shift, "Come on," murmured Peter, impatiently; at last the guards started their final patrol of the perimeter – a sign their shift was almost over. As they moved out of eyesight, on the far side of the perimeter Roberts bellowed, "Attack!"

Every soldier, and both commanders, rushed down the slope, firing indiscriminately. The guards were taken by surprise and cut down immediately; Roberts, followed by Lucy, ran to the main building's doors – they were only made out of wood – and Roberts, easily kicked them in; by this time the HART personnel had regrouped, and were waiting for their next targets. They didn't have to wait long, as soon as the commander kicked the doors in they started shooting at the startled *Proagnon* soldiers, who were immediately slaughtered. Once the shooting battle was over Roberts looked around at the fallen enemy soldiers and carried on down the main corridor, the HART soldiers following him.

More enemy troops appeared from the side corridors, left and right, and again another shooting fight started. The M-14s, -15s, and -16s rattled off volleys of cartridges into the air; in response the Russian made AK-47s, some fitted with silencers to prevent 'jumping', when the AK-47s without silencers fired their barrels seemed to 'jump' slightly upwards, and left, thus the silencers prevented this.

The weapons fired and a fierce firefight ensued, many soldiers on both sides were killed; twenty of the HART troopers were killed before every enemy troop was dead, it was a total bloodbath.

The men, those that were left, started to explore corridor after corridor, the place was huge. Suddenly, a man, the man Lucy had described as best she could appeared at the head of one of the corridor. "So you must be the great HART leader, Mr Peter Roberts."

"I am, yes, and just who the hell are you?"

"My name, before I kill you, is Abdul Singh – I am *Proagnon's* third in command." The man was of Iranian descent, Peter judged – well Middle-Eastern anyway - as Lucy had told him.

Peter looked Abdul in the eye,."You won't kill me," he said confidently, "all the men here are dead, and if you even do so much as approach me, my troops have orders to kill you." As if to reiterate what their leader had said the men, and Lucy, cocked their weapons in readiness. Quick as a flash Abdul produced a, small, handgun – about as big as his palm, and fired; "Fire," shouted Lucy, as their commander fell, every soldier fired but, mysteriously, Abdul Singh had disappeared.

Lucy knelt by her fallen leader, blood was coming from a wound to his shoulder, "Sir, can you here me?"

"Of course I can bloody hear you," Roberts stormed, as much as was possible. "Get Dr Schaiffer here, now!"

The Operational Commander, quickly, turned her communicator dial to Dr Schaiffer's frequency, "Dr Schaiffer," she called hurriedly. "The raid was a success but the commander is wounded."

"I'll be there as quick as I can," the doctor replied. "In the meantime keep him warm, and try to stem the flow of blood. Out."

Miss Lang turned to one of her soldiers, "Contact headquarters, tell them what's happened, and to send a *Gulfstream* with stretcher capabilities. Now!"

"Right you are ma'am," replied the soldier, he was only young, taking the TAC-SAT phone and hurrying outside. About five to ten minutes later he returned. "Headquarters informed and they will send a *Gulfstream* G-650 as soon as possible."

Dr Schaiffer arrived a few minutes later, carrying his medical kit; together with him were two other medical corpsmen carrying a stretcher between them, the medical men dismissed any offerings of help.

"Now let's see the wound," said the, head, medical man, pushing the Operational Commander aside. Lucy could see he had other things on his mind. "Not a particularly bad wound," he announced. "It will need cleaning out, the bullet removing, and strapping up after I've knitted it back together. Then Peter will have to rest the arm. Peter is, at this moment, even though it is only a minor shoulder injury, in hypovolemic shock due to blood loss, and this may result in disfigurement of some sort, or maybe a permanent disabiity."

"Unfortunately, the equipment I need is in the medical wing at headquarters," he finished.

"Shouldn't we get him there then?" asked a, now, frightened Lucy, trying to be patient.

"Of course," said the doctor, as if that thought hadn't occurred to him. "Corpsmen," he called, "get him loaded aboard." The corpsmen, looking bored, suddenly sprang into life at the sound of their immediate superior's voice; hastily they rolled Commander Roberts onto the stretcher, and carried the stretcher, and its occupant, outside to the ambulance.

Whilst they were doing this Miss Lang said to Hans Schaiffer, "I have contacted headquarters, well one of my men did, and requested a *Gulfstream* jet. A G-650 is being sent, but I would advise you send up flares – to let them know our position." Dr Schaiffer reassured her that he would.

They corpsmen loaded the stretcher aboard the M792 version of the HMMWV and once they were all aboard, the three men and their patient; the truck shot off – back to the encampment, and, hopefully, to rendezvous with the G-650. However, until the jet touched down Dr Schaiffer would take good care of the commnder, Lucy thought and hoped.

"Out," she called back to the troops, and they started on their two hour trek back to their encampment. Would the doctor go back on the G-650, or would he travel back on the BlackHawk.

The jet landed, at the encampment, signalled by flares, and the three men, with their commander, boarded the jet, and once refuelled, it took off again for the 1,100 mile journey back – as it was flying at a speed of 500mph it would manage the journey in, roughly, two hours and twelve minutes.

After he had reported the deaths of agents Harry Danto and Tammy Smith, Ronan Strobing lay on the bed, in his hotel room, and just stared at the ceiling, *Why?* He kept asking himself. *Was Harry right and there is a traitor among the HART personnel? If so will I ever get out of here alive?*

He was brought back to reality by the noise of the phone ringing; leaning over Ronan answered it, "Hello."

"Hello sir, this is reception, we have a gentleman down here – says he's your comrade, he has authentic ID – may we send him up?"

A comrade of mine but who? The Operational Commander wondered. He was intending to refuse, but instead he was curious so said, "Send him up."

"Right you are sir," replied the receptionist, and then replaced the receiver. As he heard the click Ronan replaced his receiver.

Still wondering, in puzzlement as to who this, mystery, person was he stood behind the door, and waited. Luckily he didn't have to wait long until there was a knock on his door. "Password," he demanded.

"Roberts," was the response. Although the password changed from day to day, the commander's surname could act as the password, even when it wasn't the password for that day. Ronan, unsure now, slowly, placed his hand on the door knob, and began to turn it; finally it clicked open, and began to open the door.

"Who are you?" he enquired of the man at the door. Hadn't he seen this man before, dressed in raincoat and sunglasses? Yes, he had been the man Ronan thought was a tramp, evidently he wasn't.

"I am here to kill you," the other man replied, slowly, withdrawing a knife from his inside pocket; suddenly the man leapt forward, pushing Ronan back, suddenly the man leant forward, lunging with the knife. Commander Strobing kicked out, knocking the man up and over him, and onto the, cold, marble floor; the Russian recovered quickly and lunged at the HART Operational Commander again; this time the knife connected with Ronan Strobing's left shin, and blood started to pour onto the white marble floor.

There was only one way out, he realised, he had to get to the balcony and cross to next door, or further, if he could. It was risky though, but stil he had to try and do something. Concentrating his weight, on his right leg, he lashed out, as best he could with his left, and then ran, as best he could, to the balcony area. He looked from his balcony to the next, he didn't want to risk damaging his leg too badly, if possible.

He looked back inside, his attacker was recovering and looking round for his prey. Finally spotting him on the balcony the attacker ran outside and pushed Ronan backwards; Ronan was bent, backwards, over the railings, one good shove might take him over. Summoning all the strength he could Ronan grabbed his attacker's wrist, squeezed and twisted it; thankfully the knife fell harmlessly below.

The Russian loosened his grip, smiling Ronan said, "Ready to give up?"

The assassin just gave a grunt, walked away, then turned, and cannoned into the HART agent. Both men were thrown over the edge.

CHAPTER 10

More deaths and casualties!

Ronan Strobing, the Operational Commander and remaining HART member in Russia, along with his attacker, fell through the air – both of them twisting and turning in each other's grip trying to shake the other off. As his attacker's grip slackened, albeit a little; Ronan, suddenly brought his, good, knee up and managed to knee the assassin between his legs. The Russian howled in pain and let go; taking his chance the Operational Commander pushed him back and away with his good leg, and then spotting the hotel awning below that led from the hotel outside to the pool area he dived for it. Knowing that it wouldn't be strong enough to hold his weight he just hoped that when he crashed through there would be someone underneath, even if there weren't it would break his fall. He wasn't bothered what happened to his attacker, well he was in a way, but the man had tried to kill him and nearly succeeded.

He crashed through the striped awning; luckily there was someone underneath, three people in fact – a group of three Russian women who had just stepped outside, "Oof," they said as one, as his body landed on them – knocking them all to the floor. They also muttered some incoherent words at him, he knew they were cursing him.

"Sorry to drop in unannounced," murmured the HART agent apologetically, "I was just passing and thought I'd drop in." Ronan thought adding a bit of humour might lighten the situation, but the three others obviously didn't share his sense of humour as not one laughed, or even attempted to.

The four people then disentangled themselves, as they were doing so they heard another loud *plop* and looked in the direction of the other sound. They all caught a brief glimpse of another body, possibly a man's, crashing into the hotel's empty swimming pool.

"Are you ok?" asked the elder of the three women pleasantly, as pleasantly as she could under the circumstances.

"I'm fine," he replied, smiling warmly at her. "It seems I owe you three ladies my thanks, at least you broke my fall."

Then one of the younger woman spotted the blood coming from his ankle; immediately the elder snapped at the other two, "Maria! Olga! Help him inside!"

"Yes Rula," the other two answered, sheepishly and helped the HART agent up, onto his feet, and supported him on either side.

"That looks nasty," said the one the others had referred to as Rula. "You need medical treatment. Take him to the medical department, I shall be there shortly."

Evidently the three ladies belonged to the hotel's medical staff, Ronan hadn't seen them around before.

Maria and Olga supported Ronan as they made their way through the hotel, and then into a side department, *This must be the medical wing*, he thought. He was led over to one of the two beds and placed on it face up, and then the two Russian women left the room.

After a few minutes; all three walked back into the room; all were wearing nursing type uniforms, but Rula appeared to be wearing a doctor's coat, over her uniform, as well. As they approached him he saw one of the younger ones appeared to be carrying a tray of medical instruments, together with, about, five rolls of bandage.

Rula produced a syringe, full of liquid, from the tray, and then rolled the HART agent's trouser leg up, his left one, to his knee. "Now this won't hurt a bit," she assured him; then selecting a part of the lower leg she pushed the needle in and depressed the plunger.

"Ow," he said, as the needle broke the skin. His lower leg felt strange, as if it was now a, dead, lump of meat. "What have you done to me?"

"It's a local anaesthetic," one of the younger ones replied. "Whilst we assess your wound and see if we can do anything, so kindly be quiet and let us get on with our job."

"Sorry," the Operational Commander muttered, in way of an apology.

Rula, along with the others, examined the wound, "Iodine and water," she said to one of the others. Once the iodine and water had been brought to her she cleaned the wound, and then put some iodine on it. "Stitching material," she called and the stitching material was brought to the doctor. "I am going to put you three stitches in here, to knit the wound closed, and then one of us will bandage it for you. Afterwards there is some paperwork we need to fill in."

"That is fine by me," he announced and she started her work. When they'd finished patching him up Operational Commander Ronan Strobing asked, "Would one of you ladies go and see what happened to my attacker?"

"Certainly," replied one of the younger Russians, and looked to her superior for permission. Permission was granted, and the younger nurse, Olga, left the room; whilst she was away the other nurse, Maria, bandaged Ronan's foot, under the guidance of Rula. When Maria had finished Rula pulled up a chair opposite the HART agent, together with a clipboard and a sheaf of papers, then started asking him questions such as name, age, date of birth, next of kin, address etc.

Olga, then, returned; a sad look on her face. "How is he?" Ronan Strobing asked her, but he guessed, from the look on her face, that the answer would be in the negative.

"He's dead," she answered with grim finality. "From the look of it, he must have caught his head on the side of the pool, thus cutting his forehead open; there's a nasty gash on the forehead, plus there is a great deal of blood surrounding his body, though he may have been dead before he ended up in the pool."

Rula then finished her questioning, and told Ronan he was free to go, but warned him not to put too much pressure on his left leg yet. He assured her he wouldn't but resolved to have Dr Schaiffer, or one of the medical team, look at his wound once he returned to headquarters.

The *Gulfstream* jet carrying Dr Schaffer, the two medical corpsmen, together with their patient, who was laid on the stretcher, touched down, in the HART compound, after about one hour fifty minutes. As soon as the plane had stopped and the doors open Dr Hans Schaffer hurried across the compound, and into the large building that served as HART

269

headquarters; the medical facilities were, situated, at the rear of the building.

The two corpsmen just looked at each other in puzzlement, as to where the doctor had gone. A few moments passed, and then several medical orderlies arrived at the foot of the G-650's staircase, pushing a gurney; the stretcher was, carefully, placed on the gurney, then the men who'd arrived with it pushed it back towards the building that housed the medical facilities, the corpsmen following, to see if they could offer any assistance.

Peter Roberts was taken on the stretcher inside where Dr Schaffer and a group of medics were waiting to perform the minor surgery that would be needed. At a nod from the doctor the commander was wheeled into surgery.

Dr Q silently fumed after the call he had received, he called Squeeze in again. "Our Russian agent, Alexi Yeltsin, is dead – after attempting to kill a HART agent; the other agents that travelled with the one I just mentioned, he eliminated those – one he poisoned with VX, the other he shot in the head."

"A pity," Squeeze murmured. "He was a useful assassin."

"He was that, plus that bastard Vladimir Krushkev has, now, had our other agents in Russia, Oleg Ayanseikov and Mikhail Suvorov arrested, for crimes against the Motherland."

"It is a pity Alexi did not manage to eliminate Krushkev, when he shot at him."

"Yes, a most unfortunate accident, but that's the way things go. Now tell me, what news on the new recruits, at the training camp?" Now, he saw, Squeeze visibly cringed. "What is it?" he demanded, banging his, black, gloved fist on the desk that separated them.

"Well sir," she began, "we had contact with Abdul Singh about five hours ago. Apparently members of HART launched a surprise attack on the camp this morning."

"And how did our, new, soldiers do?" he enquired.

"That's just it, sir, they're all dead. Abdul managed to escape, and is, even now, on his way back to Iran, to see his cousin Miranda Ochas, in Qom."

"Well, I'm glad he survived," roared her superior. "He is useful and still could be."

"You know he plots to overthrow you, and become leader himself."

"I know he does," replied the *Proagnon* leader, with contempt in his voice. "I will deal with him when I am good and ready. Now go." She left his office, still wondering if Dr Q was still fit to lead *Proagnon*, or should she side with agent Singh? Even if he did overthrow Dr Q would he still want her as a member of *Proagnon*? With these thoughts, going round in her head, she walked away and down the main corridor, passing other soldiers on the way.

In China, a group of four SU-27SK, single seat, jet fighter aircraft were now lifting off from their base in Shangpang, to the east of the country. The pilots had their orders which had been relayed to them by their commander, Colonel Wong Tan, in turn these had been relayed to him by contact, via encrypted email, with Dr Q. The jets were to travel to the mountains of Saudi Arabia, and search for signs of any intruders, as reports had reached Dr Q that there were strangers in the mountain area.

Also leaving the base in Shangpang squadrons of four J-8 Jianjihi-8, four J-11 (SU-27 Flankers), and four MiG-21 – J-7 Fishbed aircraft. However, instead of following the SU-27s the pilots of these fighter aircraft had orders to fly directly to the *Proagnon* underground bunker. All had maximum speeds in excess of 1,000mph, all had one crew member (as was usual in fighter aircraft) and all three could carry various weaponry including nuclear bombs.

The SU-27's were travelling at 1,555mph, and the distance, from their base to their destination was about 3110 miles so the planes should cover the distance in about 2 hours. When they reached the mountain region the jets circled round the area, and then the lead pilot, Sergeant San Nomuri, ordered fighters three and four to circle the southern mountain area, whilst fighter two, piloted by Seiko Chan, and himself circled the northern mountain region.

Seiko Chan dropped his plane low so he could see more, on the ground. Suddenly, he saw a brief flash; he wasn't sure what it was – maybe the sun catching something on the mountainside – so he ignored it, after all there were farmers in the area. Then he saw it flash again, and with it some movement – so he dived a bit lower to get a better look; there! – a group of soldiers, well people in some sort of uniform were shooting at something; the pilot radioed his leader, who in turn radioed the other pilots, and the fighters regrouped, ready for the attack!

The HART soldiers, on the ground, thought these military jets – Chinese SU-27's by the looks of the design – were just on a routine training mission, but there seemed to be something wrong with the way they were flying, plus why were their air-to-air missiles fully armed? Quite suddenly, the four jets throttled up – powered by their Russian made Lyulka-Satum AL-31F turbofan engines – and hurtled towards the northern mountain region of Al Hejaz; the first jet loosed off it's R-27 (AA-10 Alamo) missiles, these flew straight and true, into the mountains, smashing the rock face and causing rockslides. Plus the explosion threw up dust clouds and loose rocks.

The animals, who had been grazing, on the mountains panicked and ran, but the whole area was sliding away so it was unfortunate that many were killed; many of the rocks rolled down the mountainside and fell on many of the HART soldiers, burying them alive. Others were picked off using the SU-27SK's single barrel 30mm (GSh-301) cannon – which could fire up to 150 rounds. Once every fighter had made its pass and attacked the area, 75 of the original 100 HART troops lay dead, or mortally wounded.

As soon as it became clear of the jet fighter's intentions Leon and Celia had huddled in the back of a cave, hopefully they wouldn't get blocked in, and contacted HART headquarters, on the TAC-SAT phone and informed them of the situation, and requested backup by a squadron of F-16 Falcons.

The F-16s, or Falcons as they were known, were built by General Dynamics, and had been launched in 1978, whereas the Su-27s were first launched in 1992 by the Chinese, Peoples Liberation Army and Air Force (PLAAF), but designed by the Sukhoi Design Bereau. Both jet fighters were similar in look, and design; however, the F-16s had afterburners as well, which made them slightly faster as the jets could travel up to 915mph at sea level, whereas its counterpart could only fly 870mph; at altitude the SU-27 managed to outclass its rival, being able to fly at 1,555mph compared to the F-16s 1,500mph. The two planes outclassed each other in different areas as well.

In the armaments the Falcon definitely had the upper hand, having 6 AIM-9 Sidewinder air to air missiles, 6 ATGM-65 Maverick air to ground missiles, 4 AGM-119 Penguin anti ship missiles, a series of general purpose and laser guided bombs, a 20mm M61 Vulcan gatling gun – which was capable of firing 511 rounds, plus a couple of 70mm CRV7 rockets. The missiles on the F-16 could be varied, to suit its task.

The SU-27s, on the other hand were equipped, on combat missions, with the Vympel R-73 (AA-11 Archer) IR-homing short range air to air missiles – this coupled with the aircraft's RLPK-27 helmet mounted sights (HMS) the missile posed a very serious threat to any other fighter in close air combat. For further, or beyond visual range (BVR), combat the fighter was equipped with R-27 (AA-10 Alamo) semi active radar homing medium range air to air missiles, in both long and short variant, along with the fixed GSh 30mm cannon.

In a typical interception mission, the aircraft could carry four R-73 and six R-27 missiles. Alternatively, the aircraft could carry two R-73 missiles, six R-27 missiles, and two KNIRTI SPS-171/L005 Sorbtsiya active jamming electronic countermeasures (ECM) pods on the wing-tips for self-defence.

The squad of four HART Falcons arrived in less than an hour to provide air support. Detecting their enemy below them using the AN/APG-78 Active Electronically Scanned Array (AESA) radar, which had been fitted in all F-16s. "Looks like we have bandits at six o' clock, follow me in lads," the squad leader, Sergeant Winters, called over the radio. "Follow me in."

The lead F-16 dived downward to engage the enemy. Over the radio he heard, "Two, Three, Four;" a sign that the rest of the pilots were itching for a fight, and were following his lead.

What the pilots of the HART fighters didn't know was they had already been detected by the enemy's NIP Tikhomirov N001E Myech coherent pulse Doppler radar, again standard in all SU-27s, which were, or had been, in service with the PLAAF.

The Chinese jets turned to face their attackers and the lead pilots of both groups of planes were looking straight at each other; both groups were now, suddenly, unsure of what to do next. Sergeant Winters voice came over the Falcons radio again, "I know you may be worried, slightly intimidated, and eager to get this over with, just don't fire until they fire on us."

The lead enemy jet fired off a Vympel missile, which homed-in, using the technology of the HMS system; the R-73, even though the Falcon tried to avoid it, slammed into the undercarriage – throwing the jet in a spin. Sergeant Winters managed to loose off one of his own Sidewinder missiles, which homed in on the heat signature of the SU-27, and struck the lead enemy jet in the fuel tank and the plane exploded.

Sergeant Winters was struggling to get his jet back under control; meanwhile, seeing one of their prey was wounded, the other three SU-27s began to close in; the other three F-16s moved in to provide defensive cover for their comrade. Not knowing who was friend or foe Sergeant Winters decided to abandon his jet, he hit the ejection button and let his plane travel on – his parachute unfurling as he descended to the ground - an SU-27 moved in for a closer inspection – too close – the two fighters collided and exploded, now it was three to two. The Falcons pressed forward, trying to intimidate the enemy; but they weren't intimidated – even with the loss of their leader.

Suddenly the sky was filled with a mixture of missiles, both from the SU-27s and the F-16s; the HART troops, below couldn't believe the firefight that was happening above them. Slowly, the remaining two enemy jets exploded, courtesy of the heat seeking Sidewinder missiles, thus ending the air battle. Sergeant Winters had been retrieved, by then, and was now sitting in the encampment; watching the fight, along with the others. When he saw the enemy jets despatched by his men he punched the air with his fist and shouted, "That's my boys!" The remaining HART jets dipped and raised their nosecones, as if in a bow, and then turned and lit up their afterburners, and headed back westwards towards base.

Abdul Singh arrived back at *Mehrabad* Airport, just outside Tehran; passing through the airport, he was travelling light as usual – no luggage, however, he did have a knife secreted in his sock – just in case, but it wasn't visible. He found a taxi and gave the driver directions to his cousin's house in Qom.

What he wasn't aware of was the fact that the Russian man he'd left in the USA, Sergey Satov, was now staying with his cousin; she knew nothing of her cousin's activities – she knew he was involved in an organisation of some sort, but Miranda didn't know Abdul worked for *Proagnon*, if she had she would've probably disowned him.

Sergey had spent about a week with Miss Miranda Ochas, getting to know her and the surrounding area. During his days the Russian had noticed Miranda slept in a double bed in one bedroom, whilst he had been in a single bed in another room. Thinking nothing of it at first he hadn't seen anything strange in it; later on, during his stay, he had queried the lady about it, and been told that her cousin, a wealthy businessman, occasionally stayed with her.

Now the Russian was running a bit low on money so he had three choices. He could go out and start stealing again. He could just kill Miranda Ochas and make it look like an accident but too many people had seen him entering and leaving the premises so may link her Russian guest to the crime or he could just carry on staying with her but pay her in a different way, which was probably what she wanted, however he didn't like to think about that.

Even though he admitted, to himself, he enjoyed her company; and he knew she had feelings for him, it had become obvious to him Sergey could never reciprocate these feelings. His dislike for these Iranian creatures, particularly the one who'd left him in the hands of America's Federal Bereau of

Investigation, ran too deep for him to start softening to them now. Even after the dance Miranda had done the other morning he still felt nothing for her.

Sergey decided; he looked across the room at the woman and said to her, "As much as I enjoy your company Miranda, and my stay here, I feel it is time I moved on."

"Are you sure I can't persuade you to stay, my rates are very reasonable." She smiled teasingly at him, trying to gauge a reaction in his face, but there was none.

"Alas no, and I am sorry, but I do think it is time I left; however, many thanks for your kind hospitality."

"If you need anywhere to stay, in this area, again, my door is always open – although I get plenty of guests, mostly men but some women – can't understand why."

I bet you can't, he thought to himself, but the Russian knew she was really trying to get him to change his mind. However, Sergey was adamant he was going to leave; so Miranda led him to the door, and showed him out. As the Russian stood on the street, deciding which way he should go a taxi pulled up.

Inside the taxi Abdul Singh looked through the windshield, he could see a tall man standing outside his cousin's house. Although the man was turned away from him Abdul had the distinct impression he knew the man, for whatever reason.

The taxi driver turned in his seat and told the Iranian how much he required in payment. "Just one moment," Abdul responded and reached down, as if reaching into his pocket for some money. In reality, he reached into his boot and, slowly, extracted the knife; then quietly he moved over so he was sitting, in the seat, directly behind the driver.

"C'mon mate, I ain't got all day."

"Sorry," muttered his passenger. Abdul drew the knife back, and then thrust his arm forward, pushing the implement of death through the canvas back of the seat and straight into the driver's back; the driver grunted, in surprise, and then became still. The Iranian man, after extracting his knife and replacing it in his boot, shuffled back across the rear seat. It was at this moment that Sergey half turned to register the continuing engine noise of the vehicle; for one of the few times, in his life, Abdul felt fear, as he recognised the man, standing on the pavement, as none other than the Russian Sergey Satov. How had the man escaped the American law enforcement authorities?

Sergey, meanwhile, hadn't noticed that the taxi was carrying, his former friend and comrade, Abdul Singh.; he just turned back to the way he'd been facing when the vehicle pulled up, and walked away up the street, pushing past anyone who got in his way.

Once he was out of sight Abdul climbed out of the taxi, and walked inside his cousin's house, "Miranda," he called.

"Right here dearest cousin," she replied, coming out of the kitchen, and kissing him, warmly, on the cheek. "I've missed you."

He returned her kiss, and then announced, "I'm just going upstairs to freshen up. I'll be down soon." Inside he was still seething that she should let his, he presumed now, enemy into her house, maybe into her bed; still that could wait until he returned downstairs, to avail her with news of how well his business empire was doing.

Smiling at the thought of how easily he could fool his own cousin Abdul ascended the staircase, upon reaching the step the Russian had repaired, he could feel the difference compared to the other steps – it felt much firmer and steadier, definitely a job done by a man.

Reaching the top he headed, immediately, for the bathroom, Abdul entered and firstly used the toilet; once that was done he crossed to the sink, washed his hands, and then produced the knife he'd used to kill the driver of the taxi. The blade was covered in blood – so closing the bathroom door, and locking it, he didn't want any, unexpected, visitors – he cleaned the blade, as best he could, and then replaced it in his boot.

Leaving the bathroom he crossed to the bedroom, recently vacated by Sergey, and took his boots off; then placed them in the wardrobe; replacing them with an, almost, identical pair he left the room and descended the staircase. Reaching the bottom he saw his cousin, in the sitting room, seated on the green sofa. Strobe lighting was flickering across her face so, he assumed, she must have the television on; plus she was drinking a glass of, what looked like, wine – normally neither of them drank alcohol.

He strode into the room and sat beside her. "What are you doing?"

"Just having a drink and watching TV," she replied, and then asked, "why?"

"Neither of us drink that 'filth'," he indicated the alcohol she was drinking, but the way he said filth shocked Miranda – it was as though she had committed a crime. "Anyway, why are you drinking it?" he demanded, "And watching this 'filth'," indicating the TV, his cousin had it tuned to, yet, another porn channel. "All Western filth," he stormed at her. Miranda was shocked, this was most unlike her cousin; what had happened to change him in this way?

"My last guest, Sergey his name was, appreciated this filth, as you call it, and he appreciated me."

"I know what your last guest was called as I used to work with him. Now he is my greatest rival; did he ask about me Miranda? Answer me girl!"

"He said he was looking for you, but I told him I knew nothing of you. I think he went to Tehran, to meet someone, so he said; later on I found him watching some news about the Iranian police finding a Korean man's body, in one of Tehran's parks; when I asked him about it he said that the man was a friend of his."

"However," Miranda continued, "judging by the look he gave me I think, no I know, he was the one who killed that man."

"That wouldn't surprise me," Abdul responded, laying back into the sofa. "Sergey is totally ruthless, he gets rid of business rivals any way he can, even if it means killing them. I'm sure that's what he would have done to me if you had told him you were related to me, but luckily you said you weren't."

Miranda got up to switch the TV off completely, "As you say Western filth," then she returned to sit beside him. "Now dear cousin, tell me, is your business empire doing well?"

"Reasonably well," he replied. "As you may or may not know recently we opened a complex in northern Africa –

Tunisia to be exact. Anyway we had to close it down, suddenly, as it was discovered that one of our rivals – a firm called *Wacho* – had infiltrated our premises, and planted agents amongst my staff."

"A pity," said his cousin, "still there will be other complexes. Soon we will have the money to leave this horrible place." Abdul said nothing.

At HART headquarters the four Operational Commanders had returned. One by Airbus, the other three by military helicopter, the vehicles had been transported back, as well. They were now, crowded round Commander Roberts, who lay there, apparently unconscious. "Don't worry," Dr Schaffer said, striding into the room, "I have given him a mild sedative. The operation to remove the bullet was completely successful; however, we had to act fast – before he went into full trauma. Ronan, as I cannot take charge myself, you will have to act as commander, for the duration."

"Thank you doctor," replied now Commander Strobing, again, squeezing Lucy's hand. "He will be okay, won't he?"

"Of course," said Dr Schaffer, brusquely, and then hurried from the room, and back to his office; he had a phone call, or two, to make, on his private line.

He dialled the first number and when someone answered at the other end he said, into the handset, simply, They are all here." He replaced the phone, and then picked it up again and dialled the second number. This time when the receiver, at the other end, was picked up he said one word, "Activate."

In Dr Q's office the head of *Proagnon* replaced the receiver and smiled to himself; the news was excellent – it was a pity those, damned, fools in Russia had let themselves be caught so easily. Still he couldn't expect everything to go smoothly, even terrorism had its ups and downs.

As he was walking Sergey wondered whether he should take a train eastwards, or one south eastwards. If he took the train going east it would run parallel with the northern Elburz Mountain region, and pass through or by Tehran and

Emamrud, eventually the train would terminate at Mashhad; then he would need to find alternate transport into Afghanistan, and across to Kabul airport, and hope to book himself on a flight to his homeland of Russia. It would be a long journey so he decided against it.

If he took the train south eastwards, again it would be a long journey, the train would run parallel to the western Zagros Mountains, and pass through Kashan, Yazd, Kerman, and Bom, stopping at each station, to let passengers off or on, a distance of 1050 kilometres (653 miles).

The main passenger train would terminate at Bom as well, although there was a connecting train that would travel the further 350 kilometres (218 miles) to the town of Zahedan. This town was near the border with Pakistan, finally he would take another passenger train to the capital of that country, Karachi, was another 1500 kilometres (532 miles), on the way the train would make stops at Nushki, Sibi, Sikkir and Hydrebad; altogether Sergey would be travelling a distance of 2230 kilometres (1385 miles), maybe more, maybe less. Then, again, he would book himself on a flight to his homeland of Russia.

He had decided now that, at least this way, he could come back from Russia, anytime, to deal with Mr Singh. At this time if Sergey found him he may be surrounded by *Proagnon* troops, and the Russian would be killed instantly. Sergey may choose to stay with Miss Ochas again, if he was low on money or couldn't find anywhere else.

Sergey arrived at the station and purchased a ticket; he then tried to avoid the people around him, and keep to himself – as much as he could; though several people tried to engage him in conversation although he refused to acknowledge them.

The train he was due to be travelling on arrived and pulled into the station, the passenger carriages were a mixture of open carriage as the weather was quite humid, plus closed in carriages for people who preferred to stay out of the humid air.

Sergey boarded an open carriage with many other people, as he didn't mind the humid air: a mother, father and their eight children – they were all of Middle Eastern, origin, the children ranged in age from a newly born baby to a teenage girl, who could only have been one of the daughters. The father happened to notice Sergey looking at his eldest daughter – she could've been no older than thirteen, and said to the Russian; "You like my daughter, you have my daughter."

The Russian man was startled by this response, and wasn't exactly sure what the other man meant at first, but all became, more, apparent when the girl started unbuttoning her top, "No," replied Sergey, the girl stopped; then looking directly at the father Sergey asked, "do you treat all your daughters as whores?" He looked, there were four girls, the youngest only looked two, the next looked seven, the third looked eleven, whilst he had already guessed the eldest was thirteen. There were three boys, the youngest looked three, whilst the eldest looked seven; the baby, Sergey wasn't sure of the sex.

"It is the only way we can get money; we are a very poor family sir," the father replied, "occasionally I have to use my sons as well, to get money, or my wife." Sergey couldn't believe his ears, using the whole of his family as whores or, as they were known, rent boys as a way of getting money; this made the Russian feel sick. Plus he'd mentioned that he sometimes used his wife, therefore was he the father of all of the children?

He knew from his childhood teachings Iran was a reasonably wealthy country but where was the money going? Plus were the family from Iran? Putting these thoughts aside, for the moment, he settled back in the, uncomfortable and bare, wooden seating.

The newest addition to the Middle Eastern family started to cry, for some reason; his mother, who looked thin and was dressed only in rags, picked him up, and uncovered her left breast. Breast feeding on a public train whatever next? Sergey wondered; surely even Middle Eastern countries had some law against this, but as he didn't know the laws he had no choice but to put up with it.

After several hours, Sergey had to keep going inside the next carriage if he got too hot, the train terminated at Bom and passengers started to get off. Sergey got up, from his seat, and filed after them, he fully intended to board the connecting train to Zahedan. As he boarded he saw the family, who had travelled with him, occupying an adjacent, again, open air carriage.

The train pulled away, on its 200 mile journey. However, at the speed the train was going; he reckoned, no one had told him as he was a foreigner, the train was travelling at 50mph – so he would be travelling for yet another four hours, and that was minimum. Another four hours with these losers, he might go mad.

Sergey had noticed the father of the children – if indeed he was the father of them all, his wife called him Ashwin, kept standing up whenever another man came in, whispering something to them and pointing at his daughter; some nodded while some shook their heads, and then he would sit back down. The Russian could guess what was going on, he was offering his daughter to each of the men; thank God Sergey wouldn't witness what went on.

At the International School of Geneva, which taught over 3000 children – these included some in infant, primary and secondary schools; the schools were spread in three locations: La Chataignarie and the Campus de Mies, the Grande Boissiere and Pregny-Rigot. Students could take advantage of a French and English education, and then they could choose to pass the Swiss Maturity, the International baccalaureat; the French baccalaureat; the British, International General Certificate of Secondary Education (IGCSE) or the American high school degree.

Group 7A were out learning the history of the Palace of Nations; which had hosted the United Nations when it had first been set up. Now the United Nations had its main building in New York this building was now, mainly, used for teaching purposes.

They were told that the League of Nations was established in 1919, following the devastation caused by the First World War. Once this League of Nations had been formed it was decided a building was required at par with the League's aspirations for the creation of a more stable world. So it was that in 1926 an international competition was organised.

However, the jury of architects, who were assigned to review the 377 projects that were submitted, could not make any final decision as to the award. Construction began on the building in 1929 and eventually finished nine years later – the five architects for this project were Messrs Broggi (Italy), Flegenheimer (Switzerland), Lefevre (France), Nenot (France) and Vago (Hungary). Initial layout included four areas: The Secretariat, the Council, the Assemblies and the Library; the interior design had been contributed to largely by the Member States.

The building served as the headquarters of the League of Nations until the dissolution of the League in 1946; due to suspension caused by the Second World War; in 1945 the United Nations officially succeeded the League of Nations, following the ratification of the charter of the UN on 24th October that year.

The Palace's assets were then *transferred* to the United Nations Organisation, in New York; however the Palace remained as the UN's European Office and was the main complex in this region of the world, despite several requests to knock the building down and renovate it, in 2010.

During it's time the Palace had two extensions added on. In the early 1950s when three floors were added to the K building and the D building was built, to, temporarily, accommodate staff of the World Health Organisation (WHO), pending the construction of their headquarters on Avenue Appia. In the late 60s, early 70s, with the construction of the E building, it was still commonly referred to as the 'New Building'. This building, designed by a team of five architects, led by Eugene Beaudoin of France; was meant to host the headquarters of the United Nations Conference on Trade and Development, and to meet the growing need for conference facilities.

The overall complex was 600 metres long, with 34 conference rooms and 2,800 offices, making it the second largest United Nations centre after the UN's Headquarters in New York.

The complex was situated in the, magnificent, 45 hectare Ariana Park, among the majestic trees were several monuments including: *The Celestial Sphere*, donated by the United States in 1939, *The Conquest of Space*, which was donated in 1971 by the Union Soviet Socialist Republics, and *The Great Centaur*, a gift, in 1997, from the Russian Federation. Many other monuments could also be found, in the grounds, including gifts from Member States and private artists, a flag could also be found in the grounds as well as many artworks inside.

Ariana Park was bequeathed to the City of Geneva by the Revillod de Rive family's last descendant; who then made the land available to the UN for its offices, for as long as the UN existed. One of the only conditions of the bequest was that peacocks should still be allowed to roam freely about the grounds, therefore it wasn't unusual to see peacocks dancing in full splendour in the Palace grounds. The park also contained what remained of a 1668 chalet brought from the Guyere district to Geneva for the national fair in 1896. The park was situated on the right side of Geneva; and had an outstanding view of Lake Geneva.

There was also a spectacular view of the Alps from the building, and on a clear day Mont Blanc could clearly be seen. Finally, the grounds housed three nineteenth century villas: Villa la Fenetre, Villa la Bocage and Villa la Pelouse, dating from 1820, 1823 and 1853 respectively; these had originally been private residences. Thee Villa la Penettre was now the official residence of the Director General of the Geneva offices, whilst the other two were used as office space.

As the thirty students and one tutor along with the three assistant tutors left the building after thanking the receptionist for allowing them to look round the building as well as sit in at a UN discussion, and proceeded on the journey back to secondary school in the Grande Boisserie and Pregny-Rigot region. Suddenly a group of armed blue uniformed men seemed to appear. Several of the students panicked and tried to run back in the direction they'd come from; however, the men raised their, Russian built, AK-47 machine guns, and just fired indiscriminately into the group.

The lead tutor, backed up by the assistant tutors, stepped in front of the children, mainly 14 year olds, trying to offer protection; but they were, simply, cut down by the bullets from the guns. The students screamed as they were shot and the bloodied bodies fell, the remainder ran in all directions to try and escape the killers shots; one of the children was left behind though, a young looking girl in a wheelchair.

The men stared at her, and she stared back at them. "What's the matter? Never seen a person in a wheelchair before?" she demanded angrily.

"Erm no," one of the *Proagnon* men simply replied, he seemed to be the leader. "We have now though;" he raised his assault rifle as if preparing to shoot her.

"Are you going to shoot me, as you did the others?"

An evil and cruel smile crossed the leader's face, as he had a sudden thought, "Not just yet, the men could do with a bit of fun first," and he produced an evil looking knife.

Suddenly his radio, attached to the left upper chest area squawked, "Sniper one, I've got the group of remaining children in sight."

"Eliminate them, eliminate them all!" the leader announced with a harsh, cold, tone in his voice. Several shots rang out as sniper one did his duty. "Any survivors?" the leader said into his radio once the noise had died away.

"About fifteen," was the reply, slightly distorted as it came through the radio, but quite understandable.

The man who seemed to be the leader, a youngish man, then pressed a button on his radio and spoke into it, "Group one to Base one, we request air support at coordinates seven-degrees-twelve-inches North by five-degrees-twenty-inches East; the target is a group of about fifteen children. Seek, locate, destroy!"

"Request acknowledged, Base one out."

"Group one out," the young man said. Then he turned his attention to the young girl in the wheelchair, she was dressed for the wintry conditions. The sniper, also dressed in the same, or similar, uniform to his comrades appeared, carrying his SIG SSG550 sniper rifle in one hand, whilst in the other he dragged, pulled, along a male child.

"Caught this one hiding in the trees probably thinking, if he stayed there till nightfall he could escape." *The leader, surely he wasn't that bad was he?* wondered the girl, who was called Irene. She would find out she was, very, wrong soon enough. The group leader ordered the sniper to tie the boy to a tree, but make sure he could see everything that was about to happen.

Irene had been paralysed in a car accident many years ago – at the tender age of six – and had been in a wheelchair ever since; plus as her father's car had been hit the door, nearest her had buckled, and the force had more or less crushed her left arm. Since then she had learnt to adapt to various situations; it had been hard for a start, but gradually things had become easier. Her parents had been lifesavers in those early days, and the three tutor assistants, who had been with them, had been employed by the school, not primarily to look after her, but as long as they were there she had felt relatively safe.

Now they were gone, massacred by these butchers, whoever they were. Soon there would only her friend Jean and her left. The young man advanced towards her – there was nothing anyone could do to help the remaining two children now; she could cry for help but would anyone hear? Anyway, what was their fate to be? Then a roar came from overhead, the unmistakeable sound of a helicopter; looking up they all saw the helicopter, a HIND D class, pass over the tops of the trees. A few minutes later and they, all, heard the rattle of machine gun fire, followed by screams; and then came a huge explosion. A squawk came over the radio, "Mission accomplished;" and the HIND flew away The leader smiled.

The young leader was almost standing in front of her wheelchair now; he smiled at her, an evil smile, he then placed an arm under each of hers, and lifted her, bodily, forward and out of the chair. Knowing she was helpless he lay her, thin, form on the ground and ordered someone to destroy her chair. A, burly, man stepped forward and pushed the chair into the undergrowth; he threw a grenade in afterwards – after three seconds it exploded.

"Into line, all of you," the group leader ordered, standing in front of the helpless form before him; cutting her clothes off he laughed at the pale, unclothed, girl, writhing on the ground before him. He unbuckled his trousers and forced himself on her, she screamed loudly.

"No!" shouted Jean at the soldiers, "leave her alone!"

"Shut up, we will deal with you shortly," called one of the soldiers. Jean was forced to watch as each of the men took their turn and forced themselves upon his, helpless, friend. Once they had all taken two turns the lead soldier, he was called Felix, kicked the girl's body – there was no reaction, he slapped her – still nothing.

"I reckon she's dead boss," called the burly man. Felix picked the body up - she felt so light – and carried her to some bushes, away from his colleagues. After a few moments came the sound of machine gun fire; the bastard had, evidently, murdered her. *Why? Why was life like this?* Jean wondered. *What had Irene ever done to these men?*

The soldier, who was in charge of the group, returned and looked over at Jean. "Now what shall we do with you?"

"Do what you want," the boy replied angrily, "you've murdered my friends, so you might as well get on with it and kill me."

The soldier thought, "No, I want you to suffer, and die slowly," and he stalked over to the boy, and produced the knife again. The weapon had a curved blade and looked very sharp indeed. "Now, he said, patting Jean's trousers, "I think I know the best way to kill you."

"Go ahead," the boy said, thinking Felix was bluffing, ""you're going to kill me anyway."

"So much defiance in someone so young." The soldier, then, pulled Jean's trousers and underwear down; the other men laughed at what was exposed, it was so small – unlike their own. In one quick, and fluent, movement the other man brought his knife down, and cut it off.

Jean screamed and cried out but no one took any notice. He looked down, as best he could, blood was pouring down his legs; "Help me," he begged the other *Proagnon* soldiers.

"Move out," ordered their leader, the men just looked at Jean as they filed past, but none stopped to help the fourteen year old. They just shook their heads and one by one left the wooded area.

"Help me!" he shouted again, at the top of his voice, but no one came to the schoolboy's aid.

In one of Geneva's shopping malls – the Centre Balexert – located at Ave: Louis-Casai 27 (27 Louis-Casai avenue) four, undercover, HART agents were doing the weekly shopping required for the HART compound. Now, thanks to the bigger budgets they could buy more foodstuffs etc. Afterwards the two men and two women were hoping to watch a movie; after all they were in the largest and best shopping malls, in Geneva, with over 110 stores, including designer outlets, grocery stores and a movie theatre. It was a pity they didn't have more time, the ladies in the group would have, gladly, explored the designer outlets, plus the clothes shops, all day.

However, that was not to be; at around 14.20 the four personnel – they always carried their pistols, just in case – heard the sounds of shouts, screams and gunfire. Rushing out of the shop they were in, a general food shop, and to the top of the escalators, but keeping as well hidden as they could, each of the four – Roger Diamond, Cecil Parkinson, Theresa Robins and Liz Butler, carefully, peered out from their, respective, hiding places. They looked down and saw a group of several armed men, in blue uniforms, evidently from *Proagnon* as they seemed militarily trained, firing their AK-47s into a crowd of, innocent, shoppers. Roger Diamond lifted his eyes from the massacre occurring on the ground floor, looking at his colleagues he silently mouthed, "Let's do it!" The other three gave him the thumbs up to show they were ready, and moved back into the nearest shop.

Sidling over to the cashier Liz asked in a whisper, "Is there a back staircase to the ground floor?"

"Why yes," replied the cashier whispering. "From here turn left and you should reach a, round, balcony area. On the right of this area are four staircases. They lead down and round to the back area."

"Thank you ma'am," Roger whispered to her. "Everyone ready?"

The rest of the personnel nodded, and then drew their, trusty, Beretta pistols; then walked, calmly, out the shop, ignoring the, startled, looks on other customer's faces, those who hadn't been killed yet. The security guard, on duty, he was oblivious to what was happening below. "HART," announced the team leader, flashing his pass at the man, he nodded and radioed ahead, to make sure no one would obstruct the team's progress. The four personnel walked down one of the staircases and peered, carefully, at the terrorists. There were seven of them, one was laying out some wire attached to a, large, box; evidently they were planning to kill as many people as possible, and then they would destroy the mall.

Cecil raised his pistol, and, accidentally, pulled the trigger; the gun went off. "You fool," Roger said angrily, as the terrorists saw the HART personnel. The men, from *Proagnon*, raised their AK-47s, and let off a volley of shots killing more shoppers and wounding others; there was blood and bodies everywhere. The HART people moved around the columns that were scattered around, trying to find a good place to shoot from. As Roger watched three of the *Proagnon* men went down, *Was one of the others firing on his own men?* None of the undercover HART personnel had fired a single shot yet. *Or had the others been a bit trigger happy and fired too soon?* Whatever the reason it had brought the odds down to four all.

Roger was watching Theresa through his peripheral vision, all the soldiers were trained to use all aspects of their vision, suddenly she took a chance and rolled from the column she was behind, paused halfway and fired at the terrorists – she saw one fall, but before he fell he managed to fire at her – the bullets missed her by inches. Then she curled herself back up and carried on rolling to stand behind him, "You stupid fool!" he reprimanded her, "You could've been killed."

"I know darling," she said, silkily, "but I wasn't." The man she'd shot wasn't dead, just wounded. "I think you'll find that puts the odds more in our favour."

"I'll agree there," he admitted. "Okay people," he called to the *Proagnon* soldiers and shouted, "let's take this nice and easy. Surrender now and you won't be harmed."

"Never you pig!" Felix shouted back. "You want us, you can come and bloody well get us," and then he shot another shopper to prove his point. Roger weighed the odds up in his mind, an all out attack would result in more bloodshed, and, maybe, a total massacre; whereas waiting might result in the same conclusion.

Taking a chance the team leader, seeing there were very few shoppers about now, shouted, "Okay, have it your way," he signalled to the other members of the team to follow his lead, and then rolled forward, stood up and fired his weapon. The 9mm cartridge struck the *Proagnon* man in the chest and he fell – a patch of blood forming on his uniform. As the man fell he fired his own weapon – luckily the assault rifle's bullets only struck the ceiling. The other HART members came out, from their hiding places and fired their own weapons, the other two soldiers, who weren't wounded, plus the other one, who was wounded. All were shocked at the death of their leader who had been killed so easily.

"Cecil, the bomb!" shouted Roger. Cecil was another of the HART explosives experts.

"On it chief."

It was then that a, young, boy walked up to the other three. "Please ma'am," he said to Liz who was nearest, "can you help me. My tummy feels funny and I've lost my mummy." The boy looked about six; she looked at Roger, who nodded. "What was you mummy wearing?" She asked him kindly.

"A yellow overcoat and blue dress, she's got yellow hair." Roger and Theresa nodded and moved off. The *Proagnon* men had mostly been neutralised, two of the three remaining men had panicked at the death of their leader and run out. The final man, who had been wounded, had been despatched by another shot from Mr Diamond.

"My friends have gone to look for your mummy. Now would you like me to look at your tummy, for now?"

"Yes please," replied the boy as Liz lifted him, and laid him on a bench.

"What's your name?" asked Liz, more concerned now. She had two children herself, and so knew basic first aid.

"Michael Jenkins," he replied, and then added, "I'm on holiday here with my mummy." Liz pulled his shirttails from his trousers, and unbuttoned a few buttons on his shirt, to see if she could see anything; what she did see made her take a sharp intake of breath. "What is it?" he asked this lady who was being so kind to him.

It was obvious, from the developing red stain on his stomach, evidently he'd been shot. *However had some shrapnel caught and ripped into him? Or even, had one of the HART team, inadvertently, shot him?* At this time her companions came back, both shaking their heads. Liz motioned them over and whispered to them both the news of what had happened to Michael Jenkins.

"The poor boy," murmured Theresa quietly. The three of them went back to the bench where the boy lay; he had his eyes closed. "Michael," called Liz, as she knelt by him, "wake up." The boy opened his eyes. "Michael, my name is Liz; these are my friends Roger and Theresa."

"I'm sorry I closed my eyes," the boy apologised, "I just felt so tired." Then he looked up and asked, "Did your friends find my mummy?"

"We didn't," answered Theresa gently, "now I know you're tired but please try and stay awake, Liz'll look after you."

"I'll try," Michael promised her. Theresa then had to turn away so he wouldn't see her eyes filling with tears. Roger placed an arm around his fellow agent's shoulder, to comfort her.

"Now Michael," Liz began and held his hand, "how old are you?"

"Six," the boy replied. Then Liz asked him if he had any brothers or sisters – if so what were their names and ages, where he lived, what school he went to, what class he was in, what subject he liked best; anything to keep him from closing his eyes. Roger caught on to what she was doing, and led Theresa away out of earshot.

He placed a finger on her lips to silently, to tell her to keep quiet. When they were far enough away he moved his finger away, Theresa looked at him, tears now streaming down her face, and asked, "Why? Why Michael?"

"I don't know," he answered, "it saddens me as well, but you know as well as I do there are always, innocent, casualties in any war."

"Yes, but he's so young. He shouldn't die yet."

"That's just the way it goes sometimes." He held Theresa closer; it was at that moment that Cecil Parkinson arrived back.

"I've done it," he announced, "I've defused the bomb." Then he caught sight of the looks on their faces, he could see they were both upset at something – Theresa more than Roger. "What's up?" he asked.

Roger told him, in a quiet voice so the boy, Michael, wouldn't be able to hear him. Cecil just stood there, a shocked expression on his face, "Oh hell!" he finally said, in shocked disbelief.

At the bench Michael, now feeling the pain get worse, kept closing his eyes. "Michael," Liz kept calling, "stay with me." She knew the situation was hopeless – he would eventually, succumb to the effects of his injuries – but she had to keep trying. Roger had told her he'd sent for an ambulance anyway. Now the boy was finding it even harder to keep conscious, the end was approaching, but the group of four knew if they could save, just, one life all would not be in vain.

Michael looked up at her, his eyes saying a silent 'thank you', and then he closed his eyes forever. Liz called to him, there was no response; she tried again and again, still no response; finally she tried shaking him awake – still nothing; laying him back down she felt for a pulse, in his wrist – nothing, and then in his neck – nothing; then she felt for a heartbeat – there was none. With a shock she realised he was dead! Even though Liz knew this was inevitable it was still a shock; she leaned over him and broke down in tears, just as the ambulance pulled up.

However, the ambulance, slowly, turned to face the shopping mall; it was then that Liz Butler – who was watching the emergency vehicle sensed something was wrong when no one got out. She thumbed a button on her wrist communicator that would recall her colleagues. "What's wrong?" asked Cecil, reaching her first.

"That ambulance," his female colleague said, "I have this awful feeling that there is something amiss with that emergency vehicle, no-one's got out, it just seems to be waiting for something."

"What sort of feeling?" Roger had just joined them, and heard the woman's suspicions. Roger wondered what was dangerous about an ambulance, but even he thought she was right.

Theresa had, by this time rejoined the other three, "What are we waiting for?" she wanted to know. "All the shoppers and shop owners, that are still alive, have left, due to the terrorist incident."

"At least that's one good thing," the team leader said. "However, Liz has got this feeling there's something dangerous about that vehicle," he gestured outside. "So I want us all to draw our weapons, just to be sure, and make our way towards the entrance doors."

They, all, drew their Beretta pistols and, made their way, slowly, towards the main entrance. Suddenly, without warning, the medical vehicle reversed back, and then shot forward at alarming speed. The four HART members saw a figure, dressed in blue open the passenger door and jump from the ambulance, and then there was blackness as the ambulance struck the building.

CHAPTER 11

Safe again & *traitor!*

The connecting train carrying Sergey Satov, as well as the Middle Eastern family, finally arrived in Zahedan station about two hours after it had left Bom; many of the passengers – including the Middle Eastern family, who had been on board, stepped from the train onto the platform. Sergey stepped off, after them. The Russian then walked to a ticket booth in the railway station and purchased another, one way, ticket to Karachi, the capital of Pakistan, he boarded the train with the many other passengers – run by Raja railways, like the last one – and settled himself, in a seat in the same compartment as a group of men.

On the given signal the passenger train started out on its journey into the capital city of Karachi, roughly another mere 1500 kilometres (532 miles). Then he may be able to catch a Pakistan International Airlines flight to *Sheremeteyvo* airport – north of Moscow, or as Russian's knew it Moskva – in his native Motherland of Russia. His aim now was to return home; he would return, at a later date, and deal with that treacherous dog Abdul Singh.

As they journeyed though the mountains, on the eastern side, of Iran Sergey looked around him, he had never realised Iran had so many hills and mountains; plus the Middle-Eastern family weren't in this car, or any of the others he'd come through, he hoped never to see them again. The train arrived at Karachi's railway station. *Excellent!*, thought the Russian as he saw where they were; he filed off after all of the other passengers into the humid, afternoon, air.

The girl, Irene, was just coming to in the bushes where she'd been left; she tried to remember what had happened but all the fourteen year old could remember was going to the Palace of Nations, with her...her...classmates...that was it. Where were they now? She couldn't hear them, and why was she so cold?

Maybe something had happened to her friends, if so what? Had they just left her for some reason, and if so, why wasn't she in her trusty wheelchair? Putting those questions aside for one moment Irene lifted her head, slightly, to see why she was so cold; what she saw frightened her, as she was completely naked. How had that come about? So many questions and so few answers; she tried to move, try and crawl out of this place, she managed, somehow, to get onto her front. The light, from overhead, was beginning to fade and Irene knew if she didn't get out of here before nightfall she would freeze and die from hypothermia; using her one good hand she reached out, and managed to grab a tree root, and pulled herself forward. It was at times like this when she wished she hadn't been in her father's car, on that fateful evening.

Her body hurt as she moved, yet she couldn't remember why it should; after the disabled girl had managed to move herself about five metres, she was worn out and had to stop for a rest. As she lay there, flat out, she found herself desperate to urinate. Irene knew it was wrong to just urinate; but considering she was already unclothed, and nobody was watching, where was the harm in it; plus what else could she do? So she just emptied her bladder.

Once the girl felt rested enough she resumed her crawl, as best she could, forward; pulling on tree trunks, roots, and occasionally just grassy patches, and anything else that would help her. Irene eventually pulled herself level with the path; what she saw made her scream. There were bodies all over the path; they were the bodies of her, fellow, classmates; her teacher and the three teaching assistants. Beyond the path was another body, tied to a tree; but it hung limply, whoever it was, was now most definitely, dead; the body was or had been, that of a boy as she could see a dried patch of blood at the top of the legs, and something hanging between the legs, but Irene couldn't see who it was.

A sudden gust of wind caught the head, and it swung, slightly, as the gust caught it the facial features were revealed, but only for about ten seconds; the fourteen year old gasped, it was Jean. Then she put the pieces together, as best she could: they had visited the Palace of Nations; her classmates, along with herself and the teachers were returning to school; someone, or several someone's, had evidently appeared with guns – possibly machine guns – and shot at them. What had happened to her though? Where was her wheelchair? Why was she naked? Then she got a terrible pain in her stomach, and sort of remembered. The person, or people, had got rid of her chair, after lifting her out, and destroyed it; someone had, evidently, then cut her clothes off, and done something to her, perhaps she'd been raped! She hadn't seen what he, or they, had done to Jean, but imagined it hadn't been pleasant.

It was then that a small dog, probably a Jack Russell, came sniffing around her; a large, round, man appeared a few seconds later, and called the dog off, "King, King, come away;" obediently, the Jack Russell ran back to its owner, fortunately, the man was approaching from part of the path from where the bodies couldn't be seen. He needed to round a curve in the path, to his left, but he could already see her.

Once he'd seen her and made out her figure, he bounded up and knelt, "Are you okay my dear?" Then he looked, further down, the path and gasped, "ye Gods. What happened here?"

"My name's Irene," replied the, disabled, fourteen year old, "and I'm not okay. As for what happened, I think gunmen ambushed my class and, evidently, killed them all. Will you help me?"

"I'll try," he answered. "Can you walk?"

"No I can't, I'm disabled."

"Don't worry. Ole George'll look after you," he assured her, picking her up and laying her body over his shoulder. Holding her in one hand, so she didn't slip, he held the dog lead in the other hand, and started to walk away. "It's a bit cold for you to be wearing no clothes," he said as he walked. This man seemed to be kind.

"I had clothes, but someone either cut them off, or tore them off, me. Anyway, where are we going?" she enquired. The man, she thought, was in his late forties, maybe early fifties.

"We're going to my place, where my wife'll make you a warm meal; you can sit by the fire and warm yourself up, sleep in a warm bed tonight, and then, in the morning I'll take you to hospital; just to check you over; don't worry you're safe now."

Then a sudden thought struck him, "You can feed yourself can't you, sit in a proper chair, and sleep okay?"

"Yes, yes, and yes," replied Irene, a little bit irritated that there were still some people like George around; questioning her about everything all the time, but she knew if he didn't ask, he wouldn't know. "Are we nearly there yet?"

"Not far," he assured her, "about another 500 metres." About five minutes later they reached a slightly larger than normal, cottage type dwelling.

The door flew open and a woman appeared, though as Irene's face was buried in George's duffel coat she couldn't see her, "What you got there George?" his wife asked him.

"Put some soup on Martha, and make up the extra bed, and fetch some extra blankets, we got company."

"Who George?" the elder woman queried, "and who you got there?"

"A young un," he replied, "found her out in the bushes when I were walking the dog. There are a load of bodies on path leading through the park into main Geneva."

The burly man entered a, well lit, room and lay Irene down on the, brown coloured, cloth sofa, and then his wife, Martha laid a, thick, woollen blanket over her. Irene looked around, it was a modest dwelling with many of the, usual, necessities and comforts that were found in a usual family dwelling, but there was no TV, no radio, none of the luxuries that might be found in a proper home.

In front of the fireplace; George had made a fire and placed a fireguard around it – to stop the dog burning itself, she assumed. Martha had hung a pole, supported at either end by a stand, with a pot with a handle, on it. The girl assumed the pot held soup, of some kind. "Now you lay there dearie," cooed Martha, "and get rested, then when you feel up to it you can tell us what happened."

"I've already told your husband Mrs…"

"Guton," said the older lady.

"Guton, as best I can. I can't remember everything, most things. I'll try."

George was seated in his chair, across the room, reading an old paper – once he'd finished with it he got up, moved the fireguard slightly away from the fire, screwed the newspaper up and threw it on the fire – and then replaced the fireguard. "That isn't very environmentally friendly," the fourteen year old complained.

"I know," he replied, "but as we were both born when such things didn't matter no one can tell, or persuade, us to change our ways." He looked across the room to where his wife was sitting, "Have we still got any of Peter's old clothes?"

"I'll just go and look dear," she answered, and left the room.

"Peter's our one and only child, I would guess he's, slightly, older than you; but we still have some of his old clothes. I think they'll fit you," he explained to Irene. She couldn't believe her luck, it seemed to have changed so much. From the terror earlier in the day to now, a nice couple, who were being so good to her, clothing her, looking after her – Irene felt that she'd, suddenly, swapped lives with someone else.

Martha reappeared and she and her husband, assured by Irene that she felt warmer now, dressed her as best they could. Peter's clothes were, more or less, a perfect fit – however, his shoes were, slightly, too big. The sleeves on the sweater were too long but that didn't bother Irene, she was dressed, and warm, again. "C'mon," Martha said eagerly, "get up, let's look at you." George and Irene exchanged a look. "What's wrong?" asked the wife.

"My dear," George said, "the young lady cannot walk on her own, let alone stand."

His wife rounded on him angrily, "You mean you brought her here, and all the time you knew she was useless." Martha then turned and looked at the girl, "You're useless!" she shouted. Irene had encountered people with these sort of attitudes before, it didn't bother her now but it still hurt.

"Hang on Mrs Guton," Irene snapped back, "if your husband, George, hadn't come by, when he did, and rescued me I'd have died of hypothermia! Your husband saved my life! Anyway," she continued, not quite so angry now, "tell me, if Peter, your precious son, had been unable to walk, would you have called him useless?"

"No I wouldn't," the elder woman answered. Then, realising the point Irene was making she said, "I'm sorry, please forgive me, it's just I've never met anyone like you – disabled, I believe that's the word – I mean."

George was caught in the middle; on the one hand he wanted to defend his wife, yet, on the other, he was in agreement with the young girl. At a nod from Martha he helped the young girl to sit up, while his wife poured the contents of the, small, cooking pot into a bowl, and brought it over to where Irene was sitting. "Drink this, my dear, it'll warm you up."

The, disabled, fourteen year old girl, eagerly but slowly, drank the soup – it wasn't much but, at least, it was warm. "Is the bed made up, I'm sure the young lady must be tired?"

"It is George, so whenever you're ready, Irene." The girl thanked her, and finished the soup and then handed Martha the empty bowl.

After a cup of tea, and an explanation of what she thought had occurred Irene looked up at them, "I think I'll go to bed now." George lifted her up, in his big, strong, arms, and carried her into one of the bedrooms; which was situated towards the rear of the dwelling, and laid her on the bed. His wife followed with a bowl of water; a cloth and some towels.

Carefully and gingerly they undressed her, when she was naked, again, George started to feel uneasy; Irene could see he felt uneasy, eventually he said, "I think I'd better leave the room, leave you in the care of my wife." Then he left the room; once Martha had cleaned the young body, as best she could, and tucked her in bed she said, "Do you have any special requirements at night?"

"No I don't," Irene reassured the elder woman. Once Martha had left the room Irene felt safe, once more. She knew her parents would be worried, though, but due to the Guton's not having a telephone there was no way to contact them.

In the rubble of the Centre Balexert a figure stirred; pushing upwards she managed to shake the rocks, that had hit her, from her back. Looking around she couldn't see her companions anywhere – just before the bomb, it was now obvious it had been a bomb, of some sort, the female figure had thrown herself to the ground, whilst her two male colleagues had just, simply, been dumbstruck, unable to believe their eyes.

Emergency vehicles were entering the area; lights flashing and sirens blaring, there were fire engines, ambulances and police cars. Theresa Robins, slowly, stood and choked on the grey dust that hung in the air. A police officer climbed out his car – looked at the building, just a quick glance – then fetched some yellow police tape with the words 'Police: Do Not Cross' on it; he taped across, in front of the, main, doors, and got into conversation with the chief fire officer, "Have the premises been searched?"

"Yes sir," the fire officer replied. "There are just eleven, dead, bodies inside."

"Okay, I'll call the demolition team, get them to come as soon as possible and knock the rest of the building down." The police officer, a young man wandered back to his car. Suddenly a, black 4x4, Special Utilities Vehicle (SUV) hurtled into the parking lot and screeched to a halt to avoid crashing into the remains of the destroyed building.

The vehicle's doors flew open; two figures jumped out, both were armed with Beretta pistols; the driver was a man whilst the passenger was a woman. They ran across the parking lot to the building, startling the fire officer, "Which idiot put this tape here?" demanded the man, showing his HART pass to the fire officer, to show his authority in this situation.

"I think you'll find that, idiot, was me," said a voice from behind the two new figures. They turned and saw the police officer smiling at them, "Sergeant Heinz Brunit – Geneva police." Then he asked, "And who the hell are you two?"

"HART," replied the woman. "This is Ronan Strobing, whilst my name is Celia Most." If she thought just the mention of HART would clear things up she was wrong.

"You have no authority here," shouted the sergeant. "Now pack up and go home!" Just then, they all heard it, there was a knocking at the glass doors; they all turned to look .

There framed in the doorway was the figure of Theresa Robins, she was covered in dust, and was mouthing the words,

"Help me!" Ronan, thinking quickly, waved Theresa away from the doors; once she was far enough away Ronan ran up and kicked the glass door in; the glass shattered; and a thick, grey, cloud of mortar dust greeted them all.

"Celia, stay back," he called, "radio HQ, tell them someone's still alive." As she turned he kicked through the glass door again – shattering it, and made his way inside carefully, trying to avoid any points of glass that were sticking out from the doorframe, he made his way past the vehicle that was now lodged inside. It was evident that this vehicle – it looked like an ambulance – had deliberately been driven, at speed, through the main doors; and made his way around the front of the vehicle – it was now burnt out – and to the figure knelt down beyond.

He shone the flashlight around looking at all the debris, he'd been given the flashlight by the fire officer; he'd been right about the vehicle – it was an ambulance, hunched over the steering wheel was a man – probably no older than thirty five – he was dead! Turning his attention back to the situation, at hand, and Miss Robins the departmental commander asked, "Where are the others?"

"I think they're dead," she answered. "Roger Diamond and Cecil Parkinson were with me, while Liz Butler was over there attending to a young boy, who was dying anyway," she pointed a, shaking, finger. The two of them searched the rubble and, sure enough, found Roger Diamond's and Cecil Parkinson's bodies.

"Now you say Mrs Butler was over this way?"

"Yes," was the response, and so, cautiously, with glass crunching under their feet, they made their way in the direction Theresa had indicated. Liz's body had been trapped by a block of masonry that had fallen on her and crushed her; it was obvious she was dead as well.

Once they'd confirmed everything Miss Robins had said both agents made their way, slowly, back; a crack was heard from above, spurring both of them into action, "We need to move faster," Ronan told Theresa then urged her on, reaching back and grasping her hand in his free hand, he, almost, had to pull her along to keep up with him. "We're nearly there," he called back, and then a, very, loud rumble came from above. "Down!" he shouted.

Outside Celia was sitting in the SUV waiting for her male counterpart and Theresa Robins, the, possibly, only survivor, when she heard the rumbling; leaping out of the vehicle she ran across to the building, what was left of it, and demanded to know, "What's happening?"

Both men just looked at her, in puzzlement. Another loud rumble came from the building, and then the three of them stared, in horror, as part of the building collapsed. "Ronan!" Celia screamed, "Ronan!"

At *Proagnon*, in Dr Q's office, the STU-9 warbled; the leader of the terrorist organisation answered the call, "It is done," said a voice. "The first operation was a complete success, but, unfortunately, in the second operation the men were killed, as members of HART intervened. However, an ambulance carrying a bomb – I listen to all emergency calls – was deployed and now the shopping centre, containing the four HART personnel, was totally obliterated when the bomb went off."

"Also, I have just heard that a HART SUV was deployed to search for any survivors, carrying commanders Strobing and Most; apparently they found one survivor. Commander Strobing went inside, to rescue them, and then part of the building collapsed on both of them"

"You have done well my friend," replied Dr Q, "keep me informed."

"I will sir," said the voice, and replaced the receiver. The traitor then got up and left his office. As he walked along the, wooden panelled, corridor he thought to himself, *What will my next mission be?* He wouldn't have to wait long.

At the Guton household Irene awoke; after being washed and cleaned up etc. by Martha; she had some breakfast with the elder couple, King kept looking up at her, with his pleading, brown, eyes, obviously, begging for some food.

"No King," George told the, little, Jack Russell dog, "don't be bothering the young lady." King, obediently, returned to his master's side. After they'd finished their meals, the dog did get a few scraps of food, in the end; the young girl was carried out, by George, to a waiting automobile, and placed in the front passenger seat.

The car was an old, dark green, Honda Civic, the girl didn't know much about cars; as long as they went, and got a person from one place to another, she wasn't bothered. Of course, their beloved son, Peter, would have a car – probably better than this.

George opened the front, driver's, door and the Jack Russell jumped in; immediately, he bounded across and sat on Irene's lap. "King, come off," called the man.

"It's okay," she replied, "I think he just wants to see where we're going."

"If he gets too heavy for you Miss, let me know," he told her. Turning his attention back to the cottage he called, "You coming Martha?" Mrs Guton appeared at the door and shook her head. "It looks like it's just us and King."

George climbed aboard and started the car; he drove slowly down the country track, that lead from the Guton residence to the main road, the trees above overhung – making certain parts of the country track seem as if they had arches above. The rough track was long and windy, and it took a full ten minutes before they reached the main road. Then George flicked the indicator, upwards, and the car turned right towards the main city of Geneva.

The train, once new passengers were on board - most of them Pakistani men, began the five hundred and thirty-two mile journey to Karachi, capital of Pakistan; once there he intended to board an airliner at Jinnah airport, direct to *Sheremeteyvo* airport, in his native Russia, just north of Moscow.

His mode of transport seemed to have speeded up to one hundred mph – Sergey decided – so hopefully the remainder of his journey should only take another few hours. Settling back in the seat he was in the Russian fell asleep.

About an hour later another couple – a man and a girl stepped into the same, open top, compartment; both were of Iranian origin, the man whispered something to his partner, and handed her a package, which she unwrapped. It was a pistol! Knowing her task the girl marched up to Sergey and sat on the bench beside him. The man sat the other side, in case the Russian overwhelmed the girl; he drew a kosch from inside his jacket.

Fitting a silencer to the pistol she pressed it into the right, side of Sergey Satov's neck. "Wha...?" he mumbled, awakening with a start.

She hissed, "You are Sergey Satov?" She was checking his identity first; just in case. If it wasn't the two people would look fools.

"I am," he murmured, now waking fully and looking at her in puzzlement, and the gun she held, "why?"

"Good," she replied. The Russian was paying her so much attention he hadn't noticed the man on the other side. The next thing Sergey knew was an immense, shooting, pain from the back of his neck; and he fell forward, unconscious.

The Honda Civic pulled up outside the accident and emergency department of the UHHS Memorial Hospital, on West Main Street; George stopped the little car, turned and said to his passenger, Irene, "I'm going inside to fetch a wheelchair to take you inside, I won't be long. King'll look after you."

"Okay Mr Guton, I'll wait here," then she added. "I'm not going anywhere." George smiled, and then went inside; a few minutes later he reappeared, pushing a wheelchair. Opening the door he said to the Jack Russell, "King, I need you to guard the car while we're away. Will you do that?"

The little dog barked, happily, and then climbed into the driver's seat. The burly man picked the young girl up, in his arms, and transferred her into the chair; she felt ever so light.

He pushed the chair inside and told one of the nurses what she thought had happened. The nurse, evidently a junior, pressed a button on the intercom and spoke into it, after a minute or two a more senior nurse appeared. This was obvious as they wore different coloured uniforms, plus the one on reception looked to be about Irene's age, maybe a bit older.

Irene thanked George and asked him to pass on her thanks to his wife, for their hospitality, George said he would. The senior nurse then wheeled the chair away, deeper into the hospital; back in reception George Guton smiled to himself, and then left the building, his job was done.

The nurse took the disabled girl upstairs, in the elevator, and then wheeled her into a doctor's office, "Doctor Honda will be here shortly, in the meantime there are some questions for you to answer; the girl knew the drill: Name, Address, Date of Birth, Next of Kin, Telephone number, Medical History, Allergies, and other, standard, questions. It was all standard routine.

It was then that a, youthful looking, Japanese doctor entered the office, "I am Doctor Ming Honda, I have heard the report from the nurse on reception. Now please, tell me what happened?"

Irene told him, and then the nurse handed him the question sheet, "So Miss Calvert I see you're only fourteen, and believe you were raped. A very serious incident indeed; do your parents know?"

"No they don't. I haven't seen them since yesterday morning, I spent last night at my rescuer's house, so no my parents don't know. I, still, don't know if my school knows."

"I will see to it that someone informs, both, your parents, and your school," Doctor Honda assured her. "Where is your school, it doesn't say?"

"The school I go to," she announced, rather proudly, is part of the International School of Geneva. It is located in the Grande Boissiere and Pregny-Rigot."

"Right you are Miss. Once you're settled I'll bring in an expert to examine you, as I am not qualified in this, particular, medical field." When Ming Honda had finished talking he indicated to the nurse, her nametag identified her as Senior Nurse Helen Stoney, wheeled the chair from the office, down several, featureless, corridors and into another elevator.

Back in his office Ming made a call on his phone. Celia Most had been instructed, by Commander Roberts who was back in charge now, to remain at the shopping centre site to see if anyone was still alive; if not that would be another two members dead, that was on top of the 110 personnel already killed in this war, the cost of civilian lives was in its thousands, probably millions.

Slowly, excavation vehicles, along with bulldozers and, six wheeled trucks to take the stone in; arrived to clear the site; the firemen that were on site, along with the police sergeant and herself had cleared what they could but most of what was left now were large stones and chunks of masonry, plus the ambulance.

The big bulldozers began to push parts of the ruined building aside, whilst the cranes picked the collapsed masonry up and deposit the wreckage into the six wheeled, trucks for removal.

A breakdown truck had also arrived with the excavation crew, and, even now, the emergency vehicle, that had caused the explosion, was being lifted by a crane that had a magnet attached to its jib, and was placed on the breakdown truck; this was destined for the wreckers yard.

Celia watched and waited for any sign of her fellow departmental commander; if he were still alive they would return to base where, hopefully, their superior would grant them leave over Christmas and New Year. As a metallic girder was lifted Celia saw two bodies laid flat, face down, on the ground – one male, one female - with hope in her heart she ran forward, "Ronan! Ronan, can you hear me?"

The female figure groaned, "Where am I?"

"It's okay, you're safe now," Celia replied, pulling her clear – in case anything else fell. "How's Ronan?" she asked a fireman that had pulled him clear.

He felt for a pulse, as the other figure got up and shook herself, "I'm sorry, his pulse is very faint."

"He saved my life," announced Theresa, from behind them, and she kissed him. "Thank you."

"Sorry," said Mrs Most pushing her aside. Then she sat astride him and started pushing on his chest, "1...2...3...1000," and then she forced his mouth open and performed CPR on him, after checking his airway's were clear. After about five minutes departmental commander Strobing's pulse became clearer. He opened his eyes and looked into her face, "Welcome back to the world of the living," she teased.

"Thank you Celia," he muttered as she got off him and stood up. As he stood up he looked towards the ruined building; then looked over at Theresa, her eyes were moist, "Were we really under all that?" he asked her innocently.

"Yes we were," she answered, running over and hugging him fiercely. Once the other three bodies of the dead HART members had been recovered and placed in bodybags, and then loaded aboard the SUV; the two commanders thanked the police officer and the fire officers, and then boarded their own vehicle, along with Theresa and drove out onto the main road, and proceeded back to headquarters. The conflict was not going well, but once the *Proagnon* headquarters was discovered things would get better, hopefully.

At the UHHS Memorial Hospital Dr Hans Schaiffer arrived, in his official HART car, and proceeded up to the sixth floor to meet Doctor Ming Honda, at ward 6A. "Greetings Ming, what is the report?"

"Good day Dr Schaiffer," replied Ming Honda pleasantly, and then he read the report. "When she was brought in she claimed, to the best of her knowledge, that gunmen, armed with some sort of machine guns had killed all her classmates. A few escaped, but they were shot by a sniper and a helicopter, then the sniper returned pulling one of her friends along and tied him to a tree. What she says happened next doesn't bear thinking about."

"Proceed," said the superior medical man.

"Then she claims, she is disabled you see, that the leader of the gunmen put her on the ground, knowing she'd be helpless, ordered the destruction of her wheelchair, and then cut, or tore, her clothes off. She thinks he then ordered his men into line, and then they each raped her. Eventually, when she could stand it no longer she closed her eyes and feigned death."

"Serious stuff," Dr Schaiffer said. "Could she be making it up?" He peered at Doctor Honda over the man's desk, "You know some girls are very fanciful and imaginative."

"I've had the usual scans performed on her, while I waited for you to arrive, and this girl, Irene Calvert – only 14, has all the external and internal bruising that is connected with this sort of sexual assault; I called you in, my friend, as you know I am no expert on these things. The nurse also says that Irene, despite being rescued and taken to a place of safety could not settle. She had a little difficulty sleeping last night, and blames herself, for whatever reason."

"Shall we go and see our Miss Calvert?" asked Hans Schaiffer, now a little bored at the Japanese doctor's explanation. Rape was rape, you couldn't dress it up. Again it could just have been a less serious sexual assault.

The two men donned their doctor's coats; there were always two in every doctor's office, they walked through the main ward, and on to room 10 on the ward; seeing the door was closed Doctor Honda knocked, "Come in," called a, cheery, voice from inside. The doctors entered the room.

"Which one of you is Doctor Honda?" asked the plump, figure of a woman. As she was on the smallish side she looked even plumper. A man was standing behind her both medical men assumed he was her husband and, therefore, Irene's father.

"I am," replied the Japanese doctor. The woman shook him, firmly, by the hand. The other man in the room, wearing a business suit also shook the doctor's hand.

"I'm Mrs Veronica Calvert, and this is my husband David," she said, indicating the man. "We'd like to thank you."

The doctor looked embarrassed, "I think you should be thanking your daughter's rescuers. Apparently, she was brought in, this morning, by another man, I believe he was very concerned about your daughter."

Mrs Calvert turned to her daughter, who lay in the bed, "You never told me this, was he the man who raped you?" Even Mr Calvert, now, looked slightly suspicious at this new admission.

"No he wasn't mummy, he rescued me last night. I woke up, long after the other men had left; I was in some undergrowth, so I crawled, as best I could, back to the main path, where I saw the dead bodies of my friends."

"A most disturbing sight," Dr Schaiffer added, pulling up a chair.

"And who the hell are you?" demanded David Calvert suspiciously.

Before the German could answer, Ming jumped in, "May I introduce my colleague, superior and good friend Dr Hans Schaiffer." The parents exchanged looks, and then, shook hands with this new man.

"Now Irene," Dr Schaiffer prompted, once everything had been settled. "Please proceed."

"Well," continued the youngster, "a little, white, dog – a Jack Russell I think, saw me, ran over and started licking me. Presently the owner appeared, he picked me up, and carried me to his house, where he urged his wife to make up a bed for me, put some soup on, get some extra blankets – as I had no clothing on so he could've taken advantage of me at anytime but he didn't."

She paused, trying to remember what had happened next. "He, then, laid me on the sofa, in the house, while his wife covered me with some blankets to help me warm up, I had a little sleep; when I awoke, after roughly an hour, I had a little soup that the wife, Martha, had prepared and a warm drink. As I was very tired, after my ordeal George, that was his name, carried me into the bedroom their son used to use. His wife, Martha, followed carrying a bowl of water and wash cloth, plus towels."

The youngster paused again, looking round at each of them. "George, I could see he felt uncomfortable – even after carrying my, naked, body home, and he left while Martha washed me, and settled me in bed."

"This morning I had breakfast with them, and then George brought me here," Irene finished.

"Remarkable!" announced Dr Schaiffer, in his German accent. "May I enquire as to how you are feeling now?" He looked at the Japanese doctor, trying to gauge his counterpart's reaction; he couldn't.

"I feel pretty much okay, now I've been cleaned up, got some hot food inside me, and had a good rest; although I still, occasionally, get the odd pain in my stomach," she told him.

"Would it be okay if I asked your parents to leave, just for a few minutes – Doctor Honda will stay behind so you won't be alone?" Dr Schaiffer could see, this young girl looked frightened – only natural considering the ordeal the *Proagnon*, he was certain of it, soldiers had put her through. Her face brightened when he mentioned Ming could stay, and she wouldn't be alone with this German man.

"Okay," Miss Irene Calvert replied, looking towards her mother for reassurance. Her mother smiled to say it was okay; she and her husband rose, from their chairs, and started for the door.

"There's a canteen on the ground floor," said the Japanese man helpfully, "that serves food and drink, hot or cold." The parents thanked him and left to find the canteen.

When they were gone Doctor Honda watched as his superior moved, slowly – so as not to alarm her, unnecessarily - over to the hospital bed with the girl in it, "Now Irene," he said in a gentle tone. "Where does the pain hurt you the most?" He could see, in her eyes, that she was terrified at the mere mention of the pain in her stomach. "It's okay, neither of us," he gestured to Dr Honda, and then to himself, "wants to hurt you like the other men did. You're safe here."

"It hurts, the worst, down here," she squeaked at him, slowly pulling the bed covers below her hip line, Dr Schaiffer suggested to his counterpart that it might, also, be advisable to have a nurse in attendance to reassure the young lady; as he knew it'd be a long while until she, fully, trusted a man again, if ever.

Probably the reason she'd let this George person carry her to his cottage was because she had been in a state of shock, not fully realising the full extent of what had happened to her.

Dr Honda called a nurse in, and then he left to attend to other duties. Fully reassured now there was another woman in the room the girl raised the, hospital, nightgown, exposing the area between her thighs. It was very red and bruised.

Dr Schaiffer, thinking what the disabled girl had told them, placed his, left, hand on her stomach, "Does it hurt here?" he enquired. He knew she wouldn't have let him touch her, on the stomach, if the nurse hadn't been there.

"No," she replied, strength returning to her voice, "just below."

The doctor moved his hand down a little, just above her uterus. "Here?" he asked; looking into her face he knew he had got the right place.

"Yes, that's it," she replied. He curled the index finger, on his right hand and tapped it on the resting left hand.

"If it hurts while I'm tapping let me know." The girl had such an angelic face, how could any man do this sort of thing to her? Slowly, he circled the area she'd indicated, tapping his left hand as he went; there was no reaction until he tapped a more central area. Her face creased in agony, Dr Schaiffer turned to the, young nurse, who was standing in the room. "Please find Dr Honda for me."

The nurse buzzed the doctor on her pager and he was back with them moments later. "What have you found?" Honda enquired of his German friend. Dr Schaiffer told him what he suspected, and asked Ming to have a more in depth scan performed, of her lower stomach. "I'll get onto it straight away," the Japanese man said, "and thank you."

Hans Schaiffer gave instructions to his counterpart that once the results were back and if anything was found he was to be contacted straight away. He then left the room then and proceeded downstairs, in the elevator, and walked out to his official car.

From the glove compartment he produced a cellular phone and dialled a number, "Yes?" answered a voice.

"Your men failed, the girl is still alive."

"She will be dealt with."

"And what about the nurses, doctors and other patients?"

"If they get in the way they will have to suffer the consequences," answered the voice. "And you're taking a risk phoning on an open line."

The medical man said, with a hint of anger, "Many of my friends are inside. I refuse to tell you which hospital she is in."

"We fitted your phone with a tracking device; therefore we know where she is."

"I shall inform HART, or if I am forced to I shall help defend the girl."

"You are not always there my dear doctor," and the phone clicked off. Dr Schaiffer scowled at his, own, handset, and tossed it back in the glove compartment. Closing it he drove away.

At the HART compound the SUV drove in and parked up in its usual parking spot. Celia climbed out and hurried across the ground, to main headquarters; inside she journeyed to Commander Roberts office and knocked, a voice, she knew well, called, "Come in." In she walked to find Leon Bigship seated behind the desk.

"Where's Mr Roberts?" she automatically asked him.

"Dr Schaiffer had to go out, to the Memorial hospital, so Mr Roberts is standing in for him. As Ronan and yourself were out Commander Roberts asked me to fill in for him."

"And not Lucy?" she asked him.

"No, it appears Miss Lang is in charge of the shooting range; personally I think she and he have had a slight disagreement, but don't quote me." He sat back, in the, swivel, leather chair, "Anyway, what news do you have?"

"As you know the Centre Balexert was destroyed by a bomb."

"Yes I know, as one of our GlobalHawk UAVs observed. That is why you were deployed."

"Anyway, four of our agents: Roger Diamond, Cecil Parkinson, Theresa Robins and Liz Butler were inside when the building collapsed," Celia said to him.

Were they...?" he couldn't bring himself to finish the question.

"Not all of them, Theresa survived," Mrs Most concluded. "Anyway, Ronan went inside, with a flashlight given to him by one of the fire officers, to rescue her; I reported this information in, and then what was left of the building collapsed again."

"He isn't dead is he?" asked the acting commander, looking her straight in the eye. They both liked Ronan Strobing.

The female DC replied, "No he's not, thankfully, he nearly was. When they managed to extract his body from the remains of the building, he had covered Theresa's body with his own, to protect her, and so most of the masonry chunks that had fallen landed on him, his pulse was very faint so I performed CPR on him, and he's as good as new now, but resting."

"You haven't mentioned what happened to the other three bodies yet," Leon told her. "You said Theresa survived."

"Ah yes," said Celia. "We brought the other three bodies - once they'd been extracted – back with us; as we felt that it was only proper and right. Be able to bury them properly, not just leave them under a demolished building."

"Quite right," replied Leon. "It'll give us all time to mourn their loss. Thank you Celia, I assume the bodies are still in the Mega Cruiser."

"Yes, they are," Celia replied. Leon explained to her that he would make sure each of them would receive a military ceremony, and then their bodies would be flown home, to their rightful countries of origin: Roger was from Sweden, Cecil from Belgium and Liz from Portugal, along with a military escort; two soldiers each; then there would be a family ceremony and burial, or whatever.

Celia Most understood this sentiment, and nodded in agreement. All HART soldiers or agents, who were killed in the line of duty, underwent the same procedure.

The train, run by Pakistan 'Raja' Railways, carrying Sergey Satov, finally, pulled into Karachi's City Station which was one of Karachi's main railway stations; the other being Karachi Cantonment Station. As it pulled up to the platform and came to a halt, the Russian, he was a little disorientated from the blow on the head, disembarked. He walked out the station, a little unsteadily, and he had to sit on a bench to recover and get his strength back. He started to wonder who the two people had been.

The journey had been roughly 1170 miles – the first 550, in which he'd encountered the Middle Eastern family – had taken 11, long, hours – the remainder of the journey had taken only six and a quarter hours – as the train had speeded up due to there not being so many passengers on board. The Russian had set off from Qom at 11.00 (local time in Iran) and had finally arrived at his destination at seventeen and a quarter hours, plus time for stops; therefore a total of around 18 hours;

the time was now 06.30 (local time in Pakistan) as he had travelled into another time zone. He was shattered! Even his stamina couldn't keep up with this.

Once he had sufficiently recovered Sergey got up and wandered off to find a place to sleep – as he was, practically, out of money Sergey had to do with a, common, bench. As soon as he lay his head down he was asleep; the Russian awoke again at 13.30, he yawned and got up, he checked the bag that contained his one belonging – a bible – to make sure it hadn't fallen out, or been stolen.

He treasured that bible, not because he was religious but because the inside of the front cover could be peeled back – revealing a compartment that held a passport, it was fake of course; he'd had many different passports made but had more or less used them all for different reasons. Sergey then left the park, after urinating in the undergrowth, and caught a bus that would take him to *Jinnah* airport, or so he hoped. At last he found one and boarded it; it was hot and dusty so the bus was an open topped variety.

There was an underground *Metro* system in Karachi; the system, he'd learned was called *Duz*. He refused to use this, as he remembered on one occasion when, he was a young boy his parents had taken his sister, he hadn't heard from her for ages, and himself on Moscow's underground system. The doors to their carriage had stuck shut; he'd been frightened, even though he knew he only had to cross into the next carriage to get out.

The Russian found a seat next to a young girl, she looked familiar, and then a voice came from the seat behind, "Hello my friend, have you decided to take me up on my offer after all?"

Sergey cringed, it couldn't be, if so how had they got here so quick? He, slowly, looked round and couldn't believe his eyes. It was the Middle Eastern family, the parents, together with their newborn; if they were there where were the children? Then he had a sinking feeling, and realised, the girl he was next to had been the one offered to him, on the train journey, between Qom and Bom.

However, he had no choice but to stay where he was this time, for the moment. Lazily he yawned and, accidentally, touched the girl on her chest; within moments she was cuddling and kissing him, Sergey didn't want this and tried to stop her, but the more he tried the more she came onto him; he was afraid that she might, if pushed too far, pull her clothes off or something equally as awful.

The other passengers were watching with amused interest. Some wanted it to continue to the stage where she did pull her clothes off, if that's what she did; others wanted this awful spectacle to stop. The bus journey, through the streets of Karachi – with all its citizens and traffic - was long and arduous. Sergey kept trying to fend the girl off, but she kept clawing at him. Seeing this commotion, in the seat in front of him, the father, of the girl, leant forward and whispered something, in his native tongue, to his daughter, who smiled at him. She, suddenly stopped trying to come onto him, the Russian was puzzled.

As the daughter seemed to have stopped her attack on him, the Russian assumed she'd given up; finally and he began to relax, about three hours after Sergey had boarded the bus, it pulled into the kerb outside *Jinnah* airport; the Russian rose from his seat, and the girl did likewise. *Must be moving across to where I was sitting, so she can stretch her legs out*, he thought. He walked to the main exit doors and stepped, hesitantly, outside.

Unfortunately, he didn't see the car that had pulled in, two stops up and Abdul Singh got out. He walked inside the main terminal, and disappeared, and then the car drove away.

Sergey stood, looking at the outside of the front main terminal building – it was immense in size. He went inside and walked, nonchalantly, into the departure lounge for the 20.00 Pakistan International Airlines flight to *Sheremeteyvo* Airport, in Moscow; the Russian was most surprised that no airport security stopped him, here was a civilian wandering about and no one was stopping him. However, if he was stopped he had his fake passport on him.

The lounge started to fill up; some Iranians, Pakistani's, and some fellow Russians. Sergey was sitting peacefully, casually reading a newspaper he had picked up from the seat, when someone – on his left side – tapped him on the shoulder; automatically he looked round, sitting next to him was the girl, from the train and bus. "Hello," she said and smiled, pleasantly, at him.

"Erm hello," replied the Russian, puzzlement in his voice. "What are you doing here?"

"Your friend brought me through."

"Friend?" he was now even more puzzled. The girl indicated a group of people seated a couple of rows away, even though he could only see the back of their heads he thought the girl was indicating a female figure, but she was pointing at a male figure. *Ah, Miranda*, thought Sergey, *I wonder where she's going?* "I see you've stopped trying to molest me," he said to her.

She looked, up, at him and replied, "Well, it wasn't getting me anywhere, so I've decided to give up and, if you will permit it, fly to Moscow with you."

"Hmm, yes," he answered her, thoughtfully, "as long as you behave yourself, and keep your hands to yourself." He still had a bad feeling about this, but he could always take her with him and then disown, or lose, her when they got to Moscow, and then again accidents were known to happen, especially, to foreigners, in his home city of Yuroslavl. "I've suddenly realised," he said, "we don't know each other's names; I'm Sergey."

"My name's Bousseh," she told the Russian. "It means kiss." She leant closer to him, "Shall we pretend to be father and daughter, or lovers?"

"Well," he replied, "as we have a different skin colour we might as well be lovers." this startled Bousseh as she thought the man hated her after earlier. He then got up, "Don't worry," he said to her, "I'm just going to toilet. Back soon."

As Sergey Satov walked towards the airport toilets, another man got up and followed the Russian. Bousseh, now having the feeling that something bad was about to happen to her new friend, followed the second man as he went after Sergey Satov.

The Russian entered the airport toilets and found a urinal, where he could see the door from, as something inside of him kept telling him he was in danger, though he didn't know why, and it wasn't anything to do with Bousseh. He urinated, and then closed his fly and proceeded across to the sink, which was next to the row of urinals, to wash his hands; another man pushed open the door and walked in. Sergey glanced at him – the man was slightly shorter than himself but of a stockier build and seemed, vaguely, familiar – the Russian was pretty certain he knew the man, but as his back was turned to him he wasn't one hundred percent certain.

The man seemed to follow the same procedure as Sergey, the Russian took very little notice of the man, and then the door to the toilets, partially, opened and a small face looked in, it was the Iranian girl, Bousseh; but why had she followed him, didn't she know this was the men's toilet?

Once the other man had finished, Sergey was just drying his hands, he turned and snarled, "Sergey Satov." The Russian spun round to face the other man, whose voice he seemed to recognise, it was then that he saw the face of Abdul Singh, his former friend, but now sworn enemy. In his hand he held a Norinco NZ-75 (9mm) pistol.

"No!" shouted Bousseh, and burst into the toilets. She cannoned into Mr Singh; who fell to the floor; the Russian wrestled with his former friend, trying to get the gun from his hand. Sergey punched him over and over again and then tried to pull the gun away but Abdul held onto it, in his vice like grip.

"You won't get away with it this time," announced the Russian. "I shall kill you if I have to, now give it to me!"

"If you insist," replied the Iranian, on the floor, "you only had to say please," and he pulled the trigger. Sergey fell backwards. Satisfied with his work Abdul Singh quietly, yet confidently, entered one of the cubicles, deposited his NZ-75 pistol in the toilet cistern, and then stepped over the two bodies, as Bousseh had fallen backward as well, and left.

At HART headquarters Commander Roberts, who was now back in command, since Dr Schaiffer had returned, had called Ronan Strobing, Celia Most, Leon Bigship and Lucy Lang into his office. They sat on chairs, opposite him, "Now," he said, "as it is Christmas I intend to give you a break from duty. As it is the 23rd today I will let you go as soon as you are ready, but I request you all return on the 4th January. This will leave us four personnel short, but as I don't envisage anything major happening it shouldn't be a problem; however, if anything major does happen you may be recalled."

"Thank you sir," they each said. Peter smiled at them, these four were like the children he'd never had, as he'd been away too often. Well three of them were, he wasn't all that sure of Miss Lang, after all America wasn't in the EU, therefore she may see things differently to the rest of them, would she ever see them the same as his other young English protégés?

At *Proagnon* a squadron of four SU-27 planes landed in the bunker. As soon as they had all stopped and been secured, plus Dr Q had inspected them; then the leader of Proagnon returned to his office. Once he'd unlocked his desk drawer he took out his STU-9 and punched in a number. The phone rang and then a Chinese voice answered, "Hello."

"Greetings," Dr Q said into the receiver, "Dr Quantum here. Why have the SU-27s, only just arrived?"

"Only just arrived," said Minister Fang Ten, incredulously. "A squad of four jets departed weeks ago." Then he added, "I think that, maybe, the original four crashed or something has happened to them."

"I bet," Dr Q stormed down the phone, "I bet you never sent any!" At the other end he heard the receiver slam down, "Stupid Chinky," he muttered to himself and, casually, replaced his own receiver, and then returned the phone to the drawer. He did remember an air battle, in the skies above Saudi Arabia a couple of weeks back, had they been the original squad? Maybe the Chinky wasn't lying after all.

At the hospital Irene Calvert had had her scans, and Dr Honda examined the results, immediately, he phoned Dr Schaiffer. When he answered the Japanese doctor told him that he had examined the girl's scan results thoroughly, and there was no doubt in his mind now, the girl had been raped; and there was a, darkish, shadow in her womb.

Once Hans heard this he asked, "Do the parents know the results of their daughter's scan yet?"

"No, they know nothing about it yet. All they know is that their daughter was subjected to a sexual assault. They don't exactly know how bad it was."

"I suggest I, along with the parents, come over and we all talk, properly, about this seriousness of this, and the results of the scan, plus what should happen next." Ming looked at the results, while still holding the phone, just to make sure he hadn't got it wrong, but he knew he hadn't.

After the pause he said, "Yes, I think that may be advisable, I will phone her parents and have them come in."

"I shall be there, as well, soon," Dr Schaiffer said and replaced the receiver. He walked to Peter Roberts' office, and put his head round the door. "Excuse me sir, but I have to go back to the Memorial Hospital," he noticed his commander's slightly, annoyed look.

"Very well, I will attend to your duties for you until you return."

"Thank you sir," replied the doctor and left. He left the building, climbed in his car and drove out of the compound. Arriving at the hospital about half an hour later, he went inside; found Dr Ming Honda in his office, checking the scans again, curiously. Dr Shaffer examined the scans as well, and confirmed what his Japanese friend had initially thought.

Once Mr and Mrs Calvert arrived, the two doctors donned their white coats, and Dr Honda collected the scan results, and then all four of them walked to Irene's room. Inside they all found a chair to sit on and sat down. "Now then," announced Ming, addressing the parents, "secondary scans were performed on your daughter, as advised by Dr Schaiffer, and the results show a, darkish, shadow in her womb; which we can only assume is a tiny foetus. I'm sure this is as much a shock to you as much as it was to me."

"Are you sure it isn't just a smudge, or someone playing a trick?" Veronica Calvert asked, looking over at her husband who nodded in agreement.

"I have queried this with our scan developers – as I thought it was a smudge or something myself," the Japanese doctor told her, "but they assure me it is no trick. Your daughter is pregnant."

"Pregnant!" David Calvert nearly exploded. "She's barely more than a child herself. How will she be able to cope with her schoolwork, and now having the added responsibility of motherhood, Irene would never cope; get rid of it."

"Wait a moment Mr Calvert," soothed Dr Schaiffer. "What makes you think your daughter won't be able to cope?"

Mr Calvert gave Dr Schaiffer an *I could punch you* look. "Look at her," he stormed, "she's disabled, for God's sake! She can hardly take care of herself, how do you think she'll cope with the added responsibility of a baby?"

"Shut up, all of you," shouted a voice from the bed. "I am here, you know." Even Irene's father fell silent as he looked, over, at his daughter. "Doctor," she carried on, in a milder tone, "what are my options?"

Dr Honda answered her, "Well you could carry on with the pregnancy, though it may be ill advised at your age; or you could have a termination," Irene looked scared at that. "Don't worry, if you decide on this option, which I advise, all we do nowadays, is put a thick blindfold on you, to block out the flash of light and place you on a trolley with a transparent square plate covering you stomach. Then we wheel in a light atop a pole on wheels, place it at the foot of the trolley you're on, aim and fire the light at your stomach. Painless and has no side effects; in fact once finished you may go home."

Irene looked at her mother, who nodded at her, and then across at her father, who, like her mother just nodded; she could see he was hurting inside, because he hadn't been there to protect her. After getting her parents approval the girl said, "I think that the termination would be the best option for me. How soon can it be set up."

"As soon as you're ready," Ming told her.

"I'd like it done today," Irene replied, "if possible." Dr Schaiffer then excused himself, and went down to his car. He found the mobile phone and dialled the number.

"Greetings my dear doctor," said a voice once the phone was answered.

"Where are your soldiers?" Dr Schaiffer nearly shouted, "the girl's pregnant and about to have a termination." Panic filled his voice.

"Then you my dear doctor must prevent it," said the silky, smooth, tones at the other end. "If you fail you know the price."

"I do indeed," replied the doctor, "And I will do all I can." He ended the call.

In his subterranean base Dr Q called Squeeze. "Ready the hidden Geneva agents, here are their instructions."

In reply, a female voice came back, "Very good sir; all will be made ready."

Dr Schaiffer knew he, probably, couldn't do anything to prevent the termination, but he had to try. First he tried to talk Mr and Mrs Calvert out of signing the consent forms, only to learn they'd already signed them. Next he tried to bully Irene out of the termination, but David Calvert restrained him. Finally, in desperation, he tried to smash the equipment, but was spotted by Dr Honda who tried to restrain his friend, but the German man simply elbowed the Japanese man aside; Dr Schaiffer was like a wild animal.

In the end David Calvert saw, and heard, the commotion and barged into the room. Stepping over the Japanese doctor's fallen body he spun Dr Schaiffer around, and punched him – as hard as he could. Dr Schaiffer fell, groaning, and then suddenly sprang back to his feet; the two men slugged it out, exchanging punches. Unseen by either man Ming crawled away, and took a syringe from the tray of instruments; carefully, he filled it with a solution from a phial, on the side.

He didn't want to do what he had to do, but if it was necessary, to stop his friend who seemed to have become a madman, he would have to. Rising unsteadily to his feet the, small, Japanese doctor caught Mr Calvert's eye and winked. David made sure his German opponent's back was always to Ming Honda. The small doctor paused, as if readying himself, and then charged.

The needle on the end of the syringe entered Dr Schaiffer's back, and he screamed in agony - the needle pierced him in the right side of his back- he tried to lash out at his attacker, but Mr Calvert held him in a fixed position, Dr Honda pressed the plunger and the solution poured inside his colleague. Hans fell to the ground as the effects took him over; "Please," Dr Honda said to Mr Calvert, "help me move him to a trolley outside." So between the two of them they lay Dr Schaiffer's prone body on a trolley, and strapped him down. "He will sleep for hours yet."

"The damage seems only to be superficial," remarked the small doctor, checking around the room. "Your daughter's operation can still go ahead." Irene Calvert was wheeled in, her mother, Veronica, had gone home, as she didn't feel that both she and Irene's father needed to be there. He would phone her when he and their daughter were ready.

The operation was a complete success. Irene and her father left within the hour. When Dr Schaiffer finally awoke, some four hours later he shouted at staff, after finding himself restrained, "What is the meaning of this, untie me at once, I have work to do! I am Dr Hans Schaiffer!"

"Very sorry sir," apologised the two nurses who untied him. "We didn't realise who you were."

"Hmph," he snorted in disgust. As soon as he was free, the German doctor ran down the corridor to the operating theatre. He pushed the double doors, to the room, open and was greeted by an empty room. Dr Schaiffer slammed shut the double doors, and tore off, upstairs, to the room where the young girl had been; again that was empty; he even looked in the wardrobe, and under the bed. Nothing! Furiously he burst into Dr Honda's office, fearing the worst. "Where is she?" he demanded. "What have you done with her?"

Dr Honda looked up from his notes. "Who do you mean?" he asked innocently.

"You know bloody well who I mean, Irene fucking Calvert." The Japanese doctor could see he was extremely angry. "Tell me you little turd; else it won't be a doctor you'll be needing, it'll be an undertaker!"

The Japanese doctor simply said, "She's gone Hans; she left, with her parents, about three hours ago. The operation was a complete success."

"No!" Hans cried, and hurried out the office then left the hospital. It was not quite dark yet. There was a man standing across the parking lot, instantly the man produced a knife and walked across to the other man.

"Dr Schaiffer," he called, once he was standing behind him.

Dr Schaiffer turned, "Yes," he said. He looked at the man who seemed to be, reasonably, young "Do I know you?"

"I am an emissary from Dr Q, and am here at his request," having said that his knife suddenly shot forward, stabbing the medical man, who fell. Dr Schaiffer looked and seemed dead! Satisfied the man reported in, "Mission accomplished," he said into a radio attached to his lapel.

He then ran from the parking lot, down an alley where he knew a car was waiting to drive him to freedom. Seeing the car he slowed down; then the driver emerged, raised his pistol and shot the other man dead. "Mission accomplished," he said into his coat lapel, dumped the pistol he'd used in a refuse bin, got in the car and drove away.

Unseen by the knife man, a young orderly had just parked up; he climbed out his car, once he'd killed the engine, and silently watched from the shadows as the other medical man was stabbed; waiting until the man who had wielded the knife had gone, the orderly moved from the shadows and helped the wounded Hans Schaiffer inside. It was ironic this should take place outside a hospital.

Once inside he summoned help from the nurses on duty, also warning them that if they went outside, at break time, to go out in pairs; another orderly helped lift the figure of Dr Schaiffer onto a gurney, the nurses, both were young, managed to stem the flow of blood, and wheeled him into theatre. "Who's on call tonight?" one of the nurses asked the other.

"Ming the Merciless," the other replied, putting a call out to his pager; and then rejoining her colleague.

Many streets away Dr Honda was sitting in his apartment, settling down to watch TV with his wife Migonga. The noise from the pager made them both jump, "I'd better see what they want," he said, noting the number, and then leaving the room. "Yes?" he said once the phone at the other end had been answered.

"Dr Honda," was the senior nurse's response, "a stabbed man has just been brought in. He's waiting in theatre; two nurses are with him now."

"I'll be there as quick as I can," he replied, replacing the phone.

"Trouble dear?" asked Migonga Honda. She knew he'd have to go, even if someone else could be found. When she'd married him, four years ago, she'd been resigned to having to share him with his mistress, as she called the hospital.

"I have to go in," her husband said to her, "sorry I don't know what time I'll be back so I'll take my key, you needn't wait up" Migonga watched him leave, knowing he would return to her, eventually.

Ming Honda's green Vauxhall Cavalier swung into the hospital parking lot and pulled into the space reserved for him. He noted that Dr Schaiffer's official HART car was still there. In that case was he still inside or had he been kidnapped?

Dr Honda walked in and a voice came over the Tannoy system, "Will Dr Honda please report to theatre 2." The Japanese doctor hurried to where he needed to be; upon entering the theatre he gasped in astonishment, the nurses looked up at him. "What is it?" one of them asked.

"That patient is Dr Hans Schaiffer, you say someone stabbed him?" he asked as the two nurses scrubbed up, and got ready for the operation.

"He was doctor." Then he scrubbed up and prepared himself. He selected an instrument to start and the operation on Hans Schaiffer commenced.

CHAPTER 12

Hostage situation & terror on the road!

In the toilets, at *Jinnah* airport, a figure slowly raised its head. Looking around to check Abdul Singh had gone the figure slowly stood up; the other body, that had taken the bullet, lay in the position it had fallen; tears streamed down the other's face, and all the person could say was, "I'm sorry, you should never have become involved in this." Then the person kneeled and held the dead victim, "I'm sorry, I should never have let you follow me; all you wanted was love."

Just for a moment, even though it was dead, the body's face seemed to smile. Placing Bousseh's body in one of the cubicles Sergey closed her, now, sightless eyes, and left thinking, *I'll kill that bastard for what he's done, extinguishing a young life like that!*

It had all happened so quick, one moment the Russian had had the gun pointing at him, yet, if he was right Bousseh must have jumped in front of him as the Iranian had fired; now here he was, whilst she was dead.

Sitting down Sergey looked around, Abdul was nowhere to be seen; thinking that, maybe, he had got cold feet, or thinking he'd got the right person, Abdul had left, but he'd killed the wrong target, the Russian started to relax. However, the Iranian was standing in a corner – in the shadows – watching his former friend. He had to kill the man somehow, before he could return to *Proagnon*.

Eventually the flight was called and everyone began to head towards the departure gate; Abdul joined the throng of people, and pushed his way through the crowd, Sergey caught sight of the little man once and tried to make his way forward with hopes of stopping him, but by then he had disappeared; everyone boarded the aircraft that was waiting for them on the tarmac. Abdul sat at the rear of the plane, whilst Sergey contented himself with a seat closer to the front.

A voice came over the Tannoy system, "This is Pakistan airlines flight 907 direct to *Sheremeteyvo* airport in Russia, we shall be flying at an altitude of 35,000 feet, and a cruising speed of 966 kph (six hundred miles per hour). The weather is cloudy but clear with light winds, therefore we should reach our destination at roughly eight this evening, Karachi time, but as we are travelling North-West we shall arrive at roughly six this evening, Moscow time. Please observe the 'No Smoking' signs."

The aircraft began to taxi forward, to await a clear slot so it could take off; once a clear slot was found, the 787 powered down the runway, its twin engines roaring as they built up to full power. The machine rose into the air, with the ground fast disappearing behind them; once the aircraft had reached the correct altitude it levelled off and began its journey, onwards and northwards, towards Russia.

The aircraft was detected by the Admiral *Lazarev's* Fregat MR-710 3D search radar, situated on its main mast; the battle cruiser was awaiting its new orders, for deployment. However, the crew had been notified by *Proagnon* HQ, to report any suspicious aircraft – this one wasn't exactly suspicious, probably just a routine air flight to Russia. The signal that had been activated aboard, which was on a different frequency to that which was used by the jet airliner – it was only used by *Proagnon* soldiers, and there was only one still out there, or maybe two: Abdul Singh and, possibly, Sergey Satov.

The information was sent, over the terrorist's command network, back to HQ, where Dr Q looked at, and analysed, the data, on his laptop; which had bleeped to inform him that some new information had arrived, and was awaiting his attention. He viewed the information, and then wondered why Abdul was going to Russia; perhaps he had friends there, friends that would help him in his takeover of command, or maybe there was another reason. Whatever, he had to be stopped immediately.

He contacted his contact in Afghanstan, where the plane was due to fly over shortly, the contact answered and informed Dr Q that everything was ready, and he just needed to get to his destination, in the lower Hindu Kush mountain region, near the small place of Farah; where what was needed was located. He also told Dr Q that once he reached his destination he would get in contact again. The agent climbed into his cattle truck – the rear was covered in tarpaulin – at his home in Qandahat and drove to his destination just north of Farah; where he brought the vehicle to a halt, and got out.

Whilst he was waiting Dr Q contacted the pilot's lounge, within the underground complex, and he issued the order that one of the SU-27s was to shadow the Pakistan airlines flight, that had been detected, until it was over Afghanistan, and then shoot it down if their Afghan contact didn't deliver, although their leader was certain he would, however they wanted – knowing the fighting had ended there two years previous he wanted it to look like a possible re-emergence of the previous hostilities.

The lone pilot made his way to their fighter aircraft, and removed the chocs, that had been placed in front of the aircraft's wheels, to prevent the fighter rolling; climbing up into the cockpit of the jet the pilot seated himself in his seat, and then put on his harness and helmet. Then he started up the aircraft's twin turbofan engine, the plane was then ready to roll. "Squad leader Yang here," announced the pilot's voice. Once the engines were at full power the jet burst, from the bunker, into the cloudy sky. "Target at one o'clock," announced the Squadron leader. The plane suddenly accelerated to its top speed of mach 2.35 (1552mph). Catching up with the jet liner was easy enough, and then he followed it, keeping a steady pace and a steady distance between it and himself – not too close to be detected, but not too far away to lose sight of it.

On the ground the Afghan removed the tarpaulin, from the vehicle, and operated controls on the side of the vehicle, the truck body gradually separated revealing the gleaming form of the SkyStriker, which had been fitted with a high explosive warhead in the nosecone.

The missile had been kept in a cave, in one of the mountains that made up the Hindu Kush region, and had taken six years to build. Now it was needed to bring down an airliner, why? Siri Fakbar didn't know and wasn't about to ask. He contacted Dr Q again, and informed him all was ready; Karachi airport was 1200 kilometres (746 miles) from Siri's position –

yet the flight's distance, Dr Q didn't know it was 3900 kilometres (2422 miles).

Siri looked up into the sky, the Afghan had been informed that as soon as the civilian plane was detected by the truck's radar, he was to activate the SkyStriker. Closing the communications channel he got back in the vehicle's cab and settled down to wait, unaware Dr Q had other plans for him.

The radar beeped, making Siri jump – he had been asleep and totally unaware of it – he got out, raced to the back of the truck and activated the missile's control panel, after firstly ensuring the blast screen was up, and pressed a number of buttons – in a specific order; he turned, as he depressed the last button, and then he watched as the mammoth missile started its engines and began to lift off, the four booster rockets burning fuel as they powered up.

The SkyStriker lifted off and began the journey towards its intended target; the approaching missile was detected by the airliner's radar but nothing could be done The huge SkyStriker missile smashed into the fuselage, underneath, and exploded, on impact, completely obliterating the 787, killing all 240 passengers, the crew and anyone else who happened to be on board.

Squadron leader Yang was disappointed as he saw the missile strike the aircraft having just lined the plane up in the targeting crosshairs that now took the place of his visor, he contacted headquarters directly, and informed them of what had happened, and then he asked if he should return to base; Dr Q gave him instructions of another task he needed doing, the pilot confirmed his new instructions and flew towards his new destination.

He lined his new target up, in his targeting crosshairs, and then loosed two of his heat-seeking R-73 AA missiles. To avoid the missiles mistaking him for the target he cut the afterburners and cooled his plane down to the minimum system requirements for full mission operating. The two missiles sped toward the target, hit it and the target exploded in a huge fireball.

The four HART Operational Commanders were packing for the journey back to England, or America in Lucy's case. There had still been no word from Dr Schaiffer.

As Ronan was packing for his return journey there came a, loud, knock on his door. "Damn!" said Mr Strobing as he caught his skin in the zip of his suitcase. "Who the hell?" Reluctantly, he went downstairs to answer the door; he threw it open, "Yes?" He was annoyed. The sooner he was reunited with Simon the better.

"Don't speak to me like that!" said the person outside, and then shoved Ronan so he fell on his back. Next she was kissing him as if the world was going to end tomorrow.

"Steady on Lucy. I'm not going anywhere, only home to see my son for Christmas," he told her when he could talk.

"Christmas yes, but why can't we spend it together?" she asked. "We're going to be miles apart from each other."

"You know why we can't," Ronan told her, his voice tinged with anger. "My son's lost his mother and sister. I'm the only stable thing in his life, at the moment; how would it look if I took you home?"

"I suppose you're right," Lucy said, sounding a bit downhearted. "I'll go back to my, empty, apartment in Crisfield, New York." Ronan knew she was trying to make him feel bad. He knew that she knew he was right really.

"Lucy, if I could take you with me I would. Just be patient, and be happy with the time we've had together, and will have in the future. I haven't seen my son for two or three months," he said. "I haven't finished packing yet, I think I may need some help. Will you help me?"

"Of course I will," Miss Lang replied, and Ronan led the way upstairs. Between them the packing only took a further half an hour. When Lucy came across a toy train she sighed, "Ah, how sweet, is this for Simon?"

"It is," the other Operations Commander replied.

"How sweet," she said, handing it to him. "Your son'll love it," and then she said the one thing he was dreading; "I wish I had children."

"You will, one day," Mr Strobing reassured her, winking. Once they'd finished he carried the suitcase downstairs and loaded it into his HART vehicle. "Do you want a lift?" Ronan asked her.

"Yes, I might as well," Lucy answered and hurried back to her residence; collected her suitcase and loaded it aboard Commander Strobing's car. The other two Operational Commanders were already, making their way, through the snow that lay around, to headquarters to find out which flight they would be catching; the other two had to run to catch them up.

Once inside all four of them made the journey to Commander Robert's office, he looked a bit down but tried not to show it. "What flights are we on?" Leon asked him.

"Oh, you're not," he replied; they all looked puzzled at his response. "What I mean is I've managed to secure two *Gulfstream* G-550s for our use. One will fly to Robin Hood airport in England," he looked towards the English trio, "whilst the other," he turned to Miss Lang, "will take you to JFK airport in America." He paused, Both will be marked as Swiss airlines planes; and leave in five hours."

"However," their commander continued, "I need you all back as soon as possible; as I have had contact from a Dr Honda, at the Memorial Hospital. It appears our Dr Schaiffer went berserk yesterday, and tried to prevent a pregnant disabled girl from having a termination, for whatever reason. Then it appears four or five hours later he was stabbed, and had to be operated on. He's improving, though, and has given the name of his other employer, Dr Q – I assume this is the same one as the head of *Proagnon*; it turns out he was responsible for sending the *phoney* ambulance."

"I could kill him for that," Ronan snarled, "he could've killed me."

"Ronan, Ronan," Commander Roberts said to the younger man sternly. "That is the past, forget it. If we all held vendetta's for every little thing that people did to us we wouldn't get anywhere. Dr Schaiffer's paid the price, in blood."

"Sorry sir," murmured Mr Strobing realising he was condemning an injured man, maybe an already dead man.

"Thankfully," Roberts continued, "the operation was a complete success, and he is, now, out of danger. I intend to visit later and see how he is," he continued. "It is advised that he be taken off duty for a couple of weeks, and sent to our mountain residence on Cyprus to recuperate; so we will be another man short."

"We understand sir," announced Leon, leaning forward in his seat.

"Right you are. Have a good vacation."

Suddenly Gwyneth Jones burst in. "Don't you ever knock?" asked Peter Roberts, irritably.

"Sorry sir, ladies, gentlemen, but we've just received a transmission from our GlobalHawk UAV, patrolling the skies over Afghanistan."

"Get to the point," ordered the commander.

"It would appear that a civilian airliner, we think it was en route to Russia, has been blown up. There were no survivors," she was breathless. Every DC/OC looked at her in astonishment. The whole office fell deadly silent, as they took in what had just been said.

"What?" Roberts thundered, "tell me this isn't true."

"I'm sorry sir but is, see for yourself." Commander Roberts turned to face the viewing screen, with the others. A video feed appeared, downloaded from the UAV, and now transferred to the commander's office, where the pictures appeared on the screen.

A Boeing 787, it appeared to be a 787-9, suddenly a fighter jet – it was identified as an SU-27 – appeared; the fighter seemed to chase down the civilian airliner, which no doubt, was full of passengers. The jet – once it caught sight of the plane seemed to slow down – however, it stayed out of the airliner's radar range but kept the plane in sight.

Suddenly a trail of flame came from underneath the airliner; it looked as if a vehicle of some sort had launched something, probably a projectile of some sort - possibly a missile; the trail of flame became larger as the object approached, suddenly the airliner exploded – the screen was filled with flame as the plane exploded, and then the fragments fell down to the ground.

The jet that had been shadowing the airliner, suddenly, dived towards the ground, evidently seeking a new target. Once it had acquired its new target and locked on, two of the fighter's R-73 missiles were loosed and streaked towards the target on the ground; it was ascertained that these missiles were heat seeking, they all knew that to avoid being mistook for the target the pilot – whoever he was – would have to shut down nearly every system on board to minimum requirements.

As the missiles did not return it was assumed the pilot had done the shutdown correctly. The two missiles continued to streak downwards; The two R-73 missiles struck home, and there was, yet, another explosion on the ground. Whatever had launched the missile, at the plane, no longer existed; every commander strained their eyes to see what the object could have been, but none of them could see what it was. However, they all took it to be a vehicle, of some sort. Once the *vehicle* had become a ball of flame the jet fighter, evidently the pilot was satisfied, turned and flew back to its base.

In the 787 Sergey was puzzled, at first, by the explosions; though hadn't the pilot just informed them of impending danger? First there had been a small explosion under their feet. There was absolute disbelief amongst the passengers, the stewardesses tried to calm people who had become frantic, and the pilot's voice reassured them he'd sent out a distress call. Suddenly there had been a second explosion, from below, louder than the first. Then had come a third explosion, which had seemed to tear the plane in half, and then there had come a strangling sensation, then blackness.

Once the dust, from the explosion, had settled, and the flames put out, a child's teddy was discovered, on the ground. The plane was pulled apart by machinery, and the black box, actually an orange colour, was taken away for analysis.

In Commander Peter Roberts' office the six people, who were there, were dumbstruck. At last Peter spoke up, "Analysis people." He turned his chair to face his four Departmental/Operational Commanders; they were all ashen faced, the colour completely drained from their faces.

"Well sir," Leon said, "we all saw the footage, so there isn't that much to work out, we all think we saw a land vehicle launch, what was probably, a missile at the airliner, and then an SU-27 destroyed that vehicle, presumably it was a truck of some sort, but why?"

"My thoughts exactly, Mrs Jones, where was that planes final destination?" the commander asked her.

Gwyneth, who had been standing in a corner, out the way, stepped forward. "The airliner was ultimately destined for Russia, more exactly Moscow's *Sheremeteyvo* airport."

"Why should it have been heading there?" he thought aloud. He stared across the desk at the others, as if to will some explanation out of them.

Lucy, suddenly, had a flash of inspiration, "Maybe, sir – and this is a long shot, it was carrying Sergey Satov. That's not as hair brained as it sounds."

"Carry on," said Roberts. The other four were listening too, eagerly.

"We know the Russian escaped the FBI a couple of months back, and we assumed that he'd be going, automatically, home, what if he didn't and decided to bide his time? You know, wait until the heat died down, and flew – on a forged passport – on an indirect route to Russia," Lucy explained.

"Crazy," Peter replied, "every law enforcement officer in America was looking for him?"

"What if he'd already left the country, or had laid low."

"But all the airports had descriptions of him," argued the commander.

"What if they didn't get the descriptions out in time," she replied evenly.

"Supposing your theory is correct; how would they know he was on that plane?"

"Perhaps there was someone else from *Proagnon*, an enemy he'd made, on the same flight and they, somehow, had a tracker on them."

"It does sound plausible, sir," interrupted Celia.

"Plausible or not, I won't believe it until I have proof. Why would a terrorist like Sergey Satov take a civilian flight?"

"Less chance of being spotted, perhaps," she replied.

"Gwyneth," the commander barked, "find out where that plane came from and which airline owned it; once you've found that out get me a passenger list? Oh yes, afterwards, was the SU-27 tracked, back to its base?"

"It was sir," the main secretary answered. "It was traced back to Iran. As for your other requests," she continued, "I shall see to them straight away."

"Dismissed," Peter said to her and she left the office.

"What about our leave sir?" Celia queried her superior.

"I'm sorry," apologised Roberts, "but with everything happening at once I'm afraid your leave must be cut to just four days; therefore I need you back on the 27th December. However, you will get another ten days once things quieten down."

"Yes sir," they assured him, and then stood and saluted then left the office. The commander then relaxed in his swivel chair.

The four, Ronan, Celia, Leon and Lucy, left the building. "Typical!" muttered Miss Lang, "He develops a crisis," she indicated headquarters, "and so we get our leave cut by ten days." She didn't look very happy.

"Patience my dear," Celia told her, patting the younger woman's hand. "Yes, we may have had our Christmas leave cut short, but at least we've been promised an extra ten days sometime."

"Hmph," snorted the American, "I wonder when that'll be."

"Ladies, Leon, as we don't have that much time before our planes leave I suggest we get a move on," Ronan said to the others. They hurried to their HART cars, climbed in, and drove off to *Cointrin* airport.

Once they had, all checked in; the two G-550s were piloted out of their hangar and taxied round to the departure gate. First in line was the plane that was to carry the English agents, they only had 988.2 kilometres (620 miles) to go, compared to Lucy's 6197.3 kilometres (3850 miles). Once everyone was aboard each plane, the aircraft taxied to the top of the runway, and requested clearance to take off. Once the pilot, and co-pilot, gained clearance the first aircraft moved slowly forward - powered by its twin Rolls Royce Deutschland BR-72 turbofan engines - and then powered along the concrete runway, which was one thousand metres in length. When it was at maximum speed of 982km/h (610mph) the jet's nose began to lift, and the jet soared into the sky, making full use of its 99ft 7in (30.36 metre) wingspan.

"Good evening ladies, gentlemen, this is Captain Porter. We shall be flying today at 45,000ft (27945m), and cruising at 500mph (805km/h) so therefore we should be landing in, roughly, one and a half hours. Please read the safety instructions provided, and take note of the overhead signs."

Just then, through one of the port (left) windows the English trio saw a similar G-550 jet fly off at more of an angle than their jet. They all assumed it would be the plane carrying their fellow Departmental/Operational Commander; that jet would be flying in a direction that was more westerly than theirs; whereas they were travelling in a more north-westerly direction.

Approximately an hour and a quarter later the business jet, ideal for their usage, began its descent into Robin Hood Doncaster Sheffield airport; the HART members, on board, heard the two turbofan engines power up as the final descent began. "100 metres," reported the pilot, "50, 40, 30, 20, 10." Then came the initial bump as the aircraft landed, and then bounced off. Second time round the six wheels of the jet landed on the 2893m (9491ft), asphalt runway.

The jet's engines throttled back and the plane, after travelling over 1000 metres on full power, slowly drew to a stop. The three people, in the cabin area, waited until the staircase was lowered and then they walked down the steps to a wet and cold December evening, after thanking the captain and his co-pilot.

They had left at seven (Swiss time) but because of the difference of the time zones the time in England was only six-thirty. Each member grabbed their luggage, found their vehicles and began their journeys home. Celia and Ronan were in Ronan's 4X4, while Leon travelled in his Zetec, alone now that Mark Schnieder had been killed.

As they were journeying northwards up the M18, to the junction where they would merge and join the M62 and follow it eastwards toward Kingston-Upon-Hull, where they all lived – but in different areas, Celia happened to say to Ronan, "I know."

"What do you know?" he asked, staring straight ahead.

"You're having an affair with Lucy," she responded, knowingly. "I've seen the signs. The way you two look at each other, and act round one another."

"Are you going to report us?" Commander Strobing wanted to know. "You know it's your duty to."

"No I'm not," was the reply, "because it's only human nature. Her partner's dead, and your wife's been killed. No I'm not going to report you, even though I'm obliged to. I'm just going to say two things."

"And those are?" he asked, now puzzled. Surely it was her duty to report this to Commander Roberts.

"One," she replied, "good luck to you, and two, I don't want to see you thrown out of HART. You're too valuable"

"Thanks Celia," Ronan replied. They reached junction seven that would merge them for the M62 after about twenty minutes. For the other forty minutes they chatted about Celia's family.

At the *Proagnon* bunker Dr Q had gathered the blue suited soldiers into the conference room, together with Squeeze, and they were all watching, on the large viewing screen – at the head of the room – the destruction of Pakistan airlines flight 907, from Karachi to Moscow, by the missile that had been launched from a vehicle on the ground, this vehicle, in turn, had been destroyed by the, lone, SU-27. Only the second in command, along with her superior, knew the real reason the 787 had been destroyed; *If Squeeze, and anyone else, had the intention of betraying me and joining Abdul Singh's revolution*, thought Dr Q, *then those thoughts have died along with the man in that explosion. Though I wonder who was thinking of it.*

"Do we know if anyone of importance was on there?" he asked his number two, innocently, pretending he hadn't known his number three, and chief rival, had been aboard.

""Yes they were Dr Q," replied Squeeze, slightly timidly he noticed. "Abdul Singh, and if I'm correct, Sergey Satov, were on board."

"Good riddance!" the leader barked. "We can't have people like that getting too big for their boots and wanting to relieve me of my command!"

He paused, gauging the reaction, many heads nodded, whilst others just looked straight across the room; finally, his faceplate settled on his number two, she couldn't hold his stare. "Isn't that right Squeeze, my dear?"

"Yes, that's right leader," she answered, almost pathetically. "I can't think of anyone, seated round this table who would want to take over command from you." Was she simply trying to act as nothing had happened, he wondered, or reassure herself.

"Squeeze my dear," he said to her. "Please see me, in my office, afterwards." The colour drained from her face, as if she were frightened for some reason. "Dismissed," he told the soldiers, who were there. They all rose and walked from the room, Dr Q left as well, expecting his number two to follow; when he didn't hear her footsteps behind him he turned and saw her, still sitting in her chair, "Squeeze?" he queried.

"Sorry sir, I just need to go to my quarters, I will be with you soon after."

"Don't make me wait too long," he told her, authoritatively, and strode off.

"Not likely," she said to herself and walked toward her, private, quarters. How had all her dreams, all her goals collapsed around her? Sure, Dr Q had known about Abdul but not about her; how could he have found out? There again, had he really found out? Still, it was of little consequence now. Her superior had reasserted his authority and control over *Proagnon*.

It was obvious that any further efforts to relieve him of command would be dealt with in the same, or a similar, way.

Peter Roberts drove from the HART complex, in his official car, and journeyed to the Memorial Hospital, in the main city of Geneva, to see Hans Schaiffer. As he drove he wondered if he should be going to see the man at all, after all he had been a

Proagnon collaborator; but Hans was a good friend, so, in that respect, he felt he ought to go. He pulled into the parking lot, of the hospital, and parked up, going inside he went up to the ward where his friend was and went in to see him; inside the ward were eight beds, four each side of the room, facing each other.

On the right side of each bed was a locker, for personal items, a wheeled table was slotted over the end of each bed, and in the space between the locker and the next bed was a four legged table, on top of this was any medical equipment the patient may require. Hans was in the end bed on Peter's left as he walked into the ward.

Avoiding the nurses, and the occasional doctor, who were checking on the other patients – those that needed checking – he made his way over to his friend's bed. Dr Hans Schaiffer was sitting up in bed smiling at his superior; Roberts sat in the chair – a plastic affair – beside Schaiffer's bed, "Hello," began Peter, "how are you feeling?"

"Better now I've seen you," was the simple reply.

"That's as maybe," growled Peter. "Hans, why did you do it?"

"I was approached by a *Proagnon* officer, several months back, and he promised me riches beyond my wildest dreams if I cooperated, and brought the HART organisation down from the inside; if not it was instant death, same thing if I told anyone or refused. So what choice did I have?"

"I see," said Peter, not really seeing, but listening all the same. Roberts then said, slightly angered at this revelation, "Ronan nearly was killed because of you, and I'm afraid he's after your blood now." He shifted in his chair, slightly, *Damn, these plastic chairs don't half get uncomfortable after a while.*

"I shall apologise to Mr Strobing when I get out of here, probably another day or two."

Again Roberts barked, "No you won't." Hans Schaiffer looked mystified. "I am sending you to our mountain retreat in northern Cyprus for two weeks, to recuperate."

"But sir?" moaned Dr Schaiffer.

"That's an order Hans. As soon as you are discharged I will come and collect you, personally, drive you to the airport and make, damned, sure you get on that plane." Just then Dr Honda appeared; Commander Roberts had a few words with him, and then turned back to the figure of Dr Schaiffer, "Now remember what I've said. It's for the best, you know it and I know it," and he walked away, and left the hospital.

The HART personnel arrived at their, respective, homes in Hull at around eight fifteen to different reactions. Peter Most was waiting in the main sitting room, watching television with his son Mike, when his wife and Mr Strobing walked in. Mr Most rose, from the beige suite and hugged his wife. "I'm glad you're home," he said, kissing her, and then turned to Ronan. "Thank you for keeping her safe."

Ronan looked a little embarrassed, "I didn't do anything sir, Celia looked after herself. That's one of the basic things they teach us in training."

"Anyway," Peter carried on as Mike hugged his mother furiously, "I heard about Mandy and Zoe, damned shame that – losing both wife and daughter together, you have our deepest sympathies."

"Thank you sir, I'm afraid Celia and I have to return in four days."

"Oh well," he sighed, "your jobs are very demanding. I knew that when I married Celia."

"Anyway, I'll be off now, got to fetch my son," the male agent told him. "He's staying at Mandy's parent's house." Peter murmured his thanks again, and showed the younger man out.

Ronan left the house and climbed into his 4X4. He drove to his in-laws place, and got out. He tapped on the, front, door which was opened, after a few moments, by Arnold Stevens, "Oh it's you," he said sarcastically, and then called back, "put kettle on Elle we've got company."

Then a small figure pushed past the older man, "Dad," enthused Simon, "you're back." Father and son hugged each other. Even Arnold could see they'd missed each other; perhaps he'd judged his son-in-law too harshly in the past.

Consequently, his tone softened, "Come in my boy;" Ronan strode inside, and holding his son's hand they walked into the sitting room. Elle Stevens was just setting the tea things out; there were also cakes – set out on a plate – which made Simon's eyes light up.

"Come on Dad sit next to me," demanded Simon. "Tell me all about your adventures." They sat on the family's old, brown suite.

"Patience son, patience," his father muttered. Ronan sat at the left end, Simon in the middle and Mrs Stevens at the other end. Arnold, meanwhile, settled himself in one of the other brown, comfy, chairs. Arnold and Elle poured themselves tea, and selected a cake each; Ronan did likewise, and then poured his son a, small, cup of tea, Simon wasn't that keen on tea, and moved the cakes over so he could reach them better; Simon selected two cakes, but no-one told him off for getting an extra one. Elle just said, "Isn't that cute?"

"He's a growing boy," Arnold said.

Once they'd all finished, Ronan looked up at the elder members of the household, "Thank you for looking after Simon these past few months."

"What are grandparents for if they can't offer a helping hand occasionally?" asked Arnold Stevens.

"Yes, quite," replied his son-in-law. "Anyway, as you know, I've been sorting some business," Elle opened her mouth to speak but Ronan raised a hand. "I'm sorry but it's quite private. However, it has taken me to Russia, which I didn't enjoy – he thought of the two agents he'd lost, and how he, himself, had nearly lost his life, and then onto Geneva, which I didn't, particularly, enjoy – remembering the shopping centre collapse. However, I am returning, abroad, to business in a few days."

He looked down at Simon, "Simon would you like to stay here over Christmas, or come home with me?"

"I'd like to come home with you," his son answered automatically.

"Very well," said his father. "Unfortunately, I shall have to bring you back here on the morning of the 27th. Is that okay?"

"Yes," replied his son. "Your job must be important for you to return so soon."

"Grimly Ronan said, "It is, it is, really important," and then he turned to Mr and Mrs Stevens. "Do you mind?" he asked them.

"Of course not," replied Elle, "we love having Simon to stay."

"As long as it's okay with both of you," said Ronan. Then he, together with his son, left the house. As they travelled towards their own house Ronan turned to his son, and just gazed, lovingly, at him. That angelic face, he knew tragedy but not as much as his father did. Not yet, anyway.

Arriving home Ronan led his son inside.

Leon Bigship arrived home and switched on his heating, his house was cold – as were most houses that had been empty for a long time. He went upstairs and unpacked; he hadn't brought much home as he would be returning to Geneva soon, once finished he went downstairs and prepared himself a meal of steak pie and chips.

Airline food was okay but he preferred his own home cooking. Later on, he collapsed on his bed, thinking; Ronan had invited him round to share Christmas dinner with Simon and himself, so Leon wouldn't be on his own – usually Mark Schneider invited him over, but now Mark was dead.

At *Proagnon's* bunker Squeeze stepped into her superior's office, and sat down. "You wanted to see me sir," she said, in her, usual, bright cheerful manner.

"Yes I did," he said in reply. "Please be…oh you already are."

He looked directly at her, well as directly as a face behind a faceplate could look at her. "Tell me," purred the voice, "how far in Commander Singh's pocket were you?"

So he knew, thought Squeeze with alarm. How was she meant to reply to him.

"Well sir," she began, trying to pluck up as much courage as she could, "I was never *'in his pocket'* as you put it. It is true I knew of some of his plans, but I always tried to persuade him not to act too rashly."

"Carry on," her superior ordered. Evidently he was enjoying seeing her squirm.

"I told him the best way was to wait, and play the long game," she knew she was probably condemning herself; she'd noticed his pistol was lying on his desk, but she had to plough on, in a desperate bid to save herself. "Sir, do you really think I'd betray you. We've been in this together from the start."

He pointed the pistol at her and pulled the trigger, the silence in the room was audible – Squeeze closed her eyes in anticipation, there was a click. Squeeze opened her eyes, and Dr Q lowered the pistol. "I'm sorry you had to go through that," he apologised, "I just needed to know how far to push you."

"Now," he said, producing another pistol. "This one is loaded unlike the last one; so tell me, who were his co-conspirators?" Squeeze named them for him, "Thank you," he said, "you may go now." She rose and turned to leave, as she reached the door her superior, idly, raised the pistol and fired.

The bullet hit Squeeze straight in the middle of the back and she fell forward, hitting the door, and then falling to the floor. Dr Q replaced the pistol in the drawer where he'd taken it from, next he walked over to the body and kicked it – Squeeze gave a slight moan then fell silent – he pushed her into a corner and just left her. "Guards," he shouted, "I have some unwanted rubbish in my room. Please remove it."

The *Proagnon* guards who had been assigned to Dr Q's protection, opened the office door, looked down at Squeeze's lifeless form, and smiled. As one guard picked her body up their leader handed the list of co-conspirators to the other and said, "I want these people hunted down and shot, they have collaborated with Abdul Singh in his quest to overthrow me. They must all die!"

"Understood sir," replied the soldier, and the two guards left with Squeeze's body. They were good men, Dr Q thought to himself as the door closed. Then he walked back and sat behind his desk, thinking.

Pressing the intercom switch he barked, "Have Sandy Tulliver sent to my office immediately."

Dr Hans Schaiffer was discharged from the Memorial Hospital, in Geneva, on the morning of the 27th December; as good as his word Commander Peter Roberts arrived, at the hospital, to take him to the airport for his trip to Nicosia, on the island of Cyprus.

As it was well known the island was divided into two areas, the northern half which contained the Turkish Cypriot's; whilst in the southern half were the Greek Cypriot's. In 1974 there had been an attempted coup to unite the island with Greece; this had led to a Turkish invasion, which had left the capital divided since then.

Peter drove his friend; his cases had been packed and placed in the boot, to *Cointrin* airport – where a G-200 was parked outside a hangar. "Is that it?" Hans asked in disbelief. "Just a simple G-200, really Roberts, standards are dropping."

Peter rounded on him, "Look what did you expect? It's the only one left, as long as it gets you there its okay, so quit moaning." Hans knew his superior was right so he shut up. He knew there was nothing he could do.

Hans, along with his luggage, boarded the G-200 – the pilot had already filed the flight plan for the journey – and settled himself in for the flight to Nicosia International airport. Once a vacant slot was found for the jet, the plane powered up its twin Pratt & Whitney Canada PW-306A turbofan engines – each capable of producing 6040 pounds of thrust. The pilot and co-pilot taxied the Israeli manufactured business jet, to the top of the single, concrete, runway. This was 12795 feet (3900 metres) long. Once all was clear, and the pilot was given confirmation the plane could go, he and the co-pilot powered up the engines – one each side of the main body of the aircraft, towards the rear – and three dual sets of wheels on the aircraft hurtled down the runway, speeding up to its maximum speed of 867 km/h (538mph).

Once the business jet had reached this, maximum, speed it took off and flew in a south-easterly direction toward the, divided, island of Cyprus. Commander Peter Roberts watched as the aircraft began its 2050 mile journey, and then walked away and left the airport.

In the city of Hull the four day break seemed to have gone by too fast. Ronan seemed to have grown closer to his son, and Simon had loved the model of a replica steam train, complete with ten carriages. Leon, who had come to share Christmas dinner with them, and Ronan had watched, as a delighted Simon, had wheeled the train about, on the floor, most of Christmas afternoon. Once Leon had left at about eight Ronan had phoned Lucy, to see how she was. He checked the door to the sitting room was closed, blocking him off from his son, before he dialled.

"Hello," she said when she answered the phone.

"Hello Lucy," Ronan replied. "How are you?"

"Oh darling," she responded with a little squeal. "I'm fine, had my sister over for dinner. She left about fifteen minutes ago; so I've been in the shower since. So are you okay?"

"Considering it's my first Christmas without Mandy and Zoe, I'm bearing up. Simon seems cheerful enough, and I've had Leon over for dinner, didn't want him to spend it alone."

"Have you told your son about us yet?" she asked, in that silky, smooth, voice of hers.

"Not yet; he's busy playing with his new train. As soon as he's finished I will," her lover assured her.

"You'd better! I miss you."

"I will and I miss you." She blew him a kiss down the phone line, and they said their goodbyes then Ronan returned to his son. "Simon," he said, sitting down on their settee. "Just come here a minute, I want to talk to you."

"Can't it wait dad? I'm busy," his son protested.

His father replied mildly, "I'm sure you are, but, please, it's rather important." Grudgingly, Simon came over and sat next to his father. "Simon," his father began, unsure how to go on, "you know your mother and sister have gone on a long trip and won't be coming back." The boy's eyes told him that he'd understood. "Well, how would you feel if I was to bring another lady home?" It was crunch time now, the boy had been told, whatever Simon decided Ronan would abide by.

"Do you mean another lady to replace Mum?" asked his son, slightly puzzled.

"No," replied his father. "I've met someone I like, at work, and she likes me. I just need to know if you mind. She wouldn't replace your Mum; no one ever will."

Simon thought about it, and then asked, "If you like her; does that mean I'll be getting more brothers and sisters?"

"Maybe in time," Ronan replied honestly. He was slightly worried now. Simon looked at his father, and examined him, up and down.

"Will you still love me the same?" the boy asked his father.

"Of course I will, nothing will ever change that," replied his father, ruffling the boy's hair.

"Well dad," began his son, it was now the moment of truth. "if you promise me nothing will change then she can come here. If for some reason I don't like her she's not staying."

"Thank you," said Ronan, "that is all I ask."

"Next problem will be introducing her to Gran and Granpa," he said. He was pretty sure they'd object, well Elle might understand but there was the problem of Arnold.

At the Most household Peter showed his wife her present, a brand new, blue, Honda. "Thank you my darling," she enthused and kissed him; Mike, who was watching from the doorway, suddenly felt very embarrassed.

Everyone had a good time that day, but it was over, all too soon.

The jet carrying Hans Schaiffer arrived at Nicosia airport roughly four hours and ten minutes after it had begun its journey to the island of Cyprus. Once the plane had landed, and come to a halt, Mr Schaiffer was met by a HART representative and taken, by car, to the lodge deep within the mountains, on the northern part of the island.

The lodge was a small two-storey building, similar to a small house, situated on a rocky outcrop, and nestled in the middle of a pine forest. It was accessible, only, by a small road from the East. Once inside the German walked in the front door and then walked up the stairs – situated to his right – and down the upstairs corridor, to the bedroom, and began to unpack his suitcases; he had brought plenty of clothes to last him his two week stay, and, what was that, in the bottom? It was a little box, similar to a cigarette box, he opened it – there was nothing inside – so he closed it and just threw it in a waste basket, behind him.

As it landed in the bin he didn't see, as his back was to the bin, the faint red light that started to pulsate on the box, signalling something or someone.

Once he'd finished unpacking he went back downstairs, and through to one of the rooms at the back of the lodge, which served as a kitchen. Hans prepared himself a light snack and, once ready, he took himself, together with his snack through to the lodge's sitting room, at the front.

The signal was picked up by the *Proagnon* battlecruiser and relayed, via a satellite connection, to the *Proagnon* bunker headquarters.

Dr Q had met with Sandy Tulliver earlier in the day, he liked this young protégé, much younger than him – only in her early twenties. Her hair was, like her name, sandy, and her eyes were of a dazzling blue. She was the exact opposite to Squeeze, or Tanya Roberts, in those details, but he knew she would make a good replacement for his number two.

Once he'd seen her, and talked with her, he'd, suddenly, had a brainwave and decided to promote her. "Sandy," he announced to her, "as Tanya Roberts, also known as Squeeze, has departed."

"You mean dead!" she responded firmly. He liked her feisty attitude.

"If you wish to put it like that then yes, anyway I think you would be an ideal person to fill her shoes/boots," her superior responded.

"And why is that?" was the next enquiry. "Is it because of my intelligence, my youth, or my physical attributes?" He could tell, by that, she was suspicious of his motives.

"Your intelligence of course," was the reply, although he did admire her body. Sandy knew this but said nothing; she'd been watching him throughout the meeting, "Squeeze's quarters are, or were," and he gave her directions.

Later on, after lunch – he had his lunch on his own as he had to remove the faceplate - the bleeper went off to tell him an incoming message was being relayed directly to his office. Dr Q answered and was told the battlecruiser *Admiral Lazarev* had detected a signal from Cyprus, as it was very weak it was assumed the signal was coming from the mountains.

Strange, thought Dr Q, there were no agents in Cyprus; who could have activated the signal? Abdul Singh was dead, as was Sergey Satov, he knew so who was it; what about Hans Schaiffer? He'd been stabbed, but was he dead? If he wasn't it could be him, but he knew he'd failed to kill the last remaining person from the school group, so why would he activate his signal?

There was only one way to find out; plus if it was him, Dr Q was pretty certain it was now, he had to die! The leader of *Proagnon* called a, small, group of the, blue clad, soldiers to his office and gave them instructions, of what to do, on their trip to Cyprus. The soldiers, four of them, nodded that they understood their orders, and then left to carry out their mission.

The four men flew aboard a HIND helicopter, under cover of darkness, to their destination, or as near to the signal as they could, the HIND had been fitted with a tracking device. Then the four men slid down zip wires to the ground that surrounded the lodge, once all four soldiers were down the air transport powered up its twin 2200 ship Isotov TV-3-117 turbine engines, and headed back eastwards towards its headquarters.

Mr Schaiffer was sat on the green settee, watching the television, in the main room, when he heard, or thought he did, a, powerful, helicopter overhead; he dismissed it, thinking that maybe HART was, maybe, using the nearby, disused, base as a testing ground – they did once in a while; yet, he'd never heard anything in his previous four days on the island. Then there had been a kind of thunk, thunk on the ground. He sighed and got up to look out the window, he saw nothing, must've imagined it. He sat back down on the settee to relax.

After a few minutes he felt a very slight breeze in the room, as if a window had been left slightly open; again thinking nothing of it he pulled his, grey, cardigan tighter round him, even fastening the buttons, to see if that would help. It was then he smelt it, a smell like rotten eggs but there was something else there too; peering round Mr Schaiffer saw a, small, egg shaped object on the floor by the window – it fizzed and smoked. Suddenly, it exploded in a blinding, white, light; the old man, as that's what he thought of himself as now, fell forward – as if trying to save himself. Once the flash of white light had dissipated and his sight had readjusted again four figures stood in the room. "Who, who are you?" stammered Hans.

"We are *Proagnon* troops," replied the leader, and then as one the four soldiers raised their assault rifles. They were of a different design to the usual assault rifles

"Please don't kill me?" pleaded the older man.

They just looked at him, this pathetic old man, and fired.

The four Departmental/Operational Commander's had travelled back to Geneva's *Cointrin* airport, on the 27th December. They were given an extra day's rest to overcome any jet lag; once everyone was, fully, recovered Commander Roberts called the four: Celia, Leon, Lucy and Ronan, to his office.

"Yes sir," they said as they entered, each of them saluting.

"At ease people, take a seat." They sat at the desk, on the chairs provided. Gwyneth Jones was standing to one side of Roberts.

"Tell them Gwyneth," he said to her.

"Ah yes, earlier today one of our Unmanned Aerial Vehicles detected a helicopter leaving Cyprus, the helicopter in question was shown to be a HIND D class. Therefore we know *Proagnon* soldiers are on the island; over to you commander."

"I would guess they are on the island to find, capture, or kill, Dr Schaiffer. Somehow they must have detected where he is. So the question now is who do we send to rescue him?"

"Do we have to send anyone?" demanded Ronan crossly.

"We do," Peter retorted angrily. "Ronan, dismissed!"

"But sir," Ronan said. "I never…, I mean I…" However, he could see that the commander meant it, so he left, feeling ashamed of himself.

"Now perhaps we can discuss this properly, or does anyone else wish to join Mr Strobing?" The other three, as Gwyneth Jones had already left, shook their heads. "Good," he continued, "any ideas on who we send?"

"It really ought to be a, small, commando type group," said Leon, "led by one of us, as I don't, exactly, see Ronan volunteering for the mission."

"Yes, I agree the group should be small," Commander Peter Roberts agreed. "Next question is how do we get them there?"

"I thought," interjected Celia. "The area around the lodge is woodland, correct?"

"Perfectly," replied Roberts, wondering what she had in mind. "Please go on," he said from where he was seated behind his desk.

On the desk were two tray's – one red – one blue; the red tray was for any new paperwork that needed a signature or anything, once the paperwork was finished with it went into the blue tray which Mrs Jones, or whoever was on shift, would empty at the end of the day. Also, situated, on the desk were photos in frames – from happier times in Peter's life, and a globe of the world. There was the usual array of pens, pencils and writing paper that was to be found on most working desks. Although there wasn't that much on the desk, when you looked at it, it could be seen it was the desk of someone important.

"I suggest," continued Celia, "we send a couple of F-16 Falcons, or an AWACS, and drop incendiary devices into the area, thus starting fires."

"I don't like it but carry on," replied Peter.

"And then we fly the Chinooks over the area and drop water on the fires, in the pretence of fighting the fire, and, under darkness our squad of four can be dropped, down zip wires, to the area surrounding the lodge."

"It's a crazy idea," muttered Peter Roberts, "but it's just crazy enough to work." He smiled at Celia, "It's a brilliant plan."

"Thank you sir," she said, pleased with herself.

"Now who do we send on this mission?"

"I am prepared to lead it," Leon volunteered.

"Thank you," Peter said to him. "You may choose your own team. Once you have let me know and I'll give you my full backing. You are all dismissed for now."

They all left the commander's office. "Wonder where Ronan is," muttered Celia, "I admit I know how he feels, what with what happened, but I felt the commander was a bit harsh on him."

"He just needs to learn that we all need to get on with each other, whatever's happened" Commander Bigship said in response to her.

"I'll go and find him," Commander Lang, suddenly, said to them.

"I'll come with you," Celia Most told her.

Lucy was going to object, but caught the twinkle in her colleague's eye. "Okay," she said, in her New York accent. "Glad to have you along."

"See you later Leon," they called to him, and then ran off, towards the residences, giggling like schoolgirls. *Grow up*, thought Leon as he heard them giggle and continued to the building that would tell him the condition of the U.S. Navy's, now HART's ships, to see what state of readiness they were in, should they be needed.

Once Mrs Most and Miss Lang felt they were far enough away from their colleague they slowed to walking pace; any soldiers they passed would salute, the two women would salute back.

Celia lowered her voice and said to Lucy, "I know." Lucy looked surprised but feigned ignorance.

"About what?" she asked, in a voice as low as her companion's.

"The affair you're having with Commander Strobing." Commander Most said. "Tell me, how long has it been going on?"

Lucy pulled her colleague behind one of the various buildings in the compound and replied, "I don't know what you mean."

"The hell you don't," retorted her companion. "Ronan's admitted it, so why don't you be a good girl and tell me all about it."

Lucy realised the game was up, so pulled her Beretta on her friend. "Oh," sighed Celia, "and what good will killing me, if that's your intention, do? Trust me Lucy, I've been in the same position as you, once, so put the gun away and let's talk."

"I suppose you're right," murmured the other woman, putting the firearm away. "It all started the day after my fiancé, Mark Schnieder, was killed, I just needed a shoulder to cry on, and I'd always had feelings, deep down, for Commander Strobing."

"Anyway," she continued, "the day the pleasure cruiser was destroyed, and we lost three TOMCAT pilots, Commander Strobing was really low, so I went to cheer him up. One thing led to another, as it does, and we fell into bed together; at that time his wife was still alive. Since she passed away Ronan and I have been seeing each other in our residences – whenever we can, but his home life revolves around his son, he said he would broach the subject with Simon over Christmas, but he hasn't told me the answer yet."

"I see," Celia said gently, "c'mon let's find him," and she led the way over to their colleague's residence. They knocked on the door but there was no response. "Ronan," called Miss Lang through the letterbox, "open up." Still nothing!

"Where can he be?" said Lucy, in a voice that tried to relay confidence, but Celia detected a timid, slightly frightened tone in the voice.

"Guard," Celia called to a passing soldier, "I don't suppose you've seen Commander Strobing."

"Why yes I have," he said. "He drove off about ten minutes ago, headed toward the main city of Geneva."

"C'mon then," Lucy told Celia, "we'll take my car." The two of them jogged, in fact almost ran, to Miss Lang's automobile. They hurried to the HART car; Lucy got in the driver's side, whilst Celia was left with the passenger side.

When they were both belted in Lucy started the engine and drove, slowly, out of the compound.

When they emerged onto the main carriageway she really gunned the car's engine and they shot off, much to the annoyance of other motorists; there were horns honking at them. Lucy knew she had to find him, and fast, "Slow down," cried Celia. "You'll kill us both."

"Ronan's more important," the driver retorted.

"Okay, but what use are you going to be to him if you're dead?" her companion asked.

"I see what you mean," Miss Lang replied and, abruptly, slowed down, again to much horn honking. As they turned onto the A1 motorway, which connected to the city of Geneva; Lucy journeyed into the city, and then asked Celia, "Where would you look first?"

"Let's try the railway stations," she suggested. Lucy drove to both of the railway stations: Geneve-Secheron and Lancy Pont-Range. There was no sign of him at either, or at the underground stations. They checked the hospitals, just in case. In fact, they checked everywhere they could think of. Commander Strobing was nowhere to be found.

The two women were feeling cold, now, in the Geneva air, it was mostly cold when Celia said, "Shall we just check the lakes and the river before heading back?"

"Why not?" muttered her colleague. "We've checked about every other damn place." It was evident Lucy was afraid, and desperately upset, at the thought of losing him but she was trying to cover it with bravado.

The two female, HART, Departmental/Operational Commander's got back in the car and visited the three lakes: Leman Lake, Geneve Plage and Bain du Paqui. Nothing, so they began heading back through the city, at a, relatively, steady pace, they had just turned to drive over the bridge that crossed the Arve River, when they saw it: Ronan's car; pulling in behind it the two women got out and walked across.

It was then that they saw him, just standing there and looking into the distance. "Ronan," the American shouted joyfully, and ran over to him and hugged him. "Come back,"

Mrs Most heard. "We need you, your son needs you, I need you. Come home."

Ronan looked absently at her, as he seemed to consider what she'd said, and then he saw Celia Most approach; she nodded to him, confirming Lucy Lang's words. He, then, turned his head back to Lucy and met her gaze again. He seemed to, suddenly, come back to life.

"You're right," he held her tighter, and kissed her, "I will come back," and he let Miss Lang go and walked over to Celia, and hugged her, much to Lucy's annoyance.

The hug brought back memories of times long gone, when he had been with Celia Sancton, before Peter Most had come along. Mrs Most could tell there was still a flicker within Mr Strobing towards her, but she couldn't risk her marriage for a quick fling with him. "No," she told him, "this isn't right; Lucy needs you more than I do."

They then got into their cars, Celia in Lucy's while Ronan Strobing, together with Lucy Lang, climbed into his vehicle, and journeyed, in convoy, back towards headquarters. None of them noticed the nondescript, brown, van that pulled out of a side street and began to follow the vehicles; at a distance where the men, in the van, could keep the convoy in sight, but also so as not to make it too obvious they were following the two HART automobiles.

The van had been customised at some time, to enable it to move faster than an average, everyday, van. It was also fitted with a tracking device that enabled the occupants to choose a target, and then follow it with ease. There were six men aboard: the driver and passenger, both in plain clothes, and four men in the back – all armed with AK-47's.

Once all three vehicles had turned onto the motorway, and the traffic had built up, the van lurched forward. Swerving dangerously, through the other vehicles, to reach its targets, the van nearly collided with several buses, trucks and cars. "What the hell?" Ronan said, catching a glimpse of the swerving van, in the rear view mirror. Lucy hadn't noticed.

"What's wrong?" asked his travelling companion, still totally oblivious.

The van was, now, alongside Miss Lang's car; throwing the, sliding, side door open, the four gunmen, inside, peppered the automobile with machine gun fire. The car, driven by Celia Most swerved about as the van started to accelerate towards the leading car, driven by Ronan Strobing. As soon as the vehicle the gunmen were in started to accelerate towards his vehicle, Ronan having seen the automobile Celia was driving hit the, central, concrete reservation, he said to Lucy, grimly, "Hang on," and he did his best to weave in and out of the traffic ahead, but got stuck behind three, slow-moving, trucks. Were they there to aid the van containing the gunmen, by deliberately appearing in front of the HART automobile, or were the vehicles just part of the, normal, traffic?

He watched, helplessly, as the brown van loomed larger in the mirror, and he thought, *Oh well, this is it, I'm sorry Simon.* Suddenly, he had a, quick thought, and called across to Lucy, "Out." He knew it was a futile gesture but, well, he had to try. Reaching across he opened her door and clicked her belt free.

"Out," he said again, the van nearly upon them, he reached over and pushed her out; he knew she'd be okay.

"Oi!" she shouted angrily as he pushed her, still oblivious of the approaching danger. Over and over she rolled, and then looked up as she heard the, explosive, shots of gunfire.

She checked her wrist communicator was okay once she'd stopped falling. It was so she pressed the contact button, when Gwyneth appeared, on screen, Lucy pressed the transmit button and spoke rapidly, "There has been an incident on the A1 motorway heading towards the HART compound. Two HART vehicles have been shot at, and two personnel may be injured. Send someone over quickly."

"Just patching your co-ordinates in."

"Well hurry up," snapped the American. "They may be dead!"

"Two recovery trucks will be with you shortly," and with that Gwyneth shut the transmission. Lucy had always thought that Gwyneth Jones had been the wrong person for the job she was in, and had made those feelings quite clear, in the past.

About ten or so minutes later the recovery trucks, together with two ambulances arrived; swinging round into the southbound lane they discovered, first, the car Celia had been driving. The lane of the motorway the cars were on had been shut off by the Geneva police, who were on the scene, to prevent risk of injury to anyone else.

The car driven by Celia Most was recovered first, and Celia was brought out the car, she was a mess, and loaded aboard the first ambulance; once the paramedics had climbed back aboard the emergency vehicle roared away, lights flashing and sirens blaring.

All HART cars were equipped with a super reinforced petrol tank, preventing explosions as much as possible; therefore the vehicle could be placed on one of the recovery trucks, without fear of explosion. Once the vehicle was fastened down the truck left the scene, to return to the compound. Next Lucy directed the vehicles to the last point at where she'd seen Ronan's car.

The car Ronan had been driving, it was estimated had travelled a further two hundred metres, and then, evidently, skidded, before the automobile had ploughed – nose first – into the, concrete, strut of a bridge. From the look of it the car was a write off and Commander Strobing looked dead! The paramedics got out of their vehicle and looked at the scene, just shrugged, and then turned to return to their vehicle.

"No!" the American woman shouted, running up. "He's not dead, I just know he isn't." Sighing, the paramedics got the stretcher out the ambulance, and wheeled it to the side of the car, "Sorry Miss," one of the paramedics said to Lucy, "he looks dead to me."

"But he isn't," Lucy shouted. "Just take him to a hospital, please," she implored, as a last ditch effort. The man who'd spoken to her looked across at his colleague, who nodded.

"Okay Miss, if it'll make you happy." Miss Lang smiled, sweetly, at him as if to confirm it would make her very happy. They managed, carefully, to get him out and lay him on the stretcher; his face was covered in blood. Lucy hopped in the ambulance, before either paramedic could object, just to be near him. Finally, the doors to the vehicle were closed and the emergency vehicle sped away, lights and sirens going.

The vehicle pulled up outside Cantonal hospital, and the doors were flung open and the paramedics rushed their patient into the building. The American noticed, as she got out, another emergency vehicle, its lights still flashing, and doors wide open; they must have brought Commander Most here as well. She hurried after the paramedics, and managed to catch up with them before they boarded an elevator that took them to the top floor, where all emergency treatment was carried out.

Ronan was rushed into operating theatre 2A, of course Lucy wasn't allowed inside for fear of contamination, to the patient; however, just before he was pushed inside she was allowed to give him a quick kiss, and then he was taken from her. Would she see him again? Lucy was confident she would. Peeking inside theatre 2B she saw Celia, face serene, as the surgeons and doctors operated on her.

It was all too much to bear for her and she broke down in tears; first Mark had been taken from her, and now it looked as if Ronan might follow. Where was the justice in it all?

Slowly, she wandered back downstairs and outside, it was cold but she wasn't bothered; clicking on her communicator she waited until Mrs Jones answered, or whoever was on duty. The bright, young, face of Lisa Bell greeted her, "Hello Lucy."

Pressing the transmit button Lucy said, "Tell Commander Roberts that Commander's Strobing and Most are in the," she looked back, "Cantonal hospital. Both are in surgery now, and I shall stay with them until I am relieved."

"Thank you for your report; I will convey your message to Mr Roberts."

Lucy stayed outside, about an hour longer, and then returned inside the building, up to the operating theatre's 2A and B; looking inside each she saw Ronan and Celia were gone. Catching hold of a passing nurse she asked, "Where are the two patients who were brought in earlier?"

"They've been moved to the intensive care unit (ICU) ward," said the nurse, in reply, hoping she was being helpful. "Down the corridor," she pointed straight ahead, "second left, down that corridor and it's second on your right. Oh, and before you go in, please put a white gown on."

"I will," she replied, darting off the way the nurse had indicated.

CHAPTER 13

Back to the fight & the first skirmish!

Back at the lodge, in Cyprus, Dr Schaiffer raised his head, he wasn't dead! The room, however, was riddled with bullet holes; one of the men grabbed hold of Schaiffer and pulled him into a standing position. "Now Herr Schaiffer," the leader was, obviously, a fellow German. "Pierre, the bonds," the third member of the team handed his leader rope and a blindfold.

"Before I tie you up my name is Franz von Richter, and your pathetic group, HART, will never defeat us in *Proagnon*," he laughed, a mocking laugh, as he bound Dr Schaiffer's wrist, tied his arms to his body, and then blindfolded him. "Take him away Anton," and Schaiffer was dragged from the room.

The man who had been, quietly, watching the outside, suddenly turned to face his leader. "What is it Brutus?"

"Herr von Richter, there is a large plane flying overhead."

Von Richter got up from the, plush, leather sofa, and joined his colleague at the window. "So there is," he said. "It must be looking for something, as it looks like an AWACS aircraft. HART can't know we're here yet, no aircraft tracked us as we arrived. Our transport had its infrared jamming device on all the way."

The AWACS Sentry flew over the lodge, powered by its four powerful Pratt & Whitney turbofan engines. The two crew members on board waited patiently, to carry out their mission, there were at least 200 incendiary devices, to start the fires, stacked in crates around the hold. As it reached the far side of the building, where the main wooded area was, the ramp at the back dropped open slightly and the other two crew members began dropping the devices to start fires. Once this was done the aircraft, in order not to raise too much suspicion, flew back to its base in Cyprus.

"Must've found what they were looking for," said von Richter, moving back and reseating himself.

Pierre suddenly rushed in, "Herr von Richter, Herr von Richter," he was in a panic the leader saw. "There are flames outside, ferocious flames; and horrid black smoke."

"The forest must be on fire. Do not worry yourself, the lodge is set on a rocky square, the flames will not harm us." The noise of a helicopter flying overhead soon quieted them all.

Brutus called back into the room, "There is a large helicopter approaching our position. On its sides, it seems to have large containers filled with water." As it was approaching from the same side as the AWACS had come from, none of the occupants of the lodge knew it was a helicopter from HART that was using the cover of the flames to mount a rescue attempt.

"Well," began von Richter, "there you are. Maybe the AWACS aircraft detected the fire and reported in its position; and now they're using helicopters to bring in water to douse the flames."

"That is probably right," muttered Anton, who had now re-entered the main room and was now, looking out the main window. "The fire was probably started by a careless idiot." Little did any of them know that the fire had been started deliberately.

A couple of hours later and the fire was close to finally being extinguished. However, still more water was being dropped on the area as some parts of the fire were still raging; none of the terrorists noticed that on one Chinook helicopter there was a slight difference. As it hovered overhead, four zip lines were lowered down to the immediate area around the building; four black clad figures made their way down the wires to the ground below, as soon as they were down they dropped to below window view level; this was Commander Bigship's team of commandos.

Leon and the men were armed with M-16 machine guns and extra clips for them, each was also armed with two flashbang grenades – to disorientate the enemy, two smoke grenades, gas masks, and Beretta pistols. The commander had chosen, for his team, Major Shinto Howell, Sergeant Dan Anco – who was also an explosives expert, and newly promoted

Captain Theresa Robins; slowly and carefully, the four of them made their way around the building and to the rear entrance.

To avoid suspicion the Chinook helicopters still dropped water on the area where the flames had been, though most of the fire was out. The team members stood up and Leon asked Dan as they reached the back door, he almost had to shout to make himself heard, "Can you blow it?"

"Yes sir," replied the sergeant, taking from his backpack two pieces of what looked like plasticine. He attached one each side of the door, and joined them together with a piece of wire, next he attached another strand of wire to the middle of this piece; then he rolled the drum of wire out. Once all four of them were, safely, round the corner, Dan used his cigarette lighter to light the wire, as both pieces were encased in paper so burnt easily. About a half-minute later there came a loud explosion.

"Go! Go! Go!" shouted Leon, urging his squad forward; as the fire was now out, the Chinooks had moved away. They burst through the doorway, that used to contain a door, and moved through the lodge, carefully, looking for terrorists; the first one they encountered was Anton, he was silenced by a shot from Shinto Howell. "That was unnecessary," Leon told him, not particularly angry but not especially pleased. "You should know better."

"Sorry sir," Major Howell replied, "I thought he was armed." As they made their way deeper into the building they encountered Pierre, who was carrying his AK-47 assault rifle; again he was silenced by a shot from Dan Anco. Quietly and stealthily, they made their way down the corridor towards the main lounge area, Leon leading his troops. When they arrived Leon motioned to the two men to wait outside whilst Teresa and himself went inside.

"Stay concealed," he whispered to them, as he turned the handle. Standing inside the room was Franz von Richter, he was holding a gun at Dr Schaiffer's temple. Brutus stood, by his leader, silently watching. Teresa stood back from her commander, but holding her gun which was aimed at the big, silent, man.

"Welcome," announced von Richter. "You are about to witness the death of Dr Schaiffer." His face twisted into a cruel smile of satisfaction.

Leon stood there, aghast for a moment, and then out of the corner of his eye he noticed Teresa, and understood her intention, "Hold your fire," he ordered; she obeyed and, automatically, lowered the weapon. "May I enquire as to who you are?" he asked conversationally

"My name is Franz von Richter, I was recruited from the neo-Nazi movement in Germany, yes we are still in existence, the Hitler adorers, but with *Proagnon's* assistance we shall take over Germany and form a glorious new Reich." He smiled at Commander Bigship, coldly, "Now tell your associate to drop her weapon, now, or the old man gets it." He pressed the pistol more firmly against Dr Schaiffer's temple.

Leon sighed in defeat, "Okay you win, drop the gun Teresa," she dropped the machine gun on the floor.

"Good girl," murmured von Richter, somewhat patronisingly, "now kick it towards Brutus." She did as he ordered only because she didn't want Dr Hans Schaiffer's death on her conscience. "Kill her!" he ordered his colleague.

"If you do I will kill you," Leon retorted in anger, looking at the man who held his other friend hostage.

"Ah well, if you insist, I will kill Dr Schaiffer. You are in a bit of a dilemma I think."

"Not really, may I just say two things to Dr Schaiffer before you kill him?" Leon asked von Richter. Franz von Richter nodded, but told Leon to make it quick as possible as his trigger finger was getting itchy. "Okay," said the HART man, "Dr Schaiffer," the man looked up; a look of defeat in his eyes, "eyes and elbows." This was the key phrase for the two agents outside, if they hadn't been killed which Leon knew they hadn't been, to throw in flash and bang grenades.

On cue two grenades flew in and Teresa threw one of her own; suddenly, the room was lit up as bright as a Christmas tree, and the other two soldiers, having pulled the, now, unconscious Hans Schaiffer outside, regrouped outside the main room. Teresa followed them out, finally their commander made his way out. Reaching into an inside pocket he pulled out a smoke grenade, uncapped it, and rolled it into the room, slamming the door shut.

"Masks," was the next order he gave and each member of the team pulled on their gas masks, "protect Dr Schaiffer." He held the door shut.

"On it chief," said Shinto Howell, folding a cloth in half and placing it over Schaiffer's nose and mouth. The team waited about 30 seconds, and then the three male agents burst into the room; Teresa Robins having taken over the care of their German superior medical man. She untied the ropes that bound him and removed the blindfold.

Gunfire was heard in the main room, once the shooting had finished the two HART men, together with their commander, surveyed the scene; von Richter and Brutus were dead, well and truly. The furniture, especially the sofa, had numerous bullet holes in it, and the window, that had been smashed before was now totally obliterated. "I think that's a job well done," the Englishman announced to his colleagues, "now let's get out of here." The team of four, supporting Dr Schaiffer between them, strode back down the main corridor, closing the door to the main room behind them.

Once the door was closed, they all took off their gas masks and walked calmly back the way they'd come, Dr Schaiffer was now sufficiently recovered to support and walk himself.

As they passed through the entranceway, where the door used to be, the commander of the mission looked round and casually said, "Somebody ought to fix that door, anyone could get in." The others laughed, even Dr Schaiffer who wasn't known for his sense of humour.

"Radio headquarters," he told Major Howell, who was their radio operator. "Tell them mission accomplished, and ask if they could provide transport out of here," the radio operator nodded, got the radio out of his own backpack, set it up, and transmitted the message he'd been asked to relay.

About two minutes afterwards a HMMWV roared up to their position; it was an M1097 model, a cargo, equipment, or troop, carrier. "Hop in," the driver said to them, the team, along with the HART medical man climbed in the back and the vehicle roared off towards the base on Cyprus. From there a Chinook would transport them back to the main HART compound.

It was now the 31st December, and at Cantonal hospital Lucy waited by her colleagues, who were still in ICU; Commander Roberts had issued a rota for hospital watch, there was a four person rota and each did six hours. Commander Most had recovered quite a bit and had been moved into a side ward. However, there was still no change in Commander Strobing, what would she do if he died? She'd been told he had an extensive head injury and some broken ribs from where he'd hit the steering wheel; he had a bandage wrapped around his head and bandages wrapped round his chest.

Commander Lucy Lang was deadly worried now; were she to lose him as well as Mark Schnieder? That was the main reason she kept her bedside vigil on him, if it had been anyone else, even Commander Roberts, she would not have shown them so much attention. It was because she loved him and wanted to share her life with him she stayed with him, just in case.

The New Yorker had wanted to share New Year with Ronan, get drunk with him, spend the night together, and wake up in the morning with a massive hangover next to him. Now that was out of the question, here he was in hospital. "C'mon Ronan," she said, "wake up, I need you." The American had been talking to him, like this, for a day or two now, but it hadn't worked.

Then, remarkably, after two weeks of being in a coma he had started to come around; Miss Lang, who had just taken over from Stan Dennis, was there – she held his hand, tightly, and watched as he slowly opened his eyes; his bed had been moved a couple of days before to a more, private, room. As soon as he opened his eyes and saw her he muttered, "Hello Lucy," his voice was slightly slurred but she'd been informed, by the doctors who'd treated him that this was normal for a head injury, but he would lose the slur once all his brain functions were back in the right places. He tried to rise to kiss her but found it too painful.

"Don't try to sit up," she said. He could see tears welling up in her eyes as she blurted out, "Oh Ronan, I thought I'd lost you."

He sank back down onto the bedsheets, looked up and asked her, "What happened?"

"You were driving back to the compound when you were shot at," she replied.

"Good God," was all he could think of to say. "Was anyone else with me?"

Lucy thought, and then looked back at him, "Only me," she said guardedly, sipping a cup of water she'd got before she'd relieved Stan.

Commander Strobing could tell, from the look his colleague had given him, he wasn't being told the whole truth, "C'mon Commander Lang, tell me the full truth. There's something you're hiding." Lucy hesitated, should she tell him about Celia? It might only worry him, even though she'd been discharged a week ago but told to take it easy. "Please Lucy just tell me, that's an order." He knew he wasn't being told the, whole, truth, and didn't like it.

Even though they were both commander's Lucy knew Ronan outranked her in superiority and so knew when she was beaten. She caved in, "Okay, Celia Most was following in the car behind."

Ronan looked up at her, startled, his eyes wide now, "What happened to her?"

"She wasn't as badly injured and was operated on, like you, she recovered shortly after and about a week ago she was discharged." She paused, "Apparently, the mission to rescue Dr Hans Schaiffer was a success as well."

"Miss Lang," Ronan began, "I want you to know that, even though I said some bad things about that man, I didn't really wish him harm." Lucy nodded her understanding. "So I've got you for how much longer?" He wanted to make the most of the time they'd got left.

She looked over at the clock, on the cabinet beside the bed, "Oh another five hours."

"Just think what we can do in five hours," he said to her and winked. The old Ronan was still in there. After the five hours had passed and Lucy had brought him up to date with things she got up, stretched, and kissed him.

"Goodbye darling," she called back to him as her relief, Bruno Lola, arrived. Night shift, well someone had to do it. "By the way I like your turban."

Another week slowly passed, then finally Commander Strobing was discharged from the hospital, his head bandages having been removed, and a smaller dressing put around his chest. He walked from the hospital, head held high, and attended by Lucy, who fussed over him all the way to the new HART car, the Apollo II. The commander was told he was to see Dr Schaiffer, on a weekly basis, to check on how his wounds were healing.

The cars, belonging to the Departmental/Operational Commanders were all second generation Apollo's; the doors, and windows were now all bullet-proof, the front of the vehicle, where the engine was, was also mortar proof, as were the roof and the boot.

Plus the windows were now all made of tinted glass, enabling the occupants to see out, but no one could see inside. Altogether, it was a vast improvement on the previous model, the Apollo I.

Commander Lang held the door open for him and he climbed in the passenger seat and put his safety belt on.

Ronan had had to borrow most of the clothes he'd worn during his stay, from the hospital, the only thing which was really his was the uniform he'd been wearing when he was brought in, which had been cleaned by the laundry service available.

Lucy placed any other clothes that had been brought in; from his residence, in the boot, and then walked round to the driver's door and climbed in Once she'd fastened her safety belt they drove away, "It's funny this," she casually remarked, "it's usually you driving me." Commander Ronan Strobing said nothing, he was looking at the scenery all around them, as if he'd never seen it before; Lucy risked a glance at him, with all this staring at the trees, cars, fields, even people, it was as if he'd reverted to a child; maybe his brain hadn't fully recovered yet. It probably hadn't but it would, given time. She'd been told, by the doctors, to keep encouraging him, and, hopefully, increase the rate of recovery.

She held his hand, to comfort him, but he didn't really seem to notice except he looked at her strangely, as if she were new to him. "Don't worry, not far now." They were travelling, at speed – but never exceeding the speed limit of 121 km/h (75 mph,) along the A1 motorway in a north easterly direction.

The motorway followed Switzerland's east to west axis, running from St Margrethen in the north eastern canton of St Gallen area of Switzerland through to Geneva in south-western Switzerland. Along the A1 was the Baregg Tunnel tube, which had been built to reduce the traffic jams, although the Gubrist Tunnel, which remained as a point where there was, usually, a heavy traffic build-up. This motorway was one of the two most important motorways in Switzerland; the other being the A2 motorway, which ran from Basel in north western Switzerland to Chiasso in the canton of Ticino, in southern Switzerland, which was on the border with Italy.

Switzerland also had a network of two lane national roads; these roads usually lacked a median or central reservation, and some stretches were control-accessed (in that all traffic entered and exited through ramps and crossed using grade separations).

Finally they turned off and entered ramp number two that would link to other roads, and enable them to bypass the main city.

Commander Bigship, together with his team, and a still shaken Dr Schaiffer, arrived back at *Cointrin* Airport and were met by an official from HART, and the final remaining Apollo I automobile. Being able to seat three in the front and three in the back these vehicles were ideal for HART purposes; they followed the same route as the other Apollo II car, only an hour before.

When they were back at the compound all four men, and Teresa Robins reported to Commander Peter Roberts. Roberts told them what had happened to Celia Most and Ronan Strobing whilst they'd been gone. Dr Hans Schaiffer immediately asked, "Are they okay?"

"They're both okay now, at least Celia is, but Ronan seems to have reverted to a child, this is only temporary; therefore I have asked Lucy to stay with him for a few days. He has been instructed, by the hospital, to report to you, once a week, and let you examine how the healing process is going. I have given them, both, a few days off active duty. I assume your stay at the lodge was comfortable Hans."

"It was," he began, "until those *Proagnon* thugs attacked the place. Anyway, thankfully, the commando team you sent," indicating Leon Bigship and his team, "dealt with them all."

Roberts turned his chair to face the man, in charge of the team, in question. "Did you learn anything?"

Commander Leon Bigship replied, "I did sir, I learnt that their leader, Herr von Richter, I never got his first name."

"It was Franz," interjected the German doctor. "He told me when he first arrived."

"Thank you Doctor," Leon replied to the man, "Franz von Richter, he told me he was recruited from one of the many groups of neo-Nazi's who are still operating in Germany, and then with *Proagnon's* help and financial resources, they hope to conquer Germany. That's what he told me sir."

The commander's face darkened, slightly, "And does this von Richter know that there may be no one alive in Germany to rule over?"

"Evidently he didn't as he was so boastful about it all. But now he, along with his associates, at the lodge, are all dead."

"Thank you for bringing me up to date on this matter, Commander Bigship, I think we should send a squad of ten soldiers to Germany led by Major Shinto Howell; plus I'd like Dan Anco and Teresa Robins to accompany him, the other seven soldiers can be picked at their discretion. They will hunt these people down and put a stop to any plans these neo-Nazi's might have."

"Sir," protested Leon, "shouldn't I go with them as I led the raid on the lodge."

"Not this time Commander, I need you here. As we think we have located the area the enemy base is in we shall need to make plans to deal with them, should they show themselves." Commander Leon Bigship and the others nodded their understanding. "Squad dismissed, and well done; Dr Schaiffer, you're patients and your office await you." The soldiers, together with the doctor, filed out, "Leon, one moment," Peter said, "could you round up the other commander's for me please?"

"Yes sir," was the reply, and he filed out after the others.

At one half of the *Proagnon* bunker, in Iran, Sandy Tulliver knocked and entered Dr Q's office, he had his back to her. "Sir, Is there anything wrong?" she asked as she saw him fastening the clips, on his helmet, to attach it to his shoulders. "Can I help?" she asked, again, approaching his desk slowly.

"Stay where you are," he ordered her. "Do not approach me! I am fine, there is nothing wrong; please be seated, and do not concern yourself." Sandy seated herself at his desk.

The desk, although she didn't know it was the mirror image of Commander Roberts desk, at HART. Plus what she didn't know, none of the *Proagnon* soldiers did, was that the man behind the mask was the son of the man Peter Roberts had helped put in prison, and he wanted revenge for his father. The terrorist attacks were something his father had been working on before Sergeant Peter Roberts and his police team had arrested Richard Barker and the group of men with him; evidently one of the group had betrayed the other members.

Dr Q turned around to face her when he'd finished, "Please don't enter without knocking again," he said as he sat down. His laptop computer was open, and plugged into the internet, as he was preparing to check his email account.

"I did knock," protested Sandy, "you can't have heard me, for whatever reason." She looked across at her superior, who had now closed his laptop.

"No harm done," he replied. "Anyway, are your new quarters to your satisfaction, and are they comfortable? And does your new uniform fit?" He could see her uniform fitted perfectly where it needed to, but he asked anyway.

Miss Tulliver responded as he thought she would, "My quarters are fine thank you, and, after one or two alterations my uniform fits perfectly." She thought the question about the uniform was a bit of a strange one.

"Why don't you show me?" he asked, it was a reasonable enough request, but there was something in his voice, a kind of silky quality that made her want to refuse. However, if she refused, she had the worry that he may summon the two, armed, bodyguards, who guarded his office, to kill her.

She, politely, got up from her seat and stood in front of his desk. The black clad number two then became conscious of her superior examining her from her head to the tops of her legs. "Very nice," he murmured, "yes a good fit I think. However, I think I shall need to do a closer inspection;" he got up, from his own chair, and moved round to her side of the desk. Sandy, suddenly, became worried, why would he want to inspect her more closely? She then became aware of how small the office was and that thought, alone, terrified her. She wanted to shout, scream, anything, so she could get out of there.

What her leader said next really unnerved her. "Don't worry my dear, the room is totally soundproof."

Sandy Tulliver, then, wanted to bolt from the room but she felt like she couldn't move; a pair of black gloved hands came around her and started to pat her black uniform. "Yes, a perfect fit," and then, he released her and stepped back; relief washed over her, "a perfect fit in the buttock area – not too loose – however, it could be made, slightly, tighter, show you off better," he said gently. Then in a harsher tone he ordered, "See to it! You may go."

Sandy got up, from her chair in front of his desk, whilst he seated himself on the other side, and left the office to return to her quarters – along the featureless corridors, on her way there she passed many of the blue uniformed *Proagnon* soldiers.

Once she'd left her leader returned to his computer to check his email. He was most surprised to find an unopened email, from the Russian Defence Ministry. Quickly he moved the computer mouse that was built into the machine; and moved the cursor over to the envelope symbol, and clicked to open it. The, now, opened message read.

"Dr Quantum

We still have the Admiral Nakhimov and the Pyotr Velhikiy battle cruisers; both are Kirov class, as is the Admiral Lazarev, which was despatched for use, as an exhibit, in your exhibition of military equipment. We thought all our military hardware had been destroyed, but a more recent search unearthed these two ships, as well as four armoured personnel carriers, a BTR-60, -70, -80 and a MT-LB.

As you will know the BTR-60 is also amphibious, and can carry 18 crew members, whilst the -70 and -80 only carry 10 crew members, and the MT-LB can take up to 13 crew members. We would be pleased to supply these vessels, along with vehicles for inclusion in your exhibition, if you still want them.

I apologise for this oversight, as I was Mikhail Suvorov's deputy at the time, and since I replaced him I have had a more in-depth look at our records, and have visited many of the military sites.

Please would you let us know at your earliest convenience if you require this hardware.

Boris Kurenchev"

As Dr Q read further into the email a smile began to cross his face, though no-one could see it; when he had made the request, as was stated he'd been informed that all hardware had been destroyed, but now he knew different.

He, immediately, clicked on the *reply* button and composed a response.

Boris

Thank you for informing me about the military hardware is still available. My company have requested that I respond to you and ask that any hardware, you can spare, would be most gratefully received and displayed in our exhibition.

This exhibition is not open to the public yet, as we are still collecting the exhibits. Any items your country can provide will be of great use. Thank you once again.

Dr Quantum

He clicked on the *send* button, and then relaxed. The Russians, so it seemed, were back in the game; even though he'd never been to the country, personally, he was pleased.

In HART HQ, more specifically in Commander Peter Roberts' office, the four Departmental/Operational Commanders had assembled; Commander's Ronan Strobing, Celia Most, Leon Bigship and Lucy Lang were all seated opposite their superior officer, even though Ronan wasn't back to full operating capacity – it was good he was there; Lucy would be allowed to stay with him, until he fully recovered. Laid out, on the wooden desk, in front of Roberts were several sheets of paper, "There is no easy way to tell you this, but the HART forces are depleted. "Let's break it down; firstly our friend and colleague Mark Schnieder was killed because he was in the wrong place, at the wrong time along with the wrong person; three F-14 pilots, together with their radar intercept officers. Tammy Smith and Harry Danto in Russia; twenty soldiers in Africa; seventy-five soldiers in Saudi Arabia; and three in Geneva; and I've just sent a squad of ten to Germany to deal with some neo-Nazis."

"A total of 117 agents, depending on how many return from Germany; therefore we started with our standard number of compound personnel - 300, so we are down to 183; that's not counting the many civilian casualties – which must now be 100,000+. Therefore, I think we are doing quite well."

Peter Roberts took a sip of water, from a glass he'd poured earlier, and then pressed the *intercom* button, "Mrs Jones," he began, "may I be linked through to the loudspeakers?"

"Of course sir," she replied, "just linking the line now." After about a minute her voice came back over the intercom, "You're through sir." The four others, in the room, looked across at him; all of them wondering what was about to happen.

They didn't have to wait long, "Now hear this, every soldier and pilot who is fit and active is ordered to fly out to Iran, taking all military assets with us. Aircraft will land, at the airstrip and we will be using the old Hill Air Force Base at

DASHT-E KAVIR – more commonly known as The Great Salt Desert!" Roberts' voice was still strong despite his age. "And you four had better go too, I assume you've organised our sea fleet Leon."

"I have sir."

Commander Roberts pressed the *intercom* button again, "We will be taking, as well as our usual arsenal, the B-52 Stratofortress, together with all its weaponry." The other four commanders just looked at each other, Commander Strobing not fully comprehending; their superior had never ordered that aircraft into action before, either he was in a hurry to get this over with, he was getting desperate, or he'd gone totally crazy.

The plane was one of a mammoth series of long-range, high altitude strategic bombers that had originally been designed with an eight-engine turboprop system, and was a successor to the B-50 heavy bomber. The initial plans for the aircraft had to be redrawn later on to enable the aircraft to be powered by eight Pratt & Whitney turbofans; these were mounted on the high-monoplane swept—wing assemblies.

The result became the mainstay for United States military operations and had served for decades; its initial 'baptism of fire' had been in Vietnam, it had served during the Cold War, and in the War on Terror in Afghanistan.

The B-52 was crewed by five personnel, (pilot, co-pilot, radar navigator, navigator, and electronic warfare officer), and had been and still was, constantly undergoing updates and modifications to its systems and subsystems that kept it viable in the current high-tech environment.

Its ability to deliver dumb and precision munitions from its service ceiling of 50,000 feet has allowed military war-planners to harass fortified enemy positions with impunity, for decades. Various models of the aircraft have been in service, over the years, each has provided slight modifications and updates to targeted systems. The current model in the HART inventory was the latest version of the B-52H model, which was capable of carrying an internal bomb load of up to 50,000 pounds; in addition the plane had also been refined to allow for anti-ship Harpoon missiles, which could be mounted under the wings.

The Stratofortress system was also capable of delivering no fewer than twenty of the popularized and accurate cruise missiles from its internal payload. New armament tests are leading up to an improved number of other munitions for the delivering system to field.

Even with the advent of stealth technology in the form of the B-2 Spirit stealth bomber, the B-52 series shows little indication of being laid aside in favour of the new system. The B-52's internal capabilities against less than technological foes help the system to keep flying as it had been well into the next decade, and beyond.

Weaponry for the Stratofortress included twenty AGM-86B ALCM cruise missiles, twenty AGM-129 cruise missiles (both sets were internal). The exterior could be equipped with two AGM-86B ALCM cruise missiles, and two of the AGM-129 cruise missiles. Other weaponry could include free fall nuclear bombs, twelve AGM-84 Harpoon antiship missiles, twelve AGM 142A air to surface missiles, and AGM-86C CALM cruise missiles; plus JDAMS. Also the aircraft could carry 51,570lbs of class bombs or mines.

"Commander," Celia said, "if we're all going then who's going to defend and protect the compound? Also who's going to be in charge?"

"I was wondering when someone would ask that," replied the superior officer. "I will leave a, small, skeletal force to defend the place; as for who'll be in charge I will be leaving Dr Schaiffer in charge, I'm sure he knows now where his loyalties lie. Has anyone got a problem with that?" He looked across at Ronan.

"No sir," they each responded in turn.

"Good, now go get suited and booted, and let's get this show on the road."

The four HART personnel got up to leave to return to their residences. "Ronan, Lucy, stay behind for a moment please."

Lucy became worried, had he found out? If so how? However, Commander Roberts smiled at the pair, in that fatherly manner of his. "Miss Lang, I know we may have had our differences in the past, but we all need to work together now, so if you can put those differences behind you, so can I. Just for the record I think you're doing a good job of taking care of our colleague."

Commander Lang was taken aback and for a moment and didn't know what to say, but then she recovered her composure and simply said, "Thank you sir."

Next Commander Roberts turned to Ronan Strobing, "Ronan, I don't know if you can understand me but you are Commander Ronan Strobing of the Human Alliance for the Retaliation against Terrorism (HART), we all need you now more than ever." He turned back to Lucy, "Look after him and keep trying."

"Yes sir," she replied and tried to lead Commander Strobing away, but he wouldn't move.

Ronan looked his superior straight in the eye, and simply said, "Yes sir," and then saluted. Peter Roberts beamed; did that mean Commander Ronan Strobing was back? Lucy then led Ronan from the office, and they followed the same route, out the building, as the other two commanders to find them waiting outside.

Once they'd all left Roberts asked for Gwyneth Jones to come to his office. When she'd entered he said to her, "Gwyneth, I want you to do a search on our database, see if there might be any information on this Dr Q that we've missed; go to the British as well. You know the usual, father, mother, known associates, tax records, prison terms, and, most importantly, why is he the head of *Proagnon*? Plus, does he have to answer to any superiors."

"Why can't you do it? Where will you be?"

"I'm leading an assault in Iran/Iraq, therefore I am leaving Dr Schaiffer in charge until I return, keep an eye on him."

"Is that everything sir?" she asked him.

"It is," he replied. She saluted, he returned the salute, and she left his presence.

As the four personnel left headquarters, the other two had been waiting for Commander's Strobing and Lang, and began walking the distance between the building and the residences, they all heard the sound of klaxons going off all over the base. *So this was it*, they thought, *the final battle in this continuing war on terror*. Each entered their own residence, put on their, Kevlar, body armour then changed into their desert battle uniforms – though each knew the fighting could lead anywhere, they packed the clothes they'd need, as well as guns, explosives and night vision goggles (NVG); Ronan was assisted by Lucy. Once everyone was ready they met outside and strode back towards HQ; Peter met them at the door and announced, "C'mon you four, our transport is waiting."

"And that is?" Lucy wanted to know.

"Ladies and gentlemen," their superior said, "we have the use of a Pave Low IV helicopter."

The Pave Low was the upgraded version of the MH-53 heavy lift helicopter, the MH-53 had become, over the years, affectionately known as 'The Jolly Green Giant' because it had been built on the large green airframe of the MH-53B.

The original MH-53B helicopter had a retractable in-flight refuelling probe on the right side of the name, spindle-shaped jettisonable external tanks with a capacity of 2,461 litres, fitted to the sponsons and braced by struts attached to the fuselage. It had a rescue hoist situated above the right passenger door that was capable of deploying a jungle penetrator on 250 feet of steel cable.

An armament of three pintle-mounted General Electric GAU-2/A 7.62 millimetre (.308 in) six-barrelled Gatling-type machine guns, with one in a forward hatch on each side of the fuselage and one mounted on the tail ramp, with the gunner secured with a harness. A total of 1,200 pounds of armour was carried, along with a Doppler navigation radar in the forward belly.

Early HH-53Bs, the predecessor of the later built MH-53Bs featured T64-GE-3 turboshafts with 3,080 shaft horsepower, but these engines had later been upgraded to T64-GE-7 turboshafts with 3,925 shaft horsepower output. Five members of crew were standard, including a pilot, copilot, crew chief, and two pararescuemen.

The Pave Low IV was an MH-53M helicopter, which was a modified MH-53J model with the Interactive Defensive Avionics System/Multi-Mission Advanced Tactical Terminal or IDAS/MATT. The system had enhanced the present defensive capabilities of the Pave Low. It provided instant access to the total battlefield situation, through near real-time Electronic Order of Battle updates. It also provided a new level of detection avoidance with near real-time threat broadcasts over-the-horizon, so crews could avoid and defeat threats, and re-plan en route if necessary.

Over the years since these helicopters had been introduced by the United States Air Force (USAF) until they retired the aircraft in 2008 they had proved themselves very effective in the many different combat zones; since then HART had taken a few of the helicopters. Each machine was also equipped for air to air refueling.

Each helicopter now carried a crew of six, (two pilots, two flight engineers and two gunners), and could carry, in the hold, approximately 38 troops. Each one had a length of approximately 22 metres (seventy-two feet), a rotor diameter of approximately 22 metres (seventy-two feet), and a height of approximately 8 metres (twenty-five feet). The maximum takeoff weight was 20,909kg (46,000lb), 22,727kg (50,000lb in wartime) – compared to an empty weight of 14545kg (32,000lb).

The engines had been upgraded to two T64-GE-100 turboshafts, each producing 4,330 horsepower per engine, enabling the six bladed rotor system, on the aircraft, to reach a maximum speed of 196mph, although it usually travelled at its cruise speed of 173mph. The Pave Low could travel up to 683 miles without refueling, and had a service ceiling of 4878 metres (16,000ft).

The armaments were a combination of three 7.62mm Miniguns or three .50 BMG (12.7 mm) machine guns, which could be mounted on the left and right sides (immediately behind the flight deck) and on the ramp.

The five HART personnel boarded the helicopter, Commander Strobing was reluctant at first, but allowed himself to be led on by Commander Lang. The aircraft was piloted by Colonel Sebastian 'Seb' Mcintyre and alongside was Lieutenant Alice 'Ali' Havers. Mcintyre turned in his seat, "Welcome aboard Commanders, Missy."

"Thank you Sebastian," Peter said. "Alice," he said, regarding the co-pilot.

The other four members of the crew introduced themselves; once introductions had been performed the five commanders seated themselves on the benches, which ran down each side of the aircraft, and fastened themselves in. Sebastian informed them, "As our flight is 3,300 kilometres (2,050 miles) we shall have to be refuelled three times by an orbiting MC-130P Combat Shadow tanker plane"

Once all the pre-flight checks had been completed by the crew, the helicopter started up, and the machine rose into the air and began its long flight to the disused Hill Air Force Base in Iran.

After approximately thirteen hours the helicopter containing the five HART commanders landed at the base. As the helicopter was brought to a halt the five commanding personnel emerged, and then entered the main building, in the grounds.

The building looked more or less like a large old fort compound. However, it had been well maintained over the years. To one side was a residential building, inside this building there were at least ninety rooms, enough for all the HART personnel; in addition the main hall was large and spacious, and in the centre was a long dining table for dining and conferences, off to one side were offices with telephone connections for internet connecters.

The five set about setting up equipment in the offices, every one of them had brought their, personal/business, laptop computers and their STU-8's, after sorting out their quarters; the quarters were usually shared, either two females or two males, to minimize the risk of temptation. Lucy wanted to share with Commander Strobing, but she got put with Commander Celia Most; however, knowing what she did Mrs

Most persuaded Commander Leon Bigship, who was sharing with Commander Ronan Strobing to swap with Miss Lang, but not to tell Peter Roberts.

After sleeping arrangements had been made they set up the separate, or joint, offices they would be using, for the duration. Once they'd set things up the four land, sea, and air commanders reconvened in their superior's office and awaited further orders. "What is the status of our position?" Commander Roberts asked them.

"We shall know more once our soldiers and our heavy artillery arrive."

"However," said Celia, "I suggest once everything, and everyone, does arrive, we move our F-15s and F-16s, and any other attack aircraft, to the Elburz mountain range in the North, whilst our heavy assault artillery, the Abrahms, Bradleys, and any further ground based weaponry to the Zagros mountain range."

"Leon," she continued, looking over at her male counterpart, "could the sea fleet provide covering fire from the Gulf of Oman?"

"I'm sure they could," he answered, "but they may need King Abdullah's permission."

"Who's he when he's at home?" she demanded to know.

Roberts answered, "He, my dear, is the new King of Saudi Arabia, and is now the newest member of OPEC." Celia looked baffled.

"What's OPEC?" she wanted to know, "I don't know who or what that is." She became aware of Ronan and Leon peering at her, "At least I'm honest," she told them.

Again Roberts answered, "OPEC stands for Organisation of Petroleum Exploring Countries, and is made up of twelve countries, which are Iran, Iraq, Kuwait, Qatar, Saudi Aradia, the United Arab Emirates, Libya, Algeria, Nigeria, Angola, Venszeula, and Ecuador. Finally, their overall headquarters is in Vienna."

Feeling slightly silly now she said, "I see now, sir, sorry for my ignorance."

"Don't worry, Celia, we can't know everything," the commander assured her. As they were standing there a low rumbling overhead, there was no mistaking the turbofan engines, and they sounded very large, signalled the arrival of the first lot of soldiers, and whatever artillery that may have arrived with them.

The five of them walked down the old, spiral, staircase; the steps were built from stone and so some had become worn with age. Thankfully no one fell. As they arrived in the courtyard they saw a full five Apache, attack, helicopters; evidently the Galaxy had arrived, and using its roll on/roll off facility had deposited the five helicopters beyond the wall, however their tops were still noticeable, and unmistakable, above the perimeter wall. A total of seventy-three soldiers had been brought as well, on the aircraft; six of them were the pilots of the Apaches; well five, and a reserve pilot.

Still in the courtyard was the Pave Low IV – its main rotors were still turning. Peter Roberts had to shout to make himself heard, "Take the chopper to the Elburz mountain range, and land in a concealed location. Contact the rest of your squad and tell them to do the same."

Colonel Mcintyre turned and looked at his commander, through his helmet visor, and nodded in confirmation, and then saluted. Then the helicopter took off and flew north and eastwards.

The commander walked to the rear of the fort, avoiding the 67 soldiers that were now pushing past each other and rushing into the main building; he climbed up to the perimeter wall so he was overlooking the road that ran behind the buildings, the road was disused now, though it still served as a landing strip. On it, right now, were the refuelling Galaxy, along with its flight crew of eight, and the five Apaches – together with their pilots and the Apache commander-in-chief, Colonel Brad Williams. "Take those choppers, together with armaments, to the Elburz mountain range and conceal your machines."

Brad saluted, informed the pilots of each helicopter what was happening; then climbed aboard the final attack helicopter, and they all flew away, in a northerly direction.

Roberts climbed down the ladder and went back inside, "There," he said when he reached his office. His four subordinates were in their own offices - working out tactics, for the upcoming battles, together with different outcomes – on their computers. About an hour, maybe more, later; a deep growl was heard as the Galaxy's four, huge, turbofan engines rumbled into life. Once it had gained full speed it powered down the road/runway, and slowly rose into the air. Commander Roberts watched this from his office window. The plane looked beautiful, as it flew away, in the, purple, evening sky.

A few minutes later another sound was heard, indicating another plane was about to grace them with its presence; though this one sounded smaller. It was the Hercules, bringing in the other 110 troops; as there were only 110, instead of the full 128 it could carry the Hercules also brought in a small vehicle, the Dodge WC 3-4 ton field ambulance – one of the latest of the HART investments. The aircraft landed and deposited its load; and the ambulance was driven round and into the courtyard, followed by the soldiers marching behind it. Another hour later the C-130 Hercules lifted off and headed back to base.

The next transport aircraft to arrive was the C-141B Starlifter; as the exit ramp was lowered, at the rear, 10 HMMWVs were revealed, HART soldiers entered the aircraft and drove them out; then 5 M-151 Jeeps followed – driven again by more HART soldiers, also 35 TOW2B missile launchers – together with missiles – were brought out. Once the hold was empty, the aircraft was refuelled it took off again, back to base, ready if it was needed for more ferrying missions.

Next came the return of the C-5 Galaxy, the only transport aircraft capable of transporting the M1A1 Abrams, main, battle tank. Again the rear ramp was lowered and the fighting vehicle trundled out, on its caterpillar tracks.

After the transport plane had left the C-130 Hercules returned carrying a Renault VAB 4x4 Armoured Personnel Carrier, along with another 7 of the M-151 Jeeps. These vehicles were driven into the courtyard and were then parked in the special garages assigned for each vehicle. As Commander Roberts watched a smile started to appear on his face. Just the

Land Rover Defenders, and the Bradley fighting vehicles to be brought over, and then they would be ready.

The plane took off, into the, cloudy, wintry sky; behind it came the C-141 Starlifter, again. This time it was carrying the other 10 HMMWVs and two Land Rover Defenders. Each vehicle was driven into the courtyard. Once it was empty the aircraft's ramp was raised, after the plane had taken on fuel it took off again, knowing it wouldn't be needed again.

Again the Galaxy arrived, this time the rear ramp was lowered and the nose section was raised, and firstly five Bradley Fighting Systems rolled out (two M3A3 systems and three M2A2 systems), then came another Renault VAB, and finally three Avenger (Pedestal Mounted Stinger) missile launchers were brought out. Once everything was clear the nose section, together with the rear ramp were put back into their positions, the aircraft was refuelled, and the, giant, transport plane was given permission to take off.

As it rose into the, now, darkening sky Commander Roberts looked out his office window, and thought to himself, *Well that's the last one, now we're ready to start a full scale war! Just the Stratofortress to arrive now and we're ready for anything Proagnon throws at us.*

Just then his STU chirped and warbled, Roberts turned to his desk. He picked the phone's handset up, "Yes," he said into the receiver.

"Sir," replied a female voice, one tinged with a strong welsh accent. "I have trawled our database for information on, this, Dr Q; and the only information I can find is this, Sarah Taylor – who killed Mark Schnieder – or as we know her better, Squeeze, is an associate of his. Apparently, he has no superiors at *Proagnon*, just inferiors, but it also says he does report to someone on the outside, every so often. I know it's not much but it's a start; I will be contacting the British tomorrow."

"Thank you Gwyneth, and keep me updated," Peter replaced the handset and sat down. If Dr Q was known to Squeeze then it was a pity she'd apparently, disappeared. Either that or she'd been made to disappear after killing Mark Schnieder.

At *Proagnon's* hidden dry dock, both the *Admiral Nakhimov* and the *Pyotr Velhikiy* battle cruisers had arrived, complete with aircraft, a full crew of 710, and all armaments working. The two ships were, basically, the same as the *Admiral Lazarev*. The personnel carriers aboard were taken, into the bunker, the drivers were to await deployment orders.

Of course, the activity in the skies above had not been missed either.

Dr Q called for Sandy Tulliver to attend him. When she was in the office he said to her, "Ready the ground forces. We move soon!"

"Yes sir," she replied smoothly, and got up to leave.

As she strode towards the office door, Sandy could feel Dr Q's eyes following her.

"I like the alterations you've made, makes your uniform seem much tighter."

"Thank you sir, I'm just afraid it may rip." With that she left the room, walked past the guards and returned, to her quarters, further in the bunker.

Again, the STU-8, on his desk, chirped and warbled to grab Roberts attention, the next day; he picked the handset up, "Hello."

"Roberts?" the voice on the other end queried.

"Yes, I am Commander Peter Roberts of HART, the Human Alliance for the Retaliation against Terrorism; who is this?"

"You mean you don't know Roberts?" the voice asked, sneeringly. "It is a long time since we met. You have done well for yourself and so have I now, though, my friends and I are ready to DESTROY you, you and that pathetic little group of yours. We have been following your progress." The caller then put the phone down.

Peter wondered who this, mysterious, call had come from? He was now shaken and a tiny bit frightened. He was a man in his late fifties, yet the voice had sounded as though it had belonged to a younger man. Yet he didn't know who.

Commander Lang knocked and entered the office, and immediately saw something had disturbed her superior, "Sir," the American said, "sir, what is it?""

"Please sit down Lucy," he said, his voice slightly shaky. She sat opposite him, "Lucy," he began, "do you know who Dr Q is?"

"Yes, we all do. He's the head of *Proagnon*."

"He's more than that my dear. I think, I may be wrong, he knows me personally, but I can't think how, I'm pretty sure he rang me just now telling me he was now ready for his group, *Proagnon*, together with himself, to destroy us. The reason I don't know who he is, is because I am in my fifties, yet the voice belonged to someone much younger. I'm beginning to get worried now."

"Oh dear sir, I don't, really, know what to say."

"Anyway," Roberts said, leaning back in his chair, "what did you come for?" He seemed to be regaining his old composure.

"I came to say that all our ground forces have arrived, and are ready for battle."

Commander Roberts visibly relaxed, "Have we been attacked yet?"

"No sir, but it is only a matter of time, judging by your phone call." As they were speaking shouts came from outside.

Lucy and Peter raced out the office, almost bumping into the other commanders in their haste. All of them bolted outside, "What's happening Welms?" Roberts shouted up to the man in the lookout tower, Private Peter Welms.

"Three troop carriers, at least I presume they are, have stopped outside and men are pouring from them, it looks like a total of thirty, blue, uniformed men, all carrying guns – they look like AK-47 assault rifles to me. Each of the men are wearing gas masks as well."

"The first wave," muttered Peter, "it could be worse. Order a total of 5 jeeps out, all with at least three armed men aboard."

HART soldiers poured out the compound towards the enemy; five of the *Proagnon* soldiers threw what looked like, drinks cans. As each hit the ground they exploded in a cloud of orange gas. The first line of HART soldiers were now choking, and clutching their throats.

Now they had easier targets the muzzles on the assault rifles flashed, and there was the chatter of fire; several soldiers fell, and flopped onto the ground. The five jeeps containing armed personnel appeared. Commander Roberts indicated the enemy soldiers, "Do you think you can get them all?"

"Yes sir, we'll give it our best shot," replied each of the five jeep's commanders. The engines were then powered up and the vehicles roared away, moving towards the enemy's front line; each of the men were armed with M-16 machine guns, and each jeep contained – should it be needed – an M-14A rifle.

"Sir!" shouted Welms from his lookout post. "Another three men have just emerged, and are carrying what look like," Welms raised his binoculars, "rocket launchers."

"The HART leader's shoulders slumped, "Oh shit," he said, "I've just sent those men to their deaths!"

"You might not have sir they may just have appeared to discourage our men," Celia said.

"Maybe Celia, maybe, but somehow I don't think so." At that moment a violent explosion rocked the ground and a huge plume of fire rose into the air. "That's one jeep and it's crew of three lost." The remaining four Jeeps returned to the compound.

"That may be sir, but two of their men died in the explosion too," Mrs Most told him.

The commander looked at her and then said, "Two out of thirty, compared to our ten out of twenty-six. I shouldn't have sent them out."

"Sir," called Private Welms again, "the remainder of the *Proagnon* men are moving to the sides, making space for something. Oh God no!"

"What is it?" bellowed Roberts.

"One of the personnel carriers is being fitted with a large box of some kind, and is now being positioned between the two lines of soldiers."

"What?" shouted Roberts again but then the implications of what was happening hit him. "It's a fucking bomb! Order two of the M2A2 Bradleys up front to deal with it, everyone else inside, and quick!"

The Bradley Fighting Systems were brought up front, and positioned just outside the gates – both at 45 degree angles.

The BTR-70 driver got in the vehicle and started the powerful V8 engine. He revved the BTR-70 up, pressed the accelerator – hard to the floor, and the vehicle lurched forward, building up speed to 81 km/h (50mph).

The 3 man crews of the two Bradleys M2A2s watched as the mobile bomb headed for the compound.

This compound, unlike the Geneva one, had its brick walls still intact, together with its original wooden, double, gates; whereas in Geneva the walls had been done away with and, electric, fencing put up. Inside the main building was still brick built although, over the years, the walls had been reinforced with varying thicknesses of armour.

As soon as the enemy transport came into range the 'Bushmaster' Chain Gun, on one of the Bradleys, opened fire with its armour piercing 25mm rounds; even though the BTR-70s 9mm front armour was pierced and the driver killed, the vehicle kept on coming. One of the Bradleys crew decided, with his commander's permission, to use the TOW missile launchers with twin tubes. Permission was granted and the tubes were quickly loaded with anti-tank missiles; once the gunner had got the enemy vehicle in his sights he fired off the missiles.

The BTR was almost upon the compound gates when the two missiles struck it; the driver of the fighting system swerved away to avoid the huge fireball created, "I got it, I got it!" enthused the gunner, rejoining the rest of the crew.

As the smoke cleared they saw he'd destroyed the enemy vehicle, but there was no sign of the other M2A2. During the melee the *Proagnon* soldiers; and their transport vehicles had left. "Oh well," the commander reassured the gunner, who he could see was upset over the loss of the other crew, "you saved the compound." He couldn't find words to fully assure the young man that what had happened to him could have happened to any gunner.

"Yes I know, but I killed the three crew members in the other fighting system," he whimpered.

"Don't beat yourself up about it, they knew the risks, it could've happened to anyone."

The gunner was still upset, "Yes but it happened to me." The commander of the vehicle gave a signal to the driver, and the vehicle was driven back through the gates and back inside the compound. Once the machine was parked up the three crew got out and walked back inside the residential building.

Inside his makeshift office Commander Roberts was sitting at his desk, writing and signing papers when his STU-8 began warbling again. He stopped what he was doing and picked the handset up, "Hello, he said into the receiver.

The voice that spoke sent a chill down Peter's spine, "Greetings Commander Roberts, you have seen but a small demonstration of our firepower today. Expect more of the same soon. I look forward to our meeting, and our final confrontation, when I will kill you!"

"Tell me who you are?" pleaded Peter, but the receiver was put down, and the line went dead. Roberts buzzed through to each of the other four and said to them, "It appears that our communications have been compromised; be careful when using the system that you don't give any vital information away."

Peter Roberts was very unnerved now; when he received the news of the death of the crew members aboard the second Bradleys, he sighed – in this, only the first basic attack *Proagnon* had lost three soldiers out of the thirty-three men, and one vehicle, they'd sent whereas HART had lost thirteen out of twenty-nine personnel, and two vehicles. At this rate *Proagnon* would win easily; all the vehicles that had been brought in seemed to add up to nothing.

If only Gwyneth would get in contact with more information regarding Dr Q and Proagnon, the commander thought as he sat there. To keep occupied he started writing up a report on the days activities – he got so engrossed he failed to notice the time, or the winter sun go down – it was only when his STU warbled did the commander look up; he was afraid to answer it for a start in case it was him. However, he picked it up and answered, "Yes."

"Commander," it was Ronan's voice, "haven't you noticed the time? We're waiting for you in the dining room."

It was then that Commander Roberts looked at the clock above his door, it read 8.00pm, "Sorry Ronan," he apologised, "I lost track of time, I'll be there in a moment, in the meantime carry on without me."

"Okay sir," Commander Strobing replied and the line went dead. Peter replaced his own handset. Getting up he switched off his laptop computer and closed it, and then he left his office and strode to the dining hall where all the 160 remaining personnel were seated.

"Sorry for keeping you waiting," their commanding officer said, "today we have had our first skirmish with *Proagnon* soldiers and we suffered losses and casualties – friends and colleagues. We were taken by surprise today, but from this day we will learn, and become stronger, I admit much of it was my fault; I should never have put those lives in danger, but I, myself, have learnt. Tomorrow is a new day."

He sat down and then continued, "Also today I have found out that this Dr Q is known to me, personally, I don't know how yet but I, fully, intend to find out. As Dr Q contacted me on my STU-8 phone I can only guess that, somehow, our communications system has been compromised. If I find out that any of my own personnel has helped in this they will be found and dealt with. I guess that covers everything, carry on – as you were."

Peter got up and saluted, every person in the room except one saluted back; this was the person who had been placed within the HART organisation to help bring them down from the inside – already he had sabotaged the phone lines, he was awaiting his next orders now.

Roberts didn't notice this man, once he'd performed his salute he left the room.

CHAPTER 14

A new base, memories & sabotage!

D r Q leaned back in his command chair, in his office, satisfied now that he'd rattled Peter Roberts, and also with the brief attack on the HART compound. His men had been trained well.

Peter Roberts had been the man who'd got his father convicted, and put in prison, on terrorism crimes. Dr Q, only a boy at that time, had vowed revenge on Roberts as he'd left the courtroom and his father was taken away; either the man hadn't heard the boy, or just ignored the threats as those of a young child who was mad at him.

Now 22 years later and also having spent time inside plotting his revenge, to avenge his father, he was ready. His mother had died 5 years after his father was imprisoned, she was unable to cope; and his father had died in prison 2 years later - at the age of 42. Dr Q blamed Peter Roberts for both of his parent's deaths, and had sworn, on his father's grave, he would find his father's enemy, and make him pay by killing him.

He had been studying the country next door, Iraq; it had great potential for his future plans, some of Saddam Hussein's old palaces were still deserted – though inhabitants in others could, easily, be dealt with. He summoned Sandy Tulliver to his office and explained his plans to her; she agreed with her superior that the move could be most beneficial to them – as it seemed senseless to keep directing operations from, this, their bunker deep under Iran. Plus there was the chance HART may discover the bunker, in time.

Dr Q requested her to order all the troops into the tunnel that connected the underground bunker, in Iran, and follow it westwards into Iraq, where they would arrive under the capital city of Baghdad, which was situated east of the Euphrantes river – which ran from Turkey, through Syria and on through Iraq, but the Tigris river ran through the city, from north to south; plus the area was mainly desert; less people to get caught in the crossfire, in the battles, between HART and *Proagnon*, Dr Q wasn't that bothered if any more innocent civilians were killed. There would also be Bedouin tribes or nomads, the Arabic travellers of the desert.

The journey was approximately 805 kilometres (500 miles) long, therefore Dr Q ordered that all four of the armoured personnel carriers – the BTR-60, -70, -80, and MT-LB were to be used to transport weaponry: guns, bombs, missiles, together with their launchers, and grenades to the other half of the underground base, combined the vehicles would be able to transport up to 2000kg (4,400lbs), including driver – at one time, but it was a start.

The journey time, in the BTRs which would also be taking 38 soldiers (combined), would be, roughly, at their maximum speed of 81km/h (50mph), between ten and twelve hours and twenty minutes; those in the MT-LB would have a journey time, as this vehicles maximum speed was only 60km/h (37mph), of between 13 and 17 hours.

Unfortunately all four would not be able to make the journey in one go; both the BTR-60 and the MT-LB had an operational range of 500 kilometres (310 miles), so would be able to make the journey in two, the BTR-70 had a range of 400 kilometres (248 miles) so would take three goes, finally the BTR-80 had a range of 599 kilometres (372 miles) – it again would complete the journey in two.

All the armoured personnel carriers were similarly designed, with crew compartment at the front, troop compartment in the middle and engine at the back; all were diesel powered with powerful engines, plus all were amphibious – although their speed in water was greatly reduced from their road speed.

Luckily, a railway track had been built alongside the roadway; these two were separated by a central, concrete, reservation. A typical train, on this underground system, was ten carriages long – each carriage contained twenty fully armed soldiers – and the main engine of the train, this contained the driver; as each train was able to transport 200 troops at a time, the train would need to make four journeys, and at its speed of

403km/h (250mph) would take only 2 hours to reach its destination.

For the final 50 troops the train would return to its starting point and 6 of the 10 carriages would be uncoupled and three flatbed trucks would be put in their place – each flatbed truck was 33ft long and 10ft wide. Subsequently the train would now be the engine followed by a carriage then a flatbed truck, and then another carriage would follow, followed by another flatbed, and then a third, empty, carriage., then another flatbed, and finally the fourth carriage The total length, of this train, would be just over 171 metres.

The three tanks that *Proagnon* would use, the T-72, -80, and -90 were, carefully, manoeuvred onto the trucks; once everyone was aboard and the tanks loaded the train, slowly, pulled away; but with the heavier load of over 141 tonnes behind onto the flatbed trucks, its speed was reduced to 100mph thus it would take about 5 hours to reach its destination.

Each of the three battle cruiser's – the Admiral *Lazarev,* the Admiral *Nakhimov,* and the *Pyotr Velikiy* – each contained 710 men each, a total of 2130. Two men had been shot following the attack on the White House, Six soldiers had been killed on board the ships, Nine had been killed in Geneva, one had died in Russia, four pilots had been lost in the air battle, one, perhaps two, had been killed on an aeroplane, the original Squeeze had been shot by himself and finally only three men had been killed in the battle with HART. A grand total of 23 *Proagnon* personnel were dead, still leaving Dr Q with about 850 *Proagnon* troops at his disposal, and they were heading for Iraq.

Dr Q would stay behind until the end, with his number two, in case of any *accidents,* though he expected none; still it was better safe than sorry.

Once everyone, together with artillery and weapons, had arrived at the other end, and Dr Q had had confirmation of this by the STU, Sandy Tulliver and himself boarded the smaller train, that had been allocated for their use, and headed towards the new, main, headquarters of *Proagnon.* A concealed elevator took the superior, and his chief subordinate – once they had climbed off the train - up into one of the, disused, palaces of Saddam Hussein; it was a pity he was now dead, killed by hanging, after the second, there was a dispute whether it had been the second or third, Gulf War, in 2006. The two men could have worked well together.

The superior of *Proagnon* chose a downstairs room, for his sleeping quarters, whilst he chose an, old, upstairs room – which was centrally located, and had been reinforced for protection - for his, private, office from where he would control his operations. His number two and his bodyguards, those he trusted, all did the same. The two bodyguards walked along the upstairs corridors, armed with their AK-47s, checking each room and making sure there were no, extra, inhabitants, or squatters, anywhere; they found none.

Putting shades and curtains across the corridor windows, just in case anyone thought the place was ideal for them to squat in, particularly any of the Bedouin tribes, they began the set up of their new above ground headquarters.

Dr Q set up his office in the room he had chosen, which provided the most protection; his own sleeping quarters were on the floor below a trophy room used by Saddam had been converted into a bedroom, windows had been blacked out and the walls of the room, as well as the ceiling had been reinforced with about two feet of steel armour protection, before the war, for added protection.

The room, immediately, behind the trophy room was a large room with two extra long tables; one table was to be used as a dining table, whilst the other one was to have computer terminals on it and the operators were to provide computer simulations of different scenarios of the proposed battles with HART personnel. These simulations would be uploaded onto the *Proagnon* mainframe, and then downloaded onto Dr Q's, personal, laptop for his approval.

A few days later, at the Hills Air Force Base, Commander Roberts was addressing the HART soldiers again. "I know we are still in mourning after the events of a few days ago, and it still may be affecting people's judgements, but our colleagues who gave their lives would want us to carry on and not mope about. They would want us to get on with things, so let's get on with them."

"Yes sir," they all shouted with enthusiasm. One soldier followed that up by shouting, "Death to *Proagnon*."

Others followed his lead, and it became a chant; with that ringing in his ears Roberts strode from the hall and returned, along the corridor, to his office, happy in the knowledge that they could win this war.

He didn't see the HART soldier following him, this man was the new Iranian recruit – also a double agent – called Ibrahim Hasan; he had been a friend of Abdul Singh's, but now his friend was dead, or so it had been rumoured, Hasan now saw his job to bring down the HART organisation, with or without help from *Proagnon*. He had joined HART as he wanted to do good; or at least he said he did. He'd also mentioned that his whole family had been killed by terrorists, yet what he failed to mention was the family had been suicide bombers and had committed suicide. Therefore Hasan was also an explosives expert.

He'd, quickly, learnt how to shoot different types of guns, ranging from pistols to assault rifles; learnt how to recognise different bombs, missiles and grenades, and what harm each could do; then he'd learnt how things operated within the organisation, plus how to fly different aircraft – even the great C-141B Starlifter – as he had managed to obtain a pilot's license, and professed a preference for jets, or transport aircraft, rather than helicopters.

No-one thought this preference was strange though, why would they? Both machines, basically, did the same job of airlifting supplies and soldiers to areas where they were needed. Silently, and keeping to the shadows, Ibrahim watched as the HART commander walked into his office and closed the door. Re-sheathing the knife, with the serrated edge that he always carried – he had had the implement ready in case Peter had spotted him and there'd been a struggle. The Iranian was immensely strong, another of his good qualities, and walked, casually, away; there would be a reckoning, one day. As the commander hadn't spotted him he slunk further into the darkness of the shadows.

HART's superior sat at his desk and began viewing the latest satellite images, on his laptop computer; these had been sent over from HART headquarters via the secure, fibre optic, line. As he studied them his phone warbled; Peter, wasn't sure whether it was Gwyneth, with information on Dr Q, or whether it might be Dr Q himself.

He waited until the fourth warble before he picked it up, "Yes," he said.

"Roberts," the voice replied, it was him – there was no mistaking the cruel tones. "I am just informing you that I am no longer in my underground bunker, in Iran."

"Where are you then?" Roberts wanted to know.

"Around," was the, vague, response, "I will let you know when I am ready, somehow, but not before." With that the line went dead.

Peter Roberts was sure he recognised Dr Q's voice, now, but where from? He would, probably, find out eventually; but it still unnerved him, that creepy, cruel and sly, voice. If only he'd brought the voice pattern machine to Iran with him; but all he could do, for the moment, was write a list of people who he may have offended, or who may have vendettas against him; and also, hope that Mrs Jones managed to turn something up. He was surrounded by colleagues, at the moment, yet he'd never felt so alone.

Stop moping about, he told himself and start doing something. So he started typing up a list of people ready to E-mail back to Geneva. As he typed he began thinking back to when he was a young policeman, before he'd moved into the armed service, and the job he was doing now.

He'd served as a policeman, back in England, when he was in his twenties and early thirties; Officer Roberts had helped catch, and bring to trial, many criminals, by whatever means – sometimes even putting his own life in danger – was necessary, in his time. Over the years Peter had risen from a, lowly, police constable, to the rank of sergeant. It was then he'd left the force to spend time with his wife. Unfortunately, this was not to be. His superior officer, Superintendent Jack Higgins, had recommended him to a friend, who was commander of a, specialised army unit; so Peter, at the age of 36, had been persuaded to help in the fight abroad.

Over the next fourteen years he rose up the ranks from Private, all the way to Colonel. It was after this time that he, again, left to spend time with his wife. Again his leave was short lived as a new, specialised, unit was being set up; this one was worldwide, and it needed a leader, who had an outstanding, military service record; and Peter Roberts' name was put forward by his military commanding officer, Brigadier-General Samuel Sling, this recommendation was seconded by Superintendent Higgins, and so Colonel Roberts had got the job.

He had been attending a party, in London – given by one of his old army friends, when the news reached him; he left the party, as soon as was convenient, and drove home in his *Hyundai* Sport. As soon as he reached the apartment block, where he lived with his wife, Nicola, he sensed something was wrong; he stepped out of the car, and paused to look up to his apartment. As he stood there, watching, a huge explosion blew the apartment outwards; masonry and shards of glass rained down, striking all the vehicles that were in the parking lot. He, himself, had had to dive down by his own car, hoping it would shield him against the falling debris.

Then he remembered something, and that thought made him feel sick, Peter had had to leave Nicola behind that night as she had complained of an upset stomach and didn't want to show him up; had she been in the apartment; or had she felt better and gone to visit friends? If she had it would have had to have been someone who lived local to them, or someone in another apartment, as her car was still there. It was then that he saw the young man running away from the complex, Peter's time in both the police and army had taught him to use every aspect of his vision.

He was tempted to give chase, but even if he caught the bastard, what could he do? Even if Mr Roberts caught him the young man, about 25 he judged, he would struggle, and maybe break free. If he didn't he would, probably, protest his innocence to the police, and maybe Peter would be arrested – for harassment. So it was with a heavy heart, mainly because of his thought of the loss of Nicola, and partly because he'd had to let the young man go, Peter slumped on the ground and began to cry. It was then he'd realised maybe that he may have been the intended target.

After the fire personnel had managed to douse the flames of the fire, a fire officer had asked Peter if the apartment was his or someone else's. Mr Roberts had confirmed it was his, and then been told the, devastating, news that a woman's, decapitated, body had been found in the remains.

Dragging himself away from the past, and back to 2013, he had a sudden, and terrifying, thought, *What if that young man was, now, Dr Q? Then he thought, No he can't be, can he? If he is who could he be?*

His thoughts were interrupted by the sound of the STU again. Nervous now, his hands shaking slightly, he picked up the receiver. It nearly fell out his grip, as his hand was sweaty, so he had to use both hands to support the handset. "Hello," he said.

"Sir," was the reply. As the voice had, strong, welsh overtones the commander safely assumed, and rightly, that the voice belonged to Gwyneth Jones. "I have obtained some of the information you requested."

"And," Roberts prompted. He was now eager now to solve this great mystery.

"Well sir, I've been in touch with the British, and they gave me a great deal of information. Basically our Dr Q is a British citizen known as Adam Barker."

"Sorry," said Peter. "Would you mind repeating that name?"

"Adam Barker," repeated the secretary. Peter wondered who this Adam Barker was.

"Anything else?" he asked his secretary, in Geneva.

"Yes," she replied. "His father, it is thought, was a man called Richard Barker, his mother was called Maureen. Richard served seven years inside, out of ten, for terrorism crimes, and then passed away; Maureen, however, had already passed away two years before, leaving Adam – aged 17 we believe – an orphan."

"Hold on a moment please," and Commander Roberts covered the mouthpiece with his hand. Where had he heard the name Richard Barker before? Of course, he suddenly realised, 'Old Dick', Peter had broken a terrorist ring, along with other officers, what was it, twenty-two years ago, arrested 'Old Dick' and brought him to trial. His case had been heard, and then, based on evidence Sergeant Roberts had provided, and that had got the man imprisoned.

Peter recalled, now, that when he'd strode out the courtroom Richard's son, who was standing alongside his mother, had shouted something at him, something like, "I'll get you, eventually, pig, and kill you." Roberts had ignored it as just the boy letting off steam; but what if this Dr Q was Adam Barker, was Peter's past catching up with him?

Releasing the mouthpiece he said, "Sorry Gwyneth, do go on."

"Okay sir, now when Adam was 26, we believe, he was arrested as he was found responsible of causing an explosion, in an apartment complex, on 10th March 2006, and the explosion killed one person inside one of the apartments."

Now Roberts knew, and his blood ran cold; that had been the day of the party, evidently the figure he'd seen was that of Adam Barker, but why? "Yes, I know about the explosion Gwyneth."

You do commander, how?" was the innocent question.

"The apartment was mine, and the person inside was my wife, Nicola."

"I'm sorry sir; anyway Adam was found guilty and sent to prison for thirteen years, ten of his own, and the remaining three of his father's. On 14th September last year it was decided to transfer him from Belmarsh to Park Hurst, on the Isle of Wight, he began the journey next day but never made it."

"He was killed?" the commander queried.

Gwyneth cleared her throat before responding. "Quite the opposite, the vessel he was on was attacked, by a HIND helicopter – then a smaller one, it is believed to have been an ENSTROM-28F two-seater. It was last reported, by the police vessel, to be headed towards the southern coastline of England."

"Had he had any visitors in the days prior to his transfer?" Roberts asked her.

"I've checked and he had a female visitor, three days before, named Tanya Roberts, who we know now as Squeeze; and according to her file was a class 1 helicopter pilot. *Proagnon* was formed in 2004 and just did small stuff until it, properly, linked up with a number of terrorist organisations. While Dr Q, or Adam, was inside Miss Roberts maintained control; or someone did. There is no, actual, evidence of when he joined *Proagnon* and how he became the leader. Finally, it is believed, he has one superior who he reports to on a monthly basis. Nobody knows who this person is"

"Thank you for the information Gwyneth, all of it," Peter said and replaced the receiver. He had much to think about such as why had Adam Barker hunted him down now? *Did he want simple, revenge for his father? Did he, really, need to kill Peter Roberts, or was that simply just an afterthought?*

A knock, on the door, interrupted his train of thought, "Come in," he called. Commander Ronan Strobing entered the room, "Ah Ronan," Peter said, "and what news do you bring me?"

"Rioting seems to have broken out in Baghdad, Arabs from different regions of the city have started breaking into shops, looting, and fighting each other. Petrol bombs have been thrown, cars overturned, houses and apartments broken into, and their occupants killed – usually by the bullet, but some have been stabbed to death"

"Have the local police been notified?" Commander Roberts asked urgently.

"They have sir, but they can't hold the rioters back; and have, subsequently, requested assistance from HART forces, as they don't feel they can handle it if the situation escalates any further."

"Okay," his superior murmured, "we shall send a FAV (Fast Attack Vehicle) Jeep, with armed men in, to assess the situation first; if the driver feels our intervention is required he will let us know by radio."

"I shall select the two men who are to go," announced Ronan, saluted and was about to leave when Commander Roberts stopped him. "Yes sir," the younger man said.

"Please gather all the other commanders and bring them here. I have information on Dr Q."

"Right away sir," and he strode from the room. Once he'd gone Peter Roberts thought to himself, *I only hope our troops don't suffer the same fate as their comrades.*

After about ten minutes the four commanders; Ronan Strobing, Celia Most, Leon Bigship, and Lucy Lang entered the office, "You wanted to see us sir," said Celia.

"I did indeed," he responded, "I've just had a very interesting call from headquarters in Geneva. As I said earlier, I believed Dr Q's voice sounded familiar, and now I know why. It turns out he is a man named Adam Barker, the son of the man who I helped to convict, Richard Barker, and get put in prison, when I was a policeman."

The other four weren't sure what to say to this revelation, so kept quiet and just digested the information.

"Furthermore," their commander said, "it turns out he is also the man who was responsible for the explosion that killed my dear wife. So it would seem he is out for revenge, and using all this terrorist activity as a cover."

Everyone looked shocked. Unfortunately, when the other four had entered the office the last person in hadn't quite closed the door, Ibrahim Hasan stood outside listening as Peter Roberts told his story. Afterwards, he quietly walked away to have a think as to how to use this new information to his advantage.

Up in the commander's office everyone heard the roar of the powerful engine of the FAV as it revved up and roared off, to investigate the situation in Baghdad. After passing out relevant satellite photos that the his fellow commanders may need for reference Commander Roberts told them anything else they needed to know and then let them all go by telling them the meeting was over, and if they were needed further he would contact them via the wrist communicators. Every one of them left, Lucy was last out, and closed the office door. Noticing something was amiss she paused just outside the doorway, peering at something "C'mon," Commander Strobing said to her, slightly impatient.

"Hold on," she said, "the soil around this plant's been disturbed."

"What?" he demanded, returning to examine it. The plant in question was a potted cactus; at the end of the corridor, just beyond their superior's office door was a little alcove in which shelves had been built, for extra storage. Lucy was right, the soil had been disturbed, although only slightly. He looked up into the, young, American woman's face – Leon and Celia had joined them, "I wonder who did this, did any of you?" As the most senior of the four commanders he had the right to question them.

Each of them shook their head. "Oh no," said Leon, voicing all their thoughts, "we must have another traitor in our midst." They all sighed in frustration.

Ronan led his colleagues away from the commander's office for an emergency meeting in their own offices. "Have any of you noticed anyone acting suspiciously since we arrived?"

"No," they each answered, "no-one at all." Ronan studied their faces; they looked as surprised as he did. All the personnel had been trained, and the four commanders treated their personnel as good friends, and vice versa. There was one exception though, a man recruited about a month back named Ibrahim Hasan – this man seemed to be a bit of a loner – but, there again, he may still be getting used to things, and needed space and time to adjust, yet could that be classed as suspicious activity?.

The FAV raced toward Baghdad at over eighty miles an hour. The driver turned to his companion and said to him, "I wonder why the Iraqi authorities can't sort the problem."

"Hmm, yes indeed," his companion murmured. "Maybe it's to do with *Proagnon*."

"Please, don't say that, we've got enough trouble as it is."

"Slow down," the second man said, "we don't want to die before we get there." Promptly the vehicle slowed as the Jeep entered the outskirts of the city; the men saw people staring at them, probably wondering who they were. As the vehicle the two men were in neared the centre they saw policemen with riot shields, and the Iraqi military firing guns. Plus petrol bombs were been thrown and cars had been overturned. The scene was absolute carnage.

The driver slowed the FAV Jeep to a crawl whilst his companion took his M14 machinegun, from where it had been stored in the back, and climbed out. The driver noticed a man, standing on the sidewalk, watching his companion closely – and then the Iraqi started to follow him; the driver was going to get out, and go and challenge the Iraqi man when another Iraqi – this one looked like a holy man as he was wearing a cloak, but there was something about him that didn't seem right.

Suddenly the driver heard a noise that sounded like a strangled gasp. Turning he saw the first Iraqi had reached the other man from the FAV Jeep; cursing to himself the driver realised that he'd been watching the holy man so intently that he'd forgotten to watch his companion's back, as he watched his companion pitched forward and fell to the ground, a knife handle sticking out from between his shoulder blades.

Knowing he had to report this then get the hell out of there the driver quickly switched on his radio, there was only static – evidently it had either been tampered with or the signal was being jammed. He looked behind, a car and a van were parked across the street, blocking his retreat, and machineguns pointing from the windows of the car indicated he could go forward but he might kill Iraqi security forces. If he reversed he knew he'd end up with a bullet in the back of his head.

Then he saw the holy man had, somehow, disappeared; where was he? The driver was very worried now, as he turned back to the front he saw the man he was seeking approaching the Jeep. When the man was close enough he opened the cloak; he was wearing explosives around his waist, a suicide bomber. The man in the Jeep knew he was dead either way. He could get out and run but then the machineguns would cut him down. Plus the houses either side had all been boarded up.

Resigning himself to his fate he sat back to wait, there was no way out, the suicide bomber walked in front of the FAV and then leapt onto the bonnet; both Jeep, men and some surrounding buildings were destroyed in the resulting fireball.

As the vehicle exploded the security forces looked in the direction of the noise; all they saw was a van going one way, and a car going the other, yet another suicide bomber, they decided, things like that happened most days in Baghdad since the insurgents had reappeared.

Later on Dr Q and Sandy Tulliver were seated in his office watching the Iraqi news channel Al Alam when a news item appeared that said a Jeep had exploded near the centre of Baghdad; amongst on-going riots, a suicide bomber had apparently blown the vehicle up. The Iraqi military commander in the area, General Mahmoud Al-Jinra, had confirmed the vehicle hadn't belonged to their military. The two in the room knew then that the vehicle must've belonged to HART; Dr Q turned the TV off, and looked across at his number two, "Prepare the commandos," he said, "we must take the initiative while it is available to us."

"Yes commander," she replied, "right away," and she got up and left his presence. She passed the two bodyguards, and then turned right and walked down the corridor, to the end, where the elevator that would take her back down and into the underground headquarters, to make the necessary preparations.

At HART HQ Peter Roberts had also watched the news item, on one of the TV screens, with increasing concern. He had others to monitor activities inside the compound, there was even a camera linked to another of the security monitors, overlooking the road behind in case of any attack from that direction. This may not have been the work of *Proagnon* but it was still a blow for his organisation. Did he send in more soldiers, who may also suffer the same fate? Did he leave things as they were until the Iraqi security forces contacted him again, or act on this?

He, eventually, decided to leave things as they were for now, if anything, dramatic, happened he would be alerted.

Roberts kept the news channel, Al Alam, running all the time; every hour he would turn the sound on just to see if there was anything of interest to him. Al Alam was the first news channel, in this area, to report on the Gulf War, the trial of Saddam Hussein and his subsequent hanging. Even though it was an Iranian news service many people, if not all, in Iraq received it.

He turned around again and began writing a request, to the Iraqi government to have the bodies of the two HART soldiers be returned to their home countries of Brazil, for the commander (the second man), and Poland for the driver. He would also despatch telegrams informing the families, of the two dead men, of their, sad and untimely, passing. Now HART were down to 168 personnel, including himself, it may still be enough to win though the commander had his doubts.

Just then someone knocked on his door, Peter was startled – he hadn't called for anyone and he wasn't expecting anyone. Still, he thought, at least it wasn't a *Proagnon* assassin. "Enter," he called loudly.

The door opened, slowly, and Ibrahim Hasan entered the office. Roberts, although he didn't really know this latest recruit well, relaxed. "Yes agent Hasan, what can I do for you? Please sit down."

Hasan sat opposite his commander and said to Peter, in what English he could remember, "Mr Roberts, I think to buy machine," he gestured at the laptop, "like yours. Show me yours please."

Peter thought about this, somewhat, strange request, and decided he could show the man the basic working of the machine. After all everything he needed, documents, maps etc. were stored on his, external, hard disk drive. "Come here son," Roberts told the man, "and I'll show you." Commander Roberts knew, if this man were an assassin, he could easily have killed his superior by now, as soon as the door was fully open.

Hasan hurried, eagerly, round to the other side of the desk, Roberts opened the laptop and switched it on, he was using battery power at the moment – each of the two batteries lasted, roughly six hours; but he explained that the adaptor, or power-pack, could be plugged in to enable the computer to recharge the battery. Hasan knew all this already, he was just pleading ignorance; next he urged Peter to show him the underneath workings. As the commander didn't know that much about the workings of the computer he showed Ibrahim the bits he did know. The Iranian looked pleased, "Is it?" he asked.

"Yes that's everything," answered his superior, then taking a magazine, from his desk drawer, he handed it to Ibrahim. "There are a few different makes and models in here," he said. "to give you a bit of choice."

"Thank sir," replied the Iranian and left the office, as he walked away Ibrahim smiled – a plan forming in his mind, but first he had a phone call to make.

Peter smiled when Ibrahim had gone, the young man would make a good soldier eventually. Admittedly he would have to go through much more training, both physical and mental; it was good he'd already been trained to use many different weapons, and could fly aircraft.

On the streets of Baghdad blue uniformed soldiers, armed with the, old, Russian AK-47 assault rifles suddenly started to appear. The Iraqi rioting ceased, momentarily, as everyone; rioters, policemen, and security forces alike turned to look at the new arrivals. Who were these men, and whose side were they on?

From overhead the noise of a helicopter could be heard. Over the horizon, behind the police forces a Russian Mi-24 HIND appeared; another one appeared behind the rioters, they were both hovering, evidently waiting for something. Finally, a third helicopter appeared, this was a Mil Mi-6 – also Russian built. It looked like it was a control aircraft of some sort.

A signal was, simultaneously, passed between aircraft and soldiers and then all hell broke loose. The soldiers began to fire their assault rifles indiscriminately at the crowd and the police plus the security forces, killing many. The Iraqi security forces shot back, but the *Proagnon* soldiers were wearing Kevlar bullet resistant body armour; once they'd done their gruesome work the soldiers walked away to rendezvous with the third helicopter, which had landed in a field not far away.

Once the men were clear, both of the HIND helicopters began firing their machineguns into the crowd, bullets struck some of the remaining people on the ground; the rockets each HIND contained in the rocket pods under each of its twin wings were fired, and all struck the ground, or other vehicles, exploding on impact, killing more people, from both sides. The helicopters then, finally, flew lower and closer, and then deposited their twin 500kg bombs causing more devastation, plus some surrounding buildings were reduced to rubble.

There was panic from the few, remaining, survivors in the streets, as the Russian built helicopters began on their journey back to base. A few Iraqi's, actually, ran and tried to catch the men who had brought such devastation to the streets of their city, in the vain hope of making them pay. The soldiers were just boarding the Mil Mi-6 Heavy Transport Helicopter when the Iraqi's ran up to them and tried to stop them; and then the Iraqi's, mainly young men, planned to kill the soldiers – as they were all carrying knives. There were three soldiers left waiting to board, the other thirteen had already entered the cargo compartment, when they heard the noise which signalled the approach of someone. As soon as the Iraqi's, brandishing their knives, came into sight the AK-47's chattered their famous death cry; all the ten Iraqi civilians were cut down, small red marks had appeared where the bullets had struck the men's chests and they fell dead.

The final three *Proagnon* soldiers then climbed aboard the helicopter, joining the other soldiers already inside, once everyone had their harnesses on the twin Soloviev D-25V turbo-shaft engines roared into life, each engine was capable of putting out 4,100kW of power each. The main rotor head began turning, and, slowly, the machine began its ascent into the sky, to a height of 13,000ft – leaving death and destruction behind. The machine then turned north and began its, steady, journey back to its headquarters.

The palace Dr Q was using was located just south of Samarra, not exactly in Baghdad, but it would be useful for overseeing his operations.

The other main river in Iraq, the Tigris, ran through the town, therefore the sixteen *Proagnon* soldiers who had shot and killed the rioters, and the security forces, on the streets had journeyed downriver, in a BTR-60 armoured personnel carrier, which was amphibious, and had been deployed on the outskirts of the city, to march into the centre and kill anyone they came across.

Once he'd seen the news item about the carnage on the streets of Baghdad, Peter Roberts had phoned Geneva, hoping the line would remain secure for this call, and requested the C-5B Galaxy, the Hercules, together with the C-141B Starlifter be sent back as soon as possible, with any reserve personnel, along with the B-52 Stratofortress for aerial monitoring. Gwyneth said she would see to it at once.

Next he called the four other commanders into his office, where he informed them to get the remaining 168 personnel together, as they were moving again. He told them he thought he had located the *Proagnon* base and they were going to do battle with the enemy. Therefore, every soldier was to be equipped in their takedown gear.

This gear comprised of a sandy coloured uniform – ideal for where they would be fighting – face scarves, flop hats, Kevlar bullet proof vests, rappelling belts, ventilated assault boots, goggles with shatterproof lenses, gadget bags – these were worn around the waist; extra ammo for their M-16 machineguns and Beretta pistols, a flashlight, fragmentation and M560 concussion grenades, a first aid kit, Vaseline for any sore spots, and rappelling rings.

The four commanders reviewed their orders, and then Leon was asked about the status of the sea fleet. He responded, "The two destroyers H-Newhaven and H-Berlin have just entered the Indian Ocean – I managed to obtain permission from King Abdullah for us to use the Persian Gulf – but the two destroyers are holding station, at the moment. The aircraft carrier H-Moscow is waiting off the coast of South Africa awaiting further orders, and the frigate H-London has just left port, after undergoing substantial repairs on its engines."

"Excellent," replied Roberts. "How are the air forces Celia?"

"Well Commander, as you know we positioned them behind the Elburz mountain range, but they can be moved whenever you give the order sir." She snapped a quick salute.

"Thank you Celia," said her superior officer, and then he turned to Ronan and Lucy, "and what is the status of our ground forces?"

"Ground forces have all been checked and maintained, and are ready to go sir," they replied enthusiastically.

"Very well," said their superior. "Please see that all is made ready for our departure, and issue the men with canisters of neo-phosgene gas as well. Plus tell them it is advisable to wear their Parka's, it may appear warm and sunny where we're heading; but they'll need them. Make sure they're also issued with sunglass and gas masks with tinted lenses." He paused, "As our journey is 745 miles, roughly, in an eastward direction I have requested the three transport planes, from Geneva – the Galaxy, Hercules and Starlifter, to rendezvous here and help transport men and vehicles to our destination. They may be needed to ferry more equipment as the battle goes on."

"Yes sir," they all responded, saluted and filed out the room. Once they'd gone Peter thought to himself, *At last, something is happening!*

After about half an hour, possibly less, each commander communicated with their superior, via the wrist communicator, that the soldiers had all the equipment they needed, and were now ready to engage the enemy. Peter was also ready to engage the enemy, having put his Kevlar bulletproof vest on. "Let the men board the vehicles. You go ahead, I have some new satellite imagery coming through, I shall join you at the Turkish Air Force Base."

"Will do commander, out," came the responses through the communicator, as every soldier, plus the four Operational Commanders boarded the various vehicles HART had brought. No one boarded the Abrams M1A1 main battle tank as they all knew that would be brought over on the Galaxy aircraft later.

Nobody noticed the absence of one man, Ibrahim Hasan, he had been present at roll-call and answered when his name was called but had, then conveniently disappeared. He had disappeared back inside, there were 168 men to guide to vehicles so if one man disappeared who would notice; anyway he had a job to do. He wanted to kill Commander Peter Roberts, to avenge the death of his friend, Abdul Singh; the only problem was Roberts was still in the building, as Ibrahim hadn't seen the man outside.

Ibrahim sat, on the floor in his room, pondering; roughly an hour later he was still sitting there when he heard the first aircraft approaching; he risked a quick glance out the window, and saw the aircraft was the Starlifter, it landed behind the base, and lowered its rear ramp.

Soldiers loaded on board: the first 10 of the 20 HMMWVs, and then the remaining 4 of the M-151 Jeeps were driven on, again by more HART soldiers, and 84 of the HART soldiers got on board. Once everyone and every piece of equipment was on board, the ramp was raised; the aircraft was refuelled by then and it roared off towards its ultimate destination.

Next came the Hercules. Loaded on it were the final 7 M-151 Jeeps plus the two VABs. Again the ramp was raised and the transport plane followed the same route as the Starlifter before it. Finally the Galaxy arrived and took the remaining vehicles, the remaining three Bradleys, the other 10 HMMWVs, the two Land Rovers, the Dodge Ambulance plus another 82 soldiers; thus leaving Commander Roberts and himself at headquarters.

That ruined his first idea of installing a little computer program into the man's computer that would automatically delete all information on *Proagnon* from the hard disk, and even if the information was stored in an external disk drive the program would seek the information out.

Then another plan began to formulate in Hasan's mind; for this he needed certain items from his room; he walked back to his room, as he'd left it briefly to observe proceedings, and opened a secret panel. Due to him being Iranian he had always known about this base and, therefore, he knew the layout of this place. Once HART had decided to use this headquarters in Iran, for any Iranian operations, Ibrahim had always been watching them, and then HART had recruited him he had already known the layout so he knew which room had the secret panel in. It was also here that he'd become a class 1 pilot

However, because he was also a friend of Abdul Singh's he had been instructed to build the secret panel into one of the rooms, just in case it was needed someday. Hasan closed the panel, as it fitted so well he knew no one would see it unless they knew where it was.

He knew that somebody, probably one of the four Operational Commanders would check to make sure there was no one left in the building, except Commander Roberts. Just as he thought that a voice called, "Check," and closed the door to Ibrahim's room After about five minutes the Iranian operated the control that would open the panel and he stepped out; as his room was at the other end of the building from his superior's office Hasan started to open a cupboard.

Once the door had been fully opened he reached inside, turned a dial – first left and then right – pushed down on the handle, and opened the safe; withdrawing a small silver object, a laptop lithium battery, he looked at it; it would suit his purpose well. He planned to install the battery in Peter's laptop, for this he had to get the man out his office and that may prove a small problem. He could use his wrist communicator, but if he did Roberts might work out someone was either, inside or outside the headquarters.

Ibrahim sat on the floor in his room, again, pondering his dilemma; as it turned to dusk outside Hasan heard the noise of one of the transport planes returning. He listened carefully, trying to identify the sound, it must be! Thank the grace of Allah.

It was the sound of the returning Galaxy, as the M1A1 Abrams main, battle, tank had been left behind to allow more vehicles to go. The Iranian assumed that was what the plane had returned for. Ibrahim waited, by the door, in his room as the aircraft engine died down, this was his chance. Peeking out his door he walked up to a point where he could see Roberts office door, but if Roberts came out he could not see Hasan.

While Roberts was away from his office, it would to oversee the loading of the tank onto the aircraft, and then he would return for his laptop – as the commander would probably want to travel on the aircraft, the Iranian quickly nipped in the office, made sure the computer was turned off, for a start, and then he used his pocket knife to unscrew the battery cover and took the lithium battery out and replaced it with his own. He replaced the cover, screwed it back into place, and then he turned the laptop back over and switched the computer back on, which would trigger a countdown, pocketed the old lithium and nipped away; once he was out the office he, virtually, ran down the corridor.

Peter returned to his office, turned the machine off, collected the external disk drive from his desk drawer and left; his clothes and equipment were already aboard with the tank. As he walked away he heard something drop on the floor, Roberts looked down but could see nothing in the gloom. He left the building, which had served as HART headquarters for a fortnight/three weeks, and boarded the transport aircraft, ready to rendezvous with the rest of his men, in Turkey.

As the plane rose into the sky a few moments later, a massive explosion was heard, Commander Roberts looked out of one of the side windows upon hearing it; there was smoke billowing from the Iranian base; the main building had been blown outwards, and was now scattered all over the ground.

CHAPTER 15

The final conflict begins!

Once everyone had rendezvoused at the Diyarbakit air force base the vehicles, and transport planes were all stored in various garages and hangars around the base; whilst the men, and what few women there were, of HART had a good meal, and were then shown to their quarters by the few men of the Turkish military who were always on-site for just such an occurrence as this.

The compound, for want of a better word, consisted of, besides the hangars and garages, one large control tower for overseeing military operations and directing aircraft, and several long concrete outhouses – these buildings would serve as the sleeping quarters for the personnel whilst they were on the base. There were about 50 rooms to a building.

The town of Diyarbakit was situated to the west of the air force base (AFB), and 94 miles north of the border with Iraq; Turkey also shared a border to the south with Syria, to the west was a border with Iran and to the north was a border with Georgia, and the coastline with the Black Sea.

Syria was one country that wouldn't let HART operatives work inside the borders of the country; no-one knew why this was.

As they, all, sat down for the meal Commander Roberts told them what had happened at their Iranian headquarters as soon as he'd left, and told them he wanted to do an, immediate, headcount. The four commanders gathered all the men together, and proceeded to carry the headcount out.

They found there was one man missing, Ibrahim Hasan. Armed with this knowledge Peter Roberts was informed. It became evident, to the overall commander and his four Operational Commanders, who the perpetrator of that crime was and therefore who he had been after.

"Surely not sir," Celia said to him, in a surprised tone of voice. "What makes you think that?"

"Because Celia," Peter Roberts replied, looking over at her, "Two reasons: One, he never seemed to fit in, maybe it was because he was Iranian, maybe because he was a loner; and two, a couple of days earlier he had come in to see me about buying a laptop computer when he returned home. Therefore I showed him mine, no important documents were on screen, so he had plenty of time to examine it. I must check it," he said, suddenly thinking of something, "as I thought I heard something fall out when I left." He strode from the room and away towards his new office.

"Oh dear," murmured Ronan Strobing to Celia Most, who was seated on his right, once their superior had left the room, "since he's been getting those phone calls, plus now that explosion, the commander seems to have developed an inferiority complex."

"Hmm, I see what you mean," she murmured back.

"Hey can it you two," Leon said, having overheard bits of what they'd been saying. "The men are jumpy enough already."

The other two HART members, immediately, shut up and kept quiet as they finished off their meal. They then waited for their superior, but most of the soldiers left, the dining hall, to return to their quarters – the ones allocated to them – to get a good nights rest after their travelling. Again most were twin rooms, as in Iran, with Commander Roberts having the only single room.

Roberts returned to the dining hall, and looked down at his immediate subordinates. "It's gone," he said.

"What's gone?" Lucy asked him politely wondering what he meant.

"The Lithium battery from my Laptop computer," he answered hastily, "and I think I know where it is, or at least where it was."

The four of them looked at each other, and then realisation dawned on their faces, and then they looked back up at their superior. "Sir," said the American, female, commander, "you may use my Laptop until the mission is over, as

Commander Strobing and myself have been using his Laptop for the majority of our planning work."

"Very kind of you Lucy, I'd like to borrow it until our, eventual, return to Geneva."

"I will fetch it, and put it in your office, immediately."

Commander Roberts nodded his thanks, but held his hand up in a stop gesture to indicate he wanted them all to be present to hear what he had to say next. His face became graver as he surveyed them all, "Commanders! I believe we may have misjudged our opponent; from what I can recall, his father was a sneaky son of a bitch, no offence ladies," they assured him none was taken so he continued, "therefore I believe his son will have gone to great lengths to track me down, and fulfil his vendetta. Gwyneth, back in Geneva, as well as myself believe this whole terrorism operation is just a cover to draw me out, he's using it to say to me *look how powerful I am now*; his main mission is to take revenge on me, personally, for putting his father in jail, as, I believe, he holds me, personally, responsible."

"But sir," interrupted Ronan, "surely there were more men involved in his father's arrest, and imprisonment?"

"Indeed there were Commander Strobing, only problem was I was the only officer who would testify against his father at his trial."

"Therefore, he decides to try and kill you."

"Correct. He's tried once but only succeeded in killing my beautiful Nicola, now Adam's spent time inside and he's had time to plot, and work on methods, to bring about my ultimate downfall."

"Anyway, changing the subject," Peter continued, "I suggest we, all, get to bed. We've got a long few days ahead of us, if not weeks!" They all nodded their agreement at this, got up from their seats and left the room; together they walked down the corridor; that ran the full length of the building – and connected the three buildings together – the corridors, there were a couple – in case one got destroyed – all had windows in, which were shuttered at the moment, in fact they were left like that most of the time.

After about 2 minutes walking each of the personnel entered his or her, shared room; again the two women had been put together despite their protests, however, again because Celia knew about the affair between Ronan and Lucy, she'd managed to, again, persuade Leon to share with her. As commander's Bigship and Most climbed into their, separate, beds their thoughts wondered to what was happening next door. Were Ronan and Lucy in separate beds, or would they be in one, enjoying one last night of passion – in case it was their last?

The next morning they were all up early, mainly before six; some even earlier. Commander Roberts had called a mission briefing meeting, in the dining hall for six-thirty; at precisely six-thirty, though everyone was already seated in there and wearing their takedown uniforms, the door opened and Roberts walked in – full of life, as usual. "Good morning everybody," he boomed, "I trust everybody slept well." There were moans from those that hadn't, "If you didn't that's a soldier's life for you. Anyway, I've had drinks made up for you," and he indicated a tray with some glasses on, each glass contained an orange coloured drink. "Now drink up and let battle commence."

Each man took a glass and held it, unsure, "Now drink up," Roberts commanded, "down in one go." They all drank up, and then some of the soldier's ran out the room, clutching their throats.

Out of those who remained one of the men asked, "What was that? It tasted foul."

"That drink was a mixture of four raw eggs mixed together with some goat's milk, it is very good for waking people up; it always worked for me back in my military days." He smiled at the man who had asked. "Expect the unexpected! That's what my commander taught me." Once everyone had returned to the room the tactical satellite (TAC SAT) phone that was mainly used in the field, began beeping.

On impulse Roberts picked the handset up, "Yes," he said. The voice at the other end sent a chill down his spine.

"I assume this is Commander Peter Roberts?" replied the sinister, and now familiar, voice of Dr Q. The words were formed as a question.

"You know full well it is," Peter shot back. "What do you want Barker?"

"Oh you finally know who I am," was the patronising reply. "Isn't the fact that I want you dead, for what you did to my family, enough? I just want to say that I believe we should end this now, my forces against your forces, to the death and no tricks. Our final battlefield shall be the desert of Iraq."

"I think I should have the right to choose where we meet. You've been playing games with us for long enough!" With that the HART commander's gloved hand crashed down onto the table, making a few of the personnel jump.

"Now, now," chuckled the voice on the other end, "don't lose your temper! Plus you gave the right to choose our final battlefield up when you decided to give evidence against my father, ultimately leading to his imprisonment."

"Okay," Peter said reluctantly, "when?"

"Let's see," answered the voice calmly, "the time is now just past seven, local time, therefore shall we say eight."

"But that's less than an hour away," said Peter, he had resigned himself to the fact he didn't have much choice in the matter.

"Correct," sneered the sly voice, "best get a move on. I look forward to destroying you and crushing your miserable, HART, operatives." With that he put the phone down.

Commander Roberts faced his personnel, "We go into battle with *Proagnon*, in the Iraqi desert, in just under one hour. So I expect the Bradleys, together with both of the Land Rover Defenders and two FAVs, lined up near the Syrian border and facing towards Iran."

"Sir," said one of the soldiers, "what about the two VABs and the remaining seven M-151 Jeeps, plus the twenty HMMWVs? Not to mention the M1 tank?"

"They will be used to ferry extra men and equipment, if needed," replied his superior "One of the Land Rovers is, at the moment, having a canvas top fitted onto it; its role will be to carry four soldiers into the field, also aboard will be the satellite communications equipment; of course all infantry soldiers will be given hand held radios to keep in contact with each other, as well as their commander in the field. Okay, everyone fall out, and make any preparations you need to, and as quickly as you can. We will reconvene, in the grounds, as soon as every man, or woman, is ready. Operational commanders to my office – dismissed." Soldiers scurried from the room, each hoping to make as much of the time, they had left if that were the case, as they could. Peter was proud of them all, yes they'd suffered casualties, but they'd been patient and now, eight months after the Olympic stadium had been destroyed – as well as most of the people there – the end was finally in sight.

Ronan, Celia, Leon and Lucy seated themselves opposite their superior, in his makeshift office; Peter handed them some satellite imagery printouts. "These have just come in," he announced, "I know we have done this time and time again, but where should we place our forces for maximum, strategic and, tactical advantage?"

"I suggest we place the Bradleys in these two buildings here," said Commander Strobing, pointing to two buildings that were marked on the map. Now we place the infantry soldiers here – there is plenty of scrubland to conceal them."

"Hmm yes, a good idea," murmured his superior, "and the other vehicles?"

Lucy spoke up, "As you can see commander, a road runs parallel with the Syrian border and just beyond – though not in Syria itself – are a group of buildings. I suggest that, as some of these building's roofs are damaged we place the Land Rover, with the communications equipment aboard, in the furthest of these buildings, from the road."

"Yes I see," said Commander Roberts, "and I guess we use the other vehicles as routine patrol vehicles."

"That is correct sir," confirmed Commander Strobing again.

"Has anyone else," their superior said, looking at Celia and Leon, "got any changes they'd like to make, or are we all agreed on this strategy?"

"I am agreed," announced Commander Most. "I am in constant contact with our air support crews, should they be needed."

"Commander Bigship?" Roberts prompted his other commander.

"Like Celia," he replied, "I am in contact with our sea fleet, so should any of the vessels be needed they can be contacted straight away."

"Commander Most," he continued, turning to face her, "should you wish it, your air support jets can rendezvous with H-Moscow, stationed off the South African coast."

Commander Roberts spoke again, "If that is everything you may go and get ready. Each of his subordinates got to their feet. "Commander Lang," he called, she looked over at him in surprise, "you will be first in the field, with the troops, this morning."

"Yes sir," she replied, not very enthusiastically.

"And good luck, all of you!"

"Thank you sir," each of them turned, saluted, and then filed out the room.

At just gone 07.35 every soldier, dressed in their takedown uniform and, white, parka's, plus sunglasses reported for duty. Each man was assigned a task and given their instructions; hand held radios and a few TAC SAT sets were handed out, and then each man, or woman, boarded the vehicle that was to take them out into the field.

The two Bradley Infantry Fighting Vehicles, (BIFV), carried a crew of three; driver, gunner, and commander, as well as six infantrymen each; each of the Land Rovers had a crew of two and carried six additional soldiers; while each FAV carried four soldiers. *Forty-two soldiers going into battle*, thought Peter, *Not a huge amount but it's enough for now.* Lucy was also to travel, with the soldiers, in the second FAV.

Once everyone was aboard and the engines started Roberts shouted, above the engine noise, "Good luck to you all." Every vehicle that could, flashed their lights in acknowledgement, and pulled away from the Turkish AFB and southwards towards the border with Iraq. The FAVs led off at

129 km/h (eighty mph), followed by the Land Rovers – at a more sedately 89 km/h (fifty-five mph), finally there came the Bradley Infantry Fighting Vehicles at their top speed of 57 km/h (thirty-five mph).

As they headed towards the country border the soldiers, and their Operational Commander, all felt the air cool, and the ambient temperature started to drop off. When the convoy of vehicles had left the base the temperature on the leading FAV's dashboard had read fifteen degrees celsius, now it was reading just five degrees, even though the sun was shining very brightly. The personnel, in the vehicles, were glad of their parkas, which were now zipped up to the top, and the sunglasses. Plus the clothing they were wearing was of a loose fit.

As the armoured vehicles slowed and stopped the Bradley's commander, together with the infantryman disembarked, from the rear exit, and took up their positions, laying flat on their stomachs, in the scrubland – concealing themselves as much as they could; whilst the two M3A3 Bradleys took up their positions. The other vehicles took up shelter, at their allotted places; and the HART soldiers readied themselves for anything.

The buildings the Bradleys were in were set in a circular pattern; there were five other buildings in the circle – there was evidence a sixth one had stood in the gap, between where the Bradleys were situated - all had a gap between them but they were, definitely, in a circular pattern. The infantrymen wondered to themselves, what were in the other buildings? Did they contain *Proagnon* soldiers and fighting machines? In between the two buildings that contained the Bradley Infantry Fighting Vehicles a mortar launcher system was being placed on the ground and set up. The mortars were basic rocket shaped devices, but each rocket head contained a cylinder of RAC – rapid action incapacitant.

These canisters, once they hit the ground and exploded gave out a noxious, gas, two seconds after exploding the gas would incapacitate anybody who breathed the fumes in, within a twenty yard radius. The only way to not be affected by the gas was to wear a gas mask; however, after five minutes the gas would become less effective, and after ten minutes the gas would be completely dispersed.

The men lay, in their positions, waiting. Suddenly, there was the sound of an explosion, and one of the other five buildings was blown apart; the HART members watched as the dust settled, then they had the shock of their lives. There, facing them, was a T-72, Russian built, tank.

The infantrymen all knew that, as with many light or main tanks of the same period, the T-72 had a crew of 3 (driver, commander, gunner); plus the all knew, from their classes – each new soldier attended many lessons where they were taught all aspects of warfare, that the Russian built tank had a comprehensive nuclear, biological, and chemical (NBC) protection system. The inside of both hull and turret had been lined with a synthetic fabric made of a boron compound, which was meant to reduce the penetrating radiation from neutron bomb explosions. Crew's were now supplied with clean air via a complicated air filter system, this had been designed to protect from the effects of any nuclear, chemical, or biological warfare; a slight over-pressure prevented any entry of contamination via bearings and joints. Use of an autoloader that had been made for the main gun – this was a 125mm 2A46 gun - allowed for a more efficient forced smoke removal system compared to the more traditional manually-loaded ("pig-loader") tank guns, so the NBC isolation of the fighting compartment could, in theory, be maintained indefinitely; and this was typical of Russian built tanks, the main gun was also capable of firing anti-tank guided missiles (ATGMs), as well as the standard main gun ammunition, including high explosive anti-tank (HEAT) and APFDS rounds.

The main gun of the T-72 had a mean error of one metre at a range of 2,898 kilometres (1,800 metres), which was considered substandard in its later years. It had a maximum firing distance of 14,651km (9,100m), due to limited positive elevation. The limit of aimed fire was 6,440km (4,000m, with the gun-launched anti-tank guided missile, which was rarely used outside its country of origin). The T-72's main gun was fitted with an integral pressure reserve drum, which assisted in rapid smoke evacuation from the bore after firing. The 125 millimetre gun barrel was certified strong enough to ram the tank through forty centimetres of iron-reinforced brick wall, but doing so would badly deteriorate the firing precision afterwards.

There were rumours in the NATO armies of the late Cold War that claimed that the tremendous recoil of the huge 125mm gun could damage the fully mechanical transmission of the T-72.

The tank commander reputedly had to order firing by repeating his command, when the T-72 was on the move: "Fire! Fire!" The first shout supposedly allowed the driver to disengage the clutch to prevent wrecking the transmission while the gunner fired the cannon on the second order. In reality, this still-common tactic substantively improved the tank's firing accuracy and had nothing to do with recoil or mechanical damage to anything.

The vast majority of T-72s that were built did not have forward looking infra red (FLIR) thermal imaging sights, though all the T-72s (even those that had been exported to the Third World) possessed the characteristic (and inferior) 'Luna' infra red (IR) illuminator. Thermal imaging sights are extremely expensive, and the Russian FLIR system, commonly known as the 'Buran-Catherine Thermal Imaging Suite', was only introduced on the later T-80UM tank. Most T-72s found outside Russia do not have laser rangefinders; the T-72s built for export have a downgraded fire-control system and have an automatic loader.

The autoloader design is not based on the faster, but more complicated autoloader in the domestic-use-only T-64 tank series, which was also built in Russia (the T-72s are horizontally auto-fed, whereas the T-64's use vertical actuators). These systems are fast but prone to malfunctions if they are not maintained properly. Even when properly maintained they can prove to be relatively unreliable. It often takes between 6.5 and 15 seconds to load a new shell into the main gun, depending on the current position of the autoloader carousel. The autoloader has to crank the gun up three degrees above the horizontal in order to depress the breech end of the gun and line it up with the new shell. While autoloading, the gunner can still aim because he has a vertically independent sight. With a laser rangefinder and a ballistic computer, final aiming takes at least another three to five seconds, but the aiming is pipelined into the last steps of auto-loading so it proceeds concurrently. Refilling the autoloader with new shells is a real maintenance burden and requires great attention to maintain the specified sequence, but it should also be noted that the average rate of fire for this type of carousel automatic loader has been quoted to be 8 rounds per minute. Trained T-72 crews don't find the reloading much worse than loading other tank types; the separated cartridges are easier to handle.

The armour protection of the T-72 has been strengthened with each succeeding generation of tanks. The original T-72 turret was built from a conventional cast armour. It was believed the maximum thickness of 280mm, the nose armour of the machine is about 80mm and the glacis of the laminated armour is 200mm thick, which when inclined gives about 500-600mm line of sight (LOS) thickness. Later model T-72's feature composite armour protection.

The T-72M (the export version of the Russian T-72A, sometimes called a monkey model) featured a different armour protection compared to the T-72A: it also had a different composite insert in the turret cavity which granted it less protection against HEAT and armour-piercing (AP) munitions. The more modern T-72M1 featured an additional 16mm of armour on the glacis plate, which has granted an increase of 32mm horizontally against both the HEAT and AP munitions. It also featured a newer composite armour in the turret with pelletised filler agent.

Several T-72 models featured explosive reactive armour (ERA), which increased protection primarily against HEAT type weapons. Certain late-model T-72 tanks featured heavy ERA to help defeat modern HEAT and AP against which they were insufficiently protected. Later model T-72s, like the T-72B, featured improved turret armour, visibly bulging the turret front - this was nicknamed "Dolly Parton" armour by Western intelligence. The glacis was also fitted with 20mm of appliqué armour. The late production versions of the T-72B/B1 and T-

72A variants also featured an anti-radiation layer on the hull roof. Also noted was that the early model T-72s did not feature side skirts, instead the original base model featured gill or flipper type armour panels on either side of the forward part of the hull.

When the T-72A was introduced in 1979 it was the first model to feature the plastic side skirts covering the upper part of the suspension and separate panels protecting the side of the fuel and stowage panniers.

However, in contrast to recent Western tanks, the T-72 could store ammunition in the crew compartment, including in the turret. This meant if the main compartment was penetrated, ammunition cook-off could occur, which was likely to kill the crew and blast the turret high into the air. American tank crews who faced Iraqi T-72s during the two Persian Gulf Wars referred to the tank as the "jack-in-the-box".

After the collapse of the former Soviet Union, Russia had been known as the Soviet Union between 1918 and 1990, US and German analysts had a chance to examine Soviet made T-72 tanks that were equipped with Kontakt-5 ERA, and they proved impenetrable to most modern US and German tank projectiles; this sparked the development of more modern Western tank ammunition, such as the M829A2 and M829A3. The Russian tank designers then responded with newer types of Heavy Reactive Armour, including Relikt and Kaktus.

Like all Soviet-legacy tanks, the T-72's design has traded off the interior space in return for a very small silhouette and a more efficient use of armour, to the point of replacing the fourth crewman with a mechanical loader. The smaller complement increases the crew's mental and physical exhaustion (although in service, the tank crew waere supplemented by a mechanic who would travel with the military support organization). The small interior also demanded the use of shorter crewmen, with the maximum height set at 5ft 4inches. The basic design of the T-72 has extremely small periscope viewports, even by the constrained standards of battle tanks and the driver's field of vision is significantly reduced when his hatch is closed. The steering system is a more traditional dual-tiller layout instead of the steering wheel or steering yoke common in more modern Western tanks. This set-up requires the near-constant use of both hands, which complicates employment of the seven speed manual gearbox.

Exported T-72s did not have the internal lining that was standard on Russian T-72s, which consisted of a layer of synthetic material, containing lead, this provides some degree of protection against the effects of neutron radiation and electromagnetic pulses

This tank started to roll, slowly, towards the soldiers; its forty-four and a half ton weight pushed onward by its V-84 12 cylinder diesel engine; the sight of it was terrifying. The gunner appeared, from the hatch, and aimed the T-72s secondary armament, a 7.62 coaxial machine gun (capable of shooting 2,000 rounds), at the HART soldiers. A, cruel, smile crossed the man's face.

Once the tank was within range both of the, two, M3A3's, Bradleys main gun's – the 25mm cannons – opened fire, but the shots were to no avail; the T-72 was hit but no, visible, damage was done. Neither of the Bradleys crew's had faced a T-72 tank before; knowing, now, they were facing heavier enemy armour both crews launched their tube launched, optically guided, wire guidedan (TOW) anti-tank missiles, two of these missiles were carried and were ready to fire in a collapsible, armoured launch rack on the left of the main turret. The Bradley machine had to stop in order to fire these missiles, which were then reloaded by the officer in the back of the vehicle, using a special hatch which provided armour protection during the reload operation.

Each missile was equipped with a massive shaped charge, high explosive warhead and was propelled by a two-stage solid propellant motor. The range of the TOW missile was nearly 4 kilometres and the missile could reach a speed of almost Mach 1 on its way to its target. This weapon was capable of destroying most armoured vehicles in existence and it has a deadly accuracy.

The BIFV, in the building to the T-72's right fired its missiles; however, the TOW missiles, although having high explosive warheads exploded on the tank, but once the smoke cleared the men in the vehicle were aghast to see that no damage had been done. Knowing the cause was lost the driver aboard the fighting vehicle tried to start its engines, but they wouldn't start; fearing the worst, and knowing what the inevitable outcome would be if the engine didn't start, the rear hatch on the vehicle was opened and the crew started to rise from their seats.

The driver of the enemy tank saw the other vehicle's crew were in trouble and relayed this information back to the gunner. The turret, on the machine, rotated, to the right, and the gunner fired. Smoke erupted from the tank's main barrel as an anti-tank missile was ejected, and streaked towards its target.

The BIFV's radar detected the incoming projectile and gave a warning note. "We're going as fast as we can," the, light, tank's commander shouted at the computer, his back to it. As a second warning tone sounded – louder than the first – he turned back and saw the incoming missile, almost filling the screen, "Oh shit!" he exclaimed, "Now we're done for."

"What is it sir?" asked one of the others, attempting to turn.

The missile struck and the first BIFV exploded, killing its crew; debris rained down behind where the building had been.

The crew aboard the second BIFV, saw and, felt the explosion, and the driver was tempted to start their own vehicle's engines when the gunner called, "Wait!" The driver waited, while the gunner took aim at the ground under the T-72's lower, left side, track; the, main, barrel opened fire and a high explosive round was ejected. The missile struck where the gunner had aimed. Sand blew up and there came the sound of a small explosion; then the enemy tank dipped down on its left as the front of the track exploded, crippling the vehicle.

The crew aboard, now afraid to get out, sent a radio message to their headquarters, requesting assistance. A message that assistance was to arrive shortly was relayed back, so the crew felt safe in the knowledge that until help arrived their safest place was inside.

Suddenly, the men felt the tank shudder, or was it their imagination? Now they felt it again, the tank seemed to be moving, but not forwards or backwards – it seemed to be moving downwards. They were in quicksand! Realising this, the commander ordered the main barrel to be elevated as much as possible, and the hatch opened – if they were lucky they would survive. Once the hatch was fully open the three men abandoned their posts, and ascended the ladder, inside the turret; as soon as they were outside the vehicle the men started to ascend the gun barrel, using the handholds on the barrel, in the knowledge that now they were outside the tank the HART soldiers could pick them off easily.

The barrel on the Bradleys was raised so that it was pointing straight at the tank's turret – the gunner reloaded the gun, lined up the sights on the sinking vehicle's turret and fired a second high explosive projectile. The round hit and exploded, yet didn't seem to do any harm; the men atop the T-72's barrel thought they were safe but then a rumbling started up, deep within the tank. With horror and realisation of what might be happening below the men tried to escape their vehicle, intending to jump and hope for the best. Before anyone could do anything the T-72 tank erupted in flames as the vehicle exploded in a huge fireball. Sand was sprayed everywhere.

The HART soldiers cheered as the machine of death exploded, the commander of the Bradleys said to the gunner, "Good thinking and good shooting lad, although, in future, please don't give the orders to the driver I will do that."

"Sorry sir," apologised the gunner, "it's just that the idea of how to cripple, and possibly destroy the enemy vehicle suddenly came to me."

Outside the explosion had, evidently, stirred the occupants of the remaining four buildings, as doors flew open and men, women and children flew out; most had Arabic travelling clothes on, they were members of one of the Bedouin tribes. However, some had very few or no clothes on, despite the cold temperatures. Obviously they'd been in the middle of something.

Just then a couple of squads of *Proagnon* soldiers appeared, levelled their, newer, Kalashnikov AK-74, automatic, assault weapons at the crowd and fired several 5.45x39.5mm rounds into the people, killing them instantly. People screamed as the bullets hit them and they fell; the sand, which had been an orangey-yellowy-brownish colour, turned red with blood as the men, women and children were shot and fell – no one escaped.

The Kalashnikov AK-74 was a derivative of the AK-47 series assault rifle, but it was more closely associated with the AKM assault rifle, and was a smaller calibre system utilizing the Soviet 5.45x39.5mm round. Basically it retained the major features of previous Kalashnikov weapons; the AK-74 also featured a new barrel and bolt component along with a plastic and steel magazine. The AK-74 had seen considerable success since its introduction, to the Soviet, now Russian, soldiers in 1977.

The firing action of the AK-74 proved to be efficient, even when it was firing from full automatic mode. The weapon fired from a 30-round detachable box magazine with the signature Kalashnikov curve. Common with other AK rifle designs, the AK-74 also produced the AKS-74 system with a folding steel butt, making for a more compact system.

The HART infantrymen had been told not to engage the enemy, when they first appeared, but now the men could wait no longer as they observed the, now, dead Bedouins. "Bastards!" shouted one of the HART personnel. "You'll pay for that," and he let loose with his M-16 machine gun. As one of the enemy soldiers was hit and fell, the others spread out, in an arc, to make less of a target; the rest of the group's M-16's chattered while, in response, the *Proagnon* soldiers brought their AK-74's to bear on the place where the muzzle flashes, from the machine guns, were coming from and fired their assault rifles.

There came the sound of a groan from the bushes and a man staggered out, clutching his arm; there was a bright red spot on his upper arm. "Commander Lang!" shouted the commander of the infantrymen, "We have a wounded soldier here."

Lucy bolted from the FAV she was in, and made her way, cautiously, towards the wounded soldier, "What's your name lad?" she asked as she reached him.

"Scott, ma'am, Jason Scott. I'm a Private."

"Well Private Scott let's get that injury seen to eh? Come on," and she assisted and helped him round to the second Land Rover, which was also serving as a field ambulance at the moment. She sat him in the rear of the vehicle, and then said to him, "As we have no doctors, or corpsmen, with us, at the moment, I'm afraid that I'm the only one with the necessary medical skills. Now let's have a look," she examined the wound. "Ah, the bullet's still in there so I need to remove it, and quickly" She produced a long, slim, knife from her kit bag. "This may sting a bit so be prepared."

"I'm prepared," he said, a little dubiously.

Commander Lang cut the material of the parka – then that of his desert uniform, around the wound, away. Slowly, she touched his skin with the knife around the bullet hole; more slowly, the knife was pushed into the wound, Scott gritted his teeth, clenched his fist, and closed his eyes so his commander wouldn't see his eyes watering – the American felt sorry for him as she'd just learnt it was his first time in the field.

Gently, or as gently as was possible, the knife was moved around the bullet; it was then that Scott cried out. "Nearly there," she assured him.

"Bloody hurry it up," he swore at her, "it hurts like hell!"

Suddenly and quickly, the knife was pulled back sharply, there was a tinkling noise as the bullet popped out and fell onto the floor of the vehicle, and then the knife was withdrawn. "Sorry about the pain," Lucy told him, "you've been very brave," and she, lightly, kissed him. "Now you get some rest," and she left him to return to the FAV to carry on with her observation duty.

Sounds of gunfire, and of men screaming in agony, came from beyond the wall; then there came the sound of an explosion.

Lucy wanted to see what was happening, but the driver, of the FAV Jeep, placed a hand on her, young, shoulder. "No ma'am, let me go I'm expendable – you're not," she looked as if she was going to protest when he hurried from the vehicle and crossed to the corner of the wall.

The next thing Commander Lang heard was the whistling noise of a grenade as it was launched; she watched, gob-smacked, as the grenade exploded, and the driver of the Jeep's head was blown clean off, and the man fell, headless, onto the ground – blood pooling from his neck. She screamed!

Next she heard an ominous rumbling noise, and a projectile that could only have been shot by a tank hit the wall that separated the HART vehicles from the road – blasting a hole in the concrete; then a second explosion came from the top of the wall and chunks of debris rained down, there was a scream and a smashing sound; she lifted her hands from her head and looked up, what Lucy saw made her feel sick. The Land Rover Private Jason Scott had been in was now no more than mangled metalwork, and Scott's crushed body lay on the ground next to it, a, jagged, lump of concrete sticking in him She couldn't understand why the second BIFV hadn't fired, then it dawned on her that maybe it couldn't fire, for some reason.

Climbing out the, now deserted, Jeep Lucy raced into the back of the other Land Rover that contained the communications equipment; the operator looked up, startled. "Get a message to the base in Turkey, tell them we're under heavy fire, we've lost several men, a BIFV has been destroyed. Basically, we need reinforcements and fast; send the message NOW," and she pointed her Beretta 92 pistol at the man, to emphasise the urgency – she knew this was highly unprofessional – but she didn't feel professional, at the moment. Realising her mistake she checked herself, and then re-holstered her weapon.

The radio operator had been shocked at his commander's actions, but knew she wouldn't have acted that way unless the transmission was that urgent. "At once ma'am," he assured her, working the controls, tapping on his keyboard, and then pressing several lit buttons; the machine hummed away and, after about 30 seconds the lights went out and the humming stopped. "Message sent," he told her.

Lucy then climbed back out of the Land Rover and walked over to the dividing wall, or what was left of it. Dropping onto her stomach she crawled forwards to the end of the concrete construction; peeking round the corner, trying to offer as small a target as possible, she was aghast, and horrified, to see another tank. This one, though, looked smaller, and it seemed different – for some reason; then Commander Lang knew why.

The tank in question was an old Chinese Type 63, these had been built by the China North Industries Corporation (NORINCO) and had first seen service in 1963. This tank was in many ways a relative of the Soviet designed and built PT-76 troop carrier. The weapon system was fully amphibious – as Lucy had already guessed – utilising their water bilge pumps, and it had a fording speed of up to seven and a half miles an hour (propelled by dual water jets). However, its speed over land could be up to forty miles per hour.

The main gun, on the tank, which was 85mm, this could fire a variety of ammunition including HE, HEAT and smoke; its traversal was 360 degrees with a +18 or -4 capability. The equipment for its self defence included a single mounted .50 calibre machine gun, which could be used for anti-aircraft defence, and a coaxial .30 calibre machine gun that was used for anti-infantry defence.

The Type 63 could accommodate four, and was fully NBC protected – including infrared Night vision, the tank was powered by the 12150-L-12-cylinder water cooled diesel engine which generated 400 horse power at 2,0000 revolutions per minute.

Newer variants of the system have been upgraded with a more potent 105mm main gun and a redesigned and reengineered turret system. These upgraded Type 63s were designated as Type 63A.

Commander Lang, once she'd recovered from the shock of seeing this machine, then turned her attention to the second building that housed the other BIFV. She saw smoke billowing from the building – acrid black smoke, she reasoned that this could be because of one of several things; either the building had been caught by an explosion and this had set light to something inside; some *Proagnon* soldier had managed to get close enough, and rolled a gas canister, plus a smoke canister, into the building; or something had gone, badly, wrong with the Bradleys firing system.

Keeping as low as she could Lucy ran over to the rear of the building and threw the doors open – a huge, black, cloud engulfed her, and she coughed, in fact she almost choked on the fumes; then she smelt it: gas. She examined the Bradley Infantry Fighting Vehicle, as best she could; there was nothing wrong with the front, back, or sides of the vehicle; the rear entrance door was closed so that could count if the firing system had jammed, but as it was on an automatic mechanism surely the diver would have it open, as all crews on the Bradleys were instructed to keep their rear, entry, doors open in case of this happening. Had he shut it after the infantrymen had disembarked and the mechanism had jammed afterwards? Or was the reason totally different?

She then hauled herself up, onto the right side skirt, above the tracks, and on up the side of the machine; as she reached the top of the turret she found the hatch was shut, with an enormous effort Commander Lang wrenched the hatch open – sweat started to pour off her – and then the gas fumes really hit her, so much so she had to turn away, after about five minutes she turned back. As the fumes had more or less dispersed she had a better view inside the turret, and, yes, there on the floor of the BIFV was a small gas canister; but where had it come from? Lucy swung her legs inside the hatch, intending to climb down the steel ladder, when a ray of weak sunshine filtered into the building. Lucy looked above her; there was a hole – in the roof – directly above where the vehicle's hatch was.

There was no further investigation required; it was evident now some enemy soldier had climbed onto the roof, slid up to the hole and waited for his moment; once the hatch had been opened he'd dropped onto the tank like vehicle, knocked whoever had opened the hatch unconscious and dropped the body, plus a gas grenade inside, slammed the hatch down and jammed it somehow; after everything had been quiet for a certain amount of time he would have un-jammed the hatch and left.

She swung her legs out the hatch and made her was back down the side. On the floor, kicked to one side, was an iron bar. Realising this was probably what the soldier had, probably, used to jam the hatch shut Lucy kicked it, and then left the building. Now she wasn't concentrating on the mysterious silence of the Bradleys she could hear the sounds of guns being fired, and soldiers screaming and groaning as they were hit and killed.

Lucy stepped outside, and was just about to run across to shelter again when she heard a familiar click, and then a *Proagnon* soldier stepped into her line of vision, he wasn't wearing the usual, blue, uniform – his was grey. This soldier was carrying a weapon similar to the other men, but different as it had something else on it, "Ah," he said, noticing her gaze, "you are right HART Commander Lucy Lang, it is a different type of assault rifle. This is the AKS-74UB compact assault rifle, with added grenade launcher; the weapon was made in Russia, of course, and now I am going to use it to kill you. Prepare to die!" She watched as he raised the weapon, and lined it up with her forehead.

Lucy, then, closed her eyes, tightly, as she waited for the shot that would end her life; and then a shot rang out, convinced the sound had come from the killer's gun she, automatically, fell backwards, into the sand – then she realised she was still alive and, slowly, opened her eyes; towering above her was the figure of Commander Leon Bigship, his Beretta pistol smoking. "C'mon, get up! People'll think you're dead," he said drily, and then extended his arm down to her, "and we can't have that."

Lucy grasped his arm and pulled herself up, and then she hugged him. "Oh Leon, I am glad to see you. Thank you for saving my life, by the way."

Leon smiled at her, "Think nothing of it Missy. It looks like the cavalry arrived just in time."

"Hey, don't you start with the Missy business," Lucy said playfully, and then asked, "and anyway, what cavalry?"

Then she looked round and saw ten, assorted, HMMWV's, both VABs, and four M-151 Jeeps; She looked up at him and grinned, "Looks like the message was received." Then, in the background, the sound of multiple helicopters was heard; Commander Lang looked back over towards the border with Iran, and saw a, full, squad of four AH-64D Apache Longbow helicopters, on each of the machine's side wings were the standard, multi-role mission, complement of four Fire-and-Forget RIF Hellfire missiles, plus nineteen of its 70mm Hydra-70 Folding Fin Aerial Rockets (FFAR), on each wingtip were the standard two Aim-9 Sidewinder Air-to-Air missiles (ATAM) and underneath was the M230 gun armament which could fire 1,200 rounds of 30mm ammunition.

The Type 63 tank whirled its turret about and elevated its gun barrel to face these new attackers; "Hold your fire!" Commander Lang ordered, and then raced to the second BIFV, mounted the tank like vehicle and loaded a HE round into the main barrel. Lining the Type 63 up in the Bradleys gun sights so the crosshairs intersected on the rear of the enemy vehicle she fired.

The high explosive round struck the tank penetrating the outer shell and forcing its way into the compartment containing the engine; the HE round exploded and the Type 63 Light Amphibious tank, and its crew of four, was blown up – flames and smoke rising into the sky. "Yes," cried Lucy as she re-emerged from the building containing the second Bradleys, "I did it! That'll teach the fuckers to mess with us, and gas our troops."

"Yes, quite," Leon murmured thoughtfully, "calm down Lucy, you've done your job." An M-151 Jeep rolled over, "Now you can go back to headquarters knowing that you've avenged the deaths of your comrades."

Lucy boarded the Jeep, and then turned back to her fellow commander, "Leon, on my shift we've lost a Land Rover, a Bradleys with its three crewmen, one of the FAV's has been damaged, the crew of the second Bradleys has been gassed, we've lost the driver of the FAV, and five infantrymen. Not too bad. Two out of six vehicles destroyed and one damaged, together with 12 out of 42 personnel." Not much to show for six hours, but it was better than nothing."

"Very good Commander Lang," Leon saluted her then the Jeep powered up its diesel engine, and the vehicle made its way over the desert, over any rough terrain with ease, towards the main road and turned north, and then speeded up and headed off to Turkey, Commander Lucy Lang relaxed; she wouldn't see the, main, battlefield again until she took over from Commander Ronan Strobing in another eighteen hours.

Back at the battlefield Leon felt the sweat running off his forehead, in the sunlight; even though it wasn't, especially, hot, though the temperature had risen the sunlight still made them all sweat. It was a shame Commander's Most and Strobing were doing the night duties, as, Leon knew, it could get bitterly cold at night in the desert. Lucy had also told him about the patch of quicksand, that she'd been informed had started to swallow up the Soviet built T-72 tank; he got some infantrymen together and they had it marked out so, hopefully, no one would end up in it again. He wasn't, particularly, happy either about the communications vehicle been positioned behind that concrete wall.

Therefore, he got the men to move the vehicles: the Land Rover Defender mobile communications unit, as well as the two FAVs, under his supervision. Leon walked over to the wall where he saw the, headless, body of the driver, the wreckage of the other Land Rover as well as the body of Private Scott, as well as both FAVs – one damaged and the undamaged one, and, finally, the mobile communications unit. "Move those," he ordered his men, indicating the two FAVs, whilst he walked over to the Land Rover and banged on the side.

The sole occupant – the radio operator – stuck his head through the opening flap, between cab and body. "Sir," he said and saluted, as best he could with the radio headset on.

Commander Bigship looked over at him, "Get ready to ship out," he said to the man brusquely. "You're being relieved. However, please inform the soldiers at base, to take out the communications equipment, and remove the satellite dish – we shall use the vehicle, in future, as a personnel carrier."

"Right you are sir," replied the soldier, "excuse me, but what will happen to communications with Turkey?"

"One of the HMMWVs has everything we need aboard, now get moving!" the commander said in way of explanation.

"Yes commander," the soldier said, hurriedly, and popped back inside the body of the truck. After about five minutes he emerged, and walked round to the driver's door and climbed in. He started the big diesel engine and drove off northwards, building up to 50mph, towards Turkey.

Next Leon surveyed the fallen bodies; there were Bedouin, HART and *Proagnon*. "Round up our fallen troops, load the bodies in one of the Renault VABs and order it back to base, but throw the others in the quicksand." Leon knew this act might be seen as heartless, by some of his soldiers, but after all war was war – nothing in war was pretty.

"But sir?" one of the HART men started to protest, "that's cruel, they are, or were, human beings."

"If you have any better ideas implement them," Commander Bigship shot back hotly.

"Sorry sir but I just feel we shouldn't treat the dead this way, whoever they are."

"Okay," Leon replied. "You may bury the Bedouins but do what you want with the *Proagnon* soldiers."

"Thank you sir," replied the soldier, Sergeant Joseph Lakes. He turned and called, "You ten men," they looked up, "grab a digging implement and get over here on the double!" The soldiers grabbed spades, shovels and other digging implements from the nearest HMMWV, and hurried over; the sergeant indicated the dead men, women and children of the tribe of Bedouins. "Now we're going to bury these people with dignity."

"Yes Sarge," they all replied. The men then started digging and buried each of the Bedouins, once finished they placed a, simple, wooden cross to mark each grave. Leon felt useless, as he watched the men at work; once finished the soldiers turned their attention to the, fallen, enemy soldiers, "Sarge, what should we do with them?" queried one of the soldiers.

Sergeant Lakes replied, "We strips them lad, buries the bodies in unmarked graves, and then dumps the uniforms and identification tags in the quicksand. But keep the weapons, they may come in useful." Leon smiled; the man would go far in the HART organisation.

The soldiers set about their task, many laughed as they removed the underwear from the dead soldiers. "You won't be using that again mate," some laughed and withdrew their knives, intending to remove the, male, object.

"We're not sadists!" shouted the sergeant, seeing and realising what the men were thinking, "re-sheath your knives, NOW!" Reluctantly, the, ten, HART soldiers put their killing knives away.

Commander Bigship then produced his hand held radio and contacted the lead Apache pilot. Once the transmission was received Leon commanded, "Destroy that wall beyond the road; blow it to smithereens!" The vehicles were out the way, so all was safe.

"Gladly commander," responded the pilot. One of the Apache helicopters broke away from the formation of, four, and flew towards the wall; the machine hovered and then fired off two FFAR missiles. The explosion, as the missiles hit the lower section of the wall, was tremendous and knocked some of the men off their feet; when the smoke cleared there was a blank space where the concrete used to be, although some debris had fallen, into the desert.

"What shall we do with this sir?" asked another of the soldiers, indicating the wreckage of the Type 63 tank.

"Take the occupants out and bury them, if they're still in one piece – same as before, strip them then bring them out, and then deposit the uniforms and identification tags from the men we buried earlier, put them in the remains of the tank; then we bring over the HMMWV with the winch and we will push this tank into the quicksand."

"Right you are sir." Sergeant Lakes took command again, "Right boys, you heard what the officer said, now get to it!" Some of his men climbed onto the, destroyed, vehicle and lifted the hatch. Using flashlights they descended into the darkness, one soldier bringing the pile of uniforms, helmets and identification tags with him. He dumped these on the floor while his comrades searched the rest of the vehicle.

"Hey Corporal," shouted one of the soldiers, "over here, we've got one in one piece."

The Corporal, George Mctavish, wandered over, "You know what to do," he said to Private Walter Havers, then he noticed the wicked look on the young man's face. "Aye well, as the Sarge says we're not sadists but he ain't here. So if you want to do that, find a nice, discreet, corner, where no one can see you. I haven't seen you."

"Thanks Corp," Havers whispered conspiratorially; the corporal walked away to see if the others had found anything else. Havers removed the enemy soldier's clothing then smiled to himself; making sure he wasn't being observed Private Havers unsheathed his knife and in one fluid movement he removed the lot.

To prevent the others from seeing the flow of blood he moved the man's arm and placed the hand covering the blood flowing out. "Corporal," he called again, "I don't think this one's in a fit shape to be buried."

Mctavish walked back to where Private Havers was, "I see what you mean Walter, but who could've done this to him?" he asked, moving the man's hand. "Come and look lads!"

So Privates John Wilson and Victor Hughes sauntered over. "Ugh," each man cried, seeing the wound then they looked accusingly at Havers. "You did that!" they accused him.

"I did not," retorted the man, "I merely removed the man's uniform, when I saw blood in his underwear I, momentarily, stopped."

"I peeked inside, just to confirm my suspicions, and then I remembered what the Sarge said, so I removed the underwear as well; but I never did this to him."

As the other two men seemed to be ganging up on Havers, the Corporal jumped in, "Maybe it was one of the others, or maybe it'd been done before they left *Proagnon* headquarters."

"Yeah, maybe you're right," said Wilson. "It's probably because of earlier." However, Havers could still detect the doubt in his colleague's voice. The four men then ascended the ladder, with the weapons they had found, and climbed out, closing the hatch behind them.

"There were no bodies we could bring out Sarge," the corporal called, almost cheerfully; "three were burnt beyond recognition, whilst the fourth," he glanced at Havers, "was mutilated. The *Proagnon* troops had cut his lower organ off."

"I see," said Lakes, "good of you to do that." Then he turned to Commander Bigship, "I think you can order the HMMWV in now sir."

"Thank you Sergeent, carry on," the commander told him. He produced his radio again and contacted the personnel aboard the M1042 S-250 shelter carrier, which also had a winch. Once contact had been established the commander requested that the vehicle meet the soldiers, plus himself at coordinates Delta Zero.

The desert area had been divided into squares, or areas, designated with the phonetic alphabet and with numbers for easier reference.

The personnel aboard the HMMWV informed the commander that they would be with him shortly; Leon killed the radio, and his men, along with himself, found a shaded spot to wait. About ten minutes went by and the vehicle arrived. "Get aboard men," ordered Leon, "your job is done, go and get some rest."

"Thank you sir," the sergeant and his men saluted.

"But first we need to get rid of that tank," then he went to talk to the driver, "see that tank over there. Can you hook it on the winch and take it to the area just beyond the quicksand."

"Right away sir," replied the driver and, carefully, backed the vehicle up to the, destroyed, tank His passenger got out and directed whenever necessary; once the recovery vehicle was in position, and this was confirmed by the passenger, the winch was lowered, on its hydraulics, and the hooks were attached under the front bar, of the tank, and the enemy vehicle was pulled, slowly forwards, towards the patch of quicksand.

When they were as near to the edge of the quicksand as the driver, of the recovery HMMWV, dared to go the winch was lowered and the Type 63 tank unhooked; Commander Leon Bigship had had one of the pieces of wire marking the edge of the quicksand removed from its two marker poles, thus making an entrance. "Okay, now push it forward," their commander said.

The High Mobility Multipurpose Wheeled Vehicle manoeuvred behind the, destroyed, tank, and revved its, huge,

8 cylinder 6.2 litre diesel engine and started to push the Type 63, towards the quicksand area, using its bull-bar at the front; the Turbo-Hydramatic transmission groaned as the vehicle pushed the other. When the HMMWV reached the gap where the wire should've been all ten of the soldiers from the back were ordered to disembark, and give assistance. The vehicle reversed, allowing the men access to the tank and they pushed it, but it wouldn't move. "Put your backs into it," ordered the sergeant.

The men pushed harder and, slowly, ever so slowly, the tracked vehicle moved forward. When they felt they'd pushed the tank far enough forward the HART soldiers released their grip and moved away. Then they watched, from a safe distance, as the Type 63 sunk, very slowly. Smiling his satisfaction Leon ordered more men, and an engineer to recover the Bradleys and get it in working order again.

Suddenly, an aircraft shot overhead and a sonic boom was heard, throwing everyone to the ground. "What the hell?" the commander demanded. It was then that the aircraft flew overhead again – this time at a slower speed. Commander Bigship looked up, a MiG-29 FULCRUM was seen flying overhead, "Oh shit," he observed, "that's all we need." He ordered everyone to battle stations, using his radio, and then he contacted the communications HMMWV and requested it send the following message to Turkey, "We are under attack from a MiG, please contact H-Moscow and request, immediate, assistance."

The MiG turned again and loosed its two AA-10 Archer missiles. There was nothing anybody could do as the missiles streaked towards one of the two VABs; they struck the vehicle on its left, luckily the soldiers aboard had already disembarked, and the French built armoured personnel carrier exploded. Next the MiG pilot used his radar to detect the HART soldiers, on the ground. The 30mm Gsh-30L cannon opened fire, screams were heard as many personnel were hit and killed; at least 20 soldiers were killed. "Oh shit," announced the commander again, to no one in particular, as he surveyed the dead bodies, plus the wreckage of the VAB. *This isn't going well, the first phase never does.*

The MiG made a fourth pass, evidently trying to determine the best target; as it flew by the Bradleys main cannon was observed to be elevating. All of a sudden the cannon fired, and a round exploded on the MiG's undercarriage, causing another bigger, explosion.

The pilot, aboard, knew his jet was doomed and pressed the ejector button, it didn't respond; frantically now he jabbed at the button, willing the glass, above his head, to slide back and his seat to be ejected. As he watched the lights that were on - on the control panel - winked out. The pilot, his life, now, in danger, tried to divert the plane he was in northwards, towards the Black Sea, but the controls were locked, so the jet was stuck and flying eastwards.

The soldiers, on the ground, saw the round from the BIFV - its back door now open again – and the resulting two explosions; however, Leon was concerned, why hadn't the pilot ejected? Then it hit him that maybe he couldn't for some reason.

In the main city of Baghdad a street festival was happening – over 100 people lined the streets; everyone stopped what they were doing, as they heard the aircraft approach, it didn't sound as if it was going particularly fast, and it sounded as though there was something wrong with it. The MiG came into view and it seemed to be on a collision course with a block of, new, apartments, there were over 400 apartments inside – many full of young couples – if it were to plough into the building there would be many deaths.

The pilot saw what was going to happen, and sat back; his life may be ended but he would take many more with him. The aircraft smashed into the block of apartments, and the explosion was loud plus the fireball created was very extensive.

CHAPTER 16

The conflict continues!

At the, main, above ground *Proagnon* building – the ex-palace of Saddam Hussein – Dr Q and Sandy Tulliver were in one of Dr Q's, numerous, offices. Miss Tulliver was wearing her, usual, uniform of tight tunic and trousers, plus boots and gloves – all were black; her, shoulder length – wavy, blonde hair hung loose as she said to her superior, "If HART are suffering such losses, why can't I go into the battlefield, and lead our troops to their final victory?"

"Because my dear," her leader purred from across the desk, "your talents are more suited here."

"Oh really," she responded darkly, "and what talents would those be?"

"Your tactical skills, combined with your ability to guess our enemies movements in response to our own."

"You want revenge on this Peter Roberts, that's all. You're just using *Proagnon* as a cover."

"That's as maybe," Dr Q retorted annoyed," but you are not going into the battlefield until later." He looked, over, at her, "Yes, later, I think," and then he reached over and held her jaw in his hand – Sandy was a bit nervous at this as he applied a slight pressure; not much but it was enough to make her wince, slightly.

With disgust at this type of reaction he let go, and slapped her, not hard but it created a red mark on her right cheek, "Yes," he repeated, cruelly, "you shall get your wish eventually. Now leave me!" Sandy got up and left the office, her right cheek still stinging from where he'd hit her. The bodyguards, outside the office, looked at her as she walked out and closed the door behind her.

"Yes, he hit me," she told them as if they hadn't noticed; "now I shall return to my quarters, and await my next orders." She stalked away from them; when she was out of sight the bodyguards chuckled to themselves, both knew that their leader had a cruel streak in him, but he always had good reason if he hit someone. Sandy was seething with rage now, how dare her boss hit her, as he wasn't going to be let to go into the battlefield with his consent she would go against his orders, see how Dr Q liked that.

Back at the desert the temperature was definitely getting somewhat colder; the midday temperature had been 14 degrees. A couple of HMMWV's drove over the sand, to collect Commander Bigship, together with some of his men. As he boarded Leon looked at the temperature reading, it was now 8 degrees; Mrs Most would have an entertaining, few hours. She arrived in the same M-151 Jeep that had transported Commander Lucy Lang back to the HART headquarters in Turkey.

Like Lucy before him Leon was looking forward to returning to base, getting a good meal inside him, a hot shower, and a good sleep, during his 18 hours away from the desert and the front line. He gave the command to move off, to his driver, and the vehicle pulled away from the battlefield. As soon as the vehicle he was aboard passed the vehicle Celia was in she automatically took command of the HART forces. Celia's, like every commander's duty, was for the next 6 hours, and then Ronan Strobing would take command of the graveyard shift, this would last from 02.00 to 08.00.

Once Celia had taken command she set about getting the men to dig trenches wherever possible, these were mainly dug near the road – just before the actual desert started. They were digging hard to help keep warm as some of the soldiers weren't keen on the cold. The vehicles that were around – mostly HMMWVs were driven onto the sand, and covered with sandy coloured tarpaulins; there was a, small, patch of palm trees off to the northern side of the area. To the west was the road, that became a highway to Turkey plus beyond that the border with Jordan, to the east was the main area of desert, and the towns and the capital city of Iraq, Baghdad, and, eventually, the border with Iran. Finally, to the south was the border with Saudi Arabia.

Some of the troops had positioned themselves in the trenches, along with their commander; the others remained standing, but protected by the vehicles. The engineer, who had gone into the Bradleys earlier, had been trying to fix the drive – as it had been discovered that it had become disengaged, then damaged somehow, and now the Fighting Vehicle couldn't move forwards or backwards – the guns, and main cannon, still functioned correctly, as had been demonstrated with the downing of the MiG-29 jet. They'd all been saddened when they'd learned of the plane's, eventual, crash destination; over 1000 civilians had been killed, 900 in the apartment block – that reminded them of the New York tragedy 11+ years back; though this was on a much smaller scale.

If nothing could be done then the Bradleys would have to be destroyed, once the crew and the engineer were clear of the vehicle. It was still useful, as a machine of destruction, just unable to move, properly. Commander Most made perimeter inspections - in a HMMWV M1025, armoured, armament carrier – routinely once every hour.

The vehicle was equipped with basic armour and a weapon mount, which was located on the roof of the vehicle, and adaptable to mount either the M60, 7.62mm machine gun; M2 .50 calibre machine gun; or the MK 19 Grenade Launcher. The weapons platform could be traversed up to 360 degrees. The vehicle was able to climb 60% slopes and traverse a side slope of up to 40% fully loaded. The vehicle could ford hard bottom water crossings up to 30 inches without of deep water without the need for a fording kit and therefore could make water crossings of up to 60 inches with the addition of the kit. Similar vehicles in the HMMWV family were equipped with the self-recovery winch which could also be used to recover similar systems. Other models had the latest modifications applied to the vehicles. All HMMWV vehicles were built on a similar chassis but there were different models. The family included utility/cargo, shelter carrier, armament carrier, ambulance, TOW missile carrier and scout-reconnaissance configuration. The payload, each could carry, varied by body style ranging from 1920 lbs on the 4 litter ambulance to 5300 lbs on limited availability Expanded Capacity variant, but is generally in the 5/4T range. A basic armour package is standard on the Armament and TOW missile carrier models. A more heavily armoured, or Up-Armour HMMWV, was first produced in limited quantities, primarily for the Scout Platoon application. Special supplemental armour versions had later been developed for the US Marine Core requirements; unique model numbers designate these configurations.

Commander Most felt safe as the armament carrier pulled away and she began her latest patrol, all was quiet – at the moment – but she knew the peace wouldn't last forever; as if on cue, *Proagnon* troops appeared at the far side of her peripheral vision, inclining her head slightly, to the right. There, on the horizon were several blue dots, she raised her binoculars and peered through them, yes, as she'd thought *Proagnon* soldiers armed with the newer AK-74 assault rifles, however, some carried different weapons – they looked like sub-machine guns; also some carried hand held rocket, or grenade, launchers, there were about 30 men. She produced her radio, hand held, and contacted the sergeant she'd left in charge of the other HART soldiers and informed him of what she'd seen, and he should prepare the men for battle.

The message came back, "The RAC mortar launcher is still set up, and the men are ready for battle, the grenades are primed; basically everything is ready."

"Don't fire until you have a clear line of fire, I shall be with you as soon as I can, out."

"Understood ma'am, out." With that Celia thumbed the end switch. She then ordered the driver to continue with the patrol, he looked, slightly, dubiously at her. "Don't worry, I know what I'm doing," she assured him, "now drive on."

He nodded and pulled off – what Celia didn't notice was the figure in a, black, uniform standing behind the line of trees, watching them. The soldiers were just a diversionary tactic.

The figure – seizing its chance – moved forward, keeping under what cover there was available – it moved towards the graves of the Bedouins, and began to dig in the sand; with its hands, no one noticed as this person stripped one of these people and carried the clothes, sometimes dragging them over the sand, thus dirtying them, and hurried back behind the trees; where they changed into the clothes – putting them over the uniform – then sat and waited. While they were there the figure checked that they'd brought the correct equipment with them: Makarov PM 9x18mm pistol, APS Stechkin 9x18mm PM machine pistol, two smoke grenades, to cover their escape, plus two gas grenades, and a knife – for close up combat – if it got that far.

Meanwhile the *Prognon* soldiers, who had moved forward, were almost within the RACs range, "Wait one more moment lads," the sergeant, an experienced man who'd served at HART for the past four years, told them. A moment later came the order they'd all waited for, "Fire!" M-16s chattered away, knocking some of the enemy down; the AK-74 assault rifles fired back in retaliation, at the places where the muzzle flashes from the M-16s had come from, killing several soldiers, but the majority of the HART troops were dug in too deep.

"Bring up the AKS-74UBs." The soldiers carrying these weapons approached from the, rear, rank. "Those with the AKS-74U sub machine guns provide covering fire, now go!"

In 1979 a shortened variant of the AKS-74 was adopted into service – the AKS-74U carbine, which in terms of tactical deployment, bridges the gap between a sub machine gun and the assault rifle. It was, initially, intended for use mainly with special forces; airborne infantry, rear-echelon support units and armoured vehicle crews. The rifle's compact dimensions, compared to the AK-74, were achieved by using a short, 210 mm (8.3 in) barrel (this forced the designers to simultaneously reduce the gas piston operating rod to an appropriate length). In order to effectively stabilize projectiles, the barrel's twist rate was increased from 200 mm (1:8 in) to 160 mm (1:6.3 in). A new gas block was installed at the muzzle end of the barrel and a new conical flash hider was used, which featured an internal expansion chamber that could alleviate the gas pressure that was generated during firing. The flash suppressor, of the weapon, locked into the gas block with a latch placed on the right side. The forward sling loop was thus relocated to the left side. The front sight was integrated into the gas block. The AKS-74UB's were a specialized variant of the AKS-74U, this was adapted for silenced use with the PBS-5 sound suppressor.

The men with these weapons spread out, in a wide arc, trying to avoid the bullets from the M-16s. and the RACs range; the -74UBs fired their grenades, trying to reduce the numbers of the opposition, and also to destroy the RAC mortar launcher. "Gas masks on," ordered the sergeant of the HART soldiers, as a grenade exploded near to where he was – killing several of the soldiers. Once the gas masks were on the sergeant lifted his mask, momentarily, and ordered the man that was standing at the RAC launcher, who also had a mask on, "Fire when ready." The soldier smiled, as the sergeant gave the order, and gave him the thumbs up.

He pulled the mask down and gave the order; the launcher fired a mortar, two seconds after it hit the desert floor the cannister exploded and gave off its noxious contents. Every *Proagnon* soldier who didn't act fast enough to cover his airways, and breathed the fumes became disorientated and were easily cut down by fire from the M-16s. The driver aboard the HMMWV, along with his passenger had hastily put on their gas masks as she had ordered the RAC into action, at least 10 of the *Proagnon* soldiers fell, if not more.

Due to the armament carrier Celia was aboard only having the basic armour, it was vulnerable to rocket, or grenade, attack; luckily most of the grenades had already been fired. It was then that an explosion rocked the vehicle, "What the hell was that?" she, nearly, screamed at the driver.

"I have no idea," he replied, and then a thought came to him, "it might have been a mortar or, perhaps, even a landmine."

"I think you're, probably, right in your assumption of a mortar. Probably not a landmine or it would've thrown this vehicle on its side, or completely destroyed the vehicle." Another explosion rocked the vehicle, and then another, "Faster," Celia screamed at the driver, and then a gigantic explosion tipped the vehicle on its side and it just lay there; as Commander Most lay against the door, where she'd been thrown, she saw a figure approach the vehicle, out the corner of the windscreen, on the far left; it was the figure of a female Bedouin, or appeared to be, for a moment Celia thought she recognised the person – but how could she in the desert of Iraq?

The woman had blondish hair, it looked fairly clean, and seemed to be shining, as if it had just been washed a few hours earlier. Maybe she wasn't a Bedouin after all, perhaps she was from a town or city, yet why was she dressed in the clothes of a Bedouin traveller?

She turned her attention to the driver of the vehicle; he had hit his head on something and was now unconscious, therefore he wasn't much help at the moment. Celia pushed her way past him and pulled herself across the seats, opened the driver's window and called out to the Bedouin woman, "Please help me."

The woman ambled towards the vehicle that lay on its side – a slight stoop in her walk – she must be old, the HART commander figured, yet she looked young in appearance. None of the other personnel, above the noise of the battle had heard the explosion that had made the vehicle overturn, onto its side, or seen their commander's predicament; they were intent on repelling the enemy soldiers, and defending their positions. A HMMWV ambulance stood on stand by, should it be required.

Once the woman had reached the vehicle, that had overturned and now lay on its right side, Celia said to the woman as she came within earshot, "You're a life saver, could you help me with the door? It seems to be stuck." Then she realised if the woman was old she would be frail, and therefore, unable to help; so Celia hurriedly said, quickly, "You see those men over there," she pointed as best she could, "the ones in the sandy coloured uniforms. Would you ask one of them to come over and provide assistance?"

The woman said nothing for a moment, therefore Commander Most wasn't sure if she hadn't heard correctly or whether she was deaf. She was just about to repeat the question when the woman replied, "No I can't help you, you see I'm not an old woman," and she stood up straight. It was then Celia noticed the rock held in the woman's left hand, whilst the right held a canister of some sort. The rock looked heavy, due to it being of a medium size, as the woman brought it up to eye level, "Plus I am not a mere Bedouin woman," she threw the Arabic clothes off, revealing a smart, black, uniform underneath, "I am a *Proagnon* agent, and I am here to kill you."

With that she thrust the rock in Celia's face, knocking her out cold; as she crumpled and fell back inside the High Mobility Multipurpose Wheeled Vehicle – she was still, slightly conscious of everything - the woman, Sandy Tulliver, laughed evilly as the HART commander fell, "And now, my dear Commander Celia Most, for your final death." Sandy activated the gas grenade, dropped the device in after Celia, and then slammed the window shut and placed the rock on top.

Celia watched, bleary eyed, as the grenade fell and gave a small popping sound, and then a cloud of brown, coloured, gas escaped from the crack that had developed in the casing.

Then the world for HART Commander Celia Most went black as she lost consciousness.

CHAPTER 17

Mutiny & the conflict continues!

The driver of the ambulance that was on stand by, happened to look over to the east – he'd just woken up after having a short sleep – and saw the overturned HMMWV. Starting up his vehicles' V8, 6.2 litre diesel engine, he then swung the ambulance round and headed off into the desert, towards the stricken armament carrier, bouncing over rocks that were sticking out of the ground. The other HMMWV vehicle; that was stationed there, and had a winch on, for recovery operations, saw where the ambulance was headed and decided his vehicles recovery capabilities may be needed, so he followed. HART soldiers looked up – wondering what was happening; their eyes followed the two vehicles – whilst trying not to get killed – and then they saw the disabled HMMWV, it must be the one their commander was in as no other HART vehicles had gone out in the desert.

The M1035 soft top ambulance, capable of carrying 2 litter patients – all ambulances had basic armour – drew to a halt behind the HMMWV M1025 armament carrier; the driver – a giant of a man, Private Sam Gonzales, - jumped out and, immediately, saw the window was blocked – cutting off the air flow, pushing the rock away, effortlessly, he pulled open the side window, and then the smell hit him – gas. Going back for a couple of gas masks he put his own on and went back to the overturned vehicle, and then looked in through the window, there were two bodies – one was evidently the driver, whilst the other, he saw to his horror, was that of Commander Most. They, both, looked dead.

Gonzales, having once been a strongman in a circus before being recruited by HART, in 2010, managed to pull open the door. Taking his gas mask off – as the gas had mostly dispersed – he shouted at the two figures, "Can either of you hear me," there was no response; therefore he indicated, to the driver of the other HMMWV that this vehicle needed to be pulled the correct way up so Gonzales could carry out a proper assessment. The recovery HMMWV, once the ambulance had backed away, moved in and attached its ropes to the side of the armament carrier, and then returned to his own vehicle and pulled forward – pulling the ropes taut as he went, with a huge clang the M1025 righted itself, and then one of the ropes snapped. The driver of the recovery vehicle then climbed out and detached the ropes from the recovered vehicle; putting these back on his own HMMWV the man climbed back into the driver's side, and headed back the way he'd come, satisfied his job was over.

Gonzales brought the ambulance up, again, and climbed out. He approached the armament carrier and peered in, properly this time; things were the just the same as when he'd looked in earlier, only this time everything was viewed at a different angle. Slipping on his surgical gloves Gonzales climbed into the vehicle and moved the two bodies apart, it then became apparent that the driver of the vehicle was very dead, but Commander Most's breathing was very shallow, her pulses in her neck and wrist were very faint, and her heartbeat was very faint as well.

Dragging her body out he hoisted her up and over his shoulder, and carried her to the ambulance, he lay her on the desert floor beside the vehicle and opened the door at the back of the vehicle, in case his first idea failed. Even though he was a black man, and many regarded his height of seven foot a disadvantage, he had been accepted into the HART ranks like any other soldier.

Moving back to Celia's, prone, body he knelt down and proceeded to perform CPR on her, he pressed on her chest as he'd been shown to do, but it didn't seem to be working. "Sorry ma'am," he apologised as he undid her tunic top; then, trying his best to avert his eyes he tried again, "1-2-3-1000," he kept repeating – blowing into her; at last, after about a minute she sat upright, coughed and then fell back down. "Hold on in there commander," he reassured her, "you're not going to die, not on my watch." Private, and Medic, Sam Gonzales hoisted her over his shoulder and carried her over to the ambulance – where he lay her on the stretcher and strapped her down; as he was doing so his mind wandered back to the driver of

Commander Most's vehicle, and he became sad – tears started to build in his eyes and then ran down his cheeks as he realised there was nothing that could be done to save the man. If Sam had been more observant – instead of deciding to have a nap – he might have been able to save both of them.

Once his mind returned to the job in hand he said to the commander's prone form, ""I'm only strapping you in because this may be a rough ride;" when Gonzales had finished he shut the rear door, and walked round to the driver's door. After getting in he started the engine and pressed the accelerator, the vehicle lurched forward – again bouncing over the rocks sticking out the sand; the journey only took about ten minutes. Then Gonzales looked at the panel, which told him the time, date and temperature, and other things that were essential in military vehicles; the time was 23.30, on the 17th January 2013, plus the temperature was now -10, never before had he known it drop so low but he knew anything was possible; he contacted the base in Turkey and told them to inform the medical wing to expect a new patient, he gave them as much information as he could, saying the patient – he thought – had been gassed but was still alive, just. Her companion, the driver of the vehicle, was dead though, Gonzales hadn't been in time to save him.

The medical staff, on duty, told him they would be ready for the patient, upon arrival of the emergency vehicle, so he pressed the accelerator in the ambulance, as far as it would go. The vehicle seemed to shoot along the highway, at a speed of 55mph – its top speed, thankfully Sam Gonzales noted drivers of other vehicles saw the ambulance coming and got out his way – however, one vehicle – a slow moving cattle truck – hadn't seen him coming so, once the route was clear on the other lane of the road Sam swung his vehicle out and charged past. The whole journey took about two hours; at 01.33 the vehicle came to a halt, outside the medical wing, and members of staff loaded the stretcher with Commander Most on, onto a gurney At 01.42 she was wheeled to the operating room, as a precaution.

Commander Strobing, who knew nothing of his fellow commander's plight, had taken charge at 01.58; he wondered what had happened to Celia as he hadn't seen any HART vehicle travelling northwards as he was travelling southwards, to take command, he asked but no one seemed to know as the HMMWV that had recovered the commander's patrol vehicle had left, to be replaced by another one. Ronan wasn't looking forward to this shift as it had been termed the graveyard shift, like all other nighttime shifts. After a while Commander Strobing settled back and waited for an attack, anything to relieve the boredom he felt; still, he would get to see the sun rise, hopefully. Then a figure strode up to him, Ronan drew his Beretta 9000 pistol. "Halt, friend or foe?" The figure was tall, so he thought he knew who it was.

"Friend, Gonzales. I have come to tell you, sir, that Commander Most has been admitted to the headquarters medical wing, I took her there myself, having suffered the effects of a gas attack."

"Is she all right?" he asked, concern in his voice.

"We don't know," replied the giant, "all that can be done is being done," then noting the look, by flashlight, on the commander's face he assured him, "they won't let her die. You care very much for her." The last bit was a statement, not a question.

"I do Sam, we've known each other a long time," Ronan said. "You know, I, actually, proposed to her once, but she turned me down – yet we've always remained good friends – and I still care deeply for her." He couldn't believe he was opening up about this especially to Sam Gonzales, yet he, like all the HART personnel knew – this man was, and always had been, a good listener. Sam didn't judge people and say if they were wrong or right, he just listened; therefore he'd earned the nickname the gentle giant.

The soldiers, around the two men, said nothing – as they all respected Ronan, together with Sam. Off to the east was the sound of a helicopter landing, "Not one of ours," muttered Sam. "I should order the troops to prepare for an attack if I were you."

"Are you sure?" asked the commander, taken aback by the certainty of the medic's voice.

"As sure as onions is onions," the black man said. Ronan should have known better, Sam's father had been a helicopter pilot, and had hoped his son would want to do the same thing, but Sam had preferred to go into the circus, as a strongman, and then he'd left and studied medicine, he felt it better to cure people instead of killing them. As far as Sam was concerned, if people wanted to kill each other that was fine, as long as it didn't involve him. He was there to help afterwards though.

"Soldiers, prepare yourselves for an imminent attack," their commander called to them. "Lieutenant Smith, you're in charge."

Right-o sir," replied the lieutenant. The commander then got up and walked away towards the other end of the, recently dug, trench. "May I enquire what you're going sir?"

"You may, I'm off for a jimmy." After a few minutes the commander returned to rejoin his soldiers. "It sure is cold," Ronan murmured and put his gloves on, and zipped up his parka; strangely the medic didn't seem to feel the cold as much as the other soldiers did, particularly the older ones.

Ronan then happened to look at his watch, 03.06, as he was bored – nothing was happening, yet. As if on cue several of the *Proagnon* soldiers, all armed with the newer AKS-74UB assault rifles, with grenade launcher, appeared. M-16 machine guns, as well as some M-15s chattered away; the assault rifles fired back and several grenades were launched – creating explosions. "Fire at will," called the lieutenant, although none of the men could hear him, over the chatter of gunfire, plus explosions, from the 30mm grenades. Bodies of dead enemy soldiers soon fell, blood streaming from their wounds. However, about 20 HART soldiers were either shot or had been blown up. The battle was, now, more like a bloodbath.

Then something, some sixth sense, caused Commander Strobing to look up – into the night time, very early morning, sky – what he saw shocked him, "That's all we need," he breathed. "Gonzales," he bellowed, the man was only five feet away but the noise, from the gun battle, drowned out all normal conversational voices.

"Sir?" the giant shouted back.

"I need to get to the ambulance," Ronan shouted at the man, "contact headquarters in Turkey."

"Why?" The commander motioned upwards; the medic glanced up, "Oh I see." The commander ran to the medical vehicle, shielded by the medic; and just made it as a stray bullet hit Gonzales, in the back, and he fell to the ground.

"No!" screamed Ronan as the giant fell. "Gonzales!"

The giant looked up at the commander, "Sir, I'm not going to make it, bullet hit me in spine, sorry," and he closed his eyes, forever.

"Gonzales!" Ronan shouted, "you can't die." It was no good though. Commander Strobing climbed into the ambulance, slammed the door, and, hastily, contacted headquarters – patching the transmission through the communications vehicle. "We need air support, fast, our troops are being massacred, and a HIND has just appeared on the scene. We need help NOW!"

Commander Roberts voice came back, "I'll see what I can do. You know what the time is?"

"03.30 sir."

"Don't try to be funny Strobing. You know what I mean."

"Gonzales is dead sir," Ronan said, matter-of-factly. "He died protecting me, doing his job, like Harry Danto did."

"What?" bellowed the commander, coming wide-awake in an instant. "Air support will be with you in the next few minutes."

"Thank you sir, out." Ronan replaced the microphone, and exited the vehicle. He'd just got back to the trenches when there was an explosion; he looked back and saw the ambulance – or rather what was left of it. A column of flame and smoke, plus the burning framework, was all that was left of the vehicle. The commander shivered, he might still have been in there, he looked for the body of Sam Gonzales – but nothing remained.

Ronan broke down in tears, he hadn't known the man long but how the man had died brought back poignant and painful memories of the mission to Russia; "Are you all right sir?" asked Lieutenant Ben Smith.

Yes, I'll be okay in a minute, just laying some ghosts to rest." Lieutenant Smith nodded, in understanding; although Ronan Strobing was the commander Ben Smith had seen more action in the field. Smith returned to the soldiers and saw, to his horror, that five more men had fallen, they were down to 15 soldiers to fight off 5 enemy soldiers; although HART had more soldiers, the enemy had assault rifles with grenade launchers, so they needed to make every shot they fired count.

Then overhead helicopter rotors were heard, the commander glanced up, overhead was an AH-64D Longbow Apache helicopter, the Mi-24 HIND's closest counterpart; it was armed with the, usual, Multi Role armaments. The HIND faced its rival and loosed off 10 of its 2-4 80mm S-8 rockets, the Apache's crew had anticipated something like this and, the two crew members pulled back on their collective columns as soon as the machine's Fire Control Radar (FCR) had detected the incoming missiles, and detected the aircraft they had come from.

The Apache locked onto the other aircraft using its FCR and readied itself to retaliate by firing its AIM-9 Sidewinder air-to-air missiles, but first it had to avoid the incoming missiles. The Apaches twin rotor systems, powered by its, updated, powerful T700-GE-701C engines enabled the helicopter to move out of harms way relatively easily. Once the HIND's rockets had passed underneath, harmlessly, the Apache launched its own missiles; both struck their target, causing the enemy machine to lose power to the rotors and it started to fall, slowly at first and then it started falling faster and faster. The two *Proagnon* pilots managed to eject – not that it would do them much good, both of the pilots aboard the Apache knew Commander Strobing was out for blood, after the death of the man from the ambulance.

They saw, out their cockpit, that their colleagues on the ground were in trouble, so co-pilot/gunner sought the enemy soldiers out using the AH-64D's Target Acquisition Designation System (TADS). Once located the gunner brought the helicopter's 30mm cannon to bear and fired; *Proagnon* soldiers were cut down, in an instant. Then came a huge explosion that rocked the Apache's crew, detecting a huge heat source which hadn't been there a moment ago.

The Apache helicopter flew upwards, as fast as it could, as both pilots realised the heat source was the result of the explosion between the downed HIND and the HMMWV that had been left just sitting there, in the desert; flames and a column of smoke rose upwards.

Meanwhile the two pilots who had ejected from the enemy aircraft were now running for their lives. Commander Strobing, now the fighting had died down, had commandeered an M-151 Jeep and was, at this moment, bouncing the vehicle around the desert, in pursuit, at speed, of the two airmen. No one had stopped him – even though he should've known better, all Ronan could think about was the, pleading, look on Sam's face as his life had slipped away, plus the thought of losing his good friend Celia Most.

He gunned the Jeep into its top gear and sped off in pursuit. He reached the two, fleeing, airmen rather quickly; he slowed down to keep pace with them, then with one hand on the wheel he stood up and took his Beretta 9000 handgun out – as the vehicle drew alongside the pair he pointed the handgun at each of them in turn and fired two times, hitting both men. "Those two are for Commander Most, and these two," he fired again, "are for Sam Gonzales." The two men fell, dead!

The commander re-holstered his weapon, and then drove the Jeep, at a more sedately pace, back to where the HART soldiers were. As Ronan dismounted Lieutenant Smith came up to him and confronted him, "Sir, with all due respect, I know you're the commander."

"Cut the bull and get on with it Ben," retorted the commander sharply at his subordinate.

"Some of the lads, together with myself, feel you shouldn't have killed those men like that, in cold blood."

"Okay, and what should I have done," Ronan disliked his authority being questioned, "invited them back for a tea party!"

"No, we should've sent some men out to capture them, and then interrogated them."

"As I recall your men were somewhat busy!" Commander Strobing snapped at the man. He was angry.

"Therefore sir, I am relieving you of your command."

Ronan snapped at the lieutenant, "The hell you are!" The soldiers were watching the confrontation between their two commanding officers with interest. Those who still wanted

Ronan as commander, and knew they'd have probably done the same in his position, moved to collect in a huddle, behind him; those who felt they would benefit from a change at the top, and felt the commander had acted rashly and without proper thought, moved behind the lieutenant. "This is mutiny, this is. What do you hope to gain by it?"

"When I am in command," Lieutenant Smith announced, as he stared into Commander Strobing's eyes, "we'll do things by the book; and not just be mavericks."

"You want to do things by the book," Commander Strobing retorted, "in case you haven't noticed lieutenant, this is a battlefield; and when you're being fired upon you don't, exactly, have time to remember everything the book says." He held Smith's gaze as he spoke.

"Appreciated sir, but if we don't follow what the manual, on good soldiering, says, we become as bad as the enemy. I also appreciate you're angry but killing in cold blood never solved anything. All I am saying is we should have a temporary change of command, until you're fully over the death of Sam Gonzales."

"Fine," said the commander, slipping off his jacket which designated him as commander and handing it over to Ben. "We'll see if you can do a better job, sir," and Ronan Strobing saluted the new commander.

"Thank you sir," said Commander Ben Smith.

"No, thank you sir," Ronan said and they both laughed.

Smith said, "I admit I have disagreed with some of your ideas, in the past, but I have the utmost respect for you, and I hope this, temporary, change of command will be a very short one."

Ex-commander Ronan Strobing looked at his watch; the time was 05.02, and said quietly to himself, "Only three hours to go, then I'm off duty. It's been a long night, too long."

Meanwhile Commander Smith was issuing his first order, "Move that wreckage," he ordered, indicating the, mangled, wreckage of the crashed HIND – interwoven with the HMMWV armament carrier. Men, together with a High Mobility Multipurpose Wheeled Vehicle wrecker, were deployed to the site to clear the vehicles away. It was a long job, but after approximately two and a half hours much of the wreckage was cleared; the sun glinted, from the south, and threw a little sunlight on the surrounding area, illuminating the wreckage, slightly.

At just before eight Commander Ben Smith and Ronan Strobing left the area, in an M-151 Jeep, and headed north, along the highway towards Turkey. They passed the vehicle Commander Lucy Lang was aboard and saluted to indicate the changeover of command.

The same routine went on for the next six weeks, bringing them into early March and warmer temperatures. Since the destruction of the HMMWV ambulance, the Dodge WC-54 3-4 Battlefield ambulance had taken its place, ready to ferry any casualties back to base.

The Model WC-54 3/4 Ton Ambulance had been manufactured by the Chrysler Corporation (Dodge Brothers Division) from the years 1942 through 1945. The body work for the chassis was completed by the Wayne company. The system itself was a replacement for the WC-9 1/2 Ton Ambulance.

The Model WC-54 was able to accommodate a crew of 2 and had a capacity to fit 4 casualties on litter stretchers or 6 casualties seated and could carry an overall payload of 1,800 pounds. Overall, the WC-54 was able to carry a net weight of 5,920lbs and a gross weight of 720lbs.

The ambulance featured a four-wheel drive capability; the Model WC-54 rode on 8-ply tyres which were mounted on 16 inch wheels. The engine was the Dodge-produced Model T214 which was a 76 horsepower in-line six-cylinder power-plant. The vehicle's maximum highway speed was 54 miles per hour, just 1 mile per hour slower than its High Mobility Multipurpose Wheeled Vehicle counterpart. A high clearance enabled it to traverse off road to some degree.

During that time Commander Celia Most had made a full recovery; she had been attached to a breathing machine, and that had pumped fresh oxygen into her lungs to help get rid of the fumes from the gas grenade; as her lungs had cleared her heart beat, which had also been monitored had increased, when she'd been brought in her heart beat had been, virtually, non-existent, but after the three weeks of being attached to various machines – she'd even had to be fed through a tube which had gone from her nose, down the back of her throat and into her stomach – it'd also played hell if she'd needed to use the bathroom.

Thankfully, after the three weeks were up Celia'd been fit enough to leave the medical wing, a slight – almost negligible – trace of the gas was still found to be in her system, but as it was so small it was deemed safe to discharge her.

Commander Peter Roberts had informed Celia he wanted her to take a couple of weeks off, telling her that he – it was about time he got back into the field – would take over her shift, in the desert. Despite Celia's protests she backed down and relented to his authority, after all he was HART's commander-in-chief.

Dr Q, back at the palace, had heard reports from the men that had returned, that the HART soldiers, together with their war machines, were being easily defeated. Sensing victory was within their grasp he ordered an all out air attack, as well as continuing the land attacks. Therefore, every J-8, J-11, MiG-29, MiG-21, and Su-27 attack aircraft was deployed in hope of a quick end to the conflict.

As the jets flew away the leader returned to his office. He had noticed his number two's absence but thought nothing of it at first. Now he was more uncertain, and he started questioning his staff to see if anyone had seen her, or knew what had happened to her, but no one knew anything.

Then he questioned Mitchell Walker, Dr Q had already seen potential in this man; It eventually turned out that Mr Walker had seen Miss Tulliver leave the palace about two weeks beforehand, she'd told him, as he was on guard, that she was on a special mission.

On hearing this Dr Q became enraged and very angry, "The bitch! The stupid bitch! Going against my orders. What is she playing at? She'll end up dead. And you're a fool for not checking with me first. I ought to have you shot, but as she's, possibly, already dead, or soon will be, I'll let this go for now.

Just get out of my sight, Walker." Quickly Walker stood up, saluted his leader, he did not get a response, and then left.

Overhead the *Proagnon* jets were busy firing and deploying their various weapons. A missile that had been fired from one of the enemy planes struck the ground near the trench that had been dug by the HART soldiers; the trench contained, at the moment, ten soldiers. Commander Lang was seated in a M-151 Jeep, in case she needed to retreat, quickly.

The missile struck the desert throwing up sand everywhere. Commander Lang jumped from the Jeep, having seen what was happening, and shouted to the soldiers, "Everyone out the trench, NOW!"

The soldiers panicked and tried to make their way out, but the pilot aboard the J-11 'Flanker' saw the commotion below and seized his opportunity to inflict more damage, so he fired another of the jet's missiles which struck with deadly accuracy.

About five of the HART soldiers had managed to exit the trench when the missile struck, exploding; the soldiers were killed instantly, and the other five were buried as the trench collapsed, inwards.

"NO!" screamed Lucy, as she saw what had happened. She felt sick, the most casualties always seemed to happen on her watch. Going to the communications vehicle she ordered the radio operator to contact headquarters and request reinforcements. The radio operator relayed the request.

Lucy watched as the HMMWV's and Jeep's around her were targeted by the planes, up above, and were reduced in number; missiles destroying vehicles all around her, together with the unfortunate soldiers on board, altogether ten vehicles were destroyed plus 30 soldiers.

Just then the other VAB arrived, carrying another ten soldiers, however before anyone could disembark another couple of missiles streaked towards the VAB and struck the side of the vehicle, exploding and destroying everyone aboard. Commander Lang started to weep, everything was going wrong.

Just then more jets joined the fight, Lucy looked up. A mixture of F-14s, F-15s and F-16s had appeared, and were now battling against the *Proagnon* J-8s, J-11s, MiG-29 FULCRUMs and Sukhoi SU-27s; plus the HINDs were battling a squad of Apace AH-64D Longbows.

Although the *Proagnon* aircraft were heavily armed they were no match for the updated HART F-14 Tomcats, the F-15 Eagles or the F-16 Falcons, which had been deployed from the aircraft carrier H-Moscow which was a redesigned version of the USS Harry Truman.

This original vessel had been built in 1998, armed with 2 x Mk 57 Mod 3 Sparrow surface to air missiles, 2 x RIM-116 Rolling Airframe short-range missiles for anti-air defence, plus 3 x 20mm mk 15 Phalanx Close-in Weapon System (CIWS), it was a formidable ship. Although, since HART had obtained the ship ten years later the armaments had been doubled; and all other systems, on board, had been updated and redesigned, making the ship even more formidable.

In the helicopter fight although the HIND had more weapons systems on it, and was smaller so therefore more manoeuvrable, however it still lost out to the Longbow Apaches as one after another AIM-9 Sidewinder and FFARs hit the smaller helicopters, causing engine fires and instrument blackouts. However, one HIND did manage to drop its 500kg bomb, intending to help kill as many HART soldiers as possible, but what few HART troops remained, on the ground, had pulled back to safer ground as a Soviet built T-80 battle tank appeared. The pilot aboard the HIND, in fact it was the only one still flying, detected this change of situation too late, and could only watch – in horror – as the bomb fell towards the tank – praying death would be swift. The co-pilot had also realised what was happening as he watched with interest, but sadness; he turned to the pilot, "Is that one of ours?" he asked, already knowing what the answer would be.

BOOM!

The tank blew up, killing the three crew members instantly; the two men in the helicopter watched the spectacle of flames and smoke, and sand was sprayed far and wide – although it wasn't enough to kill the soldiers – it blinded them for a moment.

Back in the HIND the two pilots lifted their eyes, and saw an Apache out the cockpit window. "Quick, let him have it!"

ordered the pilot, but even as he spoke the words all four of the Apache's Hellfire missiles came streaking towards them. "No..."

It was then that the Mil Mi-6 transport helicopter appeared, on the horizon. The AH-64D Longbow then turned its attention to the, big, transport helicopter – as the Apaches Hellfire missiles were gone, and this aircraft had probably just been deployed to try and intimidate the opposition – the Apache launched six of their remaining thirty-four FFAR missiles. The missiles struck the Russian built Mi-6 helicopter and it blew up, and killing the five *Proagnon* crew members on board; the rotor head was blown clean off, knowing their job was done the AH-64Ds flew off in the direction of H-Moscow.

HART Pave Low IVs then flew into sight and landed on the ground, ready to transport and ferry, the few remaining, surviving, soldiers away from the battlefield, if necessary.

After three further weeks of minor skirmishes the breakthrough finally came when, purely by chance, Commander Bigship came across an, elderly, Bedouin woman – though she didn't look like a Bedouin at all; therefore with a platoon of soldiers surrounding him he had approached her and demanded to know her business, and didn't she know this was a battle zone.

She told him she had a gift for him and produced a smoke grenade from the inside of her clothes. Leon, knowing what the object was, grabbed her wrist in one hand and took the smoke grenade with the other, "Search her," he ordered his men. The wrist he had hold of didn't feel like an elderly person's wrist, the skin was, too clean and showed no sign of age; therefore he automatically had to assume she was many years younger than she seemed.

Once he'd dealt with the smoke grenade he brought his arm back round and grabbed her other wrist. "Pig," she said, biting his wrist.

"You don't want to do that lady," he said. Lieutenant Lloyd Samuels began searching her. "A gas grenade, another smoke grenade, a pistol, a machine pistol and a knife. Sir, we ain't got no lady here."

"Just who are you?" demanded the commander as Lieutenant Samuels pulled her headscarf away revealing her long blonde hair. Then, with certainty that this was no Bedouin woman he unfastened her Arabic clothing revealing the, black, uniform underneath. "Who are you?" the commander hissed again, in her ear, "tell me in the next five seconds or my men will kill you;" he nodded at his second in command.

"Draw your weapons men, and fire on my command," all the soldiers drew their Beretta pistols and aimed at the woman. Some of them looked nervous as they'd never had been ordered to shoot a woman before, even though they knew all their pistols contained blanks, they were still nervous. "Take aim," ordered the second in command loudly.

"Well?" Leon demanded, "your last chance, who are you?" He was hoping his actions would scare the blonde woman into revealing herself, but she just stared – defiantly – ahead, as if knowing she wouldn't be killed.

Finally, as the hammers, on the guns, clicked back in preparation to fire she broke, "Okay, I'll tell you, I am the second in command of *Proagnon*, Sandy Tulliver." Evidently, it seemed she wanted to change sides, for some reason. She could've been lying but the nervous tone that had now appeared, in her voice told Leon she was telling the truth.

"Wise choice Miss Tulliver," Commander Bigship said, he thought about telling her the guns had only been loaded with blanks – as the threat of them had been enough to make her talk – but decided against it; if she knew she'd been duped she might try and make a break for it. Tie her up," he ordered, "arms and legs," his sergeant, Chris Moore, found some rope and bound her arms together, and then her legs; finally he used a third length of rope to bind her arms to her legs.

She screamed as the knots were tied, thus in effect hog-tying her, "Filthy beasts," and she spat at Leon, who just loosened his grip and let her fall forward – her face hitting the sand. A couple of men hauled Sandy up and took her to one of the HMMWV cargo/troop carriers and slung her inside the back.

461

"Let's see how you like it," one of the soldiers said to her, then they both positioned themselves outside the vehicle, on guard.

Back in the battlefield Leon was saying to Lloyd, "If she's *Proagnon's* second in command, perhaps she can lead us to this Dr Q. If she's not then she'll rot in prison."

"My thoughts precisely sir, I'd better get on the radio to Commander Roberts, he'll want to interrogate her," and he bounded off to the communications vehicle, to contact headquarters. Leon smiled as his lieutenant bounded away, his men knew their stuff.

The BIFV had had to be destroyed, in the end, because of the risk that the technology inside may fall into enemy hands. So it had been, with regret that once the commander and gunner were clear, the driver had hit the self destruct switch and legged it. The switch was on a timer that gave the man 60 seconds to get out and away. Once the timer had counted down to 0 the vehicle had exploded, throwing flames and smoke into the sky.

Lieutenant Samuels returned after about ten minutes; he saluted his immediate superior, "Commander Roberts wants the prisoner taken back, under guard, straight away," he reported.

"Thank you lieutenant, you can assist in taking her back to headquarters."

"Thank you sir, it will be an honour." So he returned to the cargo/troop carrier and ordered the men, "Right you two, we are taking the prisoner back to headquarters for interrogation purposes. Now one of you will drive while the other will sit with me, in the back of the vehicle, and help guard her." The two soldiers nodded and one climbed into the driver's side of the M1038 cargo/troop carrier of the HMMWV family, this version contained a winch for recovery operations, the glass partition – between the front cabin and back body - was made of reinforced, bullet proof, glass to protect the occupants of the front cabin.

Lieutenant Samuels, together with the other guard, aimed their weapons at Sandy's body; both knew she would give them no trouble, but neither took anything for granted in these days of battle and warfare. The vehicle roared away, and after a two hour journey in a northwards direction they arrived at the Diyarbakit AFB in Turkey. When they arrived, with their prisoner, she was taken to the cells, the rope hog-tying her was untied and she was pushed into a holding cell. "Pigs!" she shouted at them.

The HART soldiers left the area and made their way back outside. They took Commander Roberts, with them, and made their way back to the battlefield; Lieutenant Lloyd Samuels was allowed to remain at headquarters as his shift was, practically, over.

Commander Bigship arrived back about four hours later, and every commander went to view this, famous, prisoner. When Celia saw Sandy she had to be restrained by Ronan, "That's the one who tried to kill me; I'll kill her."

"No you won't Celia, yes okay she's hurt you and it's dented your pride, but there is no way you're going to kill her. You're too professional for that, and believe me it'll get you nowhere." He was doing his best to calm her.

So she shouted at the woman in the cell, "You'd better watch your back," and then stormed off, the other three commanders followed her at a more sedate pace.

"I can see where she's coming from," Lucy said suddenly, "I wonder if she's the one that murdered Mark Schnieder as well."

"Ask her under interrogation," suggested Commander Bigship. "I think we're all going to get a chance." The three of them walked on in silence.

"Oh well," Commander Strobing sighed as they reached the top of the, worn, stone staircase, "soon be time for me to set out for the graveyard shift."

"I guess it will," said Leon, as he began heading towards the conference room, to see if anything new had come in, via the internet or email, from the main headquarters in Geneva.

"Are you coming Lucy?" Ronan asked his American counterpart, as he turned towards the corridor that led to their rooms.

"Hey, what you two up to?" Leon demanded to know.

"We have some extra duties to perform before I depart," replied Commander Ronan Strobing. Miss Lang just giggled.

"Okay, I guess I'll see you both later." Commander Bigship told them, however he thought he saw Ronan wink at him, but it may have been the light. So he walked away to perform his task. Meanwhile, the two land warfare commanders resumed their journey the opposite way.

About an hour later Commander Strobing – looking exhausted – joined Commander Bigship in the conference room, at one of the computer terminals; the sea warfare commander looked at his land warfare counterpart, "You look shattered."

"I know, Commander Lang likes to keep me on my toes, and on active service," Ronan replied teasingly. He was sure Leon knew, or at least suspected, about Lucy and himself.

"Do you still think you will be fit enough for your shift, or shall I contact Lieutenant Smith to cover for you?" Leon asked him.

Commander Strobing considered this, and then he answered, "I think you, maybe, ought to contact Smith and ask him to lead the HART troops, in the battlefield, as I do feel exhausted."

"Okay, will do," the sea warfare commander said to his, old, friend and contacted Ben Smith, on his wrist communicator. The communicators were okay for short range contacts, but not long range so they were, virtually, useless if a commander, in the battlefield, needed to contact headquarters.

Lieutenant Smith assured Commander Bigship he would take over command for tonight with pleasure, and hoped Commander Strobing would soon be fit enough to lead them as soon as possible. Leon thanked the man, and then turned his seat to tell Commander Strobing but he'd already gone; obviously to get as much rest as he could, figured the sea warfare commander.

However, Commander Ronan Strobing was, at this moment, walking down the main corridor; he looked at the name on each room door and finding the one he wanted, opened the door and walked inside. He looked at the figure, in the bed; slowly they opened their eyes and looked up at him,

"Hello Ronan," said the person, "I wasn't expecting you, but I'm pleased to see you."

Around 01.00 Ronan left the room, knowing he'd done his duty, and returned to his own, where he climbed into bed and, immediately, fell asleep; he'd even locked his door – which was most unlike him – as he didn't want to be disturbed. He awoke many hours later on – and found daylight shining on the walls, from the window above his head; he looked at his watch/communicator, 13.28, he'd been asleep almost 12 full hours. He rose, washed and dressed, and then went, directly, to his superior's office to report to Commander Peter Roberts.

He walked down the corridor to the commander's office. He knocked and entered when he was asked to, as he pushed the door open he smelt bacon and eggs; the commander was eating a fry up, he looked up at his subordinate, "Cracking dinner this. May not be good for the arteries, but it makes me feel good. Sit down Ronan."

The commander sat down, and his superior said, "I hear, from Commander Bigship – who has gone to the battlefield, that you were, apparently, exhausted last night so, your deputy, Lieutenant Smith had to act as the commander, in your place."

"Ah yes sir," the younger man replied, a little vaguely, "I was exhausted last night, but I'm happy to say I'm fit enough for active duty now. No problem is there sir?"" he asked, wondering why Roberts had mentioned it

"No, none at all," said the superior officer, then he looked more closely at the land warfare commander. "I have, however, now Commander Most is able to perform her duties again re-organised the daily rota. Starting next week it will be Commander Most from 08.00 to 14.00, you from 14.00 to 20.00, Commander Lang from 20.00 to 02.00, and Commander Biigship from 02.00 to 08.00. I've discussed this change of rota with the other three, but as your door was locked and yours is the only room that doesn't have a spare key, no one could discuss it with you; that is why I'm telling you now; do you agree?"

"What? Oh yes sir."

"Good," responded Roberts, "now about that prisoner."

"Yes sir," Ronan answered.

"It says in Leon's report she has alleged she the second in command of *Proagnon*; well, I've taken a look at her myself, and as we know Tanya Roberts is, or was, the second in command of *Proagnon*, so I requested, from Geneva, the file on her, and it turns out the person we have locked, up looks nothing like Miss Roberts. However, they are both wearing similar black uniforms, but whereas Tanya relied on her physical power, this Sandy Tulliver seems to rely on more conventional methods, plus her age and looks."

He took a sip of water, from the glass on his desk before continuing, "When she was captured she was carrying one gas and two smoke grenades, a handgun, an automatic pistol, plus a knife. So, whoever she is, she's still a terror suspect – *Proagnon* or not."

"I see your logic sir," Ronan said, "so why not ask her to lead us to their headquarters; if she's lying we'll know."

"That was also suggested in Commander Bigship's report, and I think that may be our best option; but he also suggests we interrogate her first."

The battles, in the desert, seemed to be drawing to a close; the ground battles had claimed many casualties. On the ground more *Proagnon* soldiers began to appear, brought aboard the BTR-60,-70, -80 and the MT-LB personnel carriers; combined the vehicles had brought in fifty armed soldiers, including the main crews of the vehicles, all were armed with an assortment of AK-74s – some with grenade launchers, some without. HART soldiers opened fire with their M-16s and tossed hand grenades at the approaching enemy soldiers. The RAC was set up in case any of them managed to get too close for comfort. Commander Bigship, whose duty it was, shouted orders at the other soldiers, who obeyed without question.

He issued orders to the crews of the High Mobility Multipurpose Wheeled Vehicles, and the M-151 Jeeps, to prepare their weapons. The HMMWV family of vehicles all had supplemental armour which was now standard.; the one Celia Most had had had her 'accident' in had been an older model, which had only had the basic armour on it, this supplemental armour had also been fitted on the Jeeps, but with modifications by HART engineers this armour had been made stronger. The HMMWV crews readied either their vehicles M60 7.62mm machine gun, their M2 .50 calibre machine gun, or their MK 19 grenade launcher. The crews on the Jeeps, the final surviving few, readied their 149-mm TOW launcher, which was the Jeep's primary armament.

Guns blazed, men fell, fireballs erupted as grenades, or vehicles; blew up; trees burnt, and there was absolute chaos as the battle raged on. Eventually, after the initial clouds of smoke had wafted away the battlefield was shown to be littered with dead bodies, of soldiers from both sides; and burnt out vehicles. Everywhere Commander Leon Bigship of HART looked around him, there were signs of death and destruction; he sighed and turned, slowly, to face the soldiers, "That's it. I guess we won that round."

The soldiers cheered and fired their weapons in the air. "Prepare to fall out and move out," ordered the commander. What men were left boarded their vehicles; and so the convoy of, assorted HMMWV's, and Jeeps roared away, on the journey back to their headquarters, in Turkey.

CHAPTER 18

The conflict finally draws to a close!

The HART destroyers H-Newhaven and H-Berlin entered the Persian Gulf, slowly, as if expecting an attack at any moment.

Both HART destroyers were based on the USS Arleigh Burke, an American vessel which had first seen service in the early 1990s. As with the H-Moscow these vessels had been updated in their design by the HART engineers; the ship, the Arleigh Burke had had 323 members of crew aboard, whereas the redesigned H-Newhaven and H-Berlin had over 500 crew members aboard, also the weapons suites consisting of: 2 x Mark 32 triple torpedo tubes, 1 x 5" Mark 45 gun, 2 x 25mm chain guns, 2 x 20mm Phalanx CIWS, 4 x 12.7mm anti aircraft machine guns, the 29 cell Mk 41 Vertical Launch Systems (VLS) which could fire RIM-66 SM-2, BGM-109 Tomahawk or RUM-139 VL-ASROC missiles, plus the 61 cell VLS, had all been upgraded to newer versions.

Plus the systems aboard the newer vessels including the AN/SPY-1D radar, the AN/SPS-67(V)2 and the AN/SPS-64(V)9 surface search radar systems, plus the AN/SQS-53C sonar array and the AN/SQR-19 tactical towed array had been upgraded. The electronic warfare system which consisted of the AN/SLQ-32(V)2 EWS while decoys are provided through CHAFF buoys, torpedo countermeasures and the Mk 36 MOD 12 decoy launching system were all newer versions.

Four, updated, General Electric LM 2500-30 gas-powered turbines operating twin shafts and delivering up to 100,000 shaft horsepower allowing for speeds in excess of 30 knots in ideal conditions supplied power for the vessels.

Helipads, on each vessel, for operations of a single Sikorsky SH-60 Seahawk LAMPS III helicopter, this was the only similarity to the original ship, a pivotal addition to the anti-submarine operation role.

The two *Proagnon* battle cruisers, the *Admiral Lazarev* and the *Pyotr Velikiy* had detected the oncoming HART vessels, the

468

plan for the men – in this situation – was to let their enemy get as close as possible, without being detected themselves, and then surprise them and blow them clean out the water.

Thanks to the upgrades provided by *Proagnon* technicians and engineers the systems – on these ships – had been upgraded. The two destroyers had been detected, firstly, by the Voskhod search radar on the foremast; this was downloaded to one of the computer terminals, and had then been confirmed by the download from the Fregat radar on the main mast. Even though there was a, concrete, wall between the battle cruisers and the searching vessels, the technicians had added a new type of computer chip, which boosted radar searches.

As the ships came nearer weapons systems aboard were readied for action. The *Proagnon* battle cruisers burst out of their dry dock and unleashed their weapons against the enemy destroyers. The crews aboard the HART ships were taken by complete surprise, but quickly retaliated; missiles were fired at each other's ship, guns chattered away, froth from the water was thrown up and across each ship's bows, swamping any men who happened to be on deck at that time. Machine gun fire hit many of the members of crew and peppered the decks; the men, that had been shot, either fell overboard or were thrown over the side railings by other sailors – who felt as the men were dead they served no further purpose – thus the water around the battling vessels started to become a bright red.

Both *Proagnon* ships had their radars taken out by missiles from the HART vessels; however, although even now they were both, electronically blind, and not to be outdone they fought back firing torpedo missiles – SS-N-15 – at the destroyers. A missile from the *Pyoyr Velikiy* struck the H-Berlin, in its bows, and created a small crack in the vessels armour.

The vessel's electronic – damage – systems registered the H-Berlin had been hit, and the captain – Glen Sawyer – was notified immediately; speaking on the ship's internal radio he commanded, "This vessel has taken a direct missile hit, in the front bows. Pull hard to port. Torpedo room, prepare our response."

A Tomahawk missile was prepared, with a High Explosive warhead, and loaded into one of the Mk 32 triple torpedo tubes. The tube was opened and firing mechanism readied; once the tube was flooded, and the weapons officer on board, Oliver Newhart, had confirmed a lock-on the Tomahawk was fired. The missile was ejected, from its tube, and flew straight towards the *Pyotr Veikiy*, "Fly, baby, fly!" enthused Oliver Newhart as he watched the missile being ejected. The Tomahawk missile struck the Russian built ship on its starboard bow. The round in the warhead exploded, creating a vast hole in the bow, thus it started taking water on.

As it started to dip at the front the captain aboard the *Kirov* class battle cruiser sent an order to the engine room. "Although that ship is slowly turning, take us to full power, as best we can, and ram it." The captain knew this would, probably, be the last command he was ever likely to issue.

The *Pyotr Velikiy* turned, slowly and sluggishly, to face its opponents port side and powered up to a speed of 16 knots – half its full speed, none of the sailors wanted to die so many tried to abandon ship – all knew they'd die in the end, many jumped overboard but once they hit the water they died instantly – forming more blood in the water – the more experienced men climbed aboard the helicopters, or used the lifeboats, and took off. The *Kirov* class battle cruiser and the H-Berlin collided, exploding. The explosion blew apart the lifeboats, plus the column of flame destroyed the helicopters, killing every sailor who had once manned the *Pyotr Velikiy*.

Two of the downed choppers crashed into the water and went down to Davy Jones' Locker; but one was headed towards the H-Newhaven, obviously intending to do as much damage as possible, but the HART destroyer had detected the incoming airborne vehicle on its radar system, and launched one of its RIM-66 SM-2 missiles, from one of its vertical missile launch systems. The projectile flew towards the burning chopper as the ship resumed its battle with the enemy; the missile hit the chopper and it exploded, the wreckage falling, harmlessly, into the sea below.

Eventually, after a further half an hour or so, the remaining *Proagnon* ship sunk beneath the waves. "Well that seems to be that," announced the captain of H-Newhaven – Sam Peters – "full steam ahead, let's go home."

"Aye, Aye skipper," First Mate James Michaels replied, then he called the order over the vessel's communications system. There was a shudder as the four General Electric LM-2500-30 gas turbines were powered up to full power – each turbine was capable of producing 25,000 horsepower, this was then transferred to its twin shafts, therefore the total power output was 100,000 shaft horsepower.

Then Captain Peters relayed a message to the radio room, "Contact headquarters in Turkey, and let them know what's happened. About the sinking of H-Berlin, and everything else; above all tell them we were victorious." With that done the destroyer headed out the Persian Gulf and began its, long, journey back to its moorings in San Francisco harbour.

The message was received at the AFB by one of the communications personnel. Immediately noting the urgency of the message he made up a carbon copy and quickly left the room with the, printed, sheet of paper; he walked along to the east side of the corridor, climbed a set of, old, worn stone steps, and ventured down the corridor, going westwards, towards Commander Roberts' office. The officer knocked, on the door, and entered when he was bid.

"Good afternoon Robert," the commander was surrounded by Commander's Most, Strobing, and Lang; evidently Commander Bigship was still on his way back from the battlefield.

The young officer looked a bit nervous in front of the four of them. "Sir, ladies, Commander Strobing; these have arrived for you in the past few minutes," and he laid three sheets of printed paper on the commander's desk, and then he saluted and left the room. Ronan picked the sheets, of paper, up and quickly read them.

"Well, these seem to confirm it," he announced, placing the sheets in front of the, overall, commander, "the war with *Proagnon* is finally over, all that remains is to locate Dr Q, capture him, and then bring about justice, for you and for the rest of the world."

CHAPTER 19

Interrogation & a deal!

"Very well," said Peter Roberts, "bring the prisoner to the conference room."

The three Operational Commanders left the office and began to walk down to the cells; upon reaching them Celia took the keys from the sergeant-at arms. She hesitated before unlocking the cell that contained the *Proagnon* agent and, alledgedly, second-in-command; once he'd handed her the keys the sergeant at arms was then dismissed from his duty. Carefully, Commander Most unlocked the cell that contained the woman in the black uniform, entered it and dragged Sandy Tulliver out. "Now you give us any trouble and I will shoot you," as if to emphasise her point Celia brought her Beretta 92 up and placed it at the base of Sandy's neck. "Right, move ahead of us."

The cell that had contained Miss Tulliver, like most of the other cells, was only a small affair. The cells all contain a single bed with wooden base, a horsehair mattress and simple bedding; also in there was a, basic, toilet and washbasin; other than that the room contained nothing else. Lighting and ventilation came from a, small, window, high up in one wall, finally a, small flap in the door gave access for the most basic of Turkish meals. The prison area below the main headquarters building hadn't been altered since the end of World War II.

The two other commanders looked at each other, both knew Celia Most wouldn't really shoot the prisoner but Sandy Tulliver didn't know that. Both Ronan's and Lucy's Berettas were still holstered but both of them had undone the button fastenings on their holsters. The *Proagnon* agent was forced forward and marched up the steps at gunpoint, and onto the conference room where Commander Roberts awaited, along with the recently returned Commander Bigship.

Sandy was marched in, and pushed onto a chair; Commander Roberts loomed over her, "Now Miss, perhaps you could answer a few questions for us."

"I suppose I could," she answered sulkily, raging at herself for being caught so easily.

"Question one," Roberts said, seating himself on a chair facing her, his Beretta 9000 drawn – in case she offered any form of resistance. "You say you are *Proagnon's* second in command, yet you look nothing like the woman on this picture." He produced the picture of Tanya Roberts, "So my question is are you sure you're the second in command?"

Sandy was aware of Commander Most standing behind her, pointing the 92 pistol at her. "I am," she answered, "Dr Q asked me to be; now this woman," she said, pointing at the picture, "I haven't seen her around for ages."

"Do you know if she's dead?"

"I don't," Sandy replied. "But as I haven't seen her for ages I assume she's either left, or is dead."

Roberts looked her straight in the eye, "No one ever leaves *Proagnon* alive, I'm sure of that," he said, in a matter of fact tone. Miss Tulliver, now, turned pale looked very scared.

Lucy moved forward and said to Sandy, "Are you the one who slept with Mark Schnieder, and then killed him?"

"No," she answered. "Who is he?" As she was hooked up to a lie detector as well, the HART commanders would know if she wasn't telling the truth, yet for every question she answered no lie was detected.

"He is, or rather was, my lover," Lucy replied, catching Ronan's eye.

"Anyway, you must have left me alive for a reason. How can I help you?"

"We left you alive for interrogation purposes; however there is one way you can help us," Roberts told the prisoner. "As you may, or may not know, the man you know as Dr Q is actually called Adam Barker;" as she looked confused, obviously Sandy didn't know that fact, "he wants revenge on me because I helped jail, and convict, his father when I was in the police. Adam swore vengeance on me then; his father died in prison and so I think Adam blames me – he even blew up the flat where I lived, killing my wife," at this point his eyes misted over, "you remind me so much of her."

"Anyway," he carried on once he'd recovered his composure, "I would like you to pretend to capture me and take me, as your prisoner to face Dr Q. We will even let you have your gun back, together with some transport facilities. Would you be prepared to do that?"

Sandy thought about it, she could warn Dr Q, or she could do as Commander Roberts requested of her; if she did that she could kill two birds with one stone, finish them both, forever! "Okay, I'll do it!" she replied with some newly found enthusiasm.

CHAPTER 20

One shall stand, one shall fall!

A couple of hours later Sandy was brought back up from the cells, and Commander Lang gave Sandy Tulliver her Makarov 9x18mm pistol, her APS Stechkin 9x18mm PM machine pistol, plus knife back. "I've had both of your guns deactivated, plus the knife is, now, blunt; these tasks were performed by some of our weaponry experts, just in case you get the thought of deciding to go back on your word. A Jeep is waiting outside to take you, together with Commander Roberts to Dr Q's residence. We have fitted the Jeep with a tracking device so we can follow your journey."

"My thanks for trusting me and allowing me to help," replied Miss Tulliver, "I won't let you down." The two women walked down the stairs, and outside, to meet the other commanders, and then they would board the Jeep that would return her, along with her prisoner, to *Proagnon* headquarters, for the final showdown between the two leaders.

Once they reached the courtyard, where the Jeep was waiting Peter Roberts said to the prisoner, "My men, and women, will be following in an old cattle truck. Once you and I have gone inside *Proagnon* they will wait for 2 minutes and then storm the building, cutting the opposition down." Sandy hadn't prepared for that, and then jokingly he added, "I am your prisoner; take me to your leader." He handed his Beretta 9000 to Commander Most.

The two of them climbed into the Jeep and they set off. As the Jeep had been fitted with a tracking device underneath, if the following vehicle lost sight of it, it could still be tracked. The convoy of two vehicles set off, another truck and Jeep would rendezvous with them later. The Jeep was driven up the slope and into the courtyard of Saddam Hussein's Babylonian palace.

Saddam Hussein built a new palace for himself overlooking the Euphrates River. It was shaped like a ziggurat (stepped pyramid), Saddam's Babylonian palace was a monstrous hill-top fortress surrounded by miniature palm trees and rose gardens. The four-storey palace extended across an area as large as five football fields. Villagers had often told news media that a thousand people were evacuated to make way for this emblem of Saddam Hussein's power.

The palace Saddam built was not merely large it was also ostentatious. Containing several hundred thousand square feet of marble, it became a showy confection of angular towers, arched gates, vaulting ceilings, and majestic stairways. Critics often commented that Saddam Hussein's lavish palace expressed exuberant excess in a land where many people died in poverty.

On the ceilings and walls of this palace hung 360-degree murals depicting scenes from ancient Babylon, Ur, and the Tower of Babel. In the cathedral-like entryway, an enormous chandelier hung from a wooden canopy carved to resemble a palm tree. In the bathrooms, the plumbing fixtures appeared to be gold-plated. Throughout Saddam Hussein's palace, pediments were engraved with the ruler's initials, "SdH."

The role of Saddam Hussein's Babylonian palace was more symbolic than functional. When American troops entered Babylon in April, 2003, they found little evidence that the palace had been occupied or even used. Saddam's fall from power brought vandals and looters at first. The smoked glass windows were shattered, the furnishings removed, and architectural details - from faucets to light switches - had been stripped away. Now it was occupied, and not by Iraqi's.

The *Proagnon* number two forced Commander Roberts out of the vehicle at gunpoint, and forced him forward, and inside the building through the, guarded, double doors.

The soldiers on duty gasped as they watched Sandy Tulliver push the commander of HART, the great Commander Peter Roberts – at least that's who they assumed it was, towards the elevator, still at gunpoint; none of them knew, or even had any suspicion, that the weapon she was carrying wasn't loaded. As they stepped inside the elevator and the doors closed Sandy breathed a huge sigh of relief, "I'm glad that bit's over."

The lift ascended to the first floor, and again Sandy pushed Roberts forward along the corridor, they entered the alcove which gave entrance to her leader's office; even Dr Q's bodyguards gasped in surprise, and looked on in awe. Then there came shouts, and the noise of weapons being fired, from downstairs, the bodyguards – unsure now – just shrugged and ran to join the firefight.

They were in the clear. Miss Tulliver pressed a switch and said into the intercom, "Sir, I have managed to capture HART's commander, and have brought him for you to interrogate."

"Excellent," hissed the voice of Dr Q, "bring him in." The automatic door slid back and they walked into the office, "So Roberts, it has ended as I foresaw, with you as my prisoner. First," he looked over at his number two, "was he easy to capture?"

"Why yes," answered Miss Tulliver, startled. "There he was, just standing on the battlefield – surveying the carnage, when I sneaked up behind him, and pressed my pistol into his spine. I warned him if he turned round I'd shoot." Peter was glad she'd stuck to her story.

"Very interesting," Dr Q responded. Suddenly, there was a flash, and a bang, from outside the office once the smoke had cleared four more members of HART joined them, in the room. "I take it Mr Roberts that these are your underlings."

"They are my operational commanders, yes."

"Greetings to you all," said Dr Q. "As we are all here, I feel an unveiling is in order," and, slowly, he undid, and removed, his helmet. Everyone recoiled in fear as the true face of Adam Barker was revealed, his face was still horribly scarred – the flesh on one side of his face had been burnt back, and he had gone prematurely bald. "Not a very nice picture is it?" As no one answered he carried on, "And now the great Peter Roberts, together with his four deputies are in my office and at my mercy. Kill them Sandy or I shall kill you!"

Sandy just handed Roberts her pistol, and he pointed it at Adam Barker, "I didn't come here as your prisoner, Barker, I came as the one to bring you to justice;" promptly the other four HART personnel drew their own weapons, and joined their commander. "You see, Barker, one shall stand and one shall fall."

Peter Roberts sat down opposite the man who had once been Adam Barker, he still was but had, obviously taken some beatings, either that or he'd tried to commit suicide at some time. "So Roberts you have me, does it make you feel big?"

"No," responded the HART leader. "Tell me Adam why did you do it?"

"Why did I want you dead? Simple, you're the one who I blame for my parent's death, so it's natural I should want you dead."

"Yes, but you're the one who blew my flat up, killing my wife. I ought to kill you. Nicola meant the world to me."

"You have your chance to kill me now. Do it!"

"No, I made a promise to bring you to justice, and I am going to honour that promise. Now let me ask you who do you report to once a month?"

"Ah," said Adam, "so you know about that, I will not tell you. As for you not killing me you're a coward. However, all I will tell you about my contact is their initials are GA." Suddenly, he pulled a pistol from a drawer, in his desk, and pointed it at Roberts, "As you refuse to kill me, I shall kill you."

Peter grabbed his adversary's wrist and squeezed, the weapon clattered onto the floor; Leon bent to pick it up, when he straightened up again Dr Q, quickly, produced another pistol and fired at Leon. Leon doubled up and fell backwards.

"Why Adam, why? He's not your enemy."

"Anyone who is under your command, Roberts, is my enemy." He found four Berettas pointed at him. Suddenly, and quite calmly, Commander Leon Bigship, helped by Commander's Lucy Lang and Celia Most, got up.

"What?" stammered Mr Barker, as he found a fifth Beretta 9000 pointed at him.

"I always instruct my personnel to wear their Kevlar body protection, even if they feel there is no risk involved in their mission."

Unnoticed by any of them Sandy Tulliver had sneaked out the office, and started hurrying down the corridor to an elevator, at the end of the corridor – only Dr Q and herself knew about it.

The elevator went from the top floor straight down and to a bunker under the palace. The bunker was unused, and only to be used in the gravest emergency. She stepped out the elevator and entered the bunker, and sat down at the computer terminal in the centre of the room and booted up the system; her fingers flew over the keyboard as she typed in commands and instructions, thus preparing the system for the purpose it had originally been constructed for; she smiled to herself, this would bring the house down, literally.

"You are to come with us and answer for your evil crimes," Peter told Adam. "Come on. Move!" The *Proagnon* leader, knowing his time was, basically, up rose from his seat; none of them noticed his finger catch a button under his desk, and press it, thus sending a, silent, signal out to any of his soldiers that were still alive.

"Okay, you win Roberts, but if I go to trial I shall tell them all what you did; and how it has affected me. Hopefully, I should just get away with being put in a mental institute." Roberts prodded his enemy with his pistol, and the six of them moved towards the palace exit.

"Where's your female friend?" the commander of HART demanded to know, suddenly noticing her absence.

"She must have escaped," sneered Adam Barker, almost casually as if he was resigned to his fate now, as he was forced, at gunpoint, down the corridor. "Evidently she got out while the going was good."

"No worries," Leon said as he was helped along by Celia Most, ""we shall track her down." As the five HART personnel, together with their prisoner neared the exit to the outside there came an ominous rumbling noise.

In the room, within the bunker – underneath the palace - where Sandy was, she had got the emergency system operational – and a hatch slid back revealing the auto destruct button. Once she was satisfied everything was working properly, Miss Tulliver took one last, long, look around, and then pressed the red, auto destruct, button.

EPILOGUE

Endings and beginnings!

Stonework fell and rained down on the six people, but as they were near enough to the exit everyone managed to escape, the collapsing building, relatively unharmed – a few minor cuts and bruises but nothing of any real significance. Adam Barker was then pushed into the back of a HMMWV cargo/troop carrier that had arrived, along with another Jeep.

The HART personnel and the *Proagnon* leader climbed aboard the vehicle, and the tailgate was closed. Once the convoy of four vehicles were ready to leave the HART soldiers started the engines, and the vehicles pulled away; they surveyed the destruction left behind them, knowing if anyone had been in that building they must be surely have perished.

Far overhead an F-16 Falcon appeared and saw the convoy. Detecting which vehicle its prey was in it swooped down, fixing the vehicle the pilot wanted in his vision the pilot built up speed, in the aircraft and did a fly past. Then the Falcon came back and started flying overhead – as if escorting the convoy of vehicles. Even when the pilot had sent out a signal to another agent he still shadowed the line of four vehicles, just in case.

The signal was received and a man, dressed in the clothing of a Bedouin travelling man, appeared from behind a group of trees that lined the road, which ran east to west. He stepped out, in front of the convoy, and so the Jeep leading the procession had to come to a, temporary, halt. "Hey, what do you think you're doing?" demanded the driver of the Jeep. "Get off the road!"

"My apologies," replied the man, "I just wanted to get a closer look at your, shiny, vehicles." The Jeep driver just snarled in response as this Bedouin – he seemed a little on the rotund side – started to walk down the line of motorized vehicles. When he reached the HMMWV he tried to engage the driver in conversation; as the driver didn't speak any Arabic he tried to get rid of the Bedouin as quickly as possible.

However, the man became very persistent and leaned closer to the truck, the driver, suddenly, realised that this man was no Bedouin but a suicide bomber, but before he could shout a warning the Arab had pressed himself against the side of the HMMWV – thus detonating the explosives he was wearing. The HMMWV exploded in a ball of flame, destroying it utterly; all that remained was a heap of burning, bent, metalwork. The other vehicles were also caught by the explosion of the first vehicle, and so, triggering a chain reaction, the convoy was completely, and utterly, destroyed.

The pilot, who had been watching – in case things had gone wrong, saw the exploding convoy and knew the agent had done his work, and so flew his aircraft away at speed.

Meanwhile, out of the wreckage of the convoy two figures pulled themselves from under the mangled metalwork – both of them were covered in blood, but they were recognisable as human figures – they pulled themselves clear of the, now, smouldering column of vehicles and collapsed, exhausted; columns of horrible, black, smoke were rising into the cloudy sky above.

A hatch slid back in the road that had once led up to the ill-fated palace, and another person emerged from the tunnel, carrying a Makarov pistol. Spying the other two figures laid on the ground the third person strode up to them, and pointed the pistol at both of them, in turn. "You have inconvenienced me, prepare to die!" With that the person fired.

Shield Crest

www.ingramcontent.com/pod-product-compliance
Lightning Source LLC
Chambersburg PA
CBHW051550100726
47898CB00001B/45